D0116740

Rivers Crossing

Also by Jim H. Ainsworth

In the Rivers' Flow
(# 1 in the Rivers Series)

Biscuits Across the Brazos

Rivers Crossing

A Novel

Jim H. Ainsworth

First Edition

#2 in the Rivers Series

The characters and events in this book are fictitious. Any similarity
to real persons, living or dead, is coincidental and
not intended by the author.

ISBN 978-0-9679483-1-7

Library of Congress Control Number: 2005906261

Designed by Darron Moore, **MOORE OR LESS DESIGN**

Printed in the United States of America

Season of Harvest Publications
Texas

Dr. Fred Tarpley, Editor

In loving memory of Nadelle,
who inspired my first novel.

If I were in prison, Mother would say three things.
First—*He's innocent and I dedicate my life to getting him out.*
Second—*He is the smartest one in that terrible place (including the warden).* Third—*Doesn't he look good in stripes?*
Everybody needs a mama like that.

Thank you...

My family for belief and support, and most of all, love.

Dr. Fred Tarpley for editing, advice, and encouragement

Darron Moore for patience in working on format and design

My readers evaluation group—
Jan, Shelly, Kendall, John, Charlotte, Charlie, Ellen, & Bill

For legal information
District Attorney F. Duncan Thomas
County Attorney Michael Bartley

Rivers Crossing

1 The flash of jagged lightning ejected Spooner Hays as it
streaked the dark, wet sky. His long, lithe form fell from
the courthouse roof like an unworthy sacrifice refused
by an angry storm god. Spooner's normal strength and agility
failed him as he grabbed for a handhold on the mossy ledge.
The courthouse oak tree seemed to rise up out of the black
dirt to gather him in its arms. Ribs cracked as the first limb
greeted him, sending sharp slivers of bone into a lung. The
tree's limbs and leaves swayed with each wind gust, making
Spooner appear to fall in slow motion.

On most summer nights, the scream and the noise of
breaking branches would have pierced still, heavy air and
carried deep into downtown Cooper, Texas. On this night,
the sounds were drowned by gusting wind and driving rain.
Spooner collided with a dog wallow on the Delta County
courthouse lawn as if it were a bull's-eye painted in the mud.
The lawn had just had its first good drink in more than six
years, so water stood in the dog wallow. His body bounced
a little as streams of brown liquid splashed up from the
puddle. Blood from the pierced lung made a gurgling sound
in Spooner's throat. Weak bubbles from labored breathing
appeared in the muddy water, floated, and burst.

If it had not been storming, someone might have seen the fall. A block away, the Sparks Theater marquee on Cooper's downtown square announced *The Searchers*, starring John Wayne, but the single showing had been over for hours. Nocturnal teenagers of summer should have been gathered on car fenders around the square until the wee hours of morning on this Northeast Texas summer night. The rain had sent them to shelter, using dried and cracked windshield wipers that had not been wet for years.

Nobody seemed to see or hear the sickening thud and splash from the mud puddle. People were already home in bed, sleeping to the rare rhythm of rainfall beating on roof-tops—dreaming peacefully about a possible end to the six-year drought. Pots and pans had been placed on floors and tables to catch water from leaky roofs. When it never rained, re-pairing roofs had seemed to be a waste of time.

Spooner Hays lay on the courthouse lawn, his arms splayed as if he were trying to fly. Nobody saw his blank stare as rain fell in one ear and mud oozed into the other. If there had been a courthouse clock, it would have struck twice as his heart took its final beat.

Sheriff Toy Roy Robbins' huge hands pushed the door of the cell open and carried Gray Boy Rivers' limp body inside. Bedbugs scattered as he eased Gray onto the cot. Gray opened one eye and moaned as a roach made its way across his cheek. He slapped it away and rolled off to the floor.

Toy closed the cell door. "It's for your own good, Cuz." The sheriff's gravelly voice echoed and bounced off the walls and floor. "Your daddy finds out what you been up to tonight, he'll likely whip both our asses."

"What time is it?" Gray's words were thick.

"It was midnight when I got the call to come to the square."

"I'm all right now, Toy. How about just lettin' me go on home? I'm done with trouble for tonight." Gray Boy hated the pleading tone in his voice.

"You're done, all right. You're stewed and tattooed. What you been drinkin', anyway?"

"Just had a few beers."

"You had more than a few, else you mixed it with some of Wheeler's rotgut. Something hit you like a ton of bricks as soon as you got in the seat of my car. I ain't about to let you drive that sickle home tonight." Toy leaned his forehead against the cell door. "You'd likely kill yourself or somebody else. 'Sides, it's raining like a cow pissin' on a flat rock."

Gray Boy was getting sicker by the minute. His voice was slurred and barely audible. "How many times I got to tell you, Toy. It's a motorcycle, not a sickle. What did you do with it? You know it ain't paid for."

"I parked it outside. Ain't nobody gonna bother it."

"I can't afford insurance. Somebody steals it, I'm shit outta luck."

Rube Carter, deputy sheriff and jailer, stuck his double chin out of his office and looked down the row of cells. "What'd he do now, Sheriff?"

Sheriff Robbins glanced back at his jailer. "Drunk on the square. Got reports about him drivin' that sickle like a bat outta hell, too, but I didn't catch him doin' that."

Rube pursed his big lips. "Too easy for them young boys to get likker, if you ask me."

"Probably went across the Red River to get it—else a boot-legger—Wheeler, most likely." Toy's voice softened. "Looks like he might have been in another fight, too." Toy leaned his huge bulk against the cell door and threaded his hammer-handle fingers through the slots. "Don't understand you, Cuz. Barely out of high school and been fightin' and drinkin' since graduation day. You wadn't raised to carry on like you been doin'." No answer came from the cell. "Can't you at

3

least sit up on that cot? Hate to see you just lay in the floor."
Toy turned and walked toward Rube, shaking his head. "If
the Good Lord had seen fit to give me that boy's body and
looks and about half his charm, I'd be spending my time in
bed with some young, pretty thang, instead of on a jailhouse
cot."

The Delta County Jail sat atop the stark courthouse like
an outhouse on a hilltop. A roof top walkway surrounded
the jail. The jailer's office and the back stairway door marked
one end of the narrow hall in front of the filthy cells. The
rooftop walkway marked the other end. Gray Boy heard Toy's
lumbering footsteps trudge down the back stairs. He pressed
his cheek to the cool and moist concrete floor of his cell.
Keeping his head still eased the nausea a little. If he could
make it past this feeling, Gray vowed never to mix Wheeler's
cheap whiskey with beer again. In fact, he'd never touch the
whiskey again. He needed time to recover before deciding
how to get out of this mess. From his position on the floor,
he looked through the bars to the other cells, straining to see
a pair of legs or any sign of other prisoners. There were none.
Good. The fewer people who knew he was in jail, the better.

The rough edges on the concrete floor were making small
pinpoint pricks in his cheek when he awoke. *I must have
passed out.* The nausea returned as he lifted his head, but he
had to get up. *No telling what this floor has had on it.* He tried
not to think about the Dairy Queen chili cheeseburger he
had consumed after Jake's baseball game. Its dead carcass was
probably somewhere in the cell with him, but he could not
remember and was grateful for that.

Threading his fingers through the holes in the cell door,
he raised himself to a sitting position and leaned his face
against the steel latticework. The cool, rough hardness of
metal felt good to his forehead. He tried not to think about
the other heads that had leaned where his was now. The over-
laid strips of steel on the cell door reminded him of the sugary

layers of cinnamon crust on his mother's apple pies. He loved those pies, but the thought made him sicker. He needed to lie back down, but he was sober enough to be unwilling to lay his cheek on the floor again. The cot, with its bedbugs, was not an option. *Did I hear voices, or was it just the alcohol? A dream maybe, or just the rain pounding on the roof?*

"Well, he finally woke up." Gray Boy opened his eyes at the voice and looked up enough to recognize Rube Carter's dirty shoes. The heels were worn down so much that Rube was walking on the sides.

"Get away, Rube. I don't need any of your bullshit tonight."

Rube grunted as he leaned down to look into Gray Boy's face. "You lookin' kinda green there, pretty boy. Still cocky though, ain't ye'? Always lettin' that alligator mouth of yours overload your hummingbird ass. From the looks of you, somebody got tired of it."

Gray managed to move his body enough to feint a move toward Rube. The fat jailer flinched and moved back a little. "Nervous about somethin', Rube? Go get Toy on the radio. I'm sick and I need to go home."

Rube leaned against the wall away from the cell and jingled the keys that dangled from his belt loop. He blew air from his nose and made a half-sneeze sound in his throat, the sound he always made when he was angry or nervous. He pulled the club he carried on his belt and ran it across the cell bars. "Don't think so. Sheriff Robbins finally went to bed, after you kept him up most of the night."

"What time is it?"

"Close to three, I guess. It ain't time for you to get out yet." Rube turned to walk away.

"Who was that I heard talking earlier?" Gray kept his eyes down and held his hand against his forehead, quelling the urge to heave.

The jailer walked back and stood in front of Gray's

cell. "You been unconscious on that floor for a long time. Probably had a whiskey dream."

Moving his hands higher in the latticework of the cell door, Gray Boy raised himself enough to stand. Trying to regain his composure before making direct eye contact, he stared at Rube's thin, white-turning-yellow shirt, trying not to notice the remnants of several meals that decorated the front or the brown rings under the armpits. A missing button caused Rube's big, hairy stomach to poke through the gap, revealing a navel that was probably butchered by an untrained midwife. Gray Boy swallowed hard to control the vomit reflex.

He rubbed his eyes with the heels of his hands. "Bullshit. I know I heard voices."

Rube put his large hands against the cell door and leaned in closer to Gray. His eyes became slits. "You listen to me, Boy. Drunk as you were when Toy brought you in here, I wouldn't be surprised if you heard the devil hisself." Rube turned and walked toward his office.

Gray Boy's cloudy gaze followed Rube as he walked down the hall. The gluttonous jailer had fed the cheeks of his ass so well that they rose above his belt loops. It looked as if he had stuffed a sack full of cotton in each side of his pants.

"I may have a little ass, but it's better than hauling around that load you carry. How does one man put that much lard on one ass?" Shouting at Rube drained what little energy Gray Boy had, and he slid down again. The flash of anger had made blood rush to his head, making it pound and slosh like a rolling watermelon. He leaned against the cell door and breathed in gasps, trying to get past the nausea. He did not pass out this time, but welcome sleep gave him temporary relief.

He awoke again with the side of his head against the cell door. The taste and feel of stomach acid as he ran his tongue across his teeth reminded him of where he was and how he got there. He looked under the cots in the adjoining cells again. Nothing. Smelling his own sour breath, he slapped his shirt pocket looking for a stick of Doublemint. Nothing.

"Anybody here?" The pelting of raindrops was his only answer.

Everyone knew that Toy seldom locked the cell door when a minor was thrown in his jail. There might be a fire, and the sheriff did not want a dead boy's burned body on his conscience. Such a thing would surely kill a sheriff's chances of getting re-elected. Gray Boy put his shoulder against his cell door, but it did not move. He shoved harder. A loud squeak from the door drifted down the hallway as the door moved a few inches. The squeak echoed and hung in the heavy air. Another push gave him enough room to squeeze through.

Light from the jailer's office cast a pale yellow glow down the gray concrete hall that ran beside the cells. Gray Boy saw his reflection in the checkerboard shadow of the cell door. His wet loafers squeaked as the eased down the hall toward the light. He knew the courthouse well. If he could get past Rube's office to the back stairway, he was almost home. No way Rube could catch him. He wasn't really escaping, just trying to buy some time to get over being sick from mixing beer and whiskey. *Toy Roy will understand.*

Gray Boy focused on the door to the back stairway and walked toward the light from the jailer's office. Toy had tossed the huge jail-cell keys across Rube's desk, and they had formed what appeared to be a cross. Gray felt a little silly as he imagined a vampire in pursuit and himself as the hero escaping from the dark castle. He pulled the keys to the back stairway door from their usual hook just inside Rube's office. He opened the door and stared down the dark steps that would take him all the way to the basement. From there, it would be easy to find his way through the hallways that led outside. He laid the keys softly on the floor and headed down the stairs.

Halfway down, he remembered the baseball. *Was it still lying on the smelly cot?* He remembered having the ball when Toy Roy had arrested him, but everything was fuzzy after that. As he turned to go back up, the door to the outside walkway creaked open. Even dimwit Rube would notice an open cell door and wet footprints. It was too late to return.

Forsaking quietness for quickness, he put both hands against the walls in the narrow stairway to brace himself as he took the steps two at a time. There was no light in the claustrophobic stairway and no handrails, but he knew the turns well. He and his friends had sneaked up the stairs many times to peek in on trials in the district courtroom. Gray was still dizzy, but the musty smells of the stairway were almost pleasant compared to the stench in the jail. The prospect of freedom, even if it was temporary, made the fogginess in his head start to go away. He was close enough to almost feel the little Mustang under him, rain and wind in his face, speeding down state highway 24 toward home. He could be there in less than ten minutes.

The bottom floor of the courthouse was half above ground, half below. Like the jail on top, the bottom floor was surrounded by an open walkway just below ground level. Exterior concrete walls held the earth at bay. Even in the middle of drought, it always had the smell of wet dirt and disinfectant. Basement floor office windows looked out on the bottoms of shrubs and the roots of small trees that had struggled to ground level in search of water. Concrete steps at each corner of the walkway led to the courthouse lawn. The place was a favored hangout for hobos and varmints. Gray Boy felt safer as the fresh fragrance of rain hit him, but he stopped short when something moved against the concrete outside wall.

Bo Creekwater was huddled in a corner against the wall, partially sheltered from the rain. He covered his head with his hands and arms, cowering like a kicked dog. A security

light on the side of the courthouse provided just enough light
for Gray Boy to see him. Bo's pant legs and brogan shoes
were soaked, but the wall had kept his upper body dry. His
high cheekbones and straight black hair suggested Indian an-
cestry, but the broad nose and large lips were more common
to Negroes.

"Don't you have enough sense to come in out of the rain,
Bo?" Gray Boy was not happy to see his retarded friend.
"You're ten steps away from a roof, dumb-ass. Get under it."
Gray felt a twinge of guilt for his impatience. "Why ain't you
home, anyway?"

"Bigmomma sick. I be stayin' with Toy Roy at the jail, uh
huh."

Gray Boy did not hear the answer. He took the four steps
to ground level in two bounds and stepped out into the full
force of the wind and rain. The Mustang was parked where
Toy Roy had promised it would be. He jumped to clear the
dark spot that he assumed was a shadow, but something
solid caught his foot. He fell hard beside the dog wallow
puddle. "What the hell?" Bracing himself with both hands,
he pushed out of the mud and looked around to see what he
had stumbled over. The oak tree blocked the security light,
making it too dark to see more than an outline of Spooner's
body.

Trembling, Gray Boy crouched and moved close enough
to put his hand on Spooner's back. He shook him. "You
hurt, Spooner?" No answer. "What're you doing out here
in the mud? You drunk?" Gray Boy heard the sound of an
approaching car and moved behind the tree. There was just
enough reflection from the car's lights to illuminate Spooner's
face. The only dead people Gray Boy had ever seen had their
eyes closed, but he knew what that blank, wide-eyed stare
meant.

The nausea returned. He heaved, but nothing came up.
Mud burned his knuckles where the skin had been knocked

off. Drained again, he sat down in the mud to stare at
Spooner's body. Another approaching car sent a torrent of
fear and adrenalin through him, and he began to shake. *I'm
not afraid—just wet and sick.* He looked in all directions to see if
anyone was watching. The rain and gusting wind forced him
to close his eyes. *I can't help you now, Spooner.* He pushed his
hand down in his jeans for the key to the Mustang.

Jake Rivers' eyes popped open. Something was wrong. He
rubbed his eyes and allowed them time to adjust. The blue
glow-in-the-dark hands and dots on the chocolate-brown face
of his birthday Timex showed a little past three. His feet
touched something wet as he pushed out of his feather bed
to pull on some jeans. In the excitement of the night before,
he had left his wet Little League uniform hanging on the
cane-bottomed chair by his bed. Water was dripping on a
bare spot where a piece of linoleum had worn away and was
running down the unlevel floor before disappearing under his
bed. Careful not to drag his feet across the splintery wood
floor, he draped the uniform over his skinny bare shoulder,
pushed open the screen door, and walked barefooted along
the front porch.

Gusts from the southeast brought rain around the corner
of the porch, slapping the lightning rods against the tall
house. The loose rods made an out-of-tune sound like the
cymbals Jake had been forced to play in the rhythm band at
school. Those days were behind him now—kid stuff. Mattie
required him to hang his wet or smelly clothes on the front
porch rail to dry and air out until her next trip to the washateria on Rainey Hill. Careful to avoid the holes where boards
had rotted away, he draped his uniform across the porch rail
and faced his number 9 toward the road. It was almost a
quarter mile down the driveway to Texas state highway 24,
but Jake wanted his number to show, just in case someone

dropped by before he got up the next morning.

He looked east, traveling in his mind's eye the three miles to Klondike and five miles farther to Cooper and the baseball diamond where it had happened. A gust full of rain chilled him a little and wet his just-dried burr. The porch wouldn't protect the uniform from all of the rain, but at least it wouldn't be dripping on the floor.

A dog-run hall split the Rivers' house into two parts— kitchen and living room on the east and bedrooms on the west. Jake's bedroom was on the north end of the hall. His father had added a porch bedroom on the south end when Tuck had been born three years before. Tuck had slept in a small bed beside his parents in that room until he was big enough to join Jake in the dog-run.

Still shoeless and shirtless, Jake tiptoed down the hall and looked into the bedroom that he had once shared with Gray and knew what was wrong. His older brother was not in his bed. Gray's motorcycle had not been parked in its usual place when Jake and his parents arrived after the ballgame, but Jake thought it might be in the abandoned dairy barn. Down the dark hall, his parents were still asleep in their porch bedroom, the only new part of the century-old house. Jake knew that his father would be up in less than an hour. A dairyman's habits die hard. Jake shivered a little at the thought of his father rising before Gray Boy came home.

Jake sighed, hoping his mother might hear, but she did not stir. He wished for his sister, but Trish had headed toward Commerce to pick up her husband as soon as the game was over. They were probably close to their home in Houston by now.

Mattie had hung a cloth curtain across the dog-run to allow Jake some privacy. He closed the curtain and pulled the light chain above his bed. The naked bulb harshly lighted the narrow bedroom, creating shadows in every corner. Jake knew it probably wasn't there, but he looked under each pillow and the feather mattress, anyway. He was certain that his brother had recovered the only ball Jake had ever hit out of the park. Gray would surely bring it when he came.

It had been only a few hours since that homerun, but Jake felt that his life had already changed for the better. He felt older than his twelve years and more confident. Laying his jeans on an arm of the chair, he reached for the light chain again. The gold-colored plating on a picture frame flickered in the corner of his eye. *Why did it always do that—calling him to look when he did not want to.* The picture had become his mother's proudest possession—a reminder of when her life had been whole.

Before Tuck died, Jake would pick up the snapshot of the Rivers siblings and melt into his little brother's eyes and thoughtful smile. Trish's jaunty, welcoming smile made him feel better when he was down. With Trish married and moved to Houston and Tuck in a lonely grave at Klondike, they seemed to be fading from the photograph, leaving Jake alone with his older brother.

Jake and Gray had the Rivers' dark skin and almost black eyes, but the similarities ended there. Gray, his penny-colored complexion framed against a white tee shirt, flashed an engaging, dimpled smile that made one want to crawl in the picture and be close to him. Gray Boy Rivers treated life like it was a lemon tree. He selected a new lemon every day, squeezed every drop out of it, and made lemonade.

Jake, skinny and shirtless, had a forced, gap-toothed smile in the picture that portrayed his lack of confidence. Much as he tried, Jake figured he would never measure up to his older brother. Before pulling the chain, he checked for Tuck's impression in the mattress. It wasn't there. It had been gone for several nights now. Maybe Tuck's work was done. Maybe the homerun ended it.

Light out and head against the pillow, he heard the Mustang roar into the driveway and pull into the dairy barn.

Jake could sleep now. He thought again of the homerun and softly mouthed, "Thanks, Tuck."

2 A squirrel stopped to inspect the unfamiliar object
in its path. The waving of a huge pair of arms and
the approach of two men sent it scurrying around
Spooner's body and up the big oak. Toy Roy Robbins'
nervousness showed as he danced across the wet lawn,
Truman Bates by his side. Toy did occasional, pirouette-like
movements in order to face Truman without slowing their
pace. Gesticulating, he skipped backward as Truman walked
forward. Truman walked under his umbrella, carefully measuring his steps in order to keep his shoes clean and dry. Toy
leaned under the umbrella to see Truman's face clearly. He
searched that face for answers and some sort of absolution for
himself and the office of sheriff. Truman's expression be-
trayed little emotion or hint as to his feelings.

Being sheriff of one of the smallest counties in the state
had looked easy to Toy when he announced for the office.
Cooper, with fewer than twenty-five hundred people, was the
largest city in the county. Toy had good intentions when he
won the election in a landslide. He had tried to understand
the complexities of law enforcement, but things were pretty
much black and white with him.

He could pick up a grown man with one of his ham-hock
hands and slam him down on the hood of his patrol car

when necessary. He could bring in most law-breakers without drawing his weapon or using his handcuffs. Criminals knew better than to try his patience. Break the law—go to jail; talk back or strike a law officer; get hit back—twice as hard. Simple. Toy's uncomplicated philosophy usually worked. When his temper got him into trouble, attorney Truman Bates usually tried to help get him out.

It had been raining cats and dogs when Clarence Anderson, the city night watchman, discovered Spooner Hays' broken body just before daybreak. At a little past time for the sun to come up, the rain had slowed to a drizzle. Drops slid down Truman Bates umbrella as he stooped to inspect the body.

Truman was quiet for what seemed like an eternity to Toy. "What do you think, Truman? He fall, or what?"

Truman stood and adjusted his spectacles. "That's Ivory's boy, all right."

Toy made a half circle around the body. "Excuse me, Truman, but I know who it is. I need to know what he's doing dead on the courthouse lawn." Toy gazed up at the oak tree. "You think he probably fell out of that tree?...and all. "

"I'm a simple country lawyer, Toy, not a detective, and certainly not a doctor. Dr. Olen is the county medical examiner. You need to get him over here to look at this boy."

"Aw, Truman, can't we just take him over to the hospital and let him look at him there? Seems like we need to get him out of this yard before he draws a crowd...and all."

Truman bent down again. "You get hold of the JP yet? He's the one with the authority to move him."

Toy nodded. "On his way."

Truman pointed to Spooner's face. "See that?" Toy nodded. "See this bruising around his neck? That looks like an hard blow." Truman extracted a fountain pen from his shirt pocket and used it to point toward Spooner's hand.

"The skin is knocked off his knuckles. Could be this boy has been in a fight. You could have a homicide on your hands." Truman pointed at Spooner's cheek. "Those scratches could be from the tree limbs; but then again, they could be from fingernails."

Toy raised both arms skyward, as if praying his way out of this predicament, and then turned back toward his mentor. "Okay, let's say foul play was involved. We still need to get him out of here as soon as Hoot gets here. Word will get down to Parkhill's Café, and we'll be up to our asses in people...and all." It was Saturday, and Toy knew that the square would soon start filling with people doing their weekly shopping, eating hamburgers, and going to the picture show.

"Looks like trouble here." Hoot Gibson's voice startled Toy. The justice of the peace stood looking over Truman's shoulder at Spooner's body.

Truman replaced his pen as he rose. "Okay, Hoot, he's all yours. If I were you, I would make some type of record of that body position. Has the tax office still got that camera?"

Charles (Hoot) Gibson shrugged his shoulders. "I imagine they do, but they're not open yet." When Charles was born during the height of the famous cowboy's silent-screen fame, people just naturally started calling him Hoot. Except for his nobody-at-home facial expression, the justice of the peace was an imposing figure. As tall as Toy, thick-bodied, still firm at the waistline, dark hair graying at the temples, a stranger would have thought him handsome, distinguished, even dynamic.

His normal stance was one he had used in the service when a superior officer shouted "ten-hut." Hoot, a veteran of the Korean War, caught a stray piece of shrapnel in his crotch during the first ground battle. He took his Purple Heart and came home to bask in the glory. In the Army, he had been Corp. Charles Gibson; in Cooper, he was Hoot again. Hoot with the vacant stare—Hoot who sometimes said and did things that were just a little out of kilter. Nobody could quite explain what was wrong with Hoot, but everybody wondered what that shrapnel had really done to him. He had run for and lost races for sheriff and county commissioner before finally being appointed to fill a vacancy caused by the death of the duly-elected justice of the peace.

Truman Bates focused his famous courtroom-noncommittal-look-of-disgust on Hoot. How could a man this persnickety about his appearance be so lacking in common sense? "Hoot, you know where the extra keys are. Use your key to the county judge's office and get the key to the tax office. The camera is probably under the counter. Hurry up."

Rance Rivers poured ground coffee into a pan, added water, and lighted the kerosene burner on the kitchen stove. He stumbled in the dark living room, forgetting Mattie's careful placement of pots and pans to catch water from the leaky roof. He peeked around the corner to see if he had awakened Jake. *Takes more than that to wake a twelve-year-old boy.*

Mattie whispered at Rance's shoulder. "He needed that homerun last night, didn't he?" The stumbling and splashing of water had awakened her.

Rance smiled. "Any man or boy who ever played baseball understands just how much he needed it. I needed it for him, too."

"He's always trying to be his big brother." Mattie moved to the table beside Jake's bed and picked up the small, bronzed boots. She carried them back to the door as if carrying an infant child. "I keep moving them to the mantle, and he keeps moving them back to his room."

Rance nodded as he took Tuck's boots. "I guess we were too tied up in our own grief to realize what Tuck's death did to Jake and the other kids."

Mattie sniffed as she took the boots from Rance and put

them back on Jake's table. She dabbed at her eyes with the sleeve of her housecoat and walked back into the kitchen. Rance followed. He poured himself a cup of coffee and gestured with the pan toward Mattie. She shook her head. "I wish you'd use the coffee pot and make decent coffee. That stuff is too strong to drink."

"Rule is, first person to bitch about the coffee gets to make it tomorrow." Rance took a seat at the chrome and gray Formica table. He looked out the window across the cistern and back porch. Rain was still falling. "Boy, ain't this nice. I think it rained all night."

Mattie stood at the window over her kitchen sink, staring at the abandoned dairy barn. "Keeps this up, the pool will be full for the first time in years." She turned back toward Rance. "If this rain had come a year ago, we might still have a dairy."

Rance shrugged a little and stared into his coffee cup. "No use crying over spilled milk. Mother Nature can be a cruel wench sometimes." He nodded toward Gray's bedroom. "What time did Gray Boy get home?"

Mattie shook her head. "You mean you didn't hear that loud thing he rides when he came home?"

"What time was it?"

Mattie's pursed her lips. "It was too dark to see good, but I think the alarm clock by the bed said after three." Mattie knew it was a lot after three.

"After three. Damn. He may be out of high school, but he still lives under my roof. I'm not puttin' up with this."

"Don't tell me. Tell him." Mattie knew something had to be done about Gray's late hours and wild behavior, but she hated conflict between her husband and oldest son.

"He's never here to tell. He avoids me on purpose. Asleep when I leave, and gone when I get back."

Mattie turned her back to Rance, took the cowboy coffee and slung it into the sink. Rance was not in the mood for a confrontation with his wife and felt one coming. He pushed his chair back and stalked out the back door, headed toward his thinking spot between the outhouse and smokehouse. A brush arbor behind the smokehouse provided some shelter for his outdoor blacksmith shop. He liked to sit on his anvil stump and think.

The rain stopped him as he stepped off the porch. It had been raining on and off for almost twelve hours now, but he was still surprised by it. Stepping back under the porch, he leaned against the cistern and took out a can of Prince Albert from one overalls pocket and OCB papers from the other. After one puff from the roll-your-own cigarette, he threw it into the yard and watched the rain melt it. *Yesterday, that cigarette might have started a grass fire.*

Mattie was making the bed as Rance passed through their porch bedroom without speaking. He slipped on the wet floor as he entered Gray's room and looked up to see if the roof had sprung another leak. The water was coming from the pile of wet clothing next to Gray's bed. A small stream of water from the clothes ran past the door and along the sloping floor from the clothes to a hole in the corner of the room. Rance could imagine it trickling down one of the bois d'arc stumps that supported the house.

Gray Boy was sprawled face down on his bed, his bare body exposed except for the sheet covering his buttocks. A fine mist drifted through the south window of the bedroom, giving the room a musty smell. The bedclothes had a wilted, wet look.

Rance recognized the familiar smell of stale beer when he kicked the end of the bed. Gray moaned and moved slightly. Rance kicked it again. "Get up, Gray."

Gray feebly moved his head and seemed to pry his eyelids apart without touching them. "Time is it?"

"Past time for boys who want to be men to be on their feet. Now get up."

"It's Saturday. I don't have to climb any telephone poles today." Gray dropped back on his pillow.

Rance kicked the bed again. "I *do* have to work, and we're gonna talk before I go. You got five minutes to get dressed and get into the kitchen."

In his own bedroom, Jake held his breath after each exchange between his brother and father, expecting the argument to escalate. He tried to concentrate on last night's moment of glory, tried not to listen to the loud voices coming from his brother's bedroom, but could not drown them out. He threw back the sheets, pulled on his jeans, and walked to the kitchen. He did not want to hear the argument or witness it, but was drawn to it by the feeling that his presence might lessen it or even end it.

"Get a shirt on, Jake. I'm tired of bare-chested boys eating at my table." Mattie spoke without looking at Jake. Jake turned and headed back toward his room. His mother shouted after him. "What do you want for breakfast?"

"Nothin'. I'm not hungry." Jake had smelled his mother's eggs and his daddy's salt pork from his room. He had never liked breakfast, and it almost gagged him to look at food in the morning since Tuck died. He missed his little brother sitting on his knee, consuming their mother's bacon-grease eggs so that he did not have to.

Rance and Gray were sitting at the table when Jake came back with his shirt on. He stopped to look at Gray, hoping for at least a mention of the baseball. Gray ignored him. Rance stared as Gray kept his head down, a pained expression on his face.

Jake felt a surge of anger and disappointment toward his brother. "How come he don't have to wear a shirt?" The words came out before he could stop them. Everyone stared at Jake. Nobody answered. Jake walked out to the porch to brush his teeth.

Rance drummed his fingers on the table. "Where were

you last night?"

"Daddy, I'm a grown man now. I got a job climbing poles for the telephone company. How long am I going to have to report to you when I come and go?"

"As long as you live under my roof. Coming in at three o'clock in the morning shows a complete lack of respect for your mother and for me." He pointed a finger at Gray. "I won't have it." Gray's nod was barely perceptible. "Do you understand me?"

Jake slowly drug the baking soda-soaked brush across his teeth as he listened through the porch window, hoping that Gray Boy would not react with anger and escalate the tension. He knew his father was probably right, but hated for his brother to be punished.

Rance leaned toward his eldest son. "Where'd you get that busted lip and the cut on your cheek? You've been fightin' again, haven't you?" Gray continued to stare at the floor, and his lack of response made Rance madder. He walked over and stood over his son. "I know you been drinking, too. Your room smells like a brewery."

Gray Boy looked up at his father. "You got a lot of room to talk about drinkin'."

Flinching at his brother's words, Jake stopped his brushing, closed his eyes, and tried with all his might to practice what his grandfather had tried to teach him. Drowning out the bickering in the once-tranquil kitchen, he summoned up the image and sound of his grandfather making plaintive, soothing music as he pulled his bow across fiddle strings, of his Aunt Exle playing the guitar, and the soft tinkle of Aunt Ola caressing the piano keys.

He held the image and sounds long enough to open his eyes and notice the changes in his damaged family. His mother was still beautiful, but she had cut her hair short after Tuck's death, and it was now flecked with gray. Her gray-green eyes still showed love, but the sparkle was gone.

His father's dark, coarse hair seemed to have been sprinkled with snow on the day of Tuck's death. At forty-four, he still looked like an Indian warrior in overalls to Jake, but the lines creeping out from his eyes had grown deeper and longer. Jake knew that Tuck would not have wanted to leave these signs of his passing.

Rance made a fist with one hand, looked at Mattie, then pointed a finger at Gray. "I want you to get that putrid pile of clothes out of the floor and mop up that mess. Then take 'em up to Rainey Hill and wash 'em yourself."

Gray's expression softened with the mention of Rainey Hill. "Yes sir."

Rance glanced at Mattie and drew a deep breath. His voice was calmer. "Gray, you can either live under my rules or move out. Make up your mind by the time I get back home tonight."

"Hey, Papa Griff." Jake spit his toothpaste water over the porch shelf into the wet yard. Griffin Rivers straightened the slicker keeping his saddle dry and stepped out of the stirrups onto the porch.

"Hey yourself, Jaker." Griffin took off his hat, ran his hand through his gray, coarse hair. He held the brim over Jake's head and let the rain run down his neck. He stamped his boots to shake water from the yellow slicker before hanging it on a porch nail.

"You ain't gonna tie him?" Jake pointed his toothbrush toward Buddy, Griffin's sorrel gelding. His reins were draped on the wet porch steps.

Griffin grinned as he whispered. "Don't tell him he ain't tied, and he'll never know." He stepped into the kitchen and sensed the coolness. "I feel like a long-tailed tomcat in a room full of rocking chairs." Griffin tried to make light of the situation, but nobody smiled. He walked to the stove for coffee. He rode the mile or so from his house most mornings for a cup of Mattie's coffee.

"Rance drank it all before you got here." Mattie avoided meeting Rance's stare. "I'll make a fresh pot."

"No need, Mattie. I just rode by to see if y'all had floated away yet. This is a damn good rain." He looked expectantly at his son, but Rance just mumbled under his breath and headed out the door. Griffin put his hat back on and stepped out on the porch.

Jake watched silently as his grandfather untied the blue wildrag from around his neck and wiped his face with it. He shook the yellow slicker before putting it back on. Picking up Buddy's wet reins, he pulled them over the horse's neck and stepped into the stirrup. Jake wanted to say something—wanted to apologize for the cool reception his grandfather had received, but he could think of no words. Papa Griff would understand. He had seen it before. *Wonder if he and Daddy fought like that?*

"Hey, Papa. What kind of music you hear today?"

"Fiddles. Kinda screechy, though." Griffin Rivers smiled and headed east toward the small shotgun house he occupied on the corner of the Rivers eighty-acre farm. Born in West Texas, the son of a ranch cowboy, he had been true to his father by keeping a horse as his only means of transportation. Griffin, a man who believed that work should never be done afoot that could be done horseback, had brought his family to this area of Northeast Texas in 1918, but had never fully accepted his own decision. "There ain't no place in Texas that's north or east, some are just a little less south and west than others," he was fond of saying.

Jake watched until his grandfather disappeared into the gray mist of distant rainfall, heading toward his house. *On days like this, Papa needs a car.*

Rance had just started to back out his '53 Chevy pickup when he saw the black '54 Ford with a star on both doors pull into his driveway off 24. He groaned as the sheriff's car came to a stop just past the entrance to the dirt driveway. Toy always did that when he was bringing bad news. From his rearview mirror, Rance watched Toy's huge bulk ease the Ford into the driveway ruts. Rance took a deep breath, trying to steel himself from taking out his frustration on his old friend. He knew that Toy hated being the bearer of bad news.

Toy seemed to be out of the Ford before it came to a complete stop behind Rance's truck. He approached Rance with agile movements more common to a smaller man. Rance stepped out of his truck, put a brogan on a tire, and stooped to tighten his leather shoestrings. "Toy." It sounded more like a warning than a greeting.

"Mornin', Rance. Good rain, huh?" Toy waited for the reply that did not come. He jingled the change in his pocket and started again. "There ain't a day goes by that I don't thank my lucky stars for having a friend like you, Rance. Why, if you hadn't took me under your wing when I was a kid, ain't no tellin' where I'd be."

Rance had to smile as he looked up to his old friend. Toy was a good four inches taller and a hundred pounds heavier. Rain dripped off both their hats. *How could I have ever taken him under my wing?*

Toy had enrolled as a freshman at Klondike when Rance was a senior. Roy Robbins and his wife had seen a toy-sized replica of Roy when their son was born, so they had named their new son Toy Roy. When his weight and name brought ridicule, Rance took up for him. He showed him how to use his size to stop the bullying. When a simple backhand slap sent one of his tormentor's teeth flying, nobody ever bullied Toy again. The abuse had taken its toll, however, and Rance knew that unresolved issues from those days could still cause Toy's temper to flare.

Rance shook his head and looked away from Toy. "I want you to stop bringing that up, Toy. Any favor I did you has long since been repaid."

"Still, I'm much obliged." Toy banged his muddy boots

against the tire of the Ford.

"Hate to rush you, Toy, but I'm on my way to work. I'll use this rain as a day to service road equipment. If you brought bad news, spit it out."

Toy made a rumbling noise in his throat as he looked toward the house. "I need to see both the boys."

Rance stiffened. "Both boys? What the hell for?"

"Now Rance, don't get bent out of shape. I got to handle this a certain way. Truman told me what I got to do, and it's better if I just tell the story once. It's probably nothin'."

Rance's heels squished in the mud as he turned and headed toward the house. Toy retrieved something from the seat of his Ford and trotted after him. Both boys had heard the conversation and were waiting on the back porch. Rance felt a hollow feeling in the pit of his stomach as he saw Gray Boy's expression. "Toy says he wants to talk to both you boys." Rance shot a questioning stare toward Jake, then watched as Mattie left her stove to move closer to the open window behind the cistern.

Toy pulled a baseball from his pocket and tossed it to Jake. Caught off guard, Jake almost let it drop into the open cistern door. "You recognize that ball, Little Rance?"

Jake liked Toy's nickname for him. He rolled the ball in his hands and examined the writing. He recognized the small, almost feminine script edged deeply into the ball's cover. *Jake Rivers 1956.* He glanced at Gray Boy, but his brother was staring at the porch boards under his feet. Jake put his arm across his face, a habit he practiced when nervous, trying to think of an answer.

Gray finally saved him. "Okay, Toy, you made your point. You know damn well that's Jake's homerun ball and that I put his name on it." He shifted his gaze toward his father. "Daddy, I spent the night in the county jail last night. I had the ball when Toy threw me in. I walked out sometime early this morning and came home."

Rance leaned against the shelf that held a wash pan and water pitcher. His release of breath sounded like a low whistle. "What did you do this time, Gray?" His words were slow and heavy.

Toy's growl broke the uncomfortable silence. "Wait, Rance. Shoot, this ain't goin' like Truman said it would." Everyone turned to face him. "I ain't out here about some stunt Gray Boy might have pulled last night. I thought I locked it, but I could have left that cell door open so he could go home if he needed to. I just don't remember. We got bigger trouble."

"What kind of bigger trouble?" Rance asked.

Toy pointed toward the ball in Jake's hand. "Spooner Hays was found dead this morning on the courthouse lawn." Jake's mouth dropped open as he stared at Toy. Toy nodded. "Yeah, Spooner Hays, King Ivory's son."

Mattie's gasp shot through the window screen. "How?"

"Don't know yet. He's over at Doc Olen's now. I hope it was just a fall out of that big oak on the courthouse lawn, but Truman says he was in some sort of scrap, too." Toy's face took on a pained expression. "Thing is, I found that ball not six feet from Spooner's dead body this morning." Toy stared at Gray. "You know how it got there?"

Everyone looked at Gray. Jake was still trying to comprehend that Spooner was dead as Gray asked, "The ball was outside? You sure?" Toy nodded. Gray looked at his father before turning back to Toy. "I had it with me when you took me to the jail. Or, at least I thought I did. I missed it when I was going down the stairs, but figured you would keep it for me."

Toy put a huge hand on the porch post and leaned against it. Jake looked up at the porch roof, wondering if the post could hold Toy's weight. "Thing is, I never saw the ball until I picked it up by Spooner's body this mornin'."

Rance looked at his oldest son, fear now replacing the

look of hurt and disappointment. "Can you explain how it got there?"

"No idea. I swear. I didn't see it there when...."

Rance moved in front of Gray. "When what?" Rance turned his glance toward Mattie and took a deep breath. "You saw Spooner's body when you left the jail, didn't you?"

Gray shook his head, trying to hold back the tears of shame that were welling up. Jake could not remember the last time he had seen his brother cry, and he felt his own eyes start to fill. It has always been that way. When his father used the razor strap on Gray's butt, Jake flinched as he felt Gray's pain. Welts would often rise on his own buttocks later. Mattie called them sympathy welts.

Rance saw the tears and realized that the situation was serious. Fear crept into his voice. "Did you see Spooner or not?"

Gray's eyes, now filled with tears, still glared defiance. He shouted as he wiped his sleeve across his nose. "Yes, damn it, I saw Spooner lying there dead."

Rance's shoulders slumped as he whispered. "And you just ran off."

Gray looked at his father, Toy, and Jake, seeking a glimmer of understanding. "He was already dead, and there wasn't anything I could do to help him."

"So you just came on home and went to sleep." Rance kept his gaze fixed on Mattie as he spoke to Gray.

"I was sick."

Toy moved away from the porch post and stepped closer to Gray. Like most people, he had always liked the boy. He saw himself as an uncle, even a big brother to Gray Boy Rivers. Gray did all the things he had wanted to do when he was a kid. "He's right, Rance. Ain't nothin' a man can do to help a person already dead."

Rance shook his head. Disgust showed. "He could have at least reported it."

Toy's double chin jiggled as he shook his head. "I was either out in the patrol car or home in bed. There wasn't anybody to report to except Rube Carter, and you know him and Gray Boy don't get along too good."

Mattie stepped out on the porch, eyes flashing. She pulled back a wisp of black hair that had fallen over one eye as she stood between her sons and Toy. "Toy, what is it you want? Stop berating these boys and get to the point."

Toy's face always flushed in Mattie's presence. He thought there was no prettier woman in Delta County. "Now, Miss Mattie, you know I'm kinda' clumsy sometimes, but I got a job to do. We got a dead colored boy not fifty feet from my jail, and I got to find out what happened to Ivory's boy before things get nasty." He paused to look toward Rance for support. "I ain't accusing you or yours of nothin'. I know these boys well enough to be sure they ain't mixed up in nothin' this serious."

Mattie's face softened as she placed a hand on each hip, but her gray-green eyes were still sending bullets in Toy's direction. "I'm still waiting for you to get to the point, Toy Robbins."

Toy looked to Rance for help. "I just found that ball with Jake's name on it next to the body. Fact is, I ain't told nobody about that ball, except Truman. Wanted to see if your boys could explain it before I said anything."

Mattie took the ball from Jake's hand. "It probably slipped out of Gray's pocket when you were taking him to...." Mattie could not say her son's name and jail in the same sentence.

Toy looked at Gray. Both knew that they had used the side entrance to the courthouse, a long way from the front lawn. Gray looked out toward the abandoned dairy barn. "I can't explain it. I could have sworn I had that ball when you threw me in the cell."

Toy stepped off the porch into the mist. "Don't say

nothin' about the ball just yet but hang onto it. I'll have to tell Buster Galt when he starts snoopin' around. Maybe we can get this thing solved before he gets back from Sulphur Springs."

Gray stiffened at the mention of Cameron Galt's father. Buster Galt was the district attorney for Delta, Hopkins, and Franklin counties. Cameron was part of the reason he had been in jail the night before. Toy opened his car door before shouting at Rance. " I almost forgot, Rance. Somebody's got to tell King Ivory. You're about the only one who can get to him without causing a commotion. I'd sure be much obliged."

3 As Rance traveled along 24 toward Klondike, he tried to form the words to tell a man that his son was dead, but he could not. He hated this mission, but he was almost relieved to escape the pressure at home and the problems with his own children and Mattie. Still, he did not want to go it alone. He pulled off 24 onto the old Klondike highway and into Hack Gentry's driveway. Rance killed the engine and pulled his pocket watch from the bib of his overalls. Hack should be finished with milking and cleaning the dairy barn about now. As he replaced the watch, he saw his best friend emerge from the dairy barn milkroom door.

Hack's milking garb always brought a smile to Rance's face. Rubber boots to his knees, a safari hardhat, khaki pants and shirt, and a sweat bandanna around his neck. Hack was a slight, wiry man with sharp features and soft, almost translucent skin. Only thinning hair indicated his fifty-six years. Everything else about Hack looked younger.

Rance's elbow hung in its usual position out the window, and Hack slapped it in a gesture of affection. "Figured you'd be up to your elbows in grease by now." Hack braced himself against the truck's door with both hands and stretched his back. "Must be getting' old. Bending over to work those milkers gets harder every day."

"Hope you got the cowshit off those hands before puttin' 'em on my door."

"Washed 'em in the dairy barn like I always do. Willie Mae doesn't allow cow manure in her house."

Rance smiled. "You're right, I should be at the county barn up to my elbows in grease, but the bulldozers are going to have to wait a little while today. Got some bad news this mornin'."

Hack's expression turned serious. "How's that?"

"They found Spooner Hays dead on the courthouse lawn." Hack stepped back and opened his mouth with surprise, but no words came out. Rance nodded. "Toy was out to the house, and he wants me to go tell Ivory. I need some company for that trip. You interested?"

"How'd it happen?"

"Jump in if you're goin'. We need to get on out there before Ivory finds out from somebody else. I'll tell you on the way."

Hack nodded. "Just let me tell the wife, and I'll be right with you." Rance watched as his friend trotted to the back door of their two-story house. A fresh coat of white paint and green gingerbread trim emphasized the contrast between the Gentry's house and the Rivers' unpainted one.

Hack and Willie Mae represented the third family generation to operate the farm. Gentry land stretched well past the Sulphur River bottom. Hack kept his dairy cattle on high, sandy land and ran stocker cows in the bottom on black gumbo, using both sides of Blue Bottom Creek for grazing. People said that Hack Gentry had bottomland stocker cows that had never seen a man, but Rance knew better. Hack checked all of his cows at least once a week, more often in good weather. When Hack returned, the jungle hardhat had been exchanged for a straw.

Klondike was only two miles from Hack's place, about equidistant between the Rivers' place and Cooper. Rance had explained all he knew about Spooner's death before they reached the Klondike cemetery. Rance barely glanced at the resting place of his two-year-old son as they passed the cemetery. The gravel road turned to mud, and the road started its downward slope toward the bottomlands. The truck started to slide as the tires reached through the soft layer of slippery, wet sand to the hardpan underneath. Hack sat up straighter for a better view of the treacherous road. Rance stayed in high gear, careful to avoid any quick acceleration or braking that might push them into the ditch or get them stuck.

"I'm starting to believe your own B.S. about being a great mud driver, but we ain't there yet."

"Good thing you're still wearing those rubber boots. You can walk for help when the gumbo gets us." The slope of the winding road grew steeper as the sand turned to black gumbo, and they made the first deep ruts in the black road. "Damn. I thought sure that somebody would have already made us some ruts before now." Rance shifted down, and the truck's tires left two wavy trails behind them.

Hack smiled and waved at the occasional group of black and brown faces that stared back from the porches of shacks along the side of the road. "Most of 'em don't have cars, and the ones that do have got better sense than to drive on roads like this. Only you and me are that dumb."

"Last Monday, you couldn't tell the road from the bar ditches down here. Now, a man who knows how to drive can get down it." Rance kept his eyes on the road.

"I suppose you were driving the maintainer that did that wonderful work, so you're now gonna take credit for the condition of the road as well as the driving."

"You, on the other hand, could get stuck in a patch of cow piss after a three-year drought." Rance slowed to a crawl as they reached Hollow Bridge. The old wooden bridge crossed Blue Bottom Creek at its deepest point. The creek marked the border of the colored community of Klondike as it wound its crooked path to the Sulphur River. Rance stopped the truck on the edge of the bridge.

Blackjack, locust, and bois d'arc limbs intertwined closely enough to form a natural roof over the creek and its banks. Droplets from the mist and the recent rains trickled from it. Tree trunks and thorny vines that grew underneath formed an almost impenetrable wall. The earth beneath had not seen daylight for many years.

Rance drummed his fingers on the steering wheel. "You're pretty good with words, Hack. You thought of what we can say to a man that just lost his only son?"

Hack shot him a surprised look. "I just came along to support you."

"Hell, I know you give the opening prayer in church nearly every Sunday. I'm not even a religious man, and you're about half Holy-Roller."

"Don't pull that on me. Deep down, you're probably the most religious man I know. Besides, you know him better than me. He's your friend. I just know him from trading with him a couple of times."

"People don't take enough care when they throw out that word—religion. Means too many different things to too many different people. You gonna keep on talkin' or open the gate?"

Ivory's gate was made of rusted barbed wire woven through perpendicular, grayed bois d'arc posts. Gumbo balled up on Hack's boots as he dragged the gate aside. He stepped back on the running board and stuck his head through the window. "You think we ought to close it?"

"No, but I think *you* ought to close it. Do you like for people to leave your gates open?"

Hack closed the gate and jumped a little as Rance pushed the horn for a long honk, followed by several shorter ones. "What's that all about?"

"It's a little signal I worked out with Ivory. I use it when he's not expecting me."

The honking ignited a cacophony of barking dogs.

"Damn. How many dogs you reckon he's got?"

"I don't imagine even Ivory knows the answer to that question. I got Shy from him. Damn good dog." Rance smiled as he eased the truck forward on the path. "Jake came with me that day. I don't think his eyes blinked once the whole time we were here."

"Thing is, I don't see any of 'em. He got 'em chained up?"

"Some are chained, some are loose. Best to keep the parts of your body you like the most inside the truck."

Hack drew his arm inside and put his hand on the window roller handle. As they drove deep along the winding road to Ivory's house, the stacks of junk that lined their path grew higher. Hack risked sticking his head out the window far enough to see the tops of the stacks.

"I've seen this once before, but I don't think it was this big. Where does he get all this junk?"

"Beats me how he gets it in and out and how it gets it stacked so high."

"Out? You mean things actually leave here?"

"Ivory trades with people all over the state. Does lots of business in Louisiana and Mississippi. Look around. A man could find just about anything he needs here." Rance pointed toward the junk wall. "There's old cars, farm implements, washing machines, tractors, and parts to just about any old machine you can think of. Ivory knows where every nut and bolt is." The road abruptly narrowed to a trail only wide enough for walking. Rance opened the door, stood on the running board, and honked the horn again. "Well, let's get this over with."

Rance started down the lane and Hack followed. "Where does this trail lead?"

Rance pointed northeast. "The creek makes a U-shape

back there. Ivory lives in a pretty good-sized house at the bottom of the U. This is the only way to approach the house unless you're a fly or can hack your way through that brush and bramble wall at the back of the house."

Hack looked up at the junk walls again. Because of curves in the pathway, he could see only a few feet in front and a few feet in back of him. "This place is like a fort. Those dogs sound like they mean business. Those ain't exactly friendly barks."

"It gets a little worse when we get close to the house, but Ivory should be waiting to call 'em off."

"Should be? What if he's not at home?" Hack's rubber boots slipped a little as he stepped onto a patchwork of red brick laid into the black gumbo in a haphazard design. The uneven surface made walking more difficult.

"That's the beginning of the walkway to the house." Rance stopped as the house came into view. With no under-pinning, foundation stumps were visible along its perimeter. A low fence made of cedar posts and split rails ran the length of the dirt yard. A steep, tin roof sloped down over the house and front porch. Vines and trees crawled over the roof's peak, making the house appear as a false front for a tree and vine wall. Axes, sledgehammers, a scythe, coyote hides, and cow skulls hung by leather strips and square nails on the front porch.

The brick pathway led through an opening in the fence and another two hundred feet to the front door. Dogs drowsed on each side of the S-shaped path. Two Dobermans, two curs, and two chows were evenly distributed along the winding lane. Tongues lolling, they seemed comfortable with visitors. Rance and Hack stepped through the gate and walked side-by-side toward the house. The dogs let them get halfway before they snarled and attacked.

"Shit!" Hack jumped away from the charging dogs. Trace chains behind the dogs rose out of the mud, snapping taut

just as the dogs reached the edge of the path. Hack took a
deep breath as his gaze followed the chains to large steel posts.
They walked the rest of the way in single file to stay away from
the edges of the path.

Rance chuckled. "The dogs Ivory keeps around the house
are usually his smartest ones. He keeps 'em tied up so they
stay mean."

"It damn sure works. What the hell is he afraid of?"

Rance shouted over the dogs' din. "He hates the thought
of anybody stealing any of his stuff. And, he likes his
privacy."

As they passed the last dog, the barking stopped as suddenly as it had begun. The silence was almost as startling as
the attack had been. Dog heads laid peacefully on paws, eyes
looked up in with innocent expressions, and snarls turned to
dog-smiles. When Rance and Hack turned back toward the
house, King Ivory was on the porch, appearing to have been
plucked from the pitch-blackness under the trees lining Blue
Bottom Creek and transported without sound to the porch.

Ivory stood shirtless, his black skin contrasting with his
painter-white overalls. His neck was bowed a little, as if Ivory
expected his head to bump the porch roof. "Hidy." His big
lips formed a wary smile. Ivory's mouth, nose, and eyes were
large to match the rest of his body. His widely spaced teeth
seemed to overfill his mouth and push against his lips. He
moved his lips like a cow chewing its cud.

Rance touched the brim of his hat. "Mornin', Ivory.
Sorry for the intrusion." Still watching the big black man,
he indicated Hack with a slight movement of his head. "You
remember Hack."

"Sho do. How you, Mr. Hack?" Ivory's local Negro
dialect conflicted with his almost regal presence. Rance
cringed a little, recognizing condescension in Ivory's tone. He
usually deflected it by a racial slur or other insult; Ivory would
respond in kind, and their real conversation could begin.

Today was not a good time for such banter.

Though seldom seen outside his junk fortress, Ivory Hays was the accepted leader of the colored population of Delta County. His hermit-like lifestyle fueled folklore in both the black and white communities. Rumored to be a practitioner of black magic, he was often referred to as King Ivory. Some claimed he was the richest man in the county, exerting complete power over the colored community and uncommon influence in the white.

"Need to talk to you a minute, Ivory. You got a place where we can sit down?"

Ivory's smile faded as he left Rance and Hack standing in embarrassed silence for several seconds before replying. "'Spose so. Come up on the porch."

The low squawk of chickens enclosed in a chicken wire fence at the edge of the porch and the grunting of pigs under the house signaled their mild displeasure at being disturbed by strangers. Rance glanced at the single chair on the front porch, then toward the open front door. He had never been inside Ivory's house. All their business had been conducted out among the piles of junk or on the porch. Ivory hesitated at the open front door. "Follow me, Mistuh Rance."

Being addressed as Mister made Rance uncomfortable again, but he let it slide. He sensed that Ivory was not pleased with their visit. Ivory ducked his head lower and entered the house. Rance and Hack followed the big man, stepping down as they entered a dark hallway. The smell of wet, old dirt filled their nostrils. Blue Bottom overflows had washed dirt and silt under the house and rotted the floor in places. The hall floorboards had decomposed so completely that Ivory's tracks could be seen in the dirt. As they moved farther into the darkness, Rance's eyes burned a little, and his nose was assaulted with the smell of old wet cedar and pine mixed with decaying, mildewed paper and cloth.

As his eyes adjusted, he tried to take in his surroundings.

Magazines with pages curled from extremes of heat, humidity, and cold were stacked with yellowed newspapers, sheets, quilts, blankets, pillows, bolts of fabric, and paper grocery sacks along each side of the hall. Ivory's wide shoulders touched the stacks as he made his way down the hall.

Rance and Hack tried to peer through doors as they passed them. The side rooms were filled, floor to ceiling, with more soft junk. Narrow trails led inside the rooms. One led to a single bed that Rance assumed to be Spooner's. Daylight crept down the hall floor as they entered an open area. If there was a doorway, it was obscured by more scrap, but they seemed to enter an open room. Hack stumbled as they stepped up. The wooden floor in this new room was rickety, but strong enough to hold them up.

A small wood cook stove and mounds of cups, saucers, and other dishes identified the room as a kitchen. Like a creeping vine, piles of soft refuse had started to take this room, too, but two windows remained partially unobstructed, allowing enough daylight for the three men to see each other. On a sunny day, the rising sun might have made the room late-morning bright. The east windows looked out on the banks of Blue Bottom Creek.

Ivory moved to a small, round table covered in newspapers, plates, glasses, cups, and saucers. He wiped the table clean with a sweep of one huge arm. The Melmac dishes, bone-and-wood-handled cutlery, and tin cups clattered as they hit the wooden floor.

"Take a seat, gentlemens." Hide-bottomed chairs with broken backs and split seats surrounded the table. Two nail kegs leaned against the wall.

Rance and Hack chose the kegs. Ivory withdrew the only chair with a good back and sat down. He put his muscled, hairless arms on the table and directed a piercing, almost confrontational stare toward both men. "Made chicory 'fore daylight this mornin'. It'd probably have to be taken with a spoon by now, but you're welcome—if you're of a mind."

Ivory's eyes were hooded and swollen, making him look older than Rance remembered. His black pupils lay in a pool of creamy-yellow, rheumy liquid. Large lower eyelids drooped, revealing pink skin underneath. He looked tired and Rance wondered if the honking had awakened him. Rance stared at the leather pouch suspended from Ivory's neck by a leather shoestring. Has that always been there? Scooting the nail keg closer to the table, he looked directly into Ivory's eyes.

"I've brought bad news, Ivory."

"I figured. Get on with it."

"They found Spooner dead in Cooper this morning."

Ivory neither moved nor spoke; his stare seemed to go completely through the two men. Rance felt his own eyes begin to burn as he unconsciously avoided blinking. He flinched as Ivory scraped back his chair and walked over to a window.

Rance began again, speaking to Ivory's back. "I don't have the words to tell you how sorry I am." He walked over and stood beside Ivory, as if he could deflect some of the pain the man was feeling. "They don't know what happened yet. Sheriff thinks he may have fallen out of that big tree on the courthouse lawn."

Ivory shook his head slowly. "Didn't fall outta no tree."

Hack stood at the other window, trying to see through the wall of trees and brush. From the window, it appeared that the creek had eroded its banks all the way to the house's foundation stumps. Hack stood on his tiptoes to look down the bank. The teetering illusion of the house sliding into the creek triggered a falling sensation, and he stepped back from the window. Mildew was mixing with the grounds of cold chicory coffee and yesterday's turnip greens. In spite of the clouds and mist, the room was getting hot.

Rance broke the tense silence. "Did you already know Spooner was dead?"

"Where is he now?" Ivory ignored the question, his East Texas Negro dialect stored away for now.

"I imagine he's at Dr. Olen's by now. Be glad to take you there."

Ivory shook his head again, still staring out the window. "No. I'll be along directly. Ask them to leave him there until I can get there. Thank you kindly for coming."

Rance and Hack acknowledged Ivory's invitation for them to leave and looked around for a door that might lead outside. A screen door led to a porch, but Ivory pointed back toward the hall. Rance turned at the opening. "Ivory, is there anything Hack and I can do to help? We can feed the dogs or any other animals that need feeding or takin' care of. We're both pretty good hands."

Ivory turned to look at Rance. "I may need your help later, but not now."

As Rance and Hack started back down the brick walkway, the dogs gave guttural warnings, but did not charge. "Rance, did you see anyplace for Ivory to sleep in that house?"

"Never thought about that, but no, I didn't."

4 Osler and Olen Bartlett, third generation doctors, were the only physicians in Delta County. Their father, leaving little doubt as to the future he expected for his progeny, named his first-born son for the famous physician, Sir William Osler. Osler Bartlett carried the mantle of both his names proudly. He wore white or gray gloves, a derby hat, and carried a cane to the Bartlett Hospital and Clinic daily. Such sartorial splendor, however, carried him over the plane of what was considered normal behavior in Cooper and Delta County.

Though Osler was considered the more brilliant of the two, younger brother Olen was revered. Olen had the demeanor Delta countians expected from their doctors. Olive complexioned, handsome but not uncomfortably so, average height, Dr. Olen was not threatening, just reassuring. He was gifted with a calm, focused, almost magical bedside manner. His mere presence was usually enough to make sick people start to feel better. Yet, he could tell and enjoyed hearing a good joke.

More importantly, everyone in Delta County knew that both brothers had turned down offers to practice medicine in several of the best hospitals in America. The Bartlett doctors had chosen to practice in one of the poorest counties in the state not only because of tradition, but because they were of the people.

Bartlett Hospital and Clinic was only two blocks east of the Delta County courthouse and a block off the downtown square. Today, it seemed like a safe haven to Toy Roy Robbins. He and justice of the peace Hoot Gibson started to relax a little the minute they laid Spooner's body on the examination table. When Dr. Olen Bartlett entered the room, both felt a huge weight lift from their shoulders.

Olen put his hands on the end of the black vinyl examination table. "Damn shame. This boy was a handsome physical specimen. Good kid, too. Right, Toy?"

Toy paced as Dr. Bartlett examined the body. "Please tell me he fell out of that oak tree, Doc...and all."

"Oh, I'm pretty sure he fell all right. Out of what or from what I don't know." Dr. Olen glanced up at Toy. "I'm also pretty sure he was in some sort of fight before the fall. Somebody beat him up pretty good, and his face is scratched, but I'd say he put up a good defense before they got the best of him."

Toy's smile disappeared. "What should I do, Doc? Just tell me and I'll do 'er...and all."

Delta County's health officer washed his hands in the sink, pulled down a clean section of gauzy towel from an antiseptic towel holder, and dried them. "You're a better sheriff than you give yourself credit for, Toy. Certainly much better than me. I'm a simple country doctor. Just use your God-given instincts."

The message had the desired effect on Toy. He liked using his instincts, even when they got him into trouble. Determination replaced doubt in his expression. "Can I leave him here till King Ivory comes to get him?"

"It's all right by me, but that's really up to the JP. Have you held an inquest yet, Hoot?"

Hoot stiffened. "Dr. Bartlett, the inquest is being held as

we speak."

"That's fine. What about an autopsy? We'll have to send him to Dallas to get that done. I don't have the skills or the equipment to do it here."

Toy looked at Hoot. The JP stared at the wall as he spoke. "Autopsy? Excuse me, Dr. Bartlett, but I would need medical advice on that matter."

"I have input in the decision, but it's really yours, Hoot. If you think there was foul play involved or any question as to the cause of death, then you can order an autopsy."

Hoot stood at attention for several minutes, staring at Spooner's body. "Sheriff, I hereby order said autopsy." Turning back to the doctor, "Can I depend on you to make the arrangements, Doctor?"

Toy leaned sideways to position himself between Hoot and his wall-stare. "You got any idea how much an autopsy's gonna cost, Hoot?"

Dr. Olen eased the sheet over Spooner's head. "I've been wrong before, but there's little doubt that he died from a broken neck as a result of a fall. Would have probably drowned in his own blood from a punctured lung if the neck had not broken. I believe an autopsy will confirm that. How's that? Now, it's up to you two fellows to determine if he was pushed or made to jump."

Hoot stiffened. "I declare this inquest to be over. Death by a fall, cause to be determined. Suspicious cuts, scratches, and bruising. No autopsy."

The doctor smiled. "I'll be needing this table before long. Why not call Carl Leslie's funeral home to come and get the body? Hoot and I can have the paperwork ready by the time Carl can get here with the ambulance."

"Doc, you know I can't do that." Toy was reluctant to tell the brilliant doctor that he had overlooked something. "Spooner's a colored boy. Besides, King Ivory told Rance for us to leave him here until he comes."

Toy's instincts told him to return to the death scene and try to trace Spooner's activities back from there. After marking the spot where the body had fallen, he started measuring distances. He examined the bark on the oak tree for mud or any evidence that Spooner had climbed it. He was looking up at its limbs in dismay when he heard Rance's voice. "Has Ivory showed up yet, Toy?" Gray Boy stood beside his father. Jake had been told to wait at the truck.

Toy shook his head. "Ain't seen hide nor hair of him, yet. Needs to be here, too."

From his seat on the truck tailgate, Jake saw the Rivers' old '39 Ford creeping along the street by the courthouse. The car rekindled few fond memories for him. He had been glad when Ivory took it away after Rance had bought their '49 Ford. The car was a late teenager when Ivory bought it and in pretty bad shape, but it was an almost total wreck now. Strands of baling wire connected the front bumper, a front fender and the hood to the body like rats clinging to a sinking ship. The back bumper hung askance. One taillight was broken, the tires were all bald; and one was nearly flat.

Shy, Jake's black and white rat terrier, sat comfortably under Jake's arm. As the brakes to the Ford squealed the rattling car to a stop, Shy jumped from under Jake's arm and ran toward the courthouse. Jake beckoned in a shouted whisper for the dog to return, but Shy was single-minded and running at top speed toward the courthouse basement. Jake jumped from the tailgate to retrieve him, but Rance signaled him to stay put.

King Ivory exited the car like a king leaving his carriage. He was dressed in the same overalls, but he had added a frayed denim shirt. His gaze swept the courthouse and its lawn before he stepped to the spot where Spooner's body had been found. Everyone else stepped respectfully back. Ivory kneeled his massive frame and studied the mud puddle and the ground around it.

He fingered the leather pouch between the buttons of his shirt as he examined the ground where his son had died. "Who has Spencer's personals?"

Toy cleared his throat, but the gravel remained in his voice. "Spencer?"

Rance stepped forward. "Spencer is Spooner's real name. Ivory is asking about his stuff, Toy. You know, what was in his pockets—things like that."

Shy ran between Toy and Ivory on his way back to Jake. Toy glanced at the dog, glad for the distraction. "Guess I never knew your boy's real name, Ivory. Sorry I didn't mention his things. Spooner had twelve dollars and some change in his pocket. I can't give that back till the DA gets here, but the money's in a safe place and you will get it when the time comes. You have my word on it."

Ivory's moist eyes looked toward the courthouse. "That all you found?"

Toy stooped to pick up a discarded carton of candy cigarettes. Bending down and rising again appeared to cause him pain. He crushed the small cardboard box. "Well, there was them two rubbers in his front pocket." Toy fidgeted as Ivory continued to stare. "Was there somethin' else we should've found? If somebody stole somethin' belonged to your boy, I need to know about it."

"My boy always carried a bone-handle Case pocketknife. I gave it to him. Wore a leather string around his neck, too."

"You sure? Cause that's all we found."

"Maybe not." Ivory shrugged and directed his attention to the basement floor of the courthouse. "What about the breed kid?"

Toy stiffened. "You mean Bo Creekwater?"

Ivory looked at Rance without speaking. "What about Bo, Ivory?"

"Just wondered if the boy around. He a good hunter, good tracker, being half-Indian. You ask him to look for the

killer?" Ivory's lapses into and out of Hollow dialect irritated
Rance, but he kept silent.

Toy's face flushed as he looked at Rance. He sensed
animosity in Ivory's tone, too. Ivory had overstepped his
bounds, but this was no time to attack a man who's just lost a
son. "Killer? Who said anything about a killer, Ivory? What
makes you think Bo found anything? Bo wadn't even here."
The words had barely escaped when he remembered that he
was to take charge of Bo last night because Beulah, his grandmother, was sick. He promised. He forgot. *Wonder where Bo
stayed last night?*

Gray Boy glanced at his father when Bo's name was mentioned, but he quickly looked back toward Toy when Rance
returned the look. Ivory did not answer Toy, but he continued to scale the courthouse, basement to roof, with his gaze.

Rance broke the silence. "Ivory, you need any help
picking up Spooner? What about services? You got plans?"

Ivory was walking toward the Ford and spoke without
turning. "Much obliged." At the car door, he turned to face
them. "Spencer in the car already." As if to answer their
questioning expressions, Ivory nodded toward the back seat.
"I brought a blanket." He opened the door and turned again.
"Preacher and our women will take care of things at the
church. Funeral will be tomorrow." Everyone's eyes turned
toward the Ford, imagining Spooner's body bundled up in the
back seat as the Ford limped its way toward The Hollow.

"Truman tells me we have a dead colored boy on our
hands." The booming voice of Buster Galt made them all
turn. Buster was taking the courthouse steps two at a time.
The Rivers and the sheriff visibly stiffened at the sound of the
district attorney's voice. A big, broad-shouldered man, Buster
wore his suit and tie like he was better suited to a football
uniform. He walked like a man in charge of things, swinging
his arms like the defensive tackle he had once been, snapping
his fingers with each step.

Buster kept his eyes on Rance as he invaded the area Toy considered his personal space. "What do we know so far? Truman says the boy probably fell out of that tree."

Toy's face grew dark, and he spoke without looking at Buster. "Happened last night. Dr. Olen says probably after midnight. The boy had been in a fight beforehand, but that could have been hours before."

Poison that he tried to keep hidden in his craw burned Toy's throat. Toy did not understand his feelings toward Buster Galt. Maybe it was because Buster knew Toy's childhood history with bullying and violence. In a safe in his courthouse office, he kept documentation of each time Sheriff Toy Roy Robbins had used what some considered excessive force. Buster enjoyed occasionally reminding Toy of those documents.

Buster turned to face Rance, but he did not step closer. "Well, Rance, have the Rivers got a dog in this fight?" The tone exaggerated politeness.

Gray flinched at the question, but Rance's reply calmed him. "What fight are we talking about, Buster?"

Buster's suit was limp from the wetness and his short, wide tie clung to his shirt. "Why, this little investigation into a death of a Negro boy. What was his name, again?" He snapped his fingers in Toy's direction.

Toy's mouth turned down as he looked at Rance. "Spooner. Spooner Hays. Ivory Hays' boy."

"Ivory Hays? The one the colored folks call King?"

"One and the same." Toy said.

Buster's swagger left him at the mention of Ivory Hays. He took a minute to compose himself. "I see why you're here now, Rance. People say you and King Ivory are buddies. That right?"

"I know the man."

"He as dangerous as they say he is?"

"Don't know him that well, Buster."

Buster and Rance had history and it showed. Both had courted Mattie in a minor contest that Rance had easily won. In weak moments or during quarrels, he had accused Mattie of regretting her decision to pass up the rich son of a district attorney for a farm boy that dropped out of high school. Mattie, responding in anger, said that Buster never cared about her—he just wanted Rance to lose the contest. Besides, she said, "Buster has that awful breath."

Buster moved into another world after high school and moved down, and then off the list of things Mattie and Rance had to argue about. A law degree from Southern Methodist University led to a stint at the Dallas County district attorney's office. His conviction rate was high, and his political prospects were good. When he married Evelyn Grant, daughter of a prominent Highland Park family, his father-in-law advised switching sides. Buster soon found himself a partner in a prominent Dallas law firm.

Ten years of almost total absence from Delta County followed. Unless they read about his well-publicized courtroom battles in one of the Dallas papers, Delta County folks almost forgot Buster until his father, Tom Galt, district attorney for Delta, Hopkins, and Franklin counties, died.

Tom's death made the front page of *The Cooper Review*. The story noted that Buster, wife Evelyn, and teenage son Cameron would be returning to the family's historic home in Cooper to take care of Buster's mother. None of the Rivers saw the article that would change their lives.

Teenage rivalries and other trivialities had been replaced by the real problems of life the day Rance saw Buster Galt using a hairpin to put a business card on the screen door of Dad Flanagan's store in Klondike. Buster turned from the screen and stuck out his hand. "Well, Rance Rivers, isn't it? Long time, no see, old friend."

Rance shook the proffered hand and took the business card that announced Buster's run for district attorney. "Hello, Buster. Looks like you're following in your daddy's footsteps." Rance cleared his throat after the words came out thin and weak.

Buster Galt was the last person Rance wanted to see that day. His appearance after all those years seemed like an evil specter, a reminder of Rance's shortcomings and mistakes. Blaming himself for Tuck's death and the loss of his dairy, he had lost his self-esteem and no longer felt respected by his wife and his children.

Buster's voice was as blustery as ever, and he easily slipped into local parlance. "Yeah, well, prosecutin' criminals don't pay as well as defendin' 'em, but it was pretty good to my daddy all those years."

Rance fingered the card as he watched Buster climb into a new Buick. A feeling of envy crept over him like a cold chill, making him try to think of reasons why Buster had succeeded while he had failed. It would have been better if Tom Galt had used the power of the district attorney's office to line his own pockets, but even Griffin vouched for the integrity of Buster's father. The Galts were not only one of the richest families in the county, but they were also one of the most admired.

Rance was still holding the business card and staring at the departing Buick when Dad Flanagan pushed open the screen door. Dad stood just inches over four feet. His head appeared to sit directly on his shoulders, and the rest of his body was shaped like one of the moonshine barrels from the still hidden in the canebrakes behind his store.

He took the business card from his screen door, tore it into several pieces, and dropped it into a spittoon. "That sumbitch didn't ask permission to use my screen or my hairpin." Dad's voice sounded as if the absence of a neck was squeezing his vocal cords.

The gesture made Rance feel better and he smiled.

"Don't see how a man could find somethin' not to like about a successful fella like Buster. He comes from a good family, got a law degree, a pretty wife, and handsome son. I hear he's one of the most successful lawyers in Dallas. What's not to like about Buster, Dad?"

"Makes you wonder, don't it? Why such a successful defense lawyer in Dallas would come back to Delta County? That boy of his is strange, too. Got a few screws loose. You say his wife is pretty? When did you ever see her? Everybody tells me she never comes out of that big house."

"You got a point. Never really saw her, but Toy says there's a picture in Buster's office. Says she's a looker and the boy takes after her."

"Buster still ain't the man his daddy was. Never will be. Too damn cocky."

"You think he'll win?"

"Hard to tell. He'll sure carry Delta County. That fellow from Sulphur Springs...." Dad paused and scratched his gray, almost perfectly round head. "Can't even remember his name—anyway, the one who followed Tom Galt—he hardly ever came over here. Spent all his time in Hopkins or Franklin counties and treated us like a bastard stepchild."

Buster's irritating voice reminded Rance that the Galt family tradition was safe. Buster Galt was now district attorney. "What did the medical examiner say? How did the JP rule?"

"The fall killed him. Why he fell, he don't know." Toy said.

"Rube see anything?"

Toy shook his head. "You know he goes out four times ever' shift. He makes one square east of the jail, then south, west, and north. Says he didn't see Spooner at all."

Buster put his hands on his hips and leaned toward Toy. "Why in hell does he do that?"

"I let him patrol like that to keep him from goin' crazy up there. Livin' in the jail like he does, he'd likely jump off the building hisself if I didn't give him some outside duties."

Buster looked down at his shoes and shook his head slowly. "Well, I figure the boy just fell, but I guess we have to treat this as a crime scene for the time being. Get civilians out of it—drag up some sawhorses or something to use as a barrier."

Rance felt some degree of satisfaction as he noticed the small inner tube-sized ring around Buster's middle and the way the waistband of his trousers had folded over his belt. Funny how a little thing like bad breath and a flabby stomach can sometimes weigh as heavy as a law degree, money, even power.

He turned toward his sons. "I think he's talking about us when he says civilians, boys. Let's go."

Jake and Gray Boy followed their father to the pickup. Shy paced the truck bed as they approached. "Ride with Shy, Jake. Be sure he doesn't try to jump out." Jake knew that Shy would never try to jump out of a moving truck, but he moved back and leaned against the cab, pulling Shy under his arm. As they pulled away from the curb, he heard his father's voice through the open windows, but could not tell if he was angry.

"Don't think you're gonna get a pass because Spooner died. Why were you in jail?"

Gray looked out the side window. "I was driving reckless, I guess."

"You guess? I knew that damned motorcycle would get you into trouble. I should never have let you have it."

"I bought it with my own money."

"You mean you're payin' for it with your own money. You could have almost bought a pretty good used car for the same price."

"I wanted the motorcycle."

"Like always, you miss the point. I'm not in the mood, and this isn't the time to argue about the cycle again. Just tell me what you did to get thrown in jail. You think I'm stupid enough to believe it was just reckless driving?"

Gray leaned his head back and stared at the roof of the cab. "That's what I was doing."

Rance lightly touched the brakes, keeping his eyes on the road. "When this truck rolls to a stop, I'm going to step out and come around to your side. I want you to look me in the eyes and tell me the truth, Son. Don't you see the river you're crossing right now?"

"All right. I was drinking. Okay? Satisfied? I was drunk and disorderly and doing donuts in the Frenches' front yard."

"I figured it was something stupid like that. What about the busted lip?"

"I got that in a fight."

"Damn, Gray Boy, you got into it again with Cameron Galt, didn't you?"

The mention of Cameron Galt shot a stabbing pain that zigzagged across Gray's kidneys, across his shoulders, and into his temple. Cameron Galt had ruined his life, but he had not fought with him last night. *If only I had.*

Cameron Galt was hurt and angry when his father told him that he would complete his senior year at tiny Cooper High School in Delta County rather than at Highland Park in Dallas. He had spent a summer with his grandparents in Cooper as a preteen and vowed never to spend more than a night among the country folks again. His father's decision to move was abrupt and not discussed. From the look on his mother's face, the move had not been discussed with her, either.

As the moving van arrived at their Dallas home, Buster was close behind in a cherry-red '55 Chevy hardtop. He tossed the keys to his son. "You can follow our furniture in your own car. Those pretty little country girls will probably lie down in the street when you drive by in that." Cameron felt better, but he knew that the car was only a temporary distraction from the pain of having his life jerked out from under him like a dirty rug.

As the movers carried the Galt furniture and cloth-ing into the historic house in Cooper, Cameron drove by the summer-empty school. As he passed the football field on the outskirts of town, he imagined himself running for touchdowns. He had made the Highland Park team, but he was not a standout. At least, not like his father had been at Cooper. Here, he would probably be all-state in at least two sports. Besides, he had the whole summer to make these country hicks appreciate him. Leaving Buster Galt's football history in his wake intrigued him. He parked the Chevy on the Cooper square and swaggered into the minty-coolness of Miller's Drugstore.

Manton Miller was behind the counter. "Help you?"

Cameron eyed the list of fountain drinks and ordered a chocolate soda. Manton slid the soda across the marble counter to him. "You're Tom Galt's grandson, aren't you?" Cameron felt flattered to be recognized already. Manton stuck out his hand, and Cameron offered a firm handshake. "I hear you're going to be a Bulldog this fall."

"Bulldog?"

Manton smiled as he wiped the counter. "Well, I call all the kids at Cooper School Bulldogs. I hear you lettered at Highland Park. Golden Glover, too."

Cameron stood a little straighter. His reputation had preceded him. "That's right. Maybe I can help out Cooper's teams next year. I need that last year of playing time before college ball."

"You going to play "B" Team or just help out the coaches in scrimmages?"

"B" team? I made varsity at Highland Park. I don't expect to play a sub team here." Cameron's face showed his indignity.

Manton kept his easy smile and soft demeanor as a customer waved a prescription at him. He leaned forward and lowered his voice. "You do know that you won't be eligible for varsity, don't you? Interscholastic League rules make transfers wait a full year to play varsity." Manton moved toward the back of the store. "Excuse me a minute will you—Cameron, isn't it? I've got to fill this prescription. The soda's on me."

Cameron Galt stood dumbly at the counter, feeling humiliated that he had not known about these rules. He left the soda untouched and walked out of the store into Texas heat. *Ineligible. We'll see about that. Daddy's probably already taken care of this.*

Cameron found his father setting up his new law office on the square. "What have you done to get around this interscholastic thing so I can play varsity here?"

Buster leaned against Tom Galt's old desk. "I thought you knew, Cameron. Those rules are there for a reason. I go out and start trying to make an exception for you, it could cost me an election.'

"You mean I can't play any sports in this hick town my senior year?"

"You can play on the alternate teams and even work out with the varsity. I imagine you can show 'em a thing or two. Should be fun."

Cameron's blue eyes blazed red. "Fun—you think it's fun to teach a bunch of hick kids how to play football and let them get all the glory? Most of 'em couldn't be water boys at Highland Park." Cameron stepped back as he spoke the words and turned toward the door. With his back to his father, he waved his right fist toward the floor. "This is all your damn fault. You couldn't wait one little year to move me to this dump. You had to run for district attorney now—no notice, no discussion, no nothing—just yank me out of school, Mother out of her home—all so the great Buster Galt can follow in his old man's footsteps."

Cameron's mother had passed on lemon-blond hair, ocean-blue eyes, and fine, almost delicate facial features to her only son. From the neck up, he was almost too pretty to be called handsome. From the neck down, Cameron was Buster Galt again with more defined muscles. It was as if another person's body was holding up Cameron's head. The contrast was so dramatic that people were prone to stop and stare.

With an eternal summer in front of him, Cameron prowled the streets of Cooper, finding little to assuage his anger or to elevate his mood. Most of the students he would get to know in the fall were working at summer jobs during the day. When he did see students his age on the square at night, he remained distant from them, preferring instead to cruise, observe, and evaluate his possible rivals.

He also roamed the back roads of Delta County's other communities in his red Chevy. He identified the prettiest girls from Charleston, Enloe, Pecan Gap, and Klondike. When those girls came to Cooper for a malt at Miller's or a picture show at Sparks on the square, Cameron made mental notes. One or more of the prettiest girls was usually on the arm of Gray Boy Rivers, a year younger than Cameron, and a junior at Klondike.

Midsummer, at a booth in Miller's, Cameron approached and stuck out his hand to Gray Boy. "Name's Cameron Tom Galt." Gray Boy took the hand in his own and felt Cameron's fingers clamp down on his smaller hand. Gray Boy frowned, then smiled and returned the squeeze with farm-hardened hands. The instant, intense dislike between the two boys was akin to dropping a lighted match into a gasoline can.

Cameron nodded his head toward the girl beside Gray in the booth. "And who might this be?"

"It *might* be just about anybody, but it *really is* Molly Beth

French."

Cameron knew he had found something to keep him from getting bored with country life.

A pothole in the Rivers' driveway shocked Gray's senses and reminded him of the pain in his back, shoulders, and head. *How much of that is imaginary and how much is leftover hangover?*

Rance stopped the truck and turned toward him. "How many times has the Galt boy got to whip you before you give it up?"

"I ain't ever going to give up. You taught me that."

The remark stung Rance enough to soften his tone. "Gray, sometimes a man has to know his limits. Cameron Galt was a Golden Gloves boxer in Dallas. Did you know that? Besides, he outweighs you at least thirty pounds. You can't be expected to compete against that."

"What choice do I have? The bastard has started following me everywhere I go again."

Rance pushed against the steering wheel; the muscles in his jaw tightened. "Well, the kid will be leaving for college again this fall. Both of you will grow up before he comes back next summer."

"They tell me he's going to start coming home most weekends. Am I just supposed to put my life on hold or stay out of Delta County until he grows up?"

"You want me to talk to Buster about his son?"

Gray Boy's head jerked toward his father. "Please promise me you will never do that."

Rance nodded. "What about the Frenches' yard? We need to haul dirt to repair the damage?"

"There's not any damage. The Mustang is light enough for me to go in a circle in wet grass without cutting any ruts."

"Well, that's good information to have. A good reason for owning a damn motorcycle." Rance opened his door and stepped out. "That French girl's going to get you into bad trouble, Gray Boy. She's just instigating trouble. Enjoying the fight between you and Galt. Makin' you look like a moon-struck kid."

Gray put distance between himself and his father as they walked toward the house. He wanted to avoid any negative discussion about someone he loved from another person he loved. He was in big trouble in almost all areas of his life and needed time to clear his mind and think.

For a fleeting moment, he felt a little safer as he plopped down on his bed and stared at the tall ceilings. This house is where he had grown up—a safe haven. *Lord, if you help me get out of this, I'll stay out of trouble from now on. What do I need to do?* He waited for answers, but thoughts of Molly Beth French soon crowded out any possible divine intervention.

Gray Boy dated many girls. All of them stirred his loins, but only two touched his heart. Molly Beth French was one—pretty, daring, and wild—a kindred spirit. She whetted and satisfied a sexual appetite that Gray Boy considered beyond his control—a creature-not-of-his-making that must be fed often.

Molly Beth would sneak out at all hours, ride on the back of his Mustang, lie her way into Dallas strip joints and bars, and drink beer. Things were almost always good with Molly Beth during those nights of fun. Lots of laughter—good sex. They attended different schools, so he seldom saw her in any situation that did not involve thrills or adventure. Taking risks satisfied their mutual craving for constant stimulation. When life slowed down and grew safe, they wrestled for control of the relationship and got on each other's nerves. Their bond seemed unable to stand the tests of ordinariness.

When Molly Beth left him feeling empty, Gray Boy dated other girls, expecting Molly Beth to pine for him and wait. Molly Beth would not wait; they would quarrel; and Gray Boy—like a young calf separated from its mother—took his emptiness and guilt to Halley Rainey. His relationship with Halley left him feeling cleaner, wholesome, more accepted by his parents.

Joe Max Rainey, Halley's father, was a Delta County commissioner and a good friend of Rance's and Hack's. He had given Rance a job when he lost the dairy. Joe Max would not let Halley ride on the back of the Mustang, so Gray had to borrow the family's '49 Ford for their dates. Halley had to be in before eleven, and Gray was expected to sit with the family on Sunday at the Klondike Church of Christ when he dated Halley on Saturday night.

Half of Gray glowed during those times with Halley; the other half suffocated. The suffocating half always sent him to other girls, feeding his needs, before finally making his way back to Molly Beth. Tension between Gray and Molly Beth rose when Cameron Galt came to Cooper.

Unable to focus on sports, Cameron made it his mission to win what he saw as a natural competition with Gray Boy Rivers. If he saw Gray with a girl, he made it his business to be with that same girl the next night or weekend. Cameron wanted Gray Boy to rise to the bait, but Gray kept disappointing him. When Cameron stopped dating other girls and focused his attention on Halley and Molly Beth, Gray Boy took notice, but said nothing.

Cameron crossed Gray's line, however, when he started following him and taunting him on his dates. Gray would not be played for a fool or a coward, especially in front of Molly Beth or Halley.

The bubble of tension burst on Cameron's graduation night. Gray Boy and Mollie Beth were sharing the Mustang seat; her arms snuggled under his armpits, her hands clenched against his flat stomach. Only a rolled blanket separated their young bodies. They had just turned off 24 toward Klondike when Gray recognized the Chevy's headlights behind him.

Cameron downshifted to make the Chevy's pipes roll and

then goosed it to pull alongside the Mustang. Gray saw two other boys in the car, but recognized neither. Cameron was probably showing out for a couple of old friends from Dallas.

Gray shouted through the wind and the roar of the Chevy's glass packs, "You always bring help, don't you, Chickenshit?" Cameron flashed a smile. Gray had to look up to see into the car from the motorcycle, making him feel even smaller and more humiliated by the taunting. He swerved close to the Chevy, rapped his knuckles on the door, put up his middle finger, smiled, and lifted the front wheels of the Mustang.

Molly Beth squealed as it shot away from the Chevy. The little motorcycle was a drag racer's dream, and Gray had it tuned to fly. He charged down Klondike's main street, the Chevy following closely behind, unable to pass or gain. Just past Dad Flanagan's, Gray turned off his light, cut across the Methodist Church parking lot through a field he had played in as a boy, then back through the Baptist Church parking lot. He passed between trees too narrow for a car to follow. The Chevy's lights were not in sight.

He stopped behind a grove of trees and looked back at Molly Beth. She removed her arms from his waist and ran her fingers through her wind-blown hair. They stepped off the Mustang to stretch. In the moonlight, shadows from the gentle swaying of oak leaves caressed her face. Gray thought she had never looked more desirable. Her hair, cut daringly short, showed the tousled look he loved.

To Gray Boy, Molly Beth always looked ready for or fresh from a roll in the blanket. Her tanned skin and sprinkling of freckles glowed under the soft light. The thrill of the ride showed in her smile. He imagined that he could feel her skin still tingling from the wind.

She reached out for his hand. "Let's go to Piss Elm Crossing and roll out the blanket." Dad Flanagan's porch light caught Gray's dimpled smile as the wheels rose again on the Mustang.

When they were satisfied that they had lost Cameron for good, Gray slowed and cut the light again as they neared their favorite parking spot. Too late, Gray saw the red Chevy lunge out of the darkness and block the dirt road. He put out his left leg and tried to turn the little motorcycle in a circle to keep from hitting the car. It turned on its side and slid along the dirt road, stopping against the car's back wheel.

Gray was on his feet instantly. He looked at Molly Beth. "You hurt?"

She looked down at a tear in her pedal-pushers. Her blouse was ripped open, leaving one breast exposed. Gray always asked her to take off her bra and lean her breasts into his back when they rode the motorcycle. Fear had replaced adventure in her expression as she fumbled with her blouse buttons. "I don't think so."

Cameron was leaning against the Chevy's fender, turning something slowly in his hand, when Gray turned. Gray felt his face and body grow hot as he walked forward. "It's time for you city boys to learn something about life in the country." He pointed toward the boys in the back seat. "Am I going to have to fight you and your chicken-shit buddies or just you, Asshole?"

Cameron was already advancing toward him. Air escaping from Cameron's lungs echoed across the bottomland cotton fields as Gray's head butted him in the stomach. Their bodies slammed against the car door. Gray backed up, took a deep breath, and hammered a fist into Cameron's jaw before he could straighten up. He heard and felt his knuckles crack against Cameron's cheekbone. The pain in his hand was blinding. Cameron staggered, but did not fall.

Gray felt adrenalin rushing through him, making the pain bearable. This was not his first fight—he liked to fight— liked smelling the blood from his knuckles mixing with blood from Cameron's jaw. The tormenting was going to end tonight. Sure that at least one of his right fingers was broken, he drew back with his left to drive his nemesis to the ground, but Cameron's head was hidden behind his shoulder. Gray hesitated before striking the blow he was sure would end the fight.

He felt the air rush out of his lungs and pain shoot across his back as a fist buried into his kidney. He had made a mistake in waiting—in underestimating Cameron. He had not even seen the fist coming; Cameron's head had barely moved.

The other fist caught Gray Boy across the neck before he could recover his breath. Choking, he gasped for breath—his eyes watered—his knees began to buckle. His father's words echoed in his ears. *Confidence is good, but don't cross the river into cockiness.*

On his knees, he felt, but did not see, the final blow across the back of his neck. He was almost grateful for the blow that stopped him from choking to death. Hard as he tried to stop, he felt himself drop face down in the dirt, heard the pitiful gagging sounds he made as his lungs clawed for a good breath. *Stand up, dammit! This can't be happening—not to Gray Boy Rivers.*

He felt the dirt suck into his mouth and nostrils. He coughed once, imagining what he must look like to Molly Beth. He wondered how she would get home. Blood from his knuckles slivered through the dry sand, but Gray did not see it. Cameron tossed a small piece of petrified wood, a perfect fit for his fist, between his hands as he walked toward the Chevy.

Gray still winced at the recollection of that year-ago fight. His little finger, though still crooked, had mostly healed, but the mental wounds were still fresh. The fight had brought an uneasy truce between him and Cameron for the rest of the year. Cameron continued to pursue Halley and Molly Beth, but he stopped following Gray. Cameron's dental surgery to replace a broken tooth did little for Gray's spirits. He expected the incident to taint the rest of his life.

Fear had intruded its ugly, unfamiliar face into Gray Boy's psyche. He was afraid of Cameron Galt. Cameron had taken his pride, shown him to be a coward, and was now after his girls. Friends thought that the old Gray Boy was back when Cameron left for college at SMU in the fall. Gray Boy played harder than ever, took bigger risks, drank more beer—trying to be someone he no longer was. Cameron stood in his past and his future like an evil apparition, ready to pounce on Gray Boy's happiness.

When Cameron returned from college to spend the summer at home, Gray saw Molly Beth in the red Chevy. He had never wanted anyone dead before, but he wanted to kill Cameron Galt. Worse, he wanted people to know that he had killed him in a fair fight. There was no way out—no way to redeem himself as long as Cameron lived. He slept fitfully.

5 Rance and Mattie's conversation drifted from the back porch through Gray's bedroom window. His eyes opened without his permission, catching the shadows of twilight creeping across the smokehouse and storm cellar door in the back yard. He pulled on a pair of jeans, walked outside, and sat beside his mother on the porch step. Mattie stopped brushing her hair and put her arm around him. The small gesture made him feel almost normal again.

Mattie patted his shoulder and squeezed. "Spooner's funeral is tomorrow. Guess we'll all go."

Rance looked up as he spoke. "Mattie, do you ever see Evelyn Galt?"

Mattie was surprised by the change of subject. "Well, we don't exactly run in the same circles, so I wouldn't necessarily see her. Why all the interest?"

"I don't really know. When I saw Buster, it got me to thinking about when he first came here. Remember how everybody talked about how beautiful she was?"

"Yep. Highland Park debutante, I hear. So you're disappointed that you never got to meet this great beauty?" Mattie's eyes twinkled.

"Just strikes me as strange that she is not in every edition of the Cooper Review. You don't even see her in the grocery store?"

Mattie's interest piqued. "To tell the truth, I wouldn't know her if I saw her, but I've heard that she never leaves the house."

"Never?"

"Well, I just assumed that never really meant seldom. But I have never seen her. Have you?"

Rance sat back down beside Mattie. "No. How about you, Gray Boy?"

"No, but if what they say about Cameron looking just like her is true, then I don't want to see the woman."

"Don't you think that's kind of strange?" Rance asked.

Mattie resumed her brushing. "I've asked some of my friends. They say she is a saint. Takes care of Buster's mother day and night—never leaves her. Mrs. Galt is senile and can't be left. Buster's wife even has her groceries delivered so she won't have to leave her mother-in-law."

"With that family money, they could afford a nurse to fill in every once in awhile, don't you think?" Rance asked.

"I think they have a colored girl come in every so often. The Shaw girl, I believe they said. Of course, Buster says that his mother gets upset when anybody tries to take care of her except Evelyn."

Rance removed his arm from Mattie's shoulder and turned to face her. "Buster says?"

Mattie squinted her eyes. "He didn't tell me in person, Rance. That's just what I was told by my friends."

Rance grinned and put his arm on her shoulder again. Mattie grabbed the hand that was draped over her shoulder. "If you ask me, Evelyn is a saint—taking care of Buster's mother while he tomcats around."

Gray and Rance turned to look at her. Mattie giggled a little. "Gray Boy, now you just heard your mother repeat gossip. You don't repeat anything I said to anybody because I don't know if it's true." She turned toward Rance. "No, I don't know who he plays around with. I just heard he's fooling around on his wife."

For the first time since Friday night, Gray felt the fog drifting away from his mind. Mattie's giggling had done it. It was good to engage in normal conversation. He seemed to be present, not far away like last night—buried in a deep hole. He turned to his father. "Why was Ivory asking about Bo today?"

Rance seemed surprised by the question. "I don't know."

"Why does he call him a breed?"

Jake was sprinkling sugar on his peanut butter and banana sandwich when the reference to Bo came over the cistern and through the open kitchen window. He grabbed his sandwich and stepped through the screen door as Rance gave the response Jake liked to hear. "That's a long story." Rance smiled as he glanced at Mattie. "You got time to hear Bo's story again?"

Mattie winked as she stood to go back to the kitchen. "I've heard this story before, and I've still got supper dishes to wash. Jake, why are you eating right after supper?" Jake shrugged. He had a sweet tooth, and there had been no dessert.

"How old is Bo, Daddy? Some people say he's in his twenties; others say he's an old man."

"I don't know exactly, but I'd say he's several years older than Gray. I expect Beulah is the only one who knows for sure. Since he was born down in The Hollow, I doubt his daddy ever recorded his birth."

Gray stood and faced his father. "His daddy? I thought he didn't have any parents, just Beulah Blandon. She really his grandma?"

"Everybody's got a daddy and a mother, Gray Boy. And yes, Beulah is his real grandmother. Bo's daddy was a full-blood Choctaw Indian they called Chock. Don't know if that was his real name or just short for Choctaw." Rance opened his pocketknife and picked up a twig for whittling.

"Choctaw hunted for a living, mostly in the bottomlands around here. Wore his hair long, braided into a ponytail, like Indians you see at the picture show. He lived mostly off what he killed, but brought hides to the square to trade for other things he needed. When Bo got big enough, he brought him along."

Jake warmed to the story as he imagined the Indian in feathers, buckskins, and moccasins. "You ever trade with him?"

"No, but Papa did once or twice. When your grandma was alive, she always had a good garden. Papa would trade vegetables for meat sometimes. Know that cougar hide on your Papa's wall?" Both boys nodded. "Well, Chock Creekwater killed that cat."

"What happened to him?" Jake asked.

Rance slid his knife down the stick and made a curl to add to the pile of shavings between his feet. "Nobody knows for sure. Every few years, he would go off looking for Bo's mother. Apparently, he just didn't come back from one of those trips."

Gray pulled his pocketknife from his jeans pocket and opened a blade. "Why was he lookin' for Bo's mother?"

Rance looked over Gray's shoulder at Jake. "Jake, go in the house and get my whet rock, will you?"

Jake frowned, recognizing that he was going to be excluded from a crucial part of the story. "Now?"

Rance stared; Jake left. Rance resumed his whittling, a more serious expression on his face. "Bo's daddy was not your normal Indian. Most Indians have skin that looks a lot like ours. Chock's was dark. Darker than a lot of colored people. He was full-blood Indian, but Papa said his own people ran him off because he looked colored."

Gray's interest piqued. "So that's why he lived down in the bottomlands?"

Rance nodded. "Partly. He hunted all along the Blue

Bottom and the Sulphur River. Guess he ran into a lot of colored people in The Hollow. He provided them with game, and they took him in. Eventually married one of 'em."

Jake whistled under his breath as he opened the screen door and handed the whet rock to his father. "Well, Jake, you managed to eavesdrop on that part, might as well hear the rest." Rance moved the knife blade softly against the whet rock. "The colored folks were not happy when Chock wanted to marry Susie Blandon, Beulah's daughter. She was just a teenager."

"Teenager?" Jake asked.

"Yeah, Papa said she was only about sixteen—real pretty." Rance glanced toward the kitchen window to see if Mattie was listening. "Colored folks didn't want them to marry, but she was pregnant, so they went along with it."

Gray walked a few feet into the yard to pick up his own whittling stick. "So that baby was Bo?"

"Yep. There are lots of stories about when he was born. They said he was a beautiful baby—took after his mama except for his hair—had that black, shiny straight hair from the beginning."

Jake thought about Bo's mangled speech, strange expressions, and messy clothes, trying to imagine him as a beautiful baby.

Rance moved his knife blade back and forth across the leather on his brogans. "Bo was done with breast feedin' before they noticed that something was wrong with him."

Susie held Bo tightly as she knocked on the door. When Beulah did not answer immediately, she began to cry. Sensing his mother's distress, Bo began to wail. Beulah, not easily upset, was frightened when she opened the door. "What's wrong with you, girl?" Called Bigmomma by her grandchildren, Beulah was a small, wiry woman, sprightly for sixty-two, but the lines in her face showed an added decade of troubles.

"He doin' it again." Susie wailed.

"Well, bring him in the house and stop that caterwaulin' in the yard."

Beulah took Bo and sat him in the living room floor. "Seem fine to me."

Susie dropped onto the small bed that Beulah kept in her living room for naps. "Well, he ain't fine, Mama. Somethin' bad wrong with this boy. I just know it."

Beulah stroked Bo's straight, black hair. "He droppin' out again, I s'pose."

"Look at him right now. Just starin' at the wall. Las' night, he started groaning and little wads of foamy spit came out the sides of his mouth. What I gonna do, Mama?" Susie began wailing again.

"Stop that, girl. I tell you what you gon' do. You gon' act like you got good sense even though you never had none. You gon' take care of this baby. He ours, even if he is half redskin."

Susie wiped her nose with the bottom of her dress and stood. "I tell you Mama, I can't. I jus' can't."

The back of Beulah's hand brought a trickle of blood to Susie's lip before the last word escaped. "Now you listen, girl. You made your bed and now you gon' lie in it. Even if I have to tie you to the bedposts." Beulah paced in front of her daughter, shame and rage on her face. "Bad enough you get yourself knocked up by that no-count redskin. Now you want to give up on your child. Over my dead body."

Susie slumped back on the bed and buried her face in her hands. "Folks in The Hollow say it ain't just the fits. Say he way behind in other things. How I gon' raise a boy like that?"

Beulah pulled her rocking chair closer to the bed. She took Susie's hand in hers. "Where that husband of yours? He any help?"

"Gone huntin'. Been gone three days. He say Bo gon' be all

right."

A sudden summer thunderstorm pushed dry leaves
against the window screen and blew Beulah's thin cur-
tains. She walked to the window to look out. "Nearly dark.
Thunderin'. Might rain. You stay here tonight. We'll think
on it tonight and decide what to do tomorrow."

Beulah made coffee at her usual time the next morning.
Following her routine, she drank two cups in the dark—her
time to think. It was her fault, she knew. She had spoiled
Susie. What was a forty-four-year-old woman with a new baby
to do?

Susie did not know that Beulah was really her grandmother, not her mother. Susie's mother had come to Beulah
with the same complaint, "I just can't." Beulah had taken her
and the baby in, only to have her oldest daughter abandon the
child a week later, never to be seen again.

As she savored the last drop of the second cup, she sighed
deeply, knowing what had to be done. Susie and Bo would
come to live with her. She had already raised Susie and two
other grandchildren for her shiftless son—one more wouldn't
be all that hard. They would deal with the Indian when the
time came. He was of no help, anyway.

She started the bacon and eggs and walked into the living
room to wake Susie and tell her about the plan. Bo was
curled up in the bed alone. Susie was gone.

"So she just left Bo and never came back?" Jake tried to
imagine life without his mother.

Rance nodded. "That's right. When Chock came to
get Bo, Beulah wouldn't let him go. Two days later, Chock
sneaked in her house and took him right out of her bed.
When Beulah woke up, they said that she ran back and forth
down the street, screaming for Bo. She searched for two days
until somebody from The Hollow finally came and told her

what had happened."

Gray pointed his knife blade at Jake in a gesture to keep quiet. "So Bo lived with Chock from then on? I still don't see what that has to do with Ivory asking about him today."

"Well, I had to tell you Bo's history before I got around to that." Rance stood and stretched. "Ivory came back from the service several years after Bo was born. He had Spooner with him, but nothing was said about Spooner's mama. He and the boy hoarded up in that U down in The Hollow and started building his junk pile. That started all sorts of stories about what had happened to him in his travels and about Spooner's mother."

Gray gave up on whittling and practiced throwing the knife and sticking it in the bottom porch step. "The ones about his being a witch doctor or practicing black magic? Is any of that true?"

"Ivory's strange, for sure. He's a hermit, builds a junk fortress around himself, has an unexplained son that looks a little too white. Colored and white are bound to talk."

"Yeah, but you know him. What do you think?"

"I don't ask and he doesn't tell, but I do know he traveled a lot in the service. He used to make trips to New Orleans in the old days; lots of that magic stuff there, I hear."

Jake wanted to get back to Bo. "So when did Bo move to town?"

Rance dropped a small wad of spit on his forearm and tested his knife by shaving a few hairs. He wiped it clean and pocketed it. "Chock, Bo's daddy, and Ivory became pretty good friends."

Gray's face showed his surprise. "Always thought Ivory was a loner...not the kind who makes friends easily. How did those two get together?"

"Seems strange on the surface till you look at it. Both had wives that ran off. Both were a little strange, both were raising sons without a mother. Probably started with Ivory selling Chock a hunting dog or something like that, but eventually, I think it was Bo who brought 'em together."

Gray folded the blade and pocketed his knife. "Retarded Bo?"

Rance drew his Prince Albert from his overalls bib. "God gave Bo plenty of shortcomings, but he is a gifted hunter and has a way with dogs. Ivory discovered that Bo could calm his meanest dogs. Took to sleeping with the dogs when he stayed with Ivory. Sounds strange, but he also had a way with Spooner. Protected him—that made him very useful to Ivory."

Jake waited while his father rolled a cigarette. "So how old was Bo when his daddy just never came back?"

Rance frowned at Jake. "Every so often, Chock would go looking for Bo's mother. On the first trip, he left Bo with Beulah. She didn't want to give him back again when he returned. After that, Bo stayed with Ivory and Spooner when his daddy left. Chock stayed gone almost a year one time."

"So Bo slept down there in Ivory's junkyard with the dogs all that time? How did Beulah get him back?"

Rance put a Zippo flame to the end of the cigarette and spit out a shred of tobacco. "Don't know for sure. He had started having seizures somewhere along through the years. That's why the colored people treat him like royalty, but I expect Ivory didn't want to deal with that."

Gray Boy stood and stretched. "They treat him like royalty because he has fits?"

"Yes. They think that the spirits are entering his body when he has those fits. When he comes out of the seizure, they believe the spirits have gone, leaving Bo with some kind of secret powers."

Jake stood beside his brother. "Is that true?"

Rance smiled. "You boys give me a lot more credit for knowing things than I deserve. Logic tells me it isn't true, but who knows? Ivory just showed up on Beulah's doorstep one day with Bo. Guess he decided Chock wasn't ever coming back. He's stayed with her ever since."

Gray stared at the trail of smoke from Rance's cigarette, thinking of the pack he had hidden in his room. "I still don't know why Ivory was asking about Bo today."

"You know as much about that as I do. I just figure that Bo is such a good hunter, Ivory might figure he could track anyone who might have been there."

Gray sat back down on the step and turned toward his father. "You know the walkway that surrounds the court-house basement?" Rance nodded. "Well, Bo was there last night when I came out. Said he was going to spend the night with Toy in the jail."

"Why didn't you say something back at the courthouse?"

"Well, Toy was keeping quiet about the baseball. Thought he probably knew Bo was there and didn't want to mention it to Buster. Maybe Buster doesn't approve of his staying in the jail."

Jake's eyebrows rose. "Bo was probably still there today. You know how crazy Shy is about Bo. Did you see him take off running to the courthouse? He was probably going to Bo. It ain't like him to run to anybody without my permission, but Bo always carries a treat for him in his pocket."

Rance shredded his cigarette and stood. "Guess I better let Toy know about that." He stopped at the screen door and turned toward Gray. "Bo's not going to tell something that we don't want to hear, is he?"

Gray shook his head. "No sir."

6 "Shy wants to go. Can he ride in the car?" Jake had his hand on the little dog's neck.

Mattie opened the front door of the black Ford and slid in. "Use your head, Jake. Of course, Shy can't go. You want to take a dog into a church during a funeral?" She looked uncomfortable, but pretty, in her navy and white polka dot dress and navy hat.

Jake's feelings were hurt. He knew that the dog wouldn't be allowed in church. "He's smart enough to stay in the car."

"Enough about the dog, Jake. Get in and shut the door." Rance, already behind the steering wheel, wore his best dark gray shirt and matching necktie. Matching pants settled over his good boots. He was hot and irritable.

Gray Boy came out of the house wearing his high-school-graduation-sport coat and penny loafers. Mattie winced when she saw him. "I can't believe he's outgrown that coat in one summer. "Gray, it's going to be hot in that church. Why don't you just wear your shirt? It looks fine."

Tension hung in the car like butter melting over flapjacks as Gray joined Jake in the back seat. He carefully laid his only sport coat on the seat between them. Mattie turned to face her sons. "Now, we're going to a colored funeral. It may be a little different. Don't stare or say dumb things. Just sit there respectfully and try to keep Spooner in your hearts."

Mattie's eyes grew shiny as they passed the New Klondike Cemetery. She turned in her seat and stared toward Tuck's grave until the cemetery was out of sight. "It's been so long since I've seen mud, I forgot how treacherous this old road can be. Rance, you think we can make it?"

Rance looked insulted. "The church sits on this side of The Hollow on sandy land. We'll make it."

Mattie placed her fingers over the rolled-down window and held on tightly as the black Ford bounced and weaved in sync with the ruts Rance had broken the day before. Mattie looked out the window at a break in the clouds. "Looks like the Good Lord is going to bring out the sun for Spooner." Clouds covered the sun as she finished her sentence. "Maybe not."

There were less than a dozen cars in the Liberty Grove Baptist churchyard, but it was filled with people who had walked to the church. Ivory's '39 Ford was parked close to the front door. Rance turned to Mattie. "Strange how our connection to the mysterious King Ivory Hays is so ordinary. An old junked-up car and a little dog." Mattie did not answer. She was searching the crowd for a familiar face, or any white face.

Weathered and warped picnic benches made from rough, green oak boards dotted the yard under several large post oaks. The church was a twin to the Church of Christ in Klondike in design, but white paint had started to peel and drop off in large flakes, revealing shiplap siding that had soaked up the rain. The fir had been patched in places with asbestos siding. Jake could smell the wet fir. Strips of uncured underpinning had warped and pulled away, revealing large bois d'arc stumps that supported the church.

The Rivers left their car and stood awkwardly in the churchyard, no other white faces in sight. Two black men who knew Rance finally approached with their wives. Rance had wired their houses in The Hollow when REA lines finally came, so they talked about light bulbs and the wonders of electricity. Their color made Jake and Gray Boy the object of stares. Jake expected his bold brother to stare back, but Gray Boy seemed even more uncomfortable than himself, alternately staring at the ground and the sky.

To take his mind off the staring eyes while his parents chatted, Jake studied his Levis and compared them to his brother's black dress slacks. For the first time ever, the comparison did not make him want to hide. Mattie always starched his first pair of Levis and put them on stretchers to dry the same as Gray Boy's, but when he wore them, his body seemed irrelevant and lost inside. The jeans seemed to be empty, standing and walking without any help from him. Gray called him "no-ass-atol" when he wore them. Now that the jeans were fading, his body had finally started to fill them. Even better, he had mastered the button fly.

Too shy to search the crowd for a familiar face, Jake stared at the church that had always seemed mysterious and unwelcoming to him. He had stood in his saddle to peek inside the church before but had never been inside. He and friends John Ray and Jerry Gervers had ridden their horses and bicycles to the edge of the mysterious and foreign land known to them as The Hollow many times. Occasionally, they ventured closer to Blue Bottom Creek.

Jake had told his friends stories of his trip inside Ivory's junk fortress. He may have exaggerated the things he saw that day, but what he saw was enough to scare the three of them. On a double-dog-dare, they planned a late night venture into King Ivory's compound, but never got much farther than the church. They visited the church often on Sunday and Wednesday nights during summer, hiding in the weeds to listen. The music was much better than in their own white churches, but the wailing and howling of the congregation was what really intrigued them. "They think God can't hear 'em if they don't yell pretty loud," John had said.

A hand on his shoulder interrupted his thoughts. "Jaker Ridge. You seem lost in thought." Hack and Willie Mae Gentry were standing behind him. Both small and fine-featured, they looked more like sister and brother than husband and wife.

"Hey, Hack. Willie Mae."

Rance and Mattie were just behind the Gentrys, and the six white faces joined the throng of people beginning to enter the church. Jake counted five steps to reach the porch. His view restricted by taller adults surrounding him, he felt a tug on his sleeve. Willie Slater, a colored boy his own age, smiled at him from among the grown-up legs. Spooner had brought Willie to the Rivers' cotton patch last year. He and Jake had become reluctant friends during the three weeks they pulled bolls together. Jake returned the smile and gave a bashful wave.

The Rivers and Gentrys sat near the back of the church, leaving the front seats for family members and closer friends. The air inside the church was heavy and musky with wet wood. Jake stared straight ahead, only occasionally daring a glimpse over his shoulder at the people still entering the church. Mattie frowned at him when he stared.

Some of the men wore tattered overalls and worn out shoes, but most were in suits and ties. Jake wondered if his father owned a suit. Flashy younger men topped their two-toned shoes with checked pants, loud shirts, and wide, short ties. Some boys his age were barefoot and wore hand-me-downs that had survived many siblings, but a few wore suits and ties. For the first time, he wondered if his own family was poorer than their colored counterparts.

Women cried without restraint, and men comforted them in muffled, deep tones. Jake looked behind him when his own pew moved, and the pew behind him creaked with protest. Toy Roy Robbins, Buster Galt, Hoot Gibson, and

Truman Bates took their seats on the bench just behind the
Rivers and Gentrys. Two rows of almost solid white faces
now joined the sea of browns and blacks. Jake tried not to
stare, but could not help but notice Truman's blue-striped
seersucker suit and the white straw hat that sat primly on his
lap. Jake felt Toy's knees touching the back of his pew, heard
and felt the heavy breathing of Buster, Toy, and Hoot mixing
with Truman's asthmatic wheeze. Most of the county's law sat
behind Gray Boy, and Jake sensed his discomfort.

Loud whispering and crying stopped abruptly as King
Ivory Hays entered the front door. The silence was broken
only by a whining sound from the back corner. Jake turned
to see Bo Creekwater crumpled in the back church pew beside
his grandmother, emitting a low, sobbing whine.

King Ivory wore a black floor-length robe. A red sash tied
at his waist trailed to the tops of his shoes. All eyes turned
as he marched down the aisle toward his son. A latigo string
attached to a small leather pouch around Ivory's neck swung
a little with each step. As he passed Jake's aisle, Jake noticed
that the ends of the red sash were touching the tops of Ivory's
muddy brogan shoes. He wondered if he was wearing his
usual faded overalls underneath that robe.

Jake had not been able to see Spooner's black casket
because of taller shoulders and heads in front of him, but he
managed a glimpse as King Ivory touched it with his hand
before taking his seat alone on the front pew. The groan of
the church bench seemed to signal the choir to stand. A hush
fell over the room as the white-robed choir began to sing.
Jake had never seen a robed choir. *Swing Low, Sweet Chariot*
wafted through the room, out the windows, and through The
Hollow.

A short stump-of-a-man with a face as black as Ivory's approached the pulpit. His prayer began with a word of appreci-
ation for the end of the drought. His voice was a low rumble
that built to a crescendo as he prayed for the soul of Spencer

Hays and the suffering of his father. Amens resonated from both men and women in the audience. When the long prayer finally ended and the preacher began his sermon, the congregation sounded its approval after each sentence with grunts and more amens.

With all eyes focused on the preacher, Jake felt free to scan the room and its occupants for signs that made this a colored church. A small black sign with white slide-in letters and numbers announced last Sunday's attendance and offering, just like the Baptist church in Klondike. He felt like an intruder on God's domain, an unworthy sinner—just as he did in white churches. Only the choir, the dark faces, and the chorus of voices that endorsed each of the preacher's utterances were different. He stole glances at his mother, father and brother. Had they been in a church together since Tuck's funeral? The movement of hand-held fans stirred the hot air and the preacher's rhythmic delivery caused Jake's mind to wander—to Spooner and happier times in the cotton patch.

Jake and Gray Boy stood up from the cotton stalks, each using slow motion to pull the twigs and leaves from cotton bolls before putting them in their sacks. The cotton was stunted from lack of rain, so even Jake could see the road. Industrious boll-pulling had slowed at the first sign of the rooster tail of dust. When the rooster tail turned into Rance's pickup as it crossed the railroad tracks, the Rivers brothers stopped work to watch.

Shy jumped over the tailgate and headed for Jake. Jake smiled at the dog's enthusiasm and kneeled to greet him. Spooner and Willie bailed out behind the dog. It was hot in the bottomland patch that day, and the air was heavy. Jake's clothes and gloves were sticky and itchy. The Rivers brothers had not spoken since the first boll was pulled that morning. Gray was in a dark mood and Jake was irritable—a combination that could easily erupt into a fight. Gray knew just how to get under Jake's skin and make him throw the first punch. With nobody around to help him, Jake kept his distance all morning.

When Spooner Hays bailed out of that pickup, Jake felt the tension start to evaporate. Spooner looked in their direction and waved. His mischievous smile was as refreshing as a glass of iced tea. He grabbed his cotton sack from the pickup and made sure Rance's head was turned before waving his middle finger toward them and grinning. Spooner and Willie started down a cotton row in their direction.

Big for his age, Spooner Hays had always walked with an ambling, disjointed gait that seemed to reflect his carefree attitude toward life. Last year, he had stooped a little, as if his movements were trying to catch up to his size. He now traveled with the easy grace of Booker T. Washington School's star athlete.

Jake and Gray Boy were awkward in their greetings. It had been a long time. Spooner stooped to pet Shy, putting the dog's chin in his hand and scratching the top of his head. Shy's tail wagged wildly. "I 'member this dog. Got him from Ivory, didn't you? What did you name him?"

Jake grinned. "You call your daddy Ivory?"

Spooner gave Jake a look that said he had asked a dumb question. "Yep." Spooner turned his tall, lanky frame toward Gray Boy and winked. "'Les I be callin' him sumbitch or horse's ass, that is."

He and Gray Boy laughed the same silly laughs they had last year. The two of them could work themselves into a giggling fit over anything. Jake usually found the stories they told or the things they said funny, but not fall-down-roll-on-your-back funny. Their laughter was contagious, however, and Jake and Willie soon joined in the hilarity.

"I named him Shiloh, Shy, for short. Where were you the day we came to get him from Ivory?"

"Now, how would I know that, Boy?" Spooner turned to direct a punch toward Gray's arm. "This brother of yo's thinks I 'member every little peckerhead white boy come to pick up a dog from my daddy. I ain't got that many fingers and toes." Another fit of laughter as Gray Boy and Spooner swapped licks. They heard Rance honk the horn, a signal to get to work.

Gray's face took on a more serious expression. "Hey, Spooner. Boys at school want me to ask you if it's true they call you Spooner because you were born with a silver spoon in your mouth?"

"That true, all right. Course, truth is, that spoon more likely up my ass than in my mouth. Why a rich boy be out here sweatin' his balls off in another man's cotton patch?"

Spooner put the cotton sack strap over his shoulder and bent down to pick a few bolls. "I'll take four rows and you take four, Gray Boy. I'll beat your white ass to the end. Las' year was the las' year your sissy white ass gon' beat me pullin' cotton. Folks in The Hollow find out some cracker beat my nigger ass pullin' cotton, I be 'shamed to go home."

Gray fell back on his sack laughing. The horn honked again, and Gray jumped to his feet. He pointed a finger at Spooner. "You're gonna be staring at my white ass until this cotton patch is in the trailer and gone to the gin. Then I'm goin' down to the Piggly Wiggly on Wednesday and let everybody know."

Spooner was already stuffing his sack, but stopped at the mention of Piggly Wiggly. "Why Wednesday?"

Gray laughed. "That's double-stamp-day, dumb-ass. More people there."

Spooner turned toward Jake. "What you waiting for, Paperwad? You and Jigger here take two rows and see if you can keep up. Otherwise, all y'all gon' be staring at my pretty black ass. Take a good look." Spooner bent, dropped his jeans, and mooned them.

જ જ જ

Jake erased the grin from his face as people began to stand
around him. Wailing filled the church as people stopped
for a final look at Spencer (Spooner) Hays. The choir softly
hummed, and the piano tinkled *Steal Away* as they made their
way down the aisle. Jake stepped aside to let his brother be
the first to see Spooner's body. Gray bit his lip and grimaced
at the casket, but quickly moved on. Jake had to stand on his
tiptoes to see inside the casket.

Spooner's chocolate skin seemed lighter. His face had a
fixed smile; the infectious grin was gone. Staring at Spooner's
long, dark eyelashes, Jake tried to grasp the enormity of death
for someone not much older than himself until Gray pulled
his sleeve and motioned for him to move on.

They waited in the churchyard until pallbearers brought
out Spooner's casket. The crowd followed King Ivory and
his son to the cemetery beside the church. Metal and wood
folding chairs sat under a tent beside the grave. Everyone
waited for King Ivory to take a seat there, but he never did.
All the chairs remained empty while the preacher finished his
last prayer for the soul of Spencer Hays.

A brisk wind cooled the mourners' sweat-soaked bodies as
they started for their cars and homes. Mattie put a finger on
Rance's shoulder. "Is that Dr. Olen standing over there?"

"Looks like him. Yep, that's his car he's leaning against."
Rance picked up his pace in a straight line for the doctor.
"Didn't see you inside, Doc."

"Got here late. I just stood in the back. Not good for
business for a doctor to be seen at too many funerals." He
winked at Mattie. "How are you, Mattie?" He laid his hand
on Mattie's shoulder, and she slipped under his arm for a hug.
"And the Rivers boys. Jake, how's that thumb?"

"All healed up. Just like you said." Jake felt a warm
glow because Dr. Olen Bartlett had remembered his mashed

thumb from over three years before.

"And Gray Boy, turning into a man." Dr. Olen had given Gray his nickname the day he delivered him. "Busted lip, black eye, cut cheek. What's that all about?" Olen winked at Rance.

"Good question, Dr. Bartlett." Hoot Gibson put his hand on Gray's shoulder and looked at the cuts. "Mr. District Attorney, looks like the colored boy isn't the only one that's been in a fight." Buster closed the car door he had just opened and walked toward them, followed by Toy and Truman.

Gray Boy jerked Hoot's hand away from his shoulder and stared at the justice of the peace. Rance stepped between his son and Hoot, nodding in Ivory's direction. "You too stupid to notice there's a funeral going on, Hoot?"

Hoot stepped back and stiffened. "This funeral service only reminds us of the need to find the killer."

Rance put his finger in Hoot's chest and used the other finger to point toward Ivory. "That man just lost his son. Your investigation and loud mouth can wait until he's out of earshot."

Buster stepped closer to Hoot. "Shut up, Hoot, and get in the car." Hoot ducked his head a little, as if to acknowledge, but not accept, the rebuff. Buster touched the brim of his hat in Mattie's direction and walked away. Truman nodded his apology and also tipped his hat. Toy shrugged and followed Hoot toward the Sheriff's car.

Hack and Willie Mae joined Rance and Mattie as the sheriff's car drove out of the churchyard. Hack pulled Rance aside. "Things looked a little tense between you and Corporal Gibson from where I was standing. Anything I can help with?"

Rance stared at the departing car. "I don't know."

7 The frequent bursts of static from the radio behind the sheriff's desk were making Gray irritable. The smell was not helping, either. A long, dark cigarette hung from the lips of the dingy-blonde dispatcher. She squinted as the smoke burned her eyes. Smoke hung in the crowded room and mixed with the stagnant odor of a butt-filled ashtray. The sheriff's office had not escaped the hint of stale urine that permeated most of the courthouse, either.

The stench of his night in jail revived in Gray's nose and throat. He opened a window and stuck his head out for a breath of fresh air. A hint of rain was still in the air and it smelled good. Green was already starting to come back to the courthouse grass below. Gray looked west, wondering if he could see home, longing to be outside, anywhere but where he was. He turned at the sound of running water and a thin sssss....sound that came from the bathroom. The thin dispatcher scowled as she dropped a wet butt into the overflowing ashtray.

"Where you at, Clarence?" Rube Carter's voice punctuated the static and increased Gray's feeling of anxiety. "Clarence, you need to report in here right now." Clarence Anderson, volunteer deputy and occasional night watchman, did regular foot patrols around the town square. Clarence knew how to use the two-way radio he carried on his belt, but he seldom answered Rube's calls. He talked only to Toy. The mental image of Clarence walking the streets, ignoring Rube, made Rance and Gray smile as they heard Toy's heavy footsteps coming up the stairs.

"You boys already off work?"

"Took off a few minutes early." Rance nodded toward Gray. "Gray Boy thought of some stuff he didn't mention when you were out at the house the other day, Toy. Go ahead, Gray."

Gray told him about seeing Bo in the open area of the courthouse basement the night Spooner died. "Thought maybe Bo might have seen somethin'."

Toy dropped his hat on the desk and rubbed a hand through his curly hair. "Yeah, I knew he was there. He was supposed to spend the night up in the jail. I promised Beulah I would look out for him, then forgot about it, what with throwing you in jail and all."

Rube's voice broke the static again. "Clarence, this is your last chance. Now, you better report in."

Toy turned in his chair, flipped a switch, and spoke into the microphone. "Rube, why do you keep callin' Clarence? What you want with him?"

Rube's voice was contrite. "Just want him to check in."

"One more time, Rube. Clarence ain't about to check in with you. He's doing the same thing he does ever' Monday. Now get off the radio."

"Over and out."

Toy turned back to face Rance and Gray. "Anyway, I guess that boy spent the night down where you saw him. Got soakin' wet. He was a mess when I found him—all nervous and shakin'. Prob'ly had another fit, too."

"I asked him why he didn't just go inside," Gray said.

Toy glanced at the blonde dispatcher and leaned closer, speaking in a whisper. "Don't say nothin', but you know that big key ring Bo carries on his belt loop?"

They both smiled and nodded. Everyone kidded Bo about the huge number of keys that threatened to pull his pants to his knees.

"Well, he's got a key to the jail stairway. Knows how to use it, too. He could have slept up there in the dry if he was of a mind to. Either something scared him out of his wits, or he just stayed down there because he wanted to watch the rain. He gets sort of—what do you call it—closetphobia—in the jail sometimes."

"Close enough. Ivory seems to think he knows something," Rance said.

"There's a good chance he saw something, but I questioned him for over an hour after I got him all dried out. Just made him more nervous. If he knows, he ain't tellin'. At least, he won't tell me. He might talk to you or one of your boys. He ain't afraid of y'all."

The dispatcher lighted up, and Gray walked to the window again to get another breath of air. "Why would Ivory even mention Bo, though? How did he know he was in the courthouse?"

Toy smiled and wiggled all his fingers in the air to indicate sorcery. "Black magic? Naw. Most everybody in town knows that Bo spends lots of nights here in the jail. Ivory would sure know about that night because he probably knows Beulah's been ailing."

Rance drummed his fingers on Toy's desk. "You think Ivory got a hold of Bo before you got to him?"

"Maybe, but he'd have to catch Bo first. That boy can run, and he don't want no truck with King Ivory. He's scared to death of that big man."

Rance leaned forward, eyebrows raised. "Scared of him? Papa told me that Ivory practically raised Bo."

"That's what the old-timers around here all say. All I know is, Bo shakes like a leaf when you mention his name."

The radio barked static. "Sheriff?"

Toy turned and flipped the switch. "What is it now, Rube?"

"DA just drove up. You said to warn you."

"Okay, boys. If Buster comes up here, nothing about the ball yet and especially nothing about Bo. Buster gets a hold of Bo, there won't be nothin' left worth keeping."

"Toy, we got no problem with you mentioning the baseball. He's bound to find out sooner or later." Rance said.

"I know, but I just need some time to work things out. He hears about the baseball or Bo, he'll light into Gray Boy and Bo at the same time. You ain't never seen Buster Galt question somebody. He's hell on wheels."

Rance grunted at the grudging admiration in Toy's voice. "He always come right up to your office when he arrives?"

"Not usually, but he probably will today. He's pushin' me pretty hard on this thing."

"Want us to leave?"

"Naw. He'll just see you walkin' down the stairs, and that would give me one more thing to explain." Toy's cut his eyes toward the stairway as they heard a big man taking the steps two at a time. Gray watched the mirror image of *Delta County Sheriff* sweep across Buster's shirt through the milky glass of the office door.

The glass shook as Buster slung the door back. He hesitated before nodding to Rance and Gray. "Anything new on the colored boy, Toy?"

"Not yet. Waiting on that picture we took to be developed. Should be here tomorrow or the day after."

Buster sat on the edge of Toy's desk, facing Rance and Gray. He fixed his stare on Gray and squared his body so that he towered over him. "What are you boys doing here?"

Gray had to look up, but met and held Buster's gaze, the hate he held for the son easily visited on the father. Though the physical features and coloring of their faces were nothing alike, father and son shared the same voice, the same intimidating expressions and movements.

Rance sensed the tension as he stood and stepped close to Buster. "Just seeing if there was anything we might do to help Toy, Buster. Spooner was a good kid. Worked for me the last three cotton harvests."

Buster stood and shook his hands and arms as if he were warming up for a ballgame. "This Hays boy dying on the courthouse lawn has got people talking everywhere I go—even in Hopkins and Franklin counties. I'm trying to cool things off, but they tell me I got to do somethin' before things get outta hand."

Rance smiled at Buster's easy slide into East Texas slang, something the DA usually tried to avoid. "What do *they* say you've got to do, Buster?"

"You figure it out, Rance. Colored boy maybe killed on our courthouse lawn. First thing you know, we'll have a snoopy reporter from Paris or even Dallas down here. That happens, he's likely to stir up our colored community and bring rabble-rousers from Dallas down here."

"I hear rumblin's that King Ivory is demandin' some sort of justice for his boy," Toy said.

Rance walked to the door and put his hand on the knob. He turned and smiled at Buster. "Worried about the colored vote, Buster? You can probably win again without it."

A faint smile crossed Buster's face and his shoulders slumped. "Boys, to tell the truth, I just want this thing to go away—far, far away. I want to call this thing an accidental death, 'cause that's probably what it was."

He walked to the open window, put both hands on the ledge, and leaned out. "Boy probably climbed that big tree on a dare, had a bad fall, and broke his damn neck. All there is to it. Thing is, that damn Hoot won't turn loose. Wants to be a damn detective."

Buster turned and gestured in Toy's direction. "Hell,

truth be known, he wants Toy's job. Figures this is his chance to get it."

Toy jabbed a pencil against his desk as Buster continued staring at him. "So—me and Toy got to stick together on this thing."

Buster shifted his gaze to the Rivers. "We'll call a spade a spade. If it was an accident, we need to jump up and say so."

He gave Toy a hard look. "If there was foul play, then we got to find out what kind—and soon. We'll have to give the colored folks their pound of flesh."

Rance and Gray walked toward the stairs. Buster held the door open and called after them. "Anything you boys can do to help would be appreciated. You know anything, anything at all, just sing out." Rance smiled and gave a two-fingered salute before turning to go down the stairs.

Sun broke through the clouds as they stepped onto the courthouse sidewalk, warming their shoulders and bringing steam from the soaked ground. "Sounds like they may be going to call it an accident." Gray's voice was cautious.

"What do you think happened, Gray Boy?"

"I suppose he could have just fallen out of that tree. I still can't figure how that ball got down here, though. I already told you that I did a lot of stupid things that night, but I kept that ball in my pocket or in my hand all the time. Doesn't make sense that I would drop it after all that. I know for sure that I didn't drop it over by the tree. I wasn't over there until...."

"Until what, Gray Boy?"

"Until I walked out of jail and tripped over Spooner's body."

Hurt showed again on Rance's face. He sat down on a small bench, scarcely noticing the wet seat. He pointed toward the spot where Spooner's body had lain. "See that spot, Gray Boy? That's where you crossed the river."

Gray stared down at the perfect crease in his Levis. "Yes, sir."

"Do you even know what I'm talking about?"

"Yes sir. I did a cowardly thing. I'm a coward."

"You said a couple of days ago that I taught you never to give up. Do you remember anything I taught you about integrity? Do you know what you should have done?"

"I should have gone back inside and used a phone or found some way to get somebody to take care of Spooner."

"Even if you knew he was dead."

Gray nodded. "Even if. I know it's no excuse, but I was awful sick."

"No, it's not an excuse. It's just the kind of thing that separates a man with character from one who hasn't got any."

"So you're saying I'm a coward and have no character."

"No, I'm not saying that, but you blamed me the other night for your continued fighting with the Galt kid. You said I taught you never to give up. How come you remember that, but don't remember about where the river is?"

"I remember about the river between right and wrong. I remember about getting' in the flow, too. You've drilled it into my head and Jake's since we were babies, but you didn't tell us that the river gets wavy sometimes. Sometimes it's hard to find the flow. You didn't tell us about split second decisions. I made a decision with a foggy head in a split second. It was wrong, and I know it now, but at the time, it seemed logical."

"You mean it seemed easy. Did it seem easy all the way home? Was it still easy when you crawled into a dry bed at home while Spooner's body laid out here in the wet?"

Gray put his hands out, palms up. "All right. I made two mistakes. One when I made the decision to leave, and a second when I didn't change it when I had the chance. I was sick and weak, but that's no excuse."

"Whose fault is it that you were sick and weak?"

"Mine. You never been sick and weak from drinking too much?"

Rance flinched. He stood and put his hands in his

pockets to keep them under control. "Yes, I have, and I know what that feels like. I was a weak, bitter man when your little brother died. I don't claim to be perfect, and I don't expect you to be. I just want you to be a better man than me—to profit from my mistakes."

"So, do we march right back in there and tell Buster about the baseball?"

"I've never lied about the baseball. I never volunteered the information because I see it as a distraction for Buster. Or maybe I'm just protecting the son I love. You think that crosses the river?"

"No, I don't."

"Have you ever lied about the baseball?"

"No."

Rance opened the door to the pickup. "Is there anything else about what you did the night Spooner died that I need to know?"

Gray picked up a rock and threw it across the lawn. He looked at the sky before facing his father. His voice quivered a little. "Yes, sir, there is. Is it okay to wait until we get home to hear the rest? I just want to tell it one time, and I want Mama, Jake, and Papa Griff to hear it."

Rance sighed heavily as he sat behind the wheel. He gripped the steering wheel and pulled back as Gray sat in the passenger seat, looking toward home. "You mentioned the flow. We haven't talked much about that since you were a little boy. You used to love Papa's stories about this family's special gift." Rance chuckled softly. "The Rivers' Flow...Jake still believes in it. Do you?"

Gray looked straight ahead. "They were good stories to grow up with. Helped me to do some things I probably wouldn't have if I hadn't believed in it. The stories helped Jake hit that home run."

"But now?"

"I guess Tuck's death took the starch out of it for me—

made it seem kinda foolish. But I think I got to believin' it again until Cameron Galt beat it out of me that night." Gray turned toward his father. "Where was it then?"

"You know what Papa would say? He'd say the Rivers' flow is the same place it always was—in your heart and in your head. It's easy to believe when things are going your way. It's when they're not—that's when you have to believe." Rance started the Chevy.

8 Jake was tying Scar, his bay gelding, to the front porch post when the pickup stopped in the driveway. Rance slid out of the truck seat and shouted over the open door. "Jake, you know better than to tie your horse to that post."

"Papa Griff does it."

"Get back on him and go get Papa. Tell him to come right away. Buddy is probably still saddled, but if he isn't, you two can double on Scar."

Jake jumped and missed the stirrup on the first try. He grabbed the saddle horn with both hands and swung into the saddle. He looked to see if his father was impressed. "What's the hurry?"

"Don't talk, Jake, just ride."

Jake liked the sound of *just ride*. He trotted to the gate and opened it from the saddle. Rance shook his head as Jake made a kissing sound and leaned forward. Scar took off in a dead run across the slippery pasture, leaving a plume of water droplets in his wake.

"Try not to slip down and kill the horse and yourself." Rance muttered under his breath.

Mattie watched Jake from the kitchen window. "He's going to kill himself on that horse. Where's he going? I just called him for supper."

Rance hung his hat on the hook behind the door. "Set another plate. Papa's comin' for supper."

"How come?"

"Gray Boy here has got something he wants to tell us." Gray's sheepish look and pale color alarmed Mattie. He avoided her look until she grabbed both shoulders and made him face her. Her face was drained of color; her eyes projected the fear she felt. "What did you do?"

Gray grabbed his mother, pulled her close, and hugged her. Memories of the worst night of his life filled his mind.

Gray Boy and a few friends had found shelter under an awning in front of the five-and-dime on the Cooper square after Jake's game. When the rain stopped, Shep Rivers, Gray's cousin, left the awning and stepped out into the street. "Sure hope it ain't done. Bet we didn't get more'n an inch or two."

Gray joined him on the brick street and looked up at the dark sky. "Hell, that's more than I can remember it raining since I was a little boy. My clothes are still wet."

"Not near enough rain to end the drought, though. Notice how it's still hot and still? Papa says that's a sign of a thunderstorm. Maybe it ain't through."

Gray nodded. "It does feel kinda creepy, just like the night James Dooley hung himself from his barn loft rafters."

"I remember that night. It never did rain, just stormed all night. Drove poor old James crazy."

"Daddy said James thought he was the cause of the drought. Thought it was punishment for running around on his wife. Felt like God was teasing him with those dry thunderstorms."

Heat lightning streaked behind them and in front of them as they stood on the square. The boys had pooled their money and were waiting for Wheeler Dodd, a local bootlegger, to return from Oklahoma with the beer they had ordered. The rise of barometric pressure and lightning filling the night with electricity made hairs stand up on the backs of their necks. The air was hot and heavy enough to cut with a knife. The slightest movement caused tiny rivulets of sweat to form and run down the boys' backs and sides.

Gray was sitting on the fender of Shep's Model A Ford sipping from a half-pint bottle and tossing the baseball when a rusty black '41 Ford eased onto the square and began a slow circle. Gray Boy jumped off the fender and pointed. "I think that's Spooner driving that old Ford."

Gray stuck the ball in his pants and tossed the bottle into the Model A. He kick-started his Mustang and pulled along-side the Ford. "Hey, Spooner. Thought that was you."

Spooner had one elbow flopped over the window ledge, one forearm on the wheel of the Ford. "Who da' hell you think it is, Cracker?" Spooner's smile seemed nervous, different.

Gray pulled a little closer to look past Spooner to the girl sitting in the front seat. "Whoeee, Spooner. Who you got with you?"

"Ain't none of your business, but this be Sadie Shaw. I already told her about you, so don't even think about it."

Gray held the clutch as he gunned the cycle. "Now, Spooner, what did you tell this innocent girl about me? She's a looker. Where you been keepin' her hid?"

"You done dipped that oversized wick of yours in just about every white girl in the county. Best leave the colored ones to me." Spooner speeded up a little, but Gray stayed alongside. Spooner nodded toward Gray. "What's that you got stuck in your pants? I know it ain't what you want the gals to think it is."

"That's Jake's baseball. He hit a homerun tonight. Come on over and shoot the bull with us, Spoon. Shep Rivers is over there—you remember him."

"'Member Shep, but don't know any of those other pasty-faced little paperwads you hangin' round with."

"That's Jimmy Joe and Jerry Doyle. They're just old country boys like you and me. Come on over. See that old truck slowin' down over there? He's bringin' us some beer from across the Red. Your girl drink Oklahoma beer? I'll let you have a couple out of my share."

Spooner was reluctant, but Gray persisted until he parked a few yards away. "See, we done run off some of your whiteass friends."

"Nope. They're just goin' to follow Wheeler out of town and pick up the beer. He ain't about to stop on the square and deliver beer to anybody, much less boys. They'll be back in a minute."

Spooner unfolded his lanky frame from the Ford and stepped onto the brick street of the town square. He motioned for the girl to join him. She kept her head down as she nestled under Spooner's arm.

Gray had to stoop to see her face. "Sadie, is it?" Gray whistled and smiled, showing his deep dimples. "What's a good-lookin' girl like you doing with this big bowl of chocolate puddin'? Everybody knows that The Spoon ain't worth the powder it'd take to kill him."

Sadie smiled as she looked up at Spooner. "He'll do in a pinch." Her caramel skin matched Spooner's. The red-faded-to-pink, sleeveless gingham dress hung straight to her knees, but could not hide the figure underneath. Her expression and lines around her mouth reflected a lifetime of smiling, but her eyes seemed full of fright.

"Yeah, but why settle for the bottom half of the chocolate pie when you could have the meringue?" Gray took a playful poke at Spooner. Spooner flinched, but did not smile. Gray barely noticed. "Hey, they're back with the beer." Molly Beth French stepped out of the car and walked toward them. Shep shrugged his shoulders behind Molly Beth as he looked at

Gray.

Molly Beth's white blouse was tied into a knot above a pair of tight jeans, leaving a sliver of belly showing. "How come I wasn't invited to this party? I had to hitch a ride with Shep."

Gray smiled and accepted Molly Beth's suggestive squeeze. "I came by after Jake's game, but you weren't at the usual place. Figured you might be out with Little Buster."

Molly Beth winced but smiled. "And I figured you were with Little Halley. Wouldn't hurt if you told me in advance sometime. I can't stay out on the street waiting for you all night, especially with it lightning and thundering."

"How was I gonna do that? You know we haven't got a phone at home. Besides, your daddy or mama would probably have answered and grounded you at the sound of my voice." Gray watched Molly Beth's face to gauge when he had gone too far. "They'd much rather answer the phone for the DA's son."

Molly Beth did not react, so Gray turned toward Spooner. "You remember Spooner. Well, this is his friend, Sadie Shaw. You guys want a beer?" Spooner shrugged a noncommittal answer, and Sadie shook her head.

Gray flashed his smile at Sadie again. "Sure?" She nodded.

"You didn't ask me, but I'll share one with you," Molly Beth said.

"You won't get much if you share with me. Hope you got a church key in your car, Shep." From the dark inside the Model A, Shep found his can opener and cracked the beers. They all slid down between the Model A and the '41 Ford. Leaning against the tires, they started on the beer.

An hour later, Shep pulled himself from his sitting position. "I gotta get home."

Gray's voice was slurred. "Any beer left?"

"Nope. Jimmy Joe and Jerry Doyle took their share, and

we drank the rest."

Gray drained the last of the can he was holding and crushed it. "We? Hell, you drank about two and Spooner drank three. Me and Molly Beth drank the rest."

Shep opened the Model A's door. "I got all I wanted and you paid for my share. Hope she'll crank." He pushed the floor starter, and the little engine sounded a smooth rhythm. Shep smiled as he looked back. "Purrs like a Singer sewing machine. I'll get rid of the cans somewhere. Better watch for Toy on the way home."

The Model A eased away, leaving the two couples exposed against the Ford's tires. Both girls were asleep. Molly Beth's head was on Spooner's shoulder, and Sadie was leaned against Gray Boy's leg. Gray Boy grinned at Spooner. "Looks like she prefers me."

Spooner held Molly Beth by the shoulders as he eased himself up. Molly Beth smiled a groggy smile and rose weakly to her feet. She leaned her head against Spooner's chest, letting her arms fall by her sides. Seeing this, Gray pulled sleepy Sadie up. When she stumbled in his direction, he kissed her lightly on the lips.

With his eyes still closed, he felt Spooner's grip on his arm as he was jerked away from Sadie. Spooner's usually creamy, friendly eyes had turned red. Gray felt the back of Spooner's hand across his jaw, felt his lip split, tasted the blood in his mouth as he staggered backward. "What the hell?"

Spooner held Sadie by the arm with one hand and used the other to point at Gray Boy. "Nobody touches my girl. Ain't no sorry-ass white man ever gon' touch her again."

Gray dragged the back of his hand across his mouth and stared at the blood. He probed with his finger, but found no loose teeth. He glanced at a trembling Sadie and a wide-eyed Molly Beth. It was the first time he had been hit in the face since the fight with Cameron. The memory ignited humiliation and rage.

Gray charged Spooner without speaking. There was nothing to say. Spooner had done the unthinkable, the forbidden. There was no thinking, no going back. Bending his knees for extra power, he threw his body into a kidney punch like the one he had received from Cameron Galt. He had learned something from that beating. Spooner's groan combined with a roll of thunder and screams from Molly Beth and Sadie.

Learning from past mistakes and acting out the scene he had replayed a hundred times in his mind, Gray did not give Spooner time to recover. Remembering his broken finger and skinned knuckles from hitting Cameron Galt on the jaw, he delivered a solid left fist to Spooner's Adam's apple. Spooner grabbed at his neck with both hands as Gray slammed a second kidney punch. Still, Spooner did not fall.

Gray stepped back and rammed his head and shoulder into Spooner, pushing them both to the brick pavement. Spooner tried to grab Gray and hold him, but Gray was on his feet instantly, kicking Spooner in the sides and the face. He could not allow Spooner to get up and use his larger size and strength. Molly Beth and Sadie flailed away at Gray, screaming for him to stop.

As suddenly as it had begun, the fight was over. Gray re-alized he was hitting his friend, held up his hands and backed away. A bolt of lightning followed almost at once by a clap of thunder punctuated the misery of the moment. Gray shifted his focus from his bleeding hands to Spooner's face. Molly Beth and Sadie were staring at him, shock in their expres-sions.

The night grew even more still, the air more oppressive. Spooner struggled to his knees, emptied his stomach on the street, and rose to his feet. They stood in a circle, everyone gasping for air. The unmistakable roar of Toy's worn out glass-pack mufflers caused a spasm in the circle. A red light reflected off a puddle in the street and a wet building wall across from the courthouse reflected headlights.

Gray's face changed from shock to alarm. "Y'all get out of here."

When Sheriff Toy Roy Robbins pulled up on the square, Gray Boy was sitting on the bricks, leaned against the Mustang, Jake's baseball nestled between his legs. A cool breeze had broken the heat and stillness.

Toy shook his head. "Suppose you stayed here to keep me from catching whoever was in that Ford I saw leavin'." Gray Boy smiled up at Toy. "Been drankin' too, ain't you? Well, you're too drunk to ride that sickle. Best you spend the night with me."

"Okay if I just ride the motorcycle to the courthouse? I'll park it in the basement."

Toy opened the trunk of the Ford, carefully picked up the front of the Mustang, and laid it half in and half out of the trunk. "She'll ride a block that way."

"You're gonna scratch it all up."

Large, widely spaced drops of rain splattered them as Toy shoved Gray into the back seat. As they moved toward the courthouse, sheets of rain pushed against the windshield.

Mattie pushed Gray away and turned toward her stove. "Jake will be back with Mr. Griffin in a few minutes. I've got to get this supper on the table."

Griffin Rivers usually left his horse saddled until a few minutes before dark every day. By twilight, he always unsaddled Buddy and rubbed his back before feeding. He had just pulled the flank strap to begin the daily ritual when Jake slid his horse to a stop.

"Whoa. Damn, Boy, how many times I got to tell you not to ride that horse so hard in this pasture?"

Jake slumped in the saddle, pride at performing his

mission draining away. "Daddy says you're supposed to come
to supper."

Griffin re-buckled the strap. "He does, does he?"

"Yep. They want you right away. Mama's settin' the table.
Somethin' is up."

Griffin tightened the front cinch, grabbed a mane-full of
hair with his left hand, put his right hand on the horn, a foot
in the stirrup, and pulled himself up. Jake enjoyed the grace
of it all. They started toward home in an easy walk. "The
cracks are all filled up now, Papa. What does it hurt for us to
run? See, Scar ain't even sweatin'."

Griffin smiled a little as he stared straight ahead. "You
ever see a horse slide on wet grass, Jake?"

"No, sir."

"Well, this wet grass is treacherous. I've seen horses turn
completely over their riders." Griffin squeezed Buddy into a
short lope, and Jake followed suit. They slowed to a walk again
behind the hay barn.

"What kind of music did you hear today, Papa?" Griffin
had often told him that a man could change his mood by
just listening to different music in his head. Jake tried, but it
almost never worked for him.

*Know why they always play background music in the picture
shows, Jake? Because music affects your mood. I just figured out
how to play music all day long.*

"I heard pianos tinklin' soft tunes most of the day.
Tonight, I'm looking forward to a little steel guitar."

Jake peeled off toward the old hay barn to unsaddle and
feed Scar. Griffin stepped off Buddy at the back porch, laying
the reins between the corner post and the shelf. He drew
some water from the cistern, poured it into the wash pan, and
washed his hands with Lava soap. Griffin took an extra long
time with the lather, gauging the mood inside the kitchen and
judging it to be somber. He was going to hear bad news.

He laid his hat on Mattie's bedspread, crown down, as he

passed through the porch bedroom and took his customary seat next to the porch door. "Evenin'."

Rance, Mattie, and Gray were already seated. Each nodded in Griffin's direction. "Where's Jake?" Rance asked.

Griffin raised in his seat enough to look out the porch window over the cistern. "He's on his way. Had to unsaddle and feed his horse."

Jake hit the porch with a thud, burst through the screen door, through the bedroom, and into the kitchen. He pulled out his chair and sat down, keeping his eyes down.

Griffin smiled. "That's about the quickest unsaddlin' and feedin' job I ever saw. After supper, you go back and rub that horse's back."

"Yes, sir."

Mattie glanced at Jake's hands as he moved toward the bowl of red beans. "You wash your hands?"

Jake frowned, pushed back his chair, and walked quickly toward the porch.

Griffin surveyed the glum faces at the table. "Jake said I was invited to supper. Are we gonna sulk or eat? Pass the cornbread, Gray Boy."

Jake smiled as he gave his hands a cursory wetting, a small amount of soap, and quick dry with a towel. He was back in time to catch the tomatoes and fried potatoes as they passed by his place at the table.

Rance took two barely-done biscuits from a plate nobody else had touched. "Let's get this over with, Gray. Spit it out."

Gray told them what had happened that terrible night. With each new revelation, Rance's face grew darker. Tears flowed unattended down Mattie's cheeks. She left the room and came back with a handkerchief to her nose.

"You and Spooner always got along so well, laughing and cutting up. Why would you say such awful things to each other? Don't you see, now he's dead and you can never take it back."

"We did it all the time, Mama. That's usually what got our laughing started. It eased the tension that was just naturally there between us. We lived in different worlds, and it was our way of bridging white and colored."

"Yes, but you see what happens when that old beer or whiskey is involved. It always gets out of hand. And you kissing his girl—Gray, you know better than that. A colored girl? And your friend's girlfriend? What if Spooner had kissed your girl?"

Jake was frightened for his brother, but he depended on his other male role models to make everything turn out right. Rance's drumbeat of fingers on the tabletop grew so loud that Jake flinched with each tap. Finding only anger and concern in his father's eyes, he turned toward his grandfather. Griffin's eyes reflected his son's disappointment and concern, but the sharp anger was not there. He waited for Rance to speak.

"So, is this finally the whole truth?"

Gray held up a palm as if taking an oath. "As God is my witness."

Everyone except Griffin jumped when Rance slapped a hand on the table. He knew it was coming. Rance scooted his chair back. "So the part about doing donuts in the Frenches' yard was a lie, right?"

"Yes, sir. Toy just took me in for causing a disturbance on the square and drinking beer in public. Guess people heard the girls scream."

"Do you realize how this looks, Gray? My God, boy, you lied to the law and to us about a possible murder. Hell, Buster Galt will be after you like a dog on a bone. You fought with Spooner and he winds up dead."

Mattie shrieked a little moan at the possibilities that raced through her mind. Jake pictured his brother in that filthy jail again.

Griffin squinted an eye toward his grandson, then his

son. "Mind if I ask a question?"

"Go ahead." Rance took out a can of Prince Albert.

Griffin pointed a finger, cocked like a pistol, at his grandson.

"Straight talk and nothing else from now on, Gray Boy. Agreed?"

Gray nodded.

"Is that the last time you saw Spooner that night?"

"Alive, yes."

"Did you hit him hard enough to kill him?"

Gray stared at his grandfather and thought before answering. His voice quivered a little. "I hit him just as hard as I could—two, three times before he fell." Gray looked at his red, skinned knuckles and shook his head, trying to fend off the thoughts that kept coming. "When he finally went down, I kicked him several times." This last at a whisper.

He looked down for a long time, drew a deep breath and began again. "But he got up and drove off. If he died from my hitting him, he died later. Even if he had, that wouldn't explain how he got on the courthouse lawn." Gray seemed to draw hope from his own conclusions. "Besides, Dr. Olen said he died from a fall."

"Did you have anything, and I mean anything, at all to do with his dying?" Rance asked.

"No."

Griffin ran a finger under his mustache. "Do you remember everything that happened that night?"

"Yes—that is, I think I do." Gray looked at his mother; fear and surprise from more, new thoughts came to his face. He turned toward his grandfather, then his father, the same thoughts crossing all their minds.

Rance reached across to put his hand on Gray's shoulder. "We might as well get it all out right now. Gray, is there any chance the two of you got together to have it out later, and you don't remember it because you were too drunk?"

Gray shook his head firmly. "Daddy, I had six, seven, maybe eight beers tops, and I was sharing those with Molly Beth." Mattie stiffened at the mention of this young girl drinking beer.

Gray glanced at his mother. "Mama, I know you don't want to hear this, but I've drunk that many beers lots of times before."

He turned back toward his father. "I drank a few swigs of bootleg whiskey before the beers; I expect that's what made me sick. There's been a few times I wanted to forget, but I always remember everything that happens when I'm drinkin'." He looked at Mattie as she got up from the table to lean against the sink.

Rance stood and stepped back from the table to stand beside Mattie. "So when we talk to Toy, we have to say that you lied at first. You and Spooner did fight; you hit him in the neck, causing him to nearly choke to death, and then you kicked him several times. You didn't see him anymore that night; your mind was clear enough to recall everything that happened, but you don't remember what happened to the baseball. That about sum it up?"

"I think I left that baseball on the bunk in the cell."

"You think." Rance stalked out of the room and headed toward the brush arbor behind the smokehouse.

Jake followed his grandfather out the back door and watched him mount Buddy. "Papa, are we in big trouble?"

Griffin laid both reins across his palm and leaned toward Jake. "Nothin' the Rivers can't handle, Jaker Ridge." The saddle squeaked as he turned Buddy toward home.

Jake called after him. "Papa, what kind of music you hear now?"

Griffin turned and smiled. "That steel guitar is tunin' up. I'll just listen to a little harmonica on the way home, though."

9 Rance parked on the street in back of the courthouse. The birds of morning announced daylight as he rolled down both windows and slumped in the seat. This deep sense of dread had filled him once before. He had stood on the edge of this cliff, on this precipice of losing a son.

Only two blocks away and two years before, he had waited on the parking lot of Bartlett Hospital for the sun to rise. He had sat in his truck then as he was sitting now—afraid—torn between the need to see his sick young son in the fresh light of a new morning and the fear of what the dark had wrought the night before. Why was it happening again?

Rance tried to recall how he felt that day. Did he want to run away and hide as he did now? Did he feel weak then, powerless to help his child? He had not helped Tuck. In fact, he had probably caused his death. Living without running water in a cold, drafty, and leaky old house he provided for his family had probably contributed to his son's death from scarlet fever and diphtheria. He had done nothing to stop it, nothing to protect the child he loved more than life. Now, he had a second chance to protect his own, and he felt powerless again.

The sun's rays crept across the square and down the street toward the courthouse. Shadows from the Delta State Bank building would keep his parking spot in the shade for a few more minutes. He pulled the railroad watch Griffin had given him from his bib. Seven-thirty. Truman would be in his office soon.

He started to build a roll-your-own cigarette, but he was starting to lose his taste for tobacco. Rance wanted a cup of Mattie's coffee. He pulled a half pint of cheap whiskey from under the seat and removed the cap. He put it to his lips, but the smell of liquor brought back memories bad enough to make him gag. He closed it and shoved it back under the seat.

Stepping out to stretch, he noticed a car behind the fire station—a '41 Ford—black—showing lots of rust. The car was pulled into some tall weeds and snuggled closely against the fire station. He walked across the street and pushed aside the weeds for a closer look. The door handle was jammed, but the window was open. He reached inside, pulled the handle, and opened the door. Mosquitoes had to be fanned away from his head as they swarmed through the open door, angry at being disturbed.

The steering wheel, especially the knob, was splotched dark red. Spots were on the front seat, too. He was about to scratch a little of the dried substance off the steering wheel with his fingernail when he sensed that he was being watched.

"No need to scratch that, Rance. It's blood all right, my boy's blood." Rance turned and looked up into Ivory's face.

"Damn, Ivory. You scared me. Beats hell outta me how such a big man can step so softly."

"Came to get the car."

"This car been here all the time? I sat less than fifty feet from it for almost two hours and didn't even notice it."

"Nobody else did either." Ivory sat down and moved the seat back to squeeze behind the wheel. He drew a rag from his back pocket and began cleaning off the steering wheel and knob.

"You think you ought to do that, Ivory? Toy and Buster

are probably going to want to get a sample of that blood and look this car over."

"Been settin' here since the boy got killed, and they ain't looked at it yet."

"That's because they either didn't see it or weren't lookin' for it. I didn't know Spooner even had a car myself till last night. I'm sure Toy didn't either."

"Law ain't lookin' for Spencer's killer. Not really. Just goin' through the motions."

Rance leaned against the door and folded his arms. "I think they are, Ivory. Fact is, I think they suspect my boy."

Ivory stepped out of the car and faced Rance. "Gray Boy?" He grunted his disapproval. "See what I mean? They ain't really lookin'. Just trying to hang this thing on somebody to clean up the mess."

"I'm glad you feel that way, but did you know that our boys had it out on the square the night Spooner died?"

Ivory shook his head. "Them two boys always wrestlin' and testin' each other. Mighta' been real friends if things were different."

"This was more than wrestling. They got mad and slugged it out with fists."

"Suppose they had any beer?"

"I know they did."

"Split-tails?"

Rance nodded. "Both beer and girls."

"I figured. Spencer can't truck with no beer. Can't handle it. Caught him drinking it las' year. Two cans make him woozy; three make him want to fight. He real protective of that little sweet thang he been seeing, too. Silly-jealous."

Ivory chuckled softly, and his face returned to the expression that Rance recognized as his old friend. "Knowing how that boy of yo's can't keep that thing of his in his britches, they probably got into it over the girl."

Rance was surprised that Ivory seemed to know more

about Gray Boy's life than he did. "You hit the nail right on the head." His expression returned to serious. "Ivory, I appreciate your not suspecting Gray. When Hoot and Buster find out about the fight and a couple of other things, it may get pretty nasty."

Rance waited for the answer that did not come. "You seem to know something that you're not telling. I'd be much obliged if you'd tell me anything that might help me clear my boy."

"I got a few notions about what happened to Spencer, but nothin' for sure yet."

Rance persisted. "Yeah, but you knew this car was parked here, for example. Why did Spooner leave it here?"

Ivory looked down the street and pointed to a streetlight. "Ever notice how dark it is right here at night? Fire station knocks off the light from the streetlamp down the street, and this 'un over here been burned out for more'n a year."

"It's obvious he wanted to leave it hidden, but there are lots better places to park and smooch his sweetie."

"Don't think his sweetie was with him when he parked here. She tol' me they had a big fight last night, and he took her home early."

"So why did he park the car here?"

"You'll be hearing from Ivory when I find that out. Ever'body gon' hear from Old King Ivory when he find out."

"I see. Been meanin' to ask you something a long time, Ivory. Now seems like the time."

Ivory sat down in the car again. "Go ahead."

"There's always been lots of talk about this black magic and voodoo stuff. Spooner's death has sure enough revived it. Any truth to it?"

Ivory smiled as he scanned the inside of Spooner's car. "A colored man comes into this ol' world with lots of things goin' agin' him. Can't blame him if he looks for some ways to equal thangs out." He pumped the accelerator a couple of times, turned the key and pushed the starter button. The engine sounded like a swarm of bumblebees. Finally, it sputtered and fired. Smoke belched out the tailpipe. Ivory ground the gears as he put it in reverse.

"Sure wish you wouldn't move that car just yet, Ivory."

Ivory eased the clutch out and started backward. The Ford creaked as it fell from the curb to the street. He shifted into first and held the clutch. "It's my car. Law find out about it, they likely to hold onto it till who knows when. I'm getting' it while the gettin's good."

As Ivory drove away, Rance looked around for the '39 Ford. No sign. *Wonder how he got here?*

Truman Bates carried an umbrella and a thin briefcase as he walked down the street beside the Delta State Bank. He walked the four blocks to his office six days a week, leaving the family's new Buick in the garage at home. With the *Dallas Morning News* and *Paris News* under his arm beside his umbrella, he unlocked the door to his office.

Truman's office was between the downtown square and the courthouse in a small lean-to that appeared as an after-thought to the bank building. The printed sign on the glass door could not be read from the street.

To keep his hands busy, Rance rolled a cigarette. He wanted to allow Truman time to get settled in before showing himself. The talk with Ivory had lifted his spirits a little. Truman turned on the lights and hung his hat and umbrella on the hall tree. Rance waited a few more minutes, shredded the cigarette, and walked across the street.

The hinges creaked as the door drug across the tile floor. A clunky Underwood typewriter gathered dust along with the receptionist-legal-secretary-desk it sat on. Truman had found that few secretaries could do legal work according to his exacting standards, so he seldom used one. They also had problems keeping client secrets.

A spider-web of cracking lines spread across a brown

leather sofa and matching chair. Gray and brown filing cabinets stood against one wall of the front room. A large blackboard hung in the only space not filled with filing cabinets. The reassuring smell of chalk and dusty books reminded Rance of a schoolroom.

A door behind the receptionist's desk opened into Truman's office. Walls in his cavernous office were lined with law books; shelves bowed from the weight. Another large chalkboard lined one wall. Several books lay open on the ledge used for research that ran the length of the bookshelves. Truman's small oak desk, two chairs that matched the oak one behind his desk, and a large table piled high with folders sat in the center of the big room. Truman had spread his newspaper on the research ledge behind his desk and had his back to Rance.

Rance tapped lightly on the doorframe. "I let myself in, Truman. Didn't see a secretary or anything."

"Well, top-o-the-morning to you, Rance. Take a seat. I haven't brewed any coffee yet, but I can." Truman's light, silky voice floated through the room as he swiveled his squeaky chair to face Rance.

"If you're going to make some, I'll have a cup. If you've already had yours, I can do without." Rance took a seat as the waves from his own rough voice and manner of speaking collided with Truman's soft, genteel tones.

"Well, you know, I usually drink some of Mama's coffee before I leave. She insists on it, but, bless her heart, she's just getting too feeble to make it. This morning, it tasted like creek water." Truman smiled a broad smile.

The lawyer took loving care of his elderly parents with good cheer and humor and was admired, even adored, by people in the community for it. A child born late in life to his parents, Truman had never left home—not really—unless you count the periodic absences necessary to obtain a university and law degree. Even during college and law school, most weekends found Truman back in Cooper.

When he graduated law school at the top of his class, he had had his choice of jobs. People said he sacrificed to return home and practice law with his aging father. Buster Galt had returned to follow in his father's footsteps as district attorney, but Truman returned for a different reason. He liked Delta County and its slower lifestyle. More than that, he liked knowing family histories and every important secret in the county.

Truman and Buster Galt were as different as night and day, but alike, too. Both were second-generation lawyers. Their third-generation historic homes were less than a hundred yards from each other. Both had gone away to law school and returned to their roots. Both had been leaders at Cooper High, though in very different ways. Truman led the student council and authored the school's alma mater, while Buster led the football team.

Although both were excellent students, Truman's intellectual capacity, seemed, well, abnormal. Truman had never married, never even shown much interest in girls. Buster loved girls and had married a Dallas debutante. The Bates and the Galts were the social and professional leaders of the community and good friends. Buster and Truman were not good friends. They got along by ignoring each other and granting grudging respect.

Rance heard the tinkling of cups and spoons, the sound of running water, and, finally, the pleasant gurgle of a percolator. The aroma of brewing coffee followed Truman back into the office. He returned to his seat. "Be ready in a jiffy."

"You mentioned your mama. How's your daddy?"

"They're both doing as well as could be expected for late eighties. How about Mr. Griffin?" Folks always called Griffin Rivers Mr. Griffin.

"Still ornery as ever. Rides his horse everywhere he goes."

Truman laughed. "I could tell you some funny stories

about Dad, but I expect you didn't come here to talk about Dad."

Rance put it off a little longer. "He's a fine man. We miss seeing him around town." Rance studied a chalk drawing on the large blackboard. "Mention of your parents brings to mind the Galts. I hear that Buster's mother is confined to her home now, too."

"Yes, unfortunately, that's true. She's a few years younger than Mama, but in worse health, I hear. Apparently, Buster's wife cares for her. Never leaves her, in fact." Truman smiled and took another sip of his coffee. "Anybody else in town we can talk about before we get down to it?"

Rance smiled. They drank coffee together while he revealed what Gray Boy had told him the night before. His face expressionless, Truman scribbled meticulous notes. "So, we have the baseball question, Gray's exit from the county jail, and now the fight. Is that everything you know so far?"

Rance shifted in his seat. "I sure as hell hope that's everything. You sound as if there might be more. I've been studying that drawing on your blackboard. What is that?"

Truman's face showed a little color as he held up a white, soft hand. "Well, you caught me. That's a drawing of the arcs and angles of several possible falls that young Mr. Hays might have taken on his death journey. I confess to an interest in the case."

"And what did you conclude?"

Truman stood by the blackboard and picked up a piece of chalk. "Assuming that Toy's measurements are accurate, that boy fell from the courthouse jail walkway, not from the tree. If you match the broken branches on the ground to the limbs they came from up high; he had to have fallen from above the tree."

"That just makes it worse for my boy."

"Not necessarily, Rance. In fact, there doesn't seem to be enough here to make a case against Gray Boy although it is enough to start rumors and put pressure on our district attorney."

"Who's bringin' the pressure?"

"Voters, I guess. They don't want the colored to get all stirred up. Folks expect their district attorney to solve crimes and put away criminals. Spooner's just another dead nigger to a lot of them, but they don't want their tranquility interrupted because of it. Nobody knows better than you that this boy was the son of the most influential man in The Hollow."

"I just saw Ivory a few minutes ago. He seems to think somebody else killed Spooner. Doesn't blame Gray Boy."

Truman raised his eyebrows. "Well, that's meaningful information. I had supposed that Ivory was behind the colored unrest. If he says somebody else did it, we best listen."

"He acts like he knows who did it."

"Perhaps he does. Ivory is not a man to be taken lightly, regardless of color."

"What do you think about all this black magic stuff?"

Truman smiled and folded one delicate hand on top of the other on his desk. "I'm in the third pew, first aisle seat at the Baptist Church every Sunday, Rance. I am not a believer in black magic or such things, but a true believer in the Holy Spirit has to believe in things he cannot see. Let's just say that opens the door to other unseen possibilities."

Truman leaned back in his chair. "Let me get the coffee pot, and you can tell me what you think."

Rance stared into his empty coffee cup until Truman returned with the pot. "I like Ivory, but it is strange for any man to live like he does. I guess his strange behavior is one of the reasons I like him. It's like escaping to another world when you visit him."

Rance held out his cup for Truman to refill. "A man needs to escape once in awhile. When you get right down to it, I always figured Ivory was acting strange to get attention and gain power. He likes being King Ivory. I sort of admired him for being brave enough to do all those crazy things. I guess I would like for the stories to be true, but I never believed them. Hell, I don't even know what black magic is."

"Do you know about his background?" Truman refilled his own cup. Fresh coffee added to the warmth of the conversation.

"Just that he lived here as a boy, made a career in the service, came back with Spooner and no mother for the boy."

"Without violating client confidentiality, I can tell you that he lived in Haiti for a short time after being released from his military obligation. Black magic and voodoo are commonly accepted religions among certain groups there."

Truman arched his eyebrows again. "He also lived in New Orleans just prior to returning home to Delta County."

Rance took a drink of coffee and smiled. "Guess that's where he gets that accent. Sounds like he's French on some days and pure East Texas colored on the next. So you think he has magic powers?"

"That's a combination of French and Creole he speaks sometimes. Picked it up in Haiti or New Orleans, I expect. As for the magic powers, no, but I think that he believes he does, and sometimes that's enough."

Rance looked at his watch. They had been visiting for almost an hour. "If he does have any, I hope he uses 'em to help me clear Gray. Guess I've been avoiding the questions I came here to ask. Do we need a lawyer, and what do we need to do now?"

"Rance, you know I'm just a simple civil lawyer. I handle wills, probate, and real estate transactions, mostly. This is a criminal matter."

"You spent time as county attorney. Always wondered why you didn't run for DA."

"Not a politician, I guess."

"Well, you're the man I want, even if I had another choice."

Truman smiled and scribbled a few notes. "All right, we've established a lawyer-client relationship this morning. As of now, I officially represent Gray Griffin Rivers." He looked up from his scribbling and smiled. "Known to us all as Gray Boy."

"As to your second question, my original thought was to keep quiet and see what happens. Now, I think it is best to go over and tell the sheriff what Gray Boy told you." Truman rose from his seat and walked toward the hall tree.

"What changed your mind?"

Truman bounced his hat in his hands as he put the umbrella in the crook of his arm. "Two things. First, they'll eventually find out about the fight. Four people were there, and only one is dead. Buster doesn't like to be made a fool of, and he'll be very angry if he finds out you kept it from him. We don't want to incur his wrath by keeping any more secrets. Second, Ivory probably knows that Gray Boy did not do it. He won't let Gray Boy go down for something he did not do."

Truman waited until he was outside to cover his light brown, fine hair with his hat. Rance realized that he had never removed his own hat in Truman's office. As an after-thought, he took it off, adjusted it, and re-covered his black, straight, coarse hair. He pointed toward the bent weed-tracks left by Spooner's car. "I'll tell you about Spooner's car on the way to the courthouse."

10 The wind felt good in Gray's face, blowing his hair and tickling his scalp as he pushed the Mustang close to its limit. Speed and wind helped him to focus. That was why he loved the motorcycle so much. Spooner had been dead for almost four days now. Three of those days had seemed like a long nightmare. Today, back at work for Gulf States Telephone in Commerce, he felt almost normal again. Climbing telephone poles required a person to keep his mind on what he was doing.

Gray's self-loathing for having left Spooner's body lying in the rain and for being too afraid and ashamed to tell the whole truth was giving way to grief. He would never be able to atone for his last acts with Spooner—never be able to apologize. The enormity of Spooner's death came in big waves, each threatening to engulf him. Tuck's death had stunned him, but sharing the grief with his family had somehow eased the pain. His death had been innocent, even virtuous—as if God had sent him to spread his goodness through the family and then taken him away.

Spooner's death was filled with guilt and wickedness, maybe evil. He could make no sense of it. There was no reason, no justification. He and Spooner were the same age. Boys that age—just out of high school—just beginning life—do not die. But Spooner had died. The same thing could happen to him.

As the wind blocked out all other sounds, Gray's imagination took flight. He imagined his own funeral—his family sitting in cold chairs under a funeral-home tent—a preacher shouting hellfire and damnation. His parents would be devastated, unable to bear the grief of losing a second son.

Trish would have come home for the funeral, weeping on Pete's shoulder. Jake would stand beside his grandfather, weeping for his big brother, his parents broken and unable to console him.

His friends would wander around the graveyard, checking out wheel covers, twin pipes, and cars in general, telling stories of Gray Boy Rivers' love for good times, girls, and beer.

"I'll tell you one thing, ain't nobody could get into more panties than Gray Boy Rivers," one would say.

"That's for sure. The girls did love Gray, and Gray loved them. He used to say that girls were like pecans—once you get the meat, there ain't nothin' left but the shell," another would opine.

They would all laugh; then someone would add, "Yep, he threw away lots of pecan shells during his time. Lived fast, loved hard, and died young, and left a beautiful memory—just like the song." They'd laugh again, then start to look through the funeral crowd for those pecan shells.

A few weeks later, Mattie would clean out his room and give his stuff to Jake. Jake would move in, admire the new things, imagine himself wearing the clothes that were too big for him now, lie down on the bed—and become Gray Boy Rivers. It would be as if he never existed. What had he really accomplished in his short life? He would be remembered for beating a friend, and being beaten by his worst enemy.

When he slept now, Spooner's open-eyed, blank stare haunted him in the dark recesses of his mind. He was sure he had not killed Spooner, but he felt somehow responsible for his death. Spooner's ghost blamed him, too. In the sober light of day, his behavior on the night of the fight made him cringe. *How could I have acted like such a damn fool? I know what I was thinking—Gray Boy Rivers don't take no shit off nobody—not even his friends.*

Of course, he did take some shit. Cameron Galt had given him plenty. Dropped him dead in his tracks in less time than it takes to light a cigarette. He had tried to take both of his best girls and may have succeeded with Molly Beth.

As he passed Camp Lake Store and the half-way point between Commerce and Cooper, he resolved to change—to make his life more memorable—and he knew just where to start. He stopped at home, took his clothes off the clothesline and turned back toward Commerce.

He turned up the steep incline on Rainey Hill and stopped beside the house. He parked his Mustang beside the back door cistern and looked inside the small shed behind the house for Halley's parents' cars. Neither was there. Nobody answered his polite knock on the back door, so he walked past the house toward the Rainey's washateria.

The bundle of clothes under his arm had hung on Mattie's clothesline since his night in jail. His skin still tingled from wind assault as the smell of bleach, washing powder, and starch mixed with the smell of stagnant pond scum off Rainey Lake. The combination was not pleasant, but it was heady and made him feel cleaner.

A symphony of singing locusts blended with the sloshing sounds of washing machines as he stopped at the washateria door. The sounds were familiar and comforting, reminding him of visits here with his mother. Concrete gutters around the small building carried the gray water, detergent, bleach, and bluing away from the building and down the hill toward the lake.

Gray looked through a window and saw Halley working a shirt through the wringer on one of the machines. He started to walk through the door or knock on the window but was afraid that the surprise would frighten her. Besides, he enjoyed watching her work. Halley's billowing skirt bounced as she ran clothes through the wringers. With her free hand, she moved wet curls and wiped the sweat off her neck. As she picked up a bundle of wrung clothes and turned to drop them in a basket, she saw him. She held the clothes for a minute as their eyes locked. Gray's dimples deepened as he eased through the open door.

"Hey, girl."

She did not mean to, but Halley returned his smile. She had practiced this meeting many times in her mind, and none of her imaginings matched what was happening. She certainly had not intended to smile.

"Hey, yourself. You caught me at a bad time. I look a mess." She did not, of course. Her large brown eyes and long, dark eyelashes complemented the freckles just under her eyes. Just enough sun had given her skin a summer glow. Soft, dark brown curls framed it all. Halley was not magazine-model-beautiful, just country girl pretty.

"You look about as good as I ever saw you."

"Thanks a lot. All this time, I thought I looked better all dressed up."

"You know what I mean. You look terrific. I like my girls to look natural."

"Your girls?"

"Now don't start twisting my words. You do that to me every time."

"A girl could get really big-headed listening to all these compliments."

"Let's just say you look good no matter what you're doing and leave it at that."

"I guess I'll take that one as a compliment and forget those other slips of the tongue." She nodded at the bundle under his arm. "You bring us some laundry business?"

Gray leaned against one of the washing machines and folded his arms. "Yeah, I guess. I'm supposed to wash these myself. Mind showing me again how to work these things?"

She folded her arms and smiled. "It's really complicated. Figure it out for yourself. Where's your detergent?"

Gray smiled and shrugged. "Wondered if you might like to go into Cooper with me tonight. Tuesday night special is on at Sparks. Probably just a shoot-em-up, but it's only a quarter for both of us to get in."

Halley's face fell. "Gray Boy, I haven't seen you up close all summer. When I did, you were with Molly Beth or some other girl. Some of those girls are my friends. You humiliated me."

The small radio on a corner table battled static and the chugging of washing machines as The Platters sang *The Magic Touch*. "Never meant to do that, Halley. You know me."

Halley turned away, picked up a shirt out of the washing machine tub, and started it through the wringer. "Oh yeah, I almost forgot. Spare me the story about feeding your cravings."

She turned and threw the shirt into a basket. "You think you're the only one with feelings? You're just selfish. You have no self-control, but you expect me to." Her eyes were glistening now.

"That's what I came by for. I've been thinking about how I've been acting. I've been selfish and I know it. I want to make it up to you. Start all over. A truce." Gray felt his body grow warm from head to toe.

He wanted to keep his thoughts pure about Halley, but everything about this girl stirred him. He might have bungled his effort to compliment her, but he could not put into words what he truly felt. He could not say that he could smell her from across the room—the shampoo mixing with sweet sweat in her hair. Even the smell of laundry detergent mixing with her bath soap intoxicated him. He could feel the warmth of her neck, imagine the smoothness of her legs under that skirt.

He could not say any of those things to Halley.

Expressing himself freely, the only way he knew how, would come out wrong somehow, and he did not want that—not this time.

Elvis had taken over for The Platters and was crooning *I Want You, I Need You, I Love You.* He did not help. "A truce?"

Halley picked up a wet basket and moved it toward the front door. Gray stepped in front of her. "Let me help." He put his hands over hers on the basket, and Halley warmed him with her eyes again. "How about it? It's just a picture show."

"I'm sure Daddy won't let me go. Everybody's already heard about your being thrown in jail last weekend."

Gray winced. He had not considered the damage that information could do to his chances with Joe Max Rainey's daughter. Turning over a new leaf would not be as easy as it had seemed a few minutes ago. He wrestled the basket from her and put it with the others by the front door.

"I'll come by about seven tonight in the car. If you can't go, maybe we can sit on the porch swing or go out by the lake." Gray started out the door.

"What about the laundry?" Halley pointed to the bundle under his arm.

"Almost forgot. Could you sell me some detergent?"

Halley held out her hand, feigning disgust toward the clothes. "Here, let me have the clothes. I'll do them for you, and you can pick them up later. Are they yours?"

Gray took the bundle from under his arm and sniffed his shirt. The clothesline had removed most of the smell, but not all. "No, I don't want you washing my nasty clothes. These are pretty bad."

She shrugged. "Don't be silly; I wash dirty clothes all day. Give 'em to me."

Gray searched her face to see if she was serious. He

had never loved her more than he did as he handed her the clothes. "Don't smell of 'em."

She put them to her nose and made a disgusted face. "Shewee. Stale beer. Shame on you."

Gray heard her, but just barely. He was on his way to the Mustang.

The Ford was in the driveway when he arrived at home. Mattie, finished with her day at the sewing factory, was sitting on the front porch, a glass of iced tea in her hand. Gray Boy parked his Mustang in the front yard. "Any chance of getting to use the Ford tonight?"

Mattie rocked in the wicker rocker. "Hello to you, too, Gray Boy. Have a nice day at work?"

He kissed her on the cheek and plopped down in the rocker with the broken leg. "Not bad. You?"

"Running a sewing machine all day in a room full of women is always fun."

"I'll bet. Worse than climbing telephone poles. How about the car?"

Mattie smiled and took a sip of tea. "The car—sounds like you've made a visit to Rainey Hill."

"Yep."

"Does that mean you're finished with that other little floozy?"

Gray Boy grinned at his mother. "It means I need the car to take Halley to the picture show. You know Joe Max will demand we come home as soon as the show is over, so I'll be back almost before it gets good and dark."

"Here comes your daddy. He'll have the say on this."

Gray's face fell as he saw Rance's pickup turn in the driveway off 24. He had hoped to have permission, maybe even be gone, before his father arrived. "You know what he's likely to say."

Rance stopped to wash his hands on the back porch before walking through the dog-run to join them. Gray jumped up to give him his chair. Rance recognized the looks on their faces. "Okay, what do you want?"

"Gray has a date with Halley Rainey tonight. Wants to use the car to take her to the picture show."

Rance looked at Mattie's glass. "Any more of that iced tea?" Mattie left for the kitchen. "Gray, you can't to into Cooper. Where are your brains? You realize what kind of deep trouble you're still in?"

Gray's expression wilted. "Guess I was just feeling innocent. Did you hear something today?"

"I told Toy and Truman Bates about the fight. Talked to Ivory, too."

"Does Ivory think I killed Spooner?"

"No, but Ivory is not our main worry. It's what the law thinks that counts."

"What does Toy say?"

"He's worried."

Gray's euphoria left him like air from a balloon. "They going to arrest me?"

Rance took the glass of iced tea. "I don't know what they're going to do. You just don't need to be cruising around town like nothing happened."

Gray stood and walked toward his motorcycle. "Okay, I'll stay at home until this thing is over, if it ever is. I need to ride over and tell Halley we won't be going."

The vigor had gone out of the wind, and the sun was blinding as he retraced his route to Rainey Hill. A slight headache reminded him of the nauseous hangover he had experienced in the jail as he turned into the steep driveway. Halley, returning to the house from the washateria, stopped and waited. He understood her look of dismay when he heard the unmistakable sound of Joe Max Rainey's '34 Chevrolet grunting up the hill behind him. They made nervous small talk while Joe Max parked his car inside the little shed.

"Gray Boy is coming by to pick up some laundry he left

today, Daddy."

Joe Max looked at the bundle of wet laundry under his daughter's arm. Halley's father was a big man, with dark red hair and a ruddy complexion "That right?" His usually jovial expression was stern as he turned toward Gray. "You start doing the laundry at your house now, Gray Boy?"

Gray felt his face grow warm. He felt small and ridiculous in front of Halley. "Just when Daddy tells me to."

"Didn't see your daddy today. I spent most of the day in the courthouse in commissioners' meetings. I can always count on Rance to take care of things when I have to be gone like that. Only man I got that can work on equipment, operate it, and manage men."

Gray felt himself shrink some more. "Yes, sir. Daddy's always been good with his hands." He chanced a smile. "Pretty good at giving orders, too." The smile did not have its usual effect.

Joe Max jingled the change in his pocket as he stared at Halley. "Halley, don't visit too long. Mama's probably got supper on the table." He ambled toward the house.

Halley and Gray Boy knew that their evening was over when Joe Max failed to invite Gray Boy to supper. Gray bit his lip as he stared at his bundle of clothes under Halley's arm. Seeing them there stirred him again. "Guess there's no reason to talk about the picture show."

Halley shook her head. "Give this a little time to blow over. He'll come around."

Gray looked toward the house before sneaking a quick kiss. He took the bundle of clothes and tied them to the Mustang. He patted the clothes. "This is where you sit." She smiled and nodded.

He felt like a small boy on a bicycle as he straddled the Mustang and kicked the starter. Joe Max Rainey had made him feel that way by refusing access to his daughter, by treating him like a boy. Halley always kindled his desire to be a grown man, even a husband and a father. Gray wanted to be a man for his woman—wanted to run away and marry her—be the man of his own house. But he had no money, no house, no car, no way to provide for a wife. He was not done being single yet, but he was tired of being treated like a boy.

The temperature had cooled to the low nineties, and the air was invigorating again as he headed east. Afraid that his father would be outside to wave him home, he did not look toward his house when he passed it. He was too old to sit around the house with his parents and little brother. A mile past the house, he eased off 24 onto the old Klondike highway.

He could not make sense of what was happening to him. He had been in the Delta County jail a half dozen times, usually for wild driving, fighting, disturbing the peace, or having beer on him or in him. Toy had always taken care of him, charging him with only one official fine. He had paid $35 out of his own pocket for speeding and reckless driving. That fine was the sum total of his written history of lawbreaking.

Only one thing had made Friday night different—the fight with Spooner—and Spooner had died. He felt a familiar hollow feeling in the pit of his stomach. Fear. Jail had always been a one-night stand for Gray Boy—a trophy of sorts. He had never considered actually losing his freedom. The heavy jail keys that lay on Rube Carter's desk swung across his mind as he eased into Klondike.

Sitting on the porch in front of his store, Dad Flanagan watched Gray approach. Gray nodded as he passed and then changed his mind and circled back. He killed the motorcycle and smiled at Dad. The porch bench was familiar to Gray—a reminder of safer times. They sat for a few minutes, listening to tree frogs and crickets announce the ending of day and the beginning of night.

Dad interrupted the night songs. "You'd likely be out

chasing poontang instead of sittin' by me if you weren't broke or in some sort of trouble. What kinda trouble you got?" The squeezed nasal tones carried down the main street of Klondike.

"I'm always broke, and usually in trouble." Talking to Dad seemed comfortable. The little storekeeper was the most non-judgmental adult Gray knew.

"What kind of trouble?"

"You probably already know. I may get blamed for Spooner's death."

"I heard. Buster Galt's probably trying to hang it on you 'cause he's too damn lazy to find out who really did it."

"You think it looks bad for me?"

Dad swung his short legs from his perch on the bench, his toes barely touching the wooden floor of the porch. "Well, I heard about the fight on the square. Don't see what that's got to do with King Ivory's kid dying a couple of hours later at the courthouse."

"I guess they're going to try to say that we got into it again at the jail, and I threw him off the top." Gray had never spoken those words, never heard them spoken. They made sense, and it scared him more.

"Did you?"

"Well, I was in the jail, but I didn't even see Spooner."

"Well, there you are. Wanna Coke?"

"You buyin?" Gray followed Dad into the store.

Dad chunked in two nickels, and they each navigated a bottle through the long slots in the machine and extracted a bottle of Coke. As Gray pushed his down in the bottle opener, he smiled. "You know, Dad, for awhile, I thought that maybe I really had killed Spooner and couldn't remember it. But I could barely lift myself when I was in that jail, much less Spooner. No way I could have wrestled him over the top."

Dad laughed his high-pitched cackle. "Another crime solved by Dad Flanagan."

When the Cokes were empty and returned to slots in the crate, Gray eased away on the cycle. He felt better again. His freedom was not going to be taken away. He turned west toward home, then made a circle in the abandoned street and headed east toward Cooper on the old highway.

It was still early. *What harm could there be in cruising the back roads for a few minutes before bedtime?* In five minutes, he was inside the Cooper city limits. Good-dark now, he cut the lights and eased down back streets, letting the Mustang slow to little more than an idle. The little machine seemed to find its way to Molly Beth's house. He raced the engine a little as he approached their usual meeting place a few feet behind her back yard. *Just habit.*

He stopped and cut the engine when he saw it. Cameron Galt's red Chevy was parked in front of the house. Gray pushed the Mustang back into the shadows as he heard voices. Cameron and Molly Beth walked down the sidewalk and got into the car. The familiar hollow feeling in his stomach returned.

11 Justice of the Peace Hoot Gibson stood over Sheriff Toy Roy Robbins' shoulder, pointing at the photograph. "Right there—definitely a baseball—knew it the minute I saw it."

Toy stood abruptly, pushing Hoot away from his shoulder. "Didn't say I didn't see it, Hoot. You been runnin' your mouth so fast, a man can't get his answer in. Besides, I don't like people lookin' over my shoulder."

Toy put his huge palm against Hoot's chest. "Move away. Get on the other side of the desk and give me room to breathe." Toy took a gulp of air and used the moment to gather his thoughts.

Hoot put both hands on top of Toy's desk and leaned toward him. "Why, that could be the murder weapon."

Toy looked at Hoot through tiny slits. "He wadn't killed by no damn baseball. He put an index finger on Hoot's forehead. If I have to tell you one more time to stand back, I'm gonna slap you across the room, Hoot. You know I don't like nobody gettin' in my face."

The justice of the peace ignored Toy's warning. "The district attorney know about this?"

"He will in a little while. Should be here any time. I'm gonna give him a full briefing on what we know and when we knew it, so I'd appreciate it if you kept your mouth shut till I get 'er done."

At sunset, Hoot Gibson gave up on Buster and went home. Toy was turning out the lights in the courthouse men's room when he heard the office door open. Buster was already shuffling paper on Toy's desk when Toy returned.

"I hear you got the picture back."

Toy's chair protested as he dropped into it and leaned back. "If you got the time, I'll give you a full report."

Buster remained calm and listened to Toy's explanation of the baseball, Gray's escape from jail, and the fight. "How much other information you been hidin', Toy?"

Toy shook his head with resignation.

"I ought to have your badge." Buster rose and paced the room. "You been lockin' up boys in the jail, not making a record, and leavin' the cells unlocked. You withheld critical evidence in a murder investigation." He put one hand on Toy's desk and leaned forward. "I could take your badge that fast," snapping his fingers in Toy's face. Toy flinched but did not reply. Buster resumed pacing. "And you damn well know it, too."

Toy unclipped the badge and slammed it down on the desk. "There it is. Take it. I'd rather give it up than have it taken away."

"Doesn't make a tinker's damn with me whether you resign or I take it. Just because you resign doesn't mean I won't bring charges."

Toy rose to leave. "A man's gotta do what a man's gotta do."

Buster whirled and pointed a finger at the chair. "Sit back down!" Toy eased back into his seat and watched Buster pace. "A little piss-ant case like this can make or break a DA—a sheriff, too. We've got to take action. I really wish it didn't, but everything points to the Rivers kid. We have to bring him in."

"That boy didn't do it. The stuff I been tellin' you ain't all I been thinkin' about. It just don't make sense that Gray Boy did it."

"Why the hell not? He had a fight with the colored kid; he was in the jail; he escaped from jail; his own baseball was right by the body; he admits seeing the body before running off and leaving it lying out in the rain."

Toy fidgeted in his chair. He made a big number one on a tablet. "Number one, those boys fought, but they were friends. Number two, Gray Boy was limp as a dishrag when I threw him in that cell. I don't believe he could have thrown a peanut over that wall on the walkway. Number three, the cell door was open, and I left it that way on purpose. That's my fault."

Buster pointed at the tablet. "None of that will stand up, Toy. Don't you know that most killings are done by friends or relatives? Second, it doesn't take an eighteen-year-old long to recover from a drunk, especially when he's fighting for his life. From what I hear, Gray Rivers was vicious when he attacked the colored kid, and the colored kid was a lot bigger. Kid's known for having a hell of a temper and for fightin'."

Buster put his finger on the number 3. "As for leaving the cell door open, that is your fault, but that hurts the kid even more. Gave him a way to get at the dead boy. Hell, if you left that door unlocked, it's about half your fault the kid's dead."

"I still say he didn't do it. I've known this boy all my life. He's a hothead and a troublemaker, but he's just trying to show everybody he's a man. Deep down, this is a good kid from a good family."

Buster put his hand on the door to leave. "Toy, face it. The boy lied to us—made a fool out of you. When you get right down to it, the most damning thing to the boy is this question—Who else could it have been? The answer is that we don't have a single person as a suspect except this kid. I don't like it any better than you do, but I want you to bring him in tomorrow for questioning."

Toy sat in his chair until the echo of Buster's steps down the deserted stairway had faded, and he was left with the burping static of the police radio. He walked down the stairs and onto the courthouse lawn. He stood beside the spot where Spooner's body had landed and looked toward the jail. Buster had said something that made his flesh crawl.

"Who else could it have been?" He had been spending too much time trying to protect Gray Boy Rivers and neglecting his real job.

Gray leaned back against his safety strap and allowed the soft breeze to wash over his sweaty clothes. It had been hot, humid, and still all day, and the breeze, however slight, was a welcome interruption. A singing mockingbird celebrated the breeze. He looked out over treetops and a stunted field of cotton. Past the small cotton patch, he could see the withered corn stalks in his Aunt Tillie's garden.

It was quiet on top of that telephone pole, and the solitude he felt at this height made him feel good—imbued with a sense of power and weightlessness—able to observe for miles without being observed. Climbing telephone poles filled some unidentified need within him. Today, sticking those spikes in the pole as he climbed assuaged his need to lash out at Cameron Galt and Molly Beth French.

Knowing that he was not authorized to climb made it even more satisfying. There was some danger associated with phone wires, but telephone lines were already starting to bore him. Maybe he would move on to a light company in the fall.

From the sun's position in the sky, he knew it was about quitting time, and he was finished with his work here. He glanced down at the phone company truck and smiled. Both doors were open, and Mule Burnett, his trainer, was sprawled across the seat. *How could he sleep in that hot truck? Oh, well, let him sleep as long as he lets me climb.*

Gray moved one foot and the strap and started down. Halfway down, he noticed a car parked in a small cluster of trees. His heart sank and the hollow feeling returned as he recognized it.

How long has Toy been there? As Gray put one foot on the ground, Toy slammed his car door and started toward him. Running crossed Gray's mind briefly, but he still had on the climbing equipment. He was still unbuckling and unhooking when Toy reached him.

"Afternoon, Gray Boy. 'Bout quittin' time, ain't it?"

Toy's bullfrog voice awakened Mule Burnett from his nap. "What's up with the lawdog, Gray?" Mule lived in Hunt County and did not recognize the Delta county sheriff.

Toy kept his eyes on Gray Boy as he waved toward Mule. "You go back to your nap, Mister. I'm just having a little talk with Gray Boy, here...and all."

"He in some kind of trouble?" Mule was already on the ground, unzipping his pants to tuck in his shirt.

Toy kept his eyes on Gray. "No trouble. Just need his help. He's comin' to Cooper with me to clear up a few things...and all."

Mule walked toward Toy and Gray. "Well, I don't know about that—you coming to get a man right off the job and all. Gray, here, is my best climber."

Toy 's patience was wearing thin. "Job's over for Gray today. It's quittin' time, anyway. You just climb back into that truck and head on home, Mister...and all."

Mule was just under six feet and built like a fireplug. He had no use for badges or the men who wore them. He bellied up to Toy, the buttons to their shirts mingling, and lifted Toy's badge for a closer look. "Says here you're sheriff of Delta County. This ain't Delta. How do we know you got any authority over here?"

Toy's eyes flamed red. He grabbed the wrist holding his badge with one hand, Mule's throat with the other, and shoved him against the telephone pole. "Now you listen to me, asshole. You interferin' with an officer of the law."

Gray stepped back and shouted. "Toy! He's my boss."

Toy glanced at Gray and took a deep breath. "Ordinarily, I don't pay no 'tention to shitheads like you, Mister. I just send a few of their teeth flying down their throat and go on about my business. Since you're Gray Boy's boss, I'm gonna let you off. Soon as I turn loose, you hightail it to that pickup and get hell outta here."

Mule's eyes bulged until Toy released him. He trotted to the pickup and spun the wheels as he left. Toy looked at Gray's slumped features. "Sorry about that peckerhead, Gray Boy, but he got under my skin."

Gray's face reflected his despair. "Hell, sounds like I'm goin' to jail for something I didn't do, anyway. Who needs a job when you're in jail?"

"It may not be that bad. I ain't arresting you—unless you make me. I'm just takin' you in for a few questions."

They rode in silence until they passed the Rivers' house on 24. Gray could see Jake riding his horse, heading toward Griffin's house. He looked so peaceful, so free of worry.

The old, unpainted house that had been a source of shame to him for most of his life now looked inviting. He longed to erase the past week from his life and return to the safety of his family, to his own bed in his own room. If he could have that back, he would never complain of drafty walls or leaky ceilings again. He would lay off the beer and stop fighting.

Toy pulled in his reserved parking space by the court-house east steps and turned to face Gray. "Now, Gray Boy, I need to put cuffs on you. Be better if we do it in the car. If we hurry up, nobody gonna see you in cuffs."

"Cuffs? You said I wasn't arrested. You never used cuffs

on me before, Toy. Why now? My mother sees me in cuffs, it'll kill her."

"DA says its procedure now. He's right, you know. I shoulda been doin' it all along. If he sees me bringin' you in without cuffs, he'll have my hide."

Gray put his hands behind his back and turned in the seat. "Is that asshole your boss, Toy? I thought you just worked for the voters."

Toy snapped the cuffs around his wrists. "In a manner of speakin', I do. But if I don't sorta do things like Buster wants, he'll see to it I don't get elected next time. So, in a way, I do work for him."

Gray felt a familiar nausea, and his eyes began to burn when Toy unlocked the stairway leading to the jail. He turned to face Toy in the narrow stairway. "You gonna lock me up, again, Toy? Do my parents know I'm here?"

"I'm just gonna put you up here for a few minutes while I go tell Truman what's happening. He'll get a hold of Rance and Mattie."

Toy removed the handcuffs and pushed the cell door closed. As the sheriff locked the door with a key almost a foot long, acid rose in Gray's throat. *I should have run. Toy would never have caught me afoot, and he would not have been able to follow me in the car. By this time, I could have been on the Mustang, heading for Louisiana. Everybody would be better off.*

He stood in the same position, arms by his sides, touching nothing, until he heard Rube Carter's shoes clopping down the hall in front of the cells. Gray braced for a confrontation, but Rube barely glanced at him as he headed toward the roof walkway.

Only a little sun filtered through the few windows in the jail, but Gray sensed that it was nearly sunset when Toy lumbered back toward him and opened the cell. "We got to put these cuffs on again, Gray Boy. Then we goin' down to let Buster ask a few questions."

"What about Truman?"

Toy's double chin quaked. "He's had to run home right quick. Something about his mama. I left word for him."

"What about Daddy?"

"I'll let him know as soon as I can. Shoot, Gray Boy, we'll be going home in a little bit, anyway."

Gray steeled himself when he saw Buster sitting in the small room just outside the district courtroom. He smelled the scents of his boyhood, of dust and books and hardwood floor polish—reminders of when he and friends found this courthouse welcoming and interesting.

Buster motioned for Gray to sit at the small table across from him. Toy took off the handcuffs.

"Toy tell you why you're here, Mr. Rivers?"

Gray stiffened. Although the face was nothing like Cameron's, the body movements and the voice were eerily identical to Cameron's. "He didn't tell me anything."

Buster glanced at Toy. "The sheriff and I are just asking routine questions about Spooner Hays' killing. Before we question you, is there anything you would like to clear up about that night?"

Buster's grating voice caused Gray's strength-sapping despair and fear to dissipate. The rage that replaced it felt better. He gripped the edges of the table until his knuckles turned white. "I have already told all that I know about that night."

Buster's smile was condescending. "Well, you told us several versions of what happened that night—and—you left out a lot of things. You can understand why we feel the need to dig a little deeper."

Gray sat perfectly still.

"The gravity of your situation just ain't sunk in on you yet, has it, boy?" Buster slithered into his country dialect.

No comment, no movement.

Blood rushed to Buster's face. "Fact is, boy, you're in

deep shit. You need my help to get out of this shithole you got yourself into. If I get cooperation, I might can help you. I don't; it's your funeral."

Toy nudged Gray from behind, signaling with his head for Gray to talk to Buster. Gray looked at Toy before facing the DA. "Just what have I got to do to get this help?"

"Come clean." Buster stepped back a few paces, put his hands behind his back, and leaned against the wall. "We got you by the balls, son. Lemme point out a few things to you." Buster made a little circle on the table with his left hand and placed one finger from his right hand in the circle.

"One, you were the only one in the jail the night the nigger was thrown from the jail roof." Another finger goes in the hole. "Two, you fought with the dead boy a few hours before he died. Dang near killed him then." A third finger is inserted. "Three, when you came down to make sure he was dead, you left your footprints right by his body. Not to mention you were dumb enough to leave your baseball at the scene."

"If I had killed him, why would I leave my baseball with my little brother's name on it, right by Spooner?"

Buster warmed up as he scooted his chair closer to the table. "You know, I couldn't figure that out at first, either. Fact is, that baseball may be your way out of this thing. You could get off easy—first offense, your youth, solid family, and all."

"Here's the way I figure it. The Hays kid somehow got up to the jail, pulled open your cell door," Buster paused to glance at Toy. "And called you out to whup your ass on that little rooftop walkway around the jail. You were too sick to fight but had to defend yourself. You didn't mean for it to happen, but Spooner fell off the roof in the scuffle. How'm I doin' so far?"

Gray relaxed a little and laid his hands on the tabletop. "So far, it's all bullshit, but don't let that stop you."

"You and your baseball run down the stairs to check to see if the colored boy's hurt. Hell, a young buck can usually take a fall like that without even breakin'a bone. Well, it's rainin' in sheets, thunder's clapping, and all of a sudden, you're lookin' into a dead boy's eyes. That kinda thing would scare the shit out of me or anybody else. You panic, drop the ball, and run off." Buster leaned back and folded his arms.

Gray turned to look at Toy, then back at Buster. "What about the lies you say I told?"

Buster smiled and leaned forward. "You were ashamed of leaving that boy out in the mud, knew that you had not meant to cause his death. You're a kid. Only natural to cover it up."

"Say all that were true—what would happen to me?"

Buster slid a pad across the table to Gray and put a pencil on top of it. "You write it all down just like we talked about it; it sounds like self-defense or an accident to me. You could get off with a slap on the wrist—maybe probation."

Gray looked in Toy's direction again and nodded his head. He stared at the floor for several seconds before facing Buster again. "You're sayin' that if I lie again, I could get out of this."

Buster rolled his eyes and stood. "God-o-mighty, Boy." He put his hands on the table and leaned into Gray's face. "Ain't nobody asking you to lie, you little sumbitch. You stupid enough to look a gift horse in the mouth?"

Gray pushed back his chair and stood. He hesitated a second before putting his palms on the table and leaning toward Buster. "Don't call me stupid, asshole."

The veins in Buster's neck vibrated; the muscles in his jaw twitched. He grabbed Gray's shirt and pulled him closer. "I'm tryin' to help you, Rivers, and you don't even know it."

Gray kept his palms on the table. He took a deep breath and tried to glance toward Toy, but Buster held his shirt tightly. "I do know one thing. You need to turn me loose right now and get out of my face. Your breath would gag a maggot."

Toy cringed as the words bounced off the walls of the tiny room. Buster's jawbones made little popping noises as he ground his teeth. He released his grip on Gray's shirt and lifted the table as if he were going to turn it over in Gray's lap. "Toy, take this little prick back to a cell; lock it this time. We'll see if that improves his attitude any."

Toy was reaching for his handcuffs when Truman walked in. He nodded toward Buster and Toy before focusing on Gray. "You look a little worse for wear, Gray Boy."

Gray's eyes still reflected rage and panic. Adrenalin rush caused a slight tremble that he tried to keep still. Truman spoke to Buster. "Mr. District Attorney, you know that Mr. Rivers is represented by counsel. Why were you questioning him out of my presence?"

"He never said anything about wanting a lawyer. Just routine. I offered him a way out of this thing."

Truman looked at Toy. "I really feel that my client isn't into anything that requires him to have an exit strategy."

Handcuffs dangling in his hand, Toy spoke to Buster with defiance in his tone. "I notified Truman that we were gonna question Gray Boy."

Truman shook his head. "What are you going to do with those cuffs, Sheriff?"

Toy glanced at Buster. Buster shrugged.

"If I could trouble you for a ride to my house, Sheriff, I will retrieve my car and take Gray to his home." Truman motioned for Gray to follow him to the door.

Buster nodded his approval to Toy and followed the three of them into the hall. "Sheriff, first thing Monday morning, I want you to get with the clerk and send out notices for my grand jury to convene."

12 Mattie put both hands over her throat when she saw Toy's black Ford pull into the driveway. Rance rose from his porch rocking chair and watched the car approach. Legs wobbly and stomach churning, he leaned against a porch post for support. Gray Boy was almost two hours overdue from work, and they feared the worst.

In the last rays of twilight, Jake was playing an imaginary game of basketball using a tennis ball and a lard bucket he had nailed to the smokehouse. The sound of crunching gravel brought his game to a stop. Daylight was about gone, anyway. He walked toward the front porch and stood behind a large bush to listen without being seen as Toy, Truman, and finally Gray left the car.

His brother looked small and beaten as he walked toward his parents. Gray's red-rimmed eyes focused on his mother, searching there for some flicker of hope, something to say that he was still loved in spite of the grief he had brought to his family. Mattie's body and mind relaxed a little when she saw her son alive, then stiffened as she wondered what had happened.

"What is it now?" Rance's voice pierced the air like breaking glass.

Toy fidgeted and looked toward Truman. Truman

removed his hat and nodded toward Mattie. "Mattie....Rance. The sheriff and I are bringing Gray Boy home from a questioning session by the district attorney."

Rance left the porch post and stood erect. "How come I'm just now finding out?"

Truman glanced at Toy. "I found out only a few minutes ago myself, Rance."

Rance walked down the porch steps and put his hand on Gray Boy's shoulder. Gray was as tall as his father now, so their gazes were level. "You all right?"

Gray's expression showed relief and gratitude at his father's concern. "Yeah."

"What happened?"

"Toy picked me up at work. Said Buster wanted to question me. We were in the middle of it when Truman walked in." Cracking at first, Gray's voice grew more defiant with each word.

Rance looked at Toy. "Why didn't you find me and tell me?"

"I stopped by the county barn, but they said you were grading roads. There was no time, Rance."

Rance pointed his hand at Toy, thumb and index finger cocked. "No time?"

To Truman, "What kind of questions?"

"From what Toy told me, Buster offered him a deal if he would confess. I put an end to the interrogation as soon as I found out about it."

Rance took a deep breath. "So we're not any worse off then we were before?"

Truman's face was expressionless. "We could be. Toy tells me there was a degree of confrontation between Gray Boy and Buster. There was a reference made to halitosis that may have made the district attorney a worse enemy than before."

Truman's bland description of the exchange between

Gray Boy and Buster struck Toy as hilarious and air shot through his nose and mouth as he tried to stifle a snigger.

Rance looked at both men. "Halitosis? What the hell are you talking about?"

Toy put a hand on Gray Boy's shoulder. "I know this is serious, but Rance, you shoulda been there when Gray Boy told Buster his breath would gag a maggot. I thought the man was gonna choke on his own spit."

Rance's expression grew sterner as Toy tried to contain his mirth. The sheriff removed his hat and made a slight bow toward Mattie. "I know it ain't no time for laughter, but it's just that it's so damn true. It's somethin' I been wantin' to say for a long time."

Mattie's lips turned up at the ends, but she quickly corrected them. Rance failed to see the humor. "You mean to tell me you insulted the man who has the power to decide how you spend the rest of your life?"

Gray stiffened. "The bastard called me stupid. Got in my face and yelled at me."

Rance threw up his hands. "We appreciate your bringing him home, boys. Unless there's something else, we'll handle it from here on out."

Toy ran his finger along the sweatband of his hat as he looked at Truman. "There's just one more thing, Rance. Buster's convening a grand jury. I expect he intends to go for an indictment."

Mattie uttered a throaty gasp. Rance's head jerked a little; his left eye twitched. "Well, men, if you'll excuse us, we need to talk."

Jake kept his vigil behind the shrub until Toy and Truman had left. Though past dark, it was still hot enough to make a standing horse sweat. But Jake felt cold—cold enough to shiver—and alone—more alone than he had since Tuck died. His parents and brother went into the house. Wishing that he had included himself in the conversation sooner, Jake walked to the back porch, hoping to listen to the conversation through the kitchen window.

Keeping his head down to avoid attention, he unwound the bristly well rope from its wooden bracket beside the cistern. He dropped the bucket into the cistern and chanced a look toward the kitchen table. Nobody was there. Muffled voices told him they were in the living room.

Mattie sat in her rocking chair, and Gray slumped on the divan as Rance paced in front of the cold woodstove. "Where's your bike?"

Gray's face showed surprise. "I forgot all about it. It's still on the parking lot at work. We need to go get it."

Rance looked at the ceiling. "After we hear what happened with Buster Galt."

"Well, he offered me a way out. Said I should say that Spooner came after me on the jail roof, we scuffled, and he fell off accidentally."

"And what did you say to that offer?"

"I said no."

"Why?"

Gray put out both hands, palms up. "Why? Because it's not true."

"The truth didn't seem all that important to you when this thing began."

Gray looked toward Mattie and shook his head. "Maybe it's because I crossed the river more than once since this nightmare began. Every time I cross it, something bad happens. I don't intend to do it again."

Mattie fanned her face with a hand-held fan she had bought at a church bazaar. "It's hot in here. Let's see if the mosquitoes will let us sit outside under the chinaberry tree."

Jake fell into step with his family as they headed for the east yard and the chairs under the tree. It was too dark to see the expression on his brother's face, but he felt the fear emanating from his body. He climbed onto a low limb to listen.

"What did Toy mean when he said that Buster is going for an indictment?" Gray Boy asked.

Rance answered without looking in Gray's direction. "It means that he intends to bring evidence to a grand jury and recommend that they try you for Spooner's death."

"Tell him more than that, Rance." Impatience was in Mattie's voice.

"A grand jury is impaneled to serve for several months at a time. I think they serve a year in Delta County—could be six months. When I served several years ago, we just met when the DA called us. They may meet on a regular schedule now. I'm just not sure."

Mattie wrung her hands. "Do you know who's on it?"

Rance's eyes opened a little wider, showing hope. "Hack was called a few months back. Maybe he's still on this one."

Gray sat straight up. "So, will I have to testify in front of this grand jury?"

"That's up to them. If they need to hear from you to decide if there is enough evidence to bring you to trial, then they will call you in for questions. But, they can decide without even talking to you."

Fear gripped Gray's heart as his mind raced. "If they decide against me, what happens then?"

"Then you go to trial."

"For murder?"

"Remember the man you insulted earlier today? He decides what charges to bring to the grand jury. I'm not familiar enough to even know the choices, but murder would be the worst."

Gray's head and shoulders slumped. "I just can't do anything right, can I? I lie; I get deeper into trouble. Today, I told the truth and stood up; I'm in deeper trouble." From his perch on the tree limb, Jake felt his brother's despair.

Mattie reached over and squeezed Gray's shoulder. "You're innocent. The grand jury will know that."

Gray rubbed his forehead with the heels of both hands. "You and Daddy are having to pay for a lawyer you can't afford. I've ruined the whole family's reputation. I'd rather be dead than go through a trial. Everybody would be better off if I were dead."

Rance stood and pointed at Gray. "Things are bad enough on your mother without your talking like that. Truman says there isn't enough evidence to convict you, but it's possible there could be a trial."

Gray stood and faced his father. "Won't make any difference. Everybody's gonna think I'm a murderer as long as I live."

Rance grabbed his son by the shoulders. "You get a hold of yourself. You can't fold up on us now. This could be a long trip." The chinaberry tree blocked the faint moonlight, casting them in total darkness. They sat in silence for several minutes until Rance spoke with authority. "Let's go get that motorcycle."

As Gray passed the tree, Jake reached out and touched his brother's arm. Gray looked up. It was too dark to see into his brother's eyes, but Jake could feel them burning into his own. He whispered to Jake. "I ain't ever going to jail again. No matter what."

Gray parked his Mustang inside the dairy barn that night and did not take it out all weekend. He only wanted to hide— to heal. At dawn on Saturday, he walked to the bottoms and spent the entire day on the banks of the Blue Bottom, watching the trickle of water from upstream rains make its slow way to the Sulphur River.

Uncle Seth, Aunt Tillie, Shep, Brenda, and Kathy came to lend their support on Sunday, but Gray just wanted to be left alone. He was devising two plans. Both involved escape. Nobody, not even Mattie, could penetrate the armor he was erecting around himself.

Monday morning, Mattie hugged him as they left for work

at the same time. Gray usually followed his mother for a mile or so before roaring past her with a grin and a casual one-handed wave as he passed. Mattie hated the Mustang, but she still treasured the daily ritual, watching her devil-may-care-son live the life she had once dreamed of. This morning, Gray Boy followed her all the way into Commerce, peeling off only when she turned toward the sewing factory, and he turned toward the telephone company.

The Mustang was parked in the front yard when she returned from work that afternoon. A warm feeling flushed her face and body when she saw Gray Boy sitting on the front porch, home and safe. Mattie's heart was lighter, almost happy, as she stopped in the kitchen to fix two glasses of iced tea.

When she stepped on the front porch and saw Gray's face, the warm feeling went away and the fear returned. She recognized the dark scowl on his face and the way he was biting the inside of his jaw; she felt the coldness touch her and goose bumps rise on her arms.

"What's wrong?" She handed him the iced tea and eased into the chair beside him.

"I got fired today."

A small squeak escaped from Mattie at yet another down-hill slide on the slippery slope that had become her son's life. "Why?"

"Who knows?"

"Gray, don't be smart with me. They gave you a reason. What was it?"

Gray's voice was filled with sarcasm. "They said they were cutting back, and I was the newest employee, but that's BS. They fired me because I'm in trouble with the law."

"They can't fire you for something like that. You haven't even been charged yet."

"Yeah, but I did get hauled off from work in a cop car, and Toy did slam my boss up against a telephone pole."

"Toy did that to your boss?"

"Damn right." Gray took a sip of his tea. "Can't blame Toy, though. They were just looking for an excuse to let me go."

They both rocked in the wicker chairs in silence until the ice in their tea melted. Gray finally spoke. "Where's Jake?"

"I expect he's at Mr. Griffin's or roaming the pasture. His horse is gone."

"Don't tell him yet."

"Why not?"

Gray spit a piece of ice into the yard. "I'm ashamed. I'm getting ready to be charged with a serious crime, and now I've lost my job."

Mattie put her hand on his shoulder. "There's no shame in either of those things. You did your job, didn't you? Somebody told your daddy that you were the best climber and quickest learner the telephone company has had in years. It's not right for them to just fire you."

She poured her diluted tea into a crack between porch boards. "As for the crime, we know you're innocent, and that's what counts."

Gray shaded his eyes and looked down 24. "Here comes Jake and Papa. Where do you reckon they've been?"

Mattie looked in the same direction. "I can barely see them. Been to Dad's store probably. Jake keeps talking your granddaddy into taking him along on some of his trips. Mr. Griffin is talking about riding all the way to the Red River with Jake, but I'm not about to give my permission for that."

"Wish I was Jake's age again. I'd be more like him."

Mattie stopped rocking and turned to face her oldest son. "Why would you say that?"

"I used to think he was just too bashful to have a good time. I even used to feel sorry for him. Now I know he was the smart one. Jake hardly ever gets into trouble. He'll mess up once in awhile, but you can't get him to repeat a mistake.

I've tried to talk him into things, but he just won't."

Mattie's eyes darted, showing her confusion and surprise. "I can't believe those words are coming out of your mouth. You've never said anything about feeling that way before."

Gray shrugged. "I never noticed it that much until the last couple of years. I've watched him. He hardly ever says anything, but he watches everything. Always watching and learning, figuring out what works and what doesn't. Papa says he stays between the banks—in the flow. Me, I just keep making the same mistakes over and over. I'm my own worst enemy."

Mattie held her hand over her heart, her eyes wide as she stared at her son until he spoke again. "Why are you lookin' at me like that?"

"Because I just can't believe it. Jake is constantly comparing himself to you and sees himself as coming up short. He worships the ground you walk on. Wants to be like you. Turns out you're doing the same thing in reverse."

"Don't see what he sees about me that's worth copying. I'm just eighteen, and my life is already permanently ruined."

"Don't talk like that. This mess is only a couple of weeks old. You're going to come out of this thing just fine." Mattie's words sounded confident, but her voice did not. "You just had more than your share of wild oats to sew."

Irritation crept into Gray's voice. "Mother, I have no job. I'll lose my only means of transportation." He rose and slung his tea across the yard. "Course, I won't need transportation 'cause I'll be in jail."

"That's enough self-pity, Gray Boy Rivers. You're better than that. Lots of people would kill to have what you've got going for you."

"Sure, just name one thing."

"All right, I will. You're good looking. People like you. You're a natural leader. You're an athlete. You're good with your hands. That's just a start on what you have going for you."

"Won't any of those things make payments on a car."

"Dammit, Gray, I can't believe I raised a son for eighteen years without knowing how he sees the world. You've always talked to me much more than Jake ever does. Why have you never told me you felt this way?"

Gray leaned against a porch post and watched the two tiny horses and riders grow as they drew closer. "I just realized it myself. The things that got me what I wanted in high school don't work in the real world."

To keep her hands from fidgeting, Mattie walked out into the yard and pulled some weeds from the flowerbed she had planted with so much pride when the children were small. Six years of drought had destroyed it. She kept her eyes down as she spoke softly. "You're dead wrong about yourself, Gray Boy. If your daddy and me have let you go on thinking that about yourself, then it's our fault."

She looked up at him with her hands on her hips. "We should have taught you better—made you feel better about yourself. All this time, I thought you were the most confident person I ever knew. Jake seemed to be the one lacking confidence. I'm a complete failure—a mother who doesn't even know her own children."

Gray kicked a stray branch off the porch. "It ain't your fault, Mama. It's mine."

Mattie walked up the porch steps and took him in her arms. "This is all going to turn out all right. You'll be proven innocent, and the phone company will be begging you to come back. Trust me on that."

Over Gray's shoulder, she saw Jake and his grandfather more clearly now. Griffin was gesturing with that Rivers trademark gesture, pointing his finger and thumb at Jake like a pistol. Watching the two of them made her feel suddenly warm and safe. She chuckled.

Gray released his hold. "What's so funny?"

"Just thinking about what you said and remembering Jake

not more than a few weeks ago."

Mattie's smile was contagious as Gray boy had to suppress a grin. "What did he do?"

"He was out here in the yard, kicking his bicycle and using the worst language I've ever heard from a twelve-year-old. I had to threaten him with a switch."

Gray laughed. "Why was he kicking it?"

Mattie laughed out loud. "Because the chain had come off and he couldn't get it back on." It was not that funny, but tears of laughter flowed down Mattie's cheeks as she slapped Gray on the shoulder. "And the back tire had gone flat after he had just spent half the day trying to patch it."

Gray smiled a confused smile as he watched his mother dab at her eyes and nose as she laughed until she coughed. "Jake never could fix anything, but he knows how to stay between the banks of the river."

Jake grabbed a guy wire supporting a utility pole on 24's shoulder as they approached their driveway. "'Member when I caught my horn on that wire and ripped my saddle off?"

Griffin chuckled. "Yep. I never saw anybody fly off a horse backward, turn a back flip holding on to his saddle, and land on the ground, still settin' his saddle. I've seen worse acts at the circus."

Jake smiled. "I don't think I could do that trick again."

"How about flying off the porch on your bicycle? Could you do that again?"

"Nope. That hurt. Wasn't anything left of my bicycle but the handlebars." Jake looked toward the house. "Looks like he's home."

Griffin frowned as he looked toward the house. "Yep. Better not let on we know about his job just yet."

"Why not?"

"Just let him tell us in his own way and in his own time. He may be upset—a little ashamed."

"Ashamed? It ain't his fault that those sunsabitches at the phone company already convicted him of somethin' he didn't do."

Griffin frowned at Jake's use of profanity. "Jake, we just know what we heard at Dad's. Beats hell outa me how that man knows things that happen in the next county five minutes after they happen."

Griffin pointed a cocked finger at his grandson again. "Whatever happened, you try to learn somethin' from it. You're lucky to have a brother like Gray Boy Rivers."

Jake was confused by his grandfather's comment, but he kept silent until he stopped to unsaddle Scar, and Griffin kept riding toward home. Jake called after him. "Why am I lucky, Papa?"

Griffin held up his horse, turned him around and rode back to Jake. He leaned down in the saddle. "Because your brother's blazing a trail for you. He's marking the turns you don't want to take—taking a lot more knocks than the average boy takes so you don't have to."

"You think he's getting' in all this trouble to help me?"

"He's not doin' it on purpose, Jake, but that's the good that can come from it. Gray's just bouncing around with life, making mistakes—serious ones—trying to find his way."

13 Rance was angry when he heard about the firing, but had half-expected it. Toy had been waiting for him when he arrived at the county barn that morning to apologize for pushing Gray's boss around. Rance drummed his fingers and stared at his plate during supper, leaving the warmed-over beans, fried squash, and breakfast biscuits to get cold on his plate.

Gray had to work. The money was important, but having something to do, anything at all, was essential. Weeks of inactivity fueled with stress about a possible jail term could take the whole family over the edge. As Mattie picked up his still-full plate, he retreated to the brush arbor behind the smoke house to think.

An hour later, he scratched on the torn screen at Gray's bedroom window. Gray lay on the bed, fully clothed, staring at the ceiling. "Gray, get up. We're going over to talk to Joe Max."

Gray swung his legs off the bed and faced his father. "Why?"

"I'll tell you in the truck. Let's go."

Thinking of Halley, Gray wanted to check himself in the mirror, but he pulled on his shoes and hustled out the door. Mattie was left to wonder as she watched her husband and

son drive away. Rance knocked on the Rainey's back door
less than ten minutes later. Gray leaned against the cistern,
searching the back yard and the road leading to the washateria for signs of Halley.

He saw her coming from the lake trail just as Joe Max
opened the door. "Evenin' Rance...Gray Boy. We just finished supper. Can I offer you a cup of coffee?"

"No thanks, Joe Max. Need to talk. Won't take long."
Rance walked backwards a few steps and leaned against the
cistern. "Come on over here, Gray."

The mutual respect between Joe Max and Rance eased
Gray's nervousness, but he kept thinking about Halley's
approach. She slowed her pace, sensing the gravity of the conversation. If she got there too soon, her father would surely
send her in the house.

Rance put his hand on Gray's shoulder and looked at Joe
Max. "You know that Gray lost his job at the phone company
today because of his trouble with the law."

Joe Max rolled the bottle of Garrett snuff he held in his
hand as he looked at Gray Boy with new eyes. "Guess everybody's heard that by now."

Gray felt his father's fingers dig into his shoulder. "Joe
Max, you know I don't make excuses for my kids. I'm not
makin' any now. Gray's done some fool things that got him
into this mess, but he didn't kill Spooner."

Joe Max rolled the toothpick he held between his lips and
folded his arms. "Never believed he did." Halley had slipped
behind a tree in time to hear her father utter words that
caused a little tingle down her spine.

"Guilty or innocent, we're looking at a long, hard ride.
This boy's got to have work."

"Sure would be better if he did."

"With Luther breaking his leg last week, we're likely to be
short a man for four or five months." Rance spoke quickly,
not allowing Joe Max time to interrupt. "What would you

think about Gray filling in for him?"

Joe Max tapped on the Garrett snuff jar, opened the lid, and took out a pinch. He placed it between his cheek and gum and moved the toothpick over to that side. "Can he operate a maintainer or bulldozer?"

Rance shook his head. "I've shown him just enough for him to be dangerous, but he's got a natural aptitude for handling and working on machinery. I'll teach him on our own time."

Gray straightened a little at his father's words. He had never thought of himself as having a natural aptitude, never heard his father say it.

Joe Max worked the toothpick and kept silent. Rance broke the silence. "He can clean up the shop and run errands till he learns. Something doesn't get done during regular hours, we'll both work free to make it up until he can do a man's work all day."

Joe Max waved his hand dismissively. "Oh, he's got the job. I'm just thinking about what he can do tomorrow. Can he drive a dump truck?"

Gray spoke before his father could. "Yes, sir." He looked around to see if Halley was listening.

Rance nodded an affirmation. "He knows how. We can see about getting him a commercial license first thing tomorrow."

Fear and despair, stubborn passengers who rode with them to Rainey Hill, drifted out of the '53 Chevy pickup and blew away on the summer breeze as Rance and Gray opened the doors. Gray looked over his shoulder as they eased down the steep driveway. A sliver of moonlight was just enough to see Halley waving. As they turned down 24 and away from Halley, Gray studied his father, a person he had never seen before.

By noon Tuesday, Gray Boy had cleaned the filthy bathroom in the county barn, swept out the shop, and changed the oil and filters in two county trucks. The bathroom was demeaning, but the work felt good. An endless list of filthy, hot, and heavy work filled his days for two weeks. He felt like rebelling only at the weekly cleaning of the bathroom. He knew that Joe Max and Rance were testing him, and he intended to pass. Between menial tasks and after work, Rance began teaching him how to drive and repair the dirt-moving equipment.

He took the test for a commercial driver's license and passed with a perfect score. Hauling dirt and gravel in county dump trucks was his favorite job, and a trip to a Red River gravel bed was planned for next week. Gray, true to his father's words, showed an immediate aptitude for driving the heavy equipment used for roadwork. When Rance made him start over on jobs that did not meet his standards, Gray was surprised to find himself willing, his old impatience and irritability missing.

He had worked at his father's side on the farm and in the dairy barn, but something was different. Rance was his boss, but they both worked for the county; both drew a paycheck. Gray almost felt equal to his father. He sensed his father's pride in him. Hot days and warm nights left him feeling a good kind of tired, bone-tired, but not weary. He spent his nights in the side yard or on the banks of the Blue Bottom, worrying about the grand jury, hoping that Buster had changed his mind.

That hope grew from a flickering candle to a torch as the days passed. Spooner had been dead more than a month when the flame went out. Rance and Gray were sitting on the tailgate of a precinct pickup, having their lunch on a shaded dirt road near Klondike, when Toy's car snaked down the winding road.

Rance saw the dust plume and recognized the car first. "Damn. He's just like a bad penny."

Toy slowed his approach to keep dust from invading

their cold biscuits and sausage. The set of his shoulders as he walked toward them told them his mission. "Afternoon, boys."

Rance held his sandwich in mid-air, half waving it at the sheriff. "Toy."

Appetite gone, Gray spit out his half-chewed bite, took a drink of tea, and waited.

Toy's embarrassed expression showed that he hated his words. "Grand jury meets next week. Thursday morning, eight sharp. There's two other cases, so yours may not be first." Rance and Gray nodded, but kept silent.

"Truman asked if it would be all right for him to drop by your place after work tonight."

Rance took a bite of his biscuit, chewed slowly as if in deep thought. "Tell him that will be fine."

Gray worried that he might lose the small amount he had eaten before Toy arrived.

Truman seemed to know when Mattie would be drying the last plate from supper. His Buick floated into the side driveway as if in slow motion. She grabbed the sink and rocked back and forth for a few seconds, afraid to go outside to join her husband and sons. Truman was already talking when she joined them.

"There's not really much we can do right now. We don't have many rights in this stage. It's just the DA and the grand jury. I've tried to talk to Buster about backing off, but he seems determined to put this to the jury." Truman rose and tipped his hat as Mattie joined them.

Rance peeled a soft curl from the small stick of hickory he was whittling. "What do you honestly think they'll do?"

Truman, a man who usually kept his body erect, sitting or standing, leaned into the small circle the Rivers family had made around him and put his hands on his knees. "I'm embarrassed to say that I don't know what they'll do. If it goes to trial, I feel certain that Gray Boy will be exonerated.

There are no witnesses to the actual crime and no conclusive evidence against him."

Gray put his elbows on his knees and clasped both hands behind his neck as if trying to keep his body under control. "Give us your best guess about whether they will indict." Gray had ingested the full meaning of words like indict during the last few weeks.

The question made Truman roll the brim of his straw hat. "On the positive side, you and your family are well known in this county. That and the lack of conclusive evidence should tip the scales in your favor."

"What about the negatives?"

Truman looked toward Mattie for help. She was folding and unfolding a frayed tissue in her lap. "Go ahead, Truman. We need to know what we're in for so we can fight."

Truman shifted and leaned on the chair arm. "The grand jurors won't be lawyers. They depend on the district attorney to explain the proceedings to them. Sometimes, this tends to create a teacher-student type of atmosphere where the jurors hear only what the DA wants them to. If the jurors get the feeling that their teacher wants an indictment, they will usually give him one."

Shy rubbed against the lawyer's leg and Truman smiled as he reached down to stroke the dog's head. "Some juries would indict this pup if the DA asked them to."

"And Buster Galt wants an indictment to cover his political ass." Rance stood and threw his whittling stick across the cow lot. He followed the stick as far as the fence, stopping to put both hands on a fence post. In the dusky rays of twilight, shadows spreading across the lot resembled two men engaged in deadly combat. He raised his head and craned his neck as if he wanted to howl like a coyote. The family circle watched him in silence.

Uncomfortable, Truman nodded toward Mattie and walked out to Rance. "I think it may be a little more than politics, Rance. Buster stands to lose more than he gains if he gets an indictment against Gray Boy."

Rance took his hands from the post and turned to face Truman. "You think he's going after him just because Gray smarted off to him? Does he have it in for him because Gray Boy had trouble with Cameron?"

"At first, I thought that was it. But Buster is quick to anger and quick to cool down. As far as the boys' fighting, I think he actually enjoys that. Says it keeps Cameron on his toes."

Rance fumbled with the Prince Albert package in his overalls bib, but left it there. "What is it then?"

"Well, there is some pressure to solve the crime, but he usually thrives on that sort of thing. He's at his best when the pressure is on."

Rance leaned against the fence post, hardly noticing the small barbs digging into his back. "We been friends a long time, Truman. Say what you mean."

"If you mention this to anyone else, Rance, I'll deny it. Buster's behavior during the last couple of weeks has been irrational at times. My father would have said, 'He's come undone.'"

Rance strained to see the expression in Truman's eyes in the moonlight. "You mean we've got an unhinged lawyer coming after my son? What in hell is wrong with him? What can we do to stop him?"

Truman held up a calming hand. "I don't know yet—and I may be overreacting. I attributed his somewhat strange behavior on this case to overwork until Dad Flanagan came to see me again last week."

Rance held out his hand as if Dad's head were under his palm. "Dad Flanagan?"

"You don't know Dad's history?"

"I've known him for more than twenty years."

"Know about his family?" Truman was warming to the

exchange, even becoming animated. Collecting and storing information about Delta County history had long been his passion. He enjoyed it much more than the law.

Rance was taken aback by the question. Dad was a loner; he had never mentioned a family. "What family?"

"Dad comes from a well-connected Dallas family. His father was a lead prosecutor in the Dallas County district attorney's office years ago."

Rance held out his palm again. "Dad Flanagan?"

"One and the same." Truman enjoyed Rance's surprise at this revelation, one of the many gems of information that he held in storage for occasional use. "Dad even spent a year in law school, planning on being a prosecutor."

"He has never said a word...."

"Probably never will. I wouldn't mention it to him. Dad was a good student, but some law professors demeaned him about his size and voice. They said he would never make a trial lawyer. Told him he would have to go to the civil side. He got mad and quit."

"Back up, Truman. What's this got to do with Gray Boy and the grand jury?"

"Maybe something. Probably nothing. Dad's been saying for quite some time that Buster didn't want to come back to Delta County. He was much too successful to just walk away. Dad says he left his old law firm under a cloud."

"What kind of cloud?"

"Dad has an idea, but it's not something I can repeat until I check it out."

Rance pointed toward Gray. "I still don't see what this has to do with Gray and the grand jury."

Truman ran his fingers down the crease in the crown of his hat. "As I said, it may be nothing. Just something I wanted you to know I'm working on. If Buster's instability is causing him to come after Gray Boy unjustly, I might be able to stop it."

"Before Thursday morning?"

Truman shook his head. "Not likely. He'll keep the pressure on, hoping that Gray Boy will plead guilty in exchange for a slap on the wrist. He as much as said that to me."

"We're not admitting to anything."

"That's what I told him. You and Gray Boy need to meet me at my office at seven. I know that the other two cases will come before yours, so we'll talk strategy."

"So does this mean Gray Boy will have to testify?"

"Probably not, but I want him there in case they do want to talk to him. I think we all want a decision as quickly as we can get it."

14 Gray Boy examined the drawing on Truman's blackboard, following the dotted line from the jailhouse walkway, to the tree limb, and, finally, the dog wallow. The line reminded him of the course his own life had taken, from top of the world to a collision inside a dark hole.

The occasional squeak of Truman's chair clashed with the lawyer's lyrical voice like a cymbal interrupting a violin. The squeaking helped Gray to hear some of what Truman was saying, but not much. Gray was dressed in his best white shirt and black slacks with new black penny loafers and matching narrow belt—all bought with his mother's sewing money. He nodded politely when each in turn, Mattie, Rance, and Truman, cautioned him not to lose his temper if he was called to testify. *If?* Not knowing was like a nail poking through the sole of his shoe.

Right now, men who held his life in his hands were having a last cup of coffee, kissing their wives or kids goodbye, parking at the courthouse. He imagined each of them walking up the steps to the courthouse, each carrying his balls in their hands. *How many did Truman say there would be?* Twelve, he thought. *Just like a regular jury—except only nine had to vote to true bill him.* True bill—another term added to his young vocabulary. It meant the same as indict. Indict meant more unknowns—waiting for a trial, the trial, and possible prison.

He walked in a daze with his parents and Truman across the street to the courthouse, making a vow never to enter the building again if this day would just turn out right. His gaze traveled up the austere outside walls of the courthouse to the jail.

Strange that he had never noticed how silly the jail looked—sitting on the regular courthouse the way it did, bars on the windows, that walkway around it. He had seen it from the inside, even absorbed it, but never paid attention to the outside while standing in the fresh air of freedom. He had never smelled it from this far before, but he could now. Prisoners were probably up there right now, using brown-stained toilets, their effluence flowing down pipes in the walls, contaminating the rest of the building and the air for a block around.

He was aware of his mother's nervous patting on his shoulder and back. It was her way of supporting him, he knew, but the patting made him nervous and a little irritable. He would not snap at her, though. Not today. Not ever again. She looked smaller today, older, dressed in that same polka dot dress with the big white collar and a bow that seemed to be hanging courtesy of hairpins. The fear in her eyes made him cringe. He had caused that.

His father's plain khaki shirt and matching pants contrasted with the shine of his only pair of good boots. Rance took great pride in those hand-made boots. The boots were obviously made of good leather, not flashy, just soft quality stuff. They had been part of the family for as long as Gray could remember. He tried to imagine his father as a young man—a perky brunette with gray-green eyes on his arm—a boot-maker in Lamar County measuring him for custom boots. *What caused him to splurge then when he wouldn't now?*

The Rance Rivers he knew would never splurge on any item of clothing. The only shiny thing he had ever seen on his father's body was a railroad pocket watch, and he kept that hidden in the bib of his overalls. Gray wondered how he could have come from this man's loins. *How could a man who took such great pride in his work and his reputation take such little notice of his appearance?* Gray was convinced that his father never looked in a mirror except when he shaved. Still, today, he looked tanned, muscular, handsome, and confident. *Never noticed that before. Clothes did not matter.*

Gray could feel eyes staring at him from every passing car, from the windows of the courthouse, and from the houses across the street. He was today's entertainment. Hell, he was the biggest show Cooper had seen in years. The headlines in next Thursday's *Cooper Review,* "Local Teen Indicted," flashed across his brain.

He heard himself groan when he saw Bo Creekwater standing by the courthouse steps. He braced himself for Bo's joyful greeting, maybe a hug, but Bo just directed a sad-eyed stare at him. If Bo was glum, Gray was in serious trouble. *He seems to know what is happening.*

His legs still felt heavy, but he was glad to be away from prying eyes as they climbed the stairs to the district court-room. Following Truman's instructions, they sat on a long bench outside the double doors. He heard Truman tell them that his case would not come up for about an hour. The smaller cases would be disposed of first. *Smaller cases. Not murder. Warm-ups for the big show.*

After sitting frozen for the better part of an hour, his legs twitched a little when Buster Galt's powerful voice summoned Sheriff Toy Roy Robbins into the courtroom. In that single utterance, Gray heard the little slithering sound that Buster often made as he used his tongue to rearrange spit. The sound raked over his skin like the blade of a rusty knife. It was the same sound Cameron made, sort of like a dog lapping water, only the Galts were lapping spit. They had formed a team, father and son, to ruin his life—probably enjoyed a good laugh at his expense every night around their dinner table.

He knew before Truman told him that the grand jury had started on his case. From the courtroom, Toy's croaking voice sneaked under the doors and behind the hinges. Gray could not hear what was being said, but he imagined it clearly.

Toy would tell about being called out to a disturbance on the square. He would tell about hauling Gray Boy Rivers to the jail and putting him in a cell—drunk. Toy would try to protect Gray as much as he could, but Buster would be there, standing over his shoulder as he gave his report. He would tell about finding the baseball. Toy, or maybe Buster, would submit written affidavits from Jimmy Joe and Jerry Doyle (cousin Shep had refused), about the drinking and from Sadie and Molly Beth about how he had hit and kicked Spooner like a vicious dog.

He saw Rube Carter coming down the stairs, huffing and puffing with each step. Three rings of keys jangled with each step as they slapped against his leg. Rube held the stair rail with one hand, causing his billy club to bounce off the railings. The holster holding his .38 revolver hung almost horizontally, buoyed by the fat on his hips. He hunched forward as he stepped off the stairs and started toward the courtroom door, as if the additional weight from the keys, the club, and the gun was threatening to tip him over.

Gray stared at the repugnant jailer, but Rube never took his eyes away from the courtroom door handles. Truman shrugged at the Rivers' questioning stares. *Bad enough that Buster Galt was in charge of his life. Adding Rube Carter was piling on.*

Gray caught Toy's nod and glance as he come out the door. *Was that a smile of encouragement or one of pity?* Toy was obviously full of information that he needed to get out. His eyes were wide, and he held one hand over his mouth, as if the secrets of grand jury proceedings might come spilling out. He paced and nodded, nodded and paced, occasionally giving Truman a meaningful look that begged him to ask the questions that Toy longed to answer. Truman remained passive and blank.

Gray tried not to think of what the repulsive jailer was doing inside the courtroom to seal his fate, but he could not keep the thoughts away. Rube was telling them about his taunts, his smart aleck attitude, and his so-called escape from jail. The jailer would pour it on, making him sound like Billy the Kid. *How would the jailer explain his own absence from duty when I just walked out of the jail?*

He jerked when he felt his father's hand on his shoulder. Truman was staring down at him. "Remember what we told you. Be calm. Hold your temper. Tell the complete truth. If they ask you a question you need help with, just ask to come out and confer with me."

Gray felt his head nod, felt his stomach roll, felt acid rising in his throat. *Not now, I can't lose it now.*

Toy escorted him into the courtroom and followed him down the rows between the spectator pews. He seemed to be traveling in slow motion as the morning sun filtering through the big windows illuminated perfect rows of dust particles. They swirled around him, warning him of the forces aligned against him in the room.

Toy showed him to a metal chair and returned to stand by the door. Gray had expected to sit in the witness box, not in a plain metal chair in the middle of the room. His naked chair faced three tables arranged in a semi-circle. Twelve people stared at him. A woman sat at a small desk behind him, a clerk or court reporter of some sort, he assumed.

Don't slump in the chair. Look them straight in the eye. He could not remember much of what Truman had said, but he could remember his parents' instructions on how to behave.

Buster administered some type of oath about secrecy

he did not hear, but he managed to say, "I do". The woman at the desk left the room with Buster. Gray felt abandoned and more alone with her leaving, somehow. Duly sworn, he sat back in the naked chair, pulled his shoulders back, and allowed himself a look at his judges. As he passed each face, he felt a little spurt of adrenalin. He knew all but four of the first eleven. When he saw the last face, it was as beautiful and kind as the face of Jesus in that painting in the First Baptist Church. Hack Gentry, his father's best friend, sat in front of a folded cardboard sign that said *Foreman*.

Hack spoke. "Gray Boy, we want to hear your version of what happened on the night in question. Just tell us in your own words."

Gray's voice came out as a whisper at first. He cleared his throat and started over. His voice began high and quivery, but as he gazed into friendly faces and kind eyes, it grew strong and steady. The words came pouring out as the cloud of despair lifted. There was no defiance in his voice, no excuses offered for his drinking or fighting with Spooner. Each word of truth seemed to refresh him and give him strength. He finished the story with Toy's visit to return the baseball.

Hack looked down the row of jurors. "Any questions?" Nobody raised a hand. "I have a couple if you don't mind, Gray. First, what do you think caused you to lash out so violently at Spooner Hays?"

Hack's question surprised Gray. "I could say he hit me first, but that sounds like something little boys say when they get caught fighting in the schoolyard." He put both of his hands together as if shaking hands with himself. "Truth is, I don't know for sure. I liked Spooner."

"Try harder. This is important." Gray turned toward the juror who had spoken. He sat at the last table—an unfamiliar face.

Gray swallowed, wondering if he should consult with

Truman. *No, that would look bad.* "I think there were two reasons. One, I had too much to drink. Alcohol makes me cocky, even mean, sometimes." He hesitated, thought of Truman again, then charged ahead. "Second, the backhand slap that Spooner gave me triggered something inside me. I got whipped pretty bad last year and I vowed never to let it happen again. When he hit me, I just went off on him before he could hit me again."

The juror's eyes were not as kind as the others. "Sounds like you've got a lot of rage in you."

Hack spoke again before Gray could respond. "I'd like to ask my second question if it's all right with everyone. Gray, did you see Spooner Hays at the jail on the night of his death?"

Gray did not hesitate. "No, sir."

Hack looked down the row of jurors. "Any other questions?"

The last juror spoke again. "You admit you had a lot of rage after the boy hit you. Are you sure you didn't get rid of that rage by pushing him off the roof when he came up to get even?"

"I never saw Spooner after that fight on the square."

"But you do admit that you were both at the jail at the same time."

"That's what I'm told."

After a few moments of silence, the last juror and Hack exchanged nods, and the juror walked out into the hall. Buster Galt and Toy followed him back in. Toy stopped to stand sentry outside the double doors. Gray squirmed in his seat. *Don't lose your temper.*

Buster paced in front of him, staring at the jurors. Finally, he turned to face Gray. "You in the habit of kissing colored girls, Mr. Rivers?"

The question was unexpected, and Gray thought of Truman again. "No, sir." Sadie was not the first colored girl he had kissed, but he was definitely not in the habit of doing it.

"You ever have sex with a colored girl?"

Gray looked toward the double doors. Truman was there, standing not thirty feet away, to advise him. *Why not use him?* "No sir." He had had sex with a colored woman, well, women, but never a colored girl. He wondered if Buster knew about the colored whore in The Hollow that he and his buddies frequented. He had not lied. The whore was definitely not a girl.

Buster whirled and grasped the arms of Gray's chair. "Ever get a girl pregnant?"

Buster's nose was inches from his own. Gray felt his body grow warm, felt his brain pounding, until he noticed the smell. *Is that peppermint? No, it's Clorets.* The jingle resonated in Gray's mind, easing his tension. *Clorets may cost a little more, but they do so much more, to dissolve bad breath away.* Buster was chewing gum for his breath. That explained some of the lapping noise. The thought almost brought a smile, but it was easy to ward off.

"No, sir." The words came out strong and clear. There had been some close calls, but he did not know of a single girl he had made pregnant.

Buster moved back and stood straight. "Isn't it true that the colored girl you kissed the night in question is carrying your child and that Spooner Hays had promised to kill you because of that?"

"I never saw that girl before that night." Gray was surprised at the question, but it was the first question he could answer without thinking about Truman's help.

Buster's face was red. He licked his lips and sucked in air, making a slight gurgling sound as bubbles of spit exploded on his tongue and in his throat. "Isn't it true that you got Sadie Shaw pregnant because Spooner Hays did the same thing to a white girl in this community?" The jurors murmured and look at each other.

Curiosity almost overcame Gray's fear. "I never met Sadie Shaw until that night. What white girl?"

Hack pushed back his chair. "Excuse me, Mr. Galt, but could you let the rest of us in on what you're talking about? What's all this got to do with the death of Spooner Hays?"

Buster walked toward the double doors and called to Toy. "Sheriff, remove Mr. Rivers." Toy escorted Gray from the room and returned to stand sentry. Truman took Gray a few steps down the hall to find out what had happened in the courtroom.

Back in front of the jury, Buster laid the true bill document on the prosecutor's table. "This boy had four motives for killing Spencer Hays. First, there was the rage. He's got a problem with anger that's documented in this file. Second, I have information that Sadie Shaw, the colored girl in question, is pregnant and that Gray Rivers may be the father. Spencer Hays was known to be violently jealous of this girl. Third, I believe this boy hates the colored. Fourth, and I remind you of the secrecy of these proceedings, I believe that Spooner Hays had impregnated a white girl that the defendant...."

The jurors were nodding when Hack interrupted. "Buster, do you have any proof or evidence of any sort that any of these accusations are true? If you do, it seems to me that you should share it with us."

Buster licked his lips. It bothered him that Hack had stopped referring to him as Mr. Galt, that he was challenging him. "The investigation is not complete, but you have my word that all four motives will eventually be proven in court."

"Very well. If you will leave the room, I think we are ready to discuss this and vote."

Buster studied the faces of the jurors until the delay became embarrassing. "I have one more witness to call."

"And who is that?"

Buster answered on his way to the double doors. "Rance Rivers."

15

Buster stuck his head out the door and motioned for Toy to come inside the courtroom. Gray leaned across his mother to speak to Truman. "You think it's over?"

Truman nodded. "Yes, I think it is. Buster will probably step out the back way, and they will vote."

Toy pushed the door open and stood facing them. His face was drained of color. He looked at Truman and jerked his head to indicate that Truman should follow. They walked a few feet down the hall and stopped.

Toy stood between the Rivers and Truman, placing his palm against the wall. "He's gone off the deep end. Talking about stuff I never even heard about. He's determined to hang that kid. Wants to question Rance now."

Truman shook his head. "I was surprised when he called Gray Boy, but to call his father?"

"Gotta go." Toy stopped in front of his old mentor. "They want to see you in there, Rance."

Rance stood and turned to face his son and wife. He took a deep breath and blew it out, making that soft whistling sound he made when he was tired. "This is a good thing. Everything I know is good for Gray Boy."

Mattie's expression had changed from fear to anger.

"Buster Galt, for some reason, has got it in for my whole family." Rance was already through the double doors.

He glanced at the jurors as he took his oath. Hack kept his gaze on the notepad in front of him. Rance knew at least eight of them well and two more by sight. Only two faces were unfamiliar. Sitting in the metal chair, he felt good taking his son's place. It was something he had wanted to do since this nightmare began. *Bring it on, Buster.*

Avoiding eye contact with Rance, Buster engaged each of the jurors as he walked in front of them. Still pacing with his back to Rance, he spoke to the jurors. "I remind each of you that you are not voting on the guilt or innocence of Mr. Gray Rivers. You are simply deciding whether or not there is sufficient evidence to bring him to trial. Your foreman has asked for evidence of the motives I listed. I have called the defendant's father to provide a part of that evidence."

Still pacing in front of the jurors, he addressed Rance. "Mr. Rivers, are you aware of the hatred your son, Gray, harbors against coloreds?"

The muscles in Rance's jaw twitched as he glanced toward Hack, seeking some unspoken explanation for the question. Hack was still staring at his notepad. With the exception of one juror seated at the end table, the other jurors also avoided eye contact with Rance. "My son does not harbor hatred of colored people."

"Were your children raised in an environment hostile to colored people?"

Rance, staring at Buster's back, squirmed in his seat. "No."

Buster turned to face him. "Is that so? Ever use racial slurs, Mr. Rivers?"

"Yes."

"Ever heard your children use racial slurs?"

"I think you need to be more specific."

"All right, I will. Do you, or any members of your family

refer to the colored population as Blacks, Niggers, Spooks or other derogatory terms?"

Rance's face grew dark; his eyes narrowed. "You still need to be more specific. You named several words."

"All right. If you want me to take the words one at a time, I will. Do you, or any member of your family, routinely refer to the colored as Blacks?"

"No, not that I recall. I guess its possible one of us could have."

Buster turned to face Rance. "Never, Mr. Rivers?"

"I believe you said routinely."

Buster smirked as he cast a meaningful gaze toward the last juror. "So, it is your testimony to this group of jurors that you, nor any member of your family, has ever referred to a colored person or persons as a Black or Nigger?"

"That's a different question than you asked before. The answer to this question is, no, that is not my testimony."

"Ever, Mr. Rivers?"

"Ever what?"

"Mr. Rivers, I remind you that this is not a trial. Rules of evidence do not apply. We are simply trying to provide information to the grand jury in order for them to make a decision with all the available facts at their disposal. You are hindering that process."

"I'd say that you're the one hindering the process, Buster. You're trying to put words in my mouth and paint me and mine as something we're not. Ask a simple question—I'll give you and these good folks a simple answer."

"Have you ever used the term Nigger?"

"Yes."

"Now we're getting somewhere."

"Do you realize that the term is hateful to colored people?"

"I suppose it is to some, but they seem to use it a lot more than I do." Rance took a deep breath. His expression was pained. "I guess it seems more like a lazy man's way of taking a shortcut. Negro doesn't exactly roll off a man's tongue. The way some people drag out Ne-e-e-gro, it seems like an insult itself. I like calling people by their names, not by their race."

Buster stopped pacing in front of the jurors and stared at Rance for several seconds. Rance kept eye contact. "Why don't you just come out and say what it is you're getting at, Buster?"

"Are you aware that your son used racial slurs to insult Spencer Hays the night of his death?"

"My son said that they insulted each other. I wasn't there, so I can't be sure of exactly what was said. I have heard them do it in the cotton patch many times."

"And you did nothing to stop it?"

"I would have stopped it if it had been one-sided or if either boy seemed to be hurt by it. Neither did."

"So you condoned it?"

Rance stared directly into Buster's eyes until Buster looked away. "I did not say I condoned it. I just chose to let the boys build their relationship their own way."

"Is it true that you have stated you would never allow your daughter to date a colored boy?"

Rance frowned at the mention of Trish. His eyes started to turn red as he glanced at Hack. "She never asked."

"If she had, would you have allowed it?"

Rance took several seconds to collect his thoughts. "No."

"Yet you claim you did not raise your children to hate the colored."

"I never taught my children to hate anybody. A white girl who marries a colored boy, or even dates one in today's world, is setting herself and the colored boy up for a lifetime of grief. Only a fool would wish that on a child or grandchild."

Buster turned away from Rance and the jurors and walked to the railing on the other side of the room. He stared out the courtroom window. Hack cleared his throat and stood. "Mr. District Attorney, are you all done? I, for one, am ready to deliberate."

Buster's mouth drooped slightly open, revealing a wad of Clorets between his teeth. "I have a few more questions for Mr. Rivers."

Hack rolled a pencil between his thumb and forefinger. "Do they pertain to racial hatred?"

No answer.

"I can't speak for the other jurors, but as for me, it's gettin' close to milkin' time. I'd like to wind this thing up."

Buster picked up the true bill form folder and slapped it against the table once before dropping it with a dramatic thump. He walked out the back entrance. Toy opened the back door and rushed down the aisle to escort Rance from the room.

Truman was waiting. "What was that all about?"

Rance shook his head. "He was trying to use me to prove that Gray Boy killed Spooner because he hated colored people."

Truman stared at Toy, who nodded firmly. "In a grand jury."

Truman's tone was incredulous. "He called the accused and the accused father in a grand jury proceeding. In all my years of practice in Delta County, I have never seen such a thing. The man has lost control of his faculties."

Gray was not interested in the technicalities of what had taken place. "What happens now?"

Toy put his hand on Gray's shoulder and winked. "Ole Hack is leadin' 'em in their deliberations. He said somethin' about being home in time to milk."

Truman herded Rance, Mattie, and Gray Boy toward the door like a mother hen. "Toy, we'll wait in my office so the jurors don't have to face us when they come out. You come report to me as soon as we have a decision."

The coffee pot was still percolating when Toy burst

through the door of Truman's office. "It's a no-bill, boys."

Gray was sitting on a tabletop. He took a deep breath of free air and exhaled. The news made him feel good, but immediately tired. Rance put his hand on Gray's arm as Mattie squeezed him around his head and shoulders.

Toy danced a little jig around the room. "Ten to two, boys." Silence filled the room as Toy realized he had revealed a secret that he was not supposed to know. Truman shot him a stern look that said to keep silent.

"So two voted against us." Rance's statement was posed as a question to Truman.

Gray sensed the tension in the room, but did not fully understand what was bothering everyone. "Am I done with this thing or not?"

Truman leaned against his desk and folded his arms. "Probably, but I can't promise. If Buster can dig up more evidence, he could come after you again."

Gray looked as if he had been struck. Mattie and Rance, heads down, pulled him toward the door.

Truman began again. "That almost never happens. Besides, since you didn't do it, there can't be anything else to dig up. He took his best shot, and he missed. He won't take the chance of embarrassing himself again."

Gray's hand was on the doorknob. "This is going to hang over me for the rest of my life."

Toy stopped jingling the change in his pocket. "You listen to me, Gray Boy. Me and Truman gonna solve this crime. All we needed was to get this thing with accusin' you out of the way. Now, we can concentrate on what really happened."

Truman help up a halting hand toward Toy. "Toy, you've got to stop promising things you can't deliver. We don't know anything for sure yet."

Toy wagged a huge finger in Truman's direction. "I know enough to be sure somethin' smells real bad."

Rance shook hands with Truman and Toy. "I guess we can settle up on this thing later, Truman. You figure up what I owe you, and I'll try to figure a way to pay it. We're grateful."

Truman nodded as Gray also shook his hand. "I didn't do much, so it won't be too bad."

When the Rivers were out of hearing, Truman turned to Toy. "I'm warning you, Toy. Don't mess this up by revealing too much. We must be methodical."

Toy nodded as he opened the door and stepped out. Truman yelled after him. "Toy, did you find out anything else about that proceeding that I would find useful?"

Toy stepped back in the door and smiled. "You mean the secret proceedings?"

Truman frowned and gave a slight nod.

"Buster had his indictment until he jumped all over Gray Boy and attacked Rance on the race thing. That pissed 'em off. Came off like he was out to get the boy and his family."

Truman smiled. "Just as I thought. I really expected to have to go to trial."

Outside in the bruising sun, Gray hesitated after opening the back door to their Ford. "Is that Ivory sitting over there?"

Rance slid from under the wheel and shaded his eyes from the sun. "That's our old Ford—and that's definitely Ivory." Rance waved a greeting, but Ivory was already driving away. "Who was that in there with him?"

Gray watched until they were out of sight. "Looked like Sadie Shaw."

Hack Gentry stood beside Buster Galt on the courthouse steps as the Rivers drove away. Buster's face was still flushed. "You should have recused yourself, Hack. You're too close to the Rivers to be impartial."

Hack looked up at the taller man. "You and everyone else

on that jury knew about my friendship with Rance and his family. The other jurors and I discussed it. They felt I could be fair, and I feel I was. Besides, I wasn't the only one who is friends with Rance."

"That boy is guilty as sin."

"You're one to talk about being unfair. What was all that crap about racial hatred? Everybody who knows Rance can tell you that ain't true. Even if it was, most of the jurors would have sided with Rance on the issue. You threw your own case out the window barking up that tree. Don't blame it on me."

Buster stalked up the stairs without replying. As he turned the doorknob to his office door, Rube Carter stepped from the dark stairway and stuck his big face close to Buster's. Beads of sweat rested on his flushed forehead, and a single droplet rested on the end of his nose. "What we gonna do now, Buster?"

The district attorney put his fist into Rube's chest and pushed him away, as if touching him was repulsive. "We? We? Listen, you lard-assed piece of filth, never use the word *we* around me again. When it comes to me and you, there is no *we*. Do I make myself clear?"

Rube stared at the floor, fingering the billy club hanging from his belt. "Yeah, but...this thing could cause us a lot of problems. It ain't gonna go away until somebody pays."

Buster opened his office door and peeked inside to be sure it was empty. He looked up and down the hall before crooking his arm and pushing it against Rube's neck until the jailer was pressed against the wall. "Us? Us? That's another word you don't use around me. Ever. You understand? Ever. This thing, as you say, will go away over time. It ain't ever gonna cause me trouble. It might cause you trouble, but not me." Buster pressed Rube's throat until he struggled for breath.

The jailer looked down and away from Buster, his face

flushing, eyes rolling back. When Buster removed his arm, Rube put his hands on his knees, coughing and struggling for breath. Holding his throat, he straightened, turned away from his tormentor, and walked toward the stairs. When he reached the third step, he stopped and looked down toward Buster, the billy club in his hand. "No matter what you say, I know things and I ain't keepin' quiet if they come after me."

Rube was already on his way up the stairs as he summoned the strength to say those words, but he was too slow for the former football star. He felt the tug on his pants leg before he had advanced four steps. Buster pulled a leg out from under him. When Rube fell, Buster grabbed the other leg and pulled the big man bumping down the stairs to the landing. Buster kicked him in the side and then put a foot across the back of his neck.

"You ignorant enough to threaten me? You? You're totally unarmed in a battle of wits with a third-grade kid, and you dare to threaten me?" Buster looked down the hall again before leaning down into Rube's face. Between clenched teeth, his voice came out as a raspy whisper. "Listen to me one last time, asshole. I will not hesitate to hang you out to dry like the garbage you are. Say one more word, I'll go into my office right now and start the paperwork to end your worthless life. You think anybody's gonna believe anything that comes out of your mouth after I get through with you?"

Buster grabbed a handful of Rube's hair and slammed his head against the floor twice. "You listening?" Rube managed a head nod. The fear in his eyes made words unnecessary. "That shit you told me about that girl being pregnant had better be right, too."

16 From the back seat of the car, Gray saw Jake and Papa Griff in the side yard. When they heard the Ford's tires crunch gravel in the driveway, they coiled their ropes and leaned against the sawhorse they had been using for roping practice. The two of them, with their ropes and practice dummy, looked innocent and tranquil to Gray, unsullied by the accusations surrounding his own life. He was envious and irritated that they could engage in something so trivial when his life was on the line.

Only a few years ago, it had been him standing there by Griffin Rivers, absorbing his grandfather's wisdom and placid, musical approach to life. That was before Papa Griff's advice and company started to bore him; started to seem irrelevant and outdated. It started going in one ear and out the other for him. Jake seemed to absorb it all and thirst for more. Had he ever been that way? He tried to recall some of his grandfather's teachings, especially the ones that would have kept him away from the unclean feeling he still felt after his experience today.

Rance delivered the good news to Griffin and Jake calmly. Griffin grabbed Gray's hand with both of his own and shook it before pulling him forward into a rough hug. Jake smiled and stood as if his arms were useless appendages, unsure of what to say or do. His sense of relief turned to joy as he saw his father pull a carton of Cokes from the back seat. The greasy sack of hamburgers from Silman's that his mother held gave Jake a reprieve from his embarrassment.

He took the sack from his mother and peered inside. "Celebration?"

They enjoyed the burgers and Cokes under tree shade in the side yard. Rance told his father that both he and Gray had testified, but he did not provide details for Jake's waiting ears. They lingered in the side yard until it began to cool a little, trying to suspend this moment of escape as long as possible. Each fervently hoping that a chapter in their lives was closed, they soaked their bodies and minds in the soothing salve of relief. Their conversation was remarkably trivial, even contrived, as they avoided discussing the accusations and actions that had brought them to the brink of disaster.

When the conversation turned to the unusually wet weather, Gray walked away from the group toward the dairy barn. The Mustang's soft rumble soon interrupted the whippoorwills. Gray stayed in the barn almost an hour, tinkering with the motorcycle's engine. When the barn door finally opened, Gray rode out; his somber mood lifted.

"Think I'll run over to Rainey Hill." He posed the statement as a question toward his parents.

Mattie smiled and nodded, but Rance spoke. "You expected over there?"

"No, sir. Just thought I would drop by and tell her the good news. She asked me to."

Rance pulled his watch from its pocket. "Don't forget that Joe Max is your boss now, not just your girlfriend's daddy. It complicates things for him a little. You have to respect that."

"Yes sir, I will."

"You need to lay pretty low for awhile until this thing dies down a little."

"I know. Just going down 24 and straight back here."

The setting sun in his face and wind blowing his hair, Gray took one hand from the handlebars and slipped on his aviator shades. The sunglasses helped with the sun, but they served a greater purpose. Behind them, the wild and crazy Gray Boy Rivers of the past came briefly alive. The new Gray Rivers quickly suppressed him.

Hot wind was scalding all of the filth from his body and soul, leaving him invigorated as he turned up the steep incline of Rainey Hill. He drove past the house to the washateria and let the Mustang idle a few seconds in front of the dark little laundry building. He slowed his return, hoping that Halley had heard the Mustang when he passed the house and would come outside to greet him.

The screen door slammed shut as he pushed down the kickstand. A smiling, but hesitant Halley approached as if someone was watching her from the house.

"I was hoping you would come by. I heard that everything turned out good, and I'm glad." Halley's speech was hurried and stiff, as if she had to crowd as many thoughts as possible into the shortest period of time.

Gray sensed that their talk was being heard. He glanced over the cistern toward the screened-in porch, but shadows kept him from seeing behind the screen. "Thanks. I'm out of trouble for now, but not completely out of the woods. I just hope Toy can figure out what really happened to Spooner before Buster Galt comes after me again." Gray's words sounded like a speech to a stranger.

Halley held her arms in front of her skirt, nervously squeezing her hands together. Gray stared at her clean shiny fingernails, no polish, at least no colored polish. He was close enough to smell the aroma of the Raineys' supper in her hair. Chicken-fried steak for sure, probably black-eyed peas and squash on the side. Halley had helped her mother prepare the meal.

The sun was gone now, and twilight softened her features, accented the whiteness of her teeth. "I thought maybe we could sit on the front porch or take a walk down by the lake."

Halley nodded. "I already asked. I have to be back here before full dark." She was already walking ahead of him toward the trail that led down to the lake. When they were out of sight of the back porch, Halley turned to Gray, taking both his hands in her own. They stood facing each other, hands swaying back and forth between them, listening to the croaks of bullfrogs on the lake. Gray leaned forward and brushed her lips with his own.

Halley pulled her hands from his and put her arms around his neck, her head on his shoulder. "I'm so glad. I was so worried."

"Yeah, me too." It sounded trite when Gray Boy heard himself whisper the words in her ear, but it was all he could manage. Is this the new Gray Boy, bashful and tongue-tied? "Maybe now your daddy will let us take in a picture show."

They walked farther down the path, close enough to cause frogs to splash into the water. "He says you're a good worker. Says you're a natural with the equipment and roads, just like your dad."

"He said that?"

"I don't think he intended for me to hear it, but I did."

"Maybe we can go to that picture show this weekend."

She stopped and took both hands in hers again. "I don't think so. I also heard him telling Mother something about your getting girls pregnant."

Gray dropped her hands and stared up at the early moon. "Damn. Everybody swore to keep those things secret."

"You mean those things are true?"

"No, they're not true. Just more of Buster and Cameron Galt trying to send me to prison."

"Cameron? What's he got to do with this?"

"Nothing. Never mind. I might as well be in prison

if I stay around here, Halley. I've never been charged with anything, but I'm already found guilty of not only killing Spooner, but knocking up every girl in the county."

Halley took his hand and pulled him back toward the house as the first sign of summer stars appeared. "What was that all about?"

Gray stopped and faced her. "See? Even you are going for it. First your daddy, now you. Imagine what people who don't know me are gonna say."

Halley smirked. "You better worry about what people who *do* know you are going to say."

Gray could not stop the grin. "See what I mean?"

They slowed their pace as the house came back into view. Joe Max would call if she stayed too long. "I know you have been hurt by all this, but you have to admit that your reputation for being fast never bothered you before."

"That was before it was all mixed in with a killing—with jail." Gray stopped, bending down to pick up a few rocks from the trail. "I'm willing to take my licks for the things I've done. I'm not ashamed of 'em."

He tossed a small rock down the driveway and grinned at Halley in the moonlight. "Well, maybe some of 'em. But I hate taking the blame for things I didn't do. You and your daddy seem ready to believe anything anybody says about me, especially if it's bad."

Halley looked toward the back porch, searching for any sign that her parents were sitting there. "That's exactly what I said to Daddy. You know what he said? He said that if you run with cur dogs, it's hard to keep smelling like a new pup. Daddy says he doesn't believe you killed anybody, but you brought a lot of your trouble on yourself by being irresponsible and not respecting women."

Hattie reached over and gently squeezed his bicep. "There, now I've said it."

Anger had been building with every word until she

touched his arm. "Is that your and your daddy's way of telling me I am not fit to take out a decent girl?"

"Daddy has his own way of thinking. I think I love you, Gray Boy Rivers, but I can't allow you to keep shaming me."

"And I can't keep letting your daddy and mine and everybody else control my life, treating me like a boy. I'm grown; I've got a job, and I plan on buying a car and getting my own place in the fall."

He grabbed both her arms as she stared nervously at the house. "If I did all that, you think your daddy would let you go out with me again?"

Halley shook her head. "I think so, but I don't know."

"If he won't, will you marry me and move away from here? Leave all my bad reputation behind and start all over somewhere else?"

Halley trembled as he squeezed her arms tight enough to hurt. "Gray, I have a year left in high school. I can't quit."

Gray dropped his hands and shook his head. "I know you can't, but what am I supposed to do for a whole year?"

The screen door's hinges squeaked as Joe Max stepped out to the cistern. He unwound the well rope and eased the bucket down into the water. As he drew it back up, his deep voice traveled through the sound of frogs and whippoorwills. "Halley? It's time." In a small gesture of defiance, Gray leaned over and gave Halley a quick kiss.

Joe Max stood by the cistern, his arm around Halley's shoulder as Gray drove by. Gray waved a friendly greeting, but he could not erase the feeling of weakness that the scene left in his mind as he headed east toward home—always somebody else in control of his life.

He had passed the three bridges of Jernigan Creek and his home was in sight before he noticed the cream and blue '54 Ford pass him a second time. The brake lights blinked a greeting as the '54 pulled off 24 onto a dirt road. He stopped a few feet past the car and killed the Mustang.

Molly Beth French had one elbow out the car window, the other wrist slung casually across the wheel. Gray looked for activity at his house as he walked toward her. Lights were on, but he was too far away to be seen.

Molly Beth was smiling, but her usual carefree attitude was missing. Her eyes were red, and they had a wild, cornered look. "I've been driving up and down the highway between your house and the Rainey's for almost an hour. I knew you'd come away from her sooner or later."

Gray put his hands on the door, one on each side of her arm. "How'd you get your daddy's car?"

"Sneaked the keys. What happened today?"

Gray tried to study her face in the moonlight, but the car kept her in the dark. Something was different. Molly Beth's voice was urgent, her movements jerky. Gray had always been attracted to her pretty face and athletic, almost tomboyish body, but her devil-may-care attitude was what kept them together. That appealing attribute was missing tonight. It was easy to take his hand away from her arm. He sensed a threat.

"Can't say. Grand jury proceedings are secret, you know." Molly Beth looked away as she spoke. "So I hear. You goin' to tell me or not?"

Gray waited for the sound of a passing car to drift away on the humid summer air. "What is it you want to know, Molly Beth?"

"About all the girls you are supposed to have screwed and left pregnant."

"What did you hear?"

"Rumors, mostly. About how there was supposed to be a white girl pregnant by a colored boy. How you got a colored girl pregnant."

"Why do you care about stories like that? I hear you and Galt are a thing now. What do you care what I did or didn't do?"

Molly Beth's voice started as a whisper, rising and then

breaking as she ended her sentence sobbing. "I care, because people are saying I'm the white girl pregnant by a colored boy."

It was not the answer Gray Boy wanted or expected. Molly Beth had been crying, and he could not fend off the sense of satisfaction it gave him to think she was crying over him. "Who says that?" He had never seen Molly Beth cry and had no idea how to comfort her. Just one more person whose life was being ruined because of him.

Molly Beth pulled a tissue from the box of Kleenex sitting beside her. Ignoring the damage to her mascara, she wiped her eyes, blew her nose, and threw the tissue in the floorboard with other used ones. "I don't know. It just got back to me. What does it matter who said it? It isn't true. Is it true about you and Sadie Shaw?"

Gray tried to wrap his brain around all the things caused by Buster Galt's vicious attack. He pointed his finger at Molly Beth. "You can thank your boyfriend's pond-scum daddy for this." Gray tensed as he saw the '55 Chevy pass slowly on 24.

The impulse was quick and seemed almost inevitable. Putting both hands on the roof of the car, he leaned in and kissed Molly Beth softly on the lips. The feel of her mouth was so familiar, her scent so sensual, he lingered to brush his lips across her neck. Memories flooded his senses before he managed to push himself back from the door.

"Oh, Gray Boy, I wish you hadn't done that."

"Everything's going to be all right, Molly Beth. Let people talk. The joke's on them. You ain't pregnant, and I never did more than kiss Sadie Shaw. A month or two will pass, and everybody will know that. I hope they feel like fools for ever believin' it." Gray watched the Chevy slow as it reached Jernigan Creek. Its brake lights blinked once before it went out of sight.

"It's kinda funny when you think about it. I may always get blamed for killing Spooner, but they sure as hell can't blame me for knocking up Sadie Shaw, and they can't say you're having a kid when you aren't."

Molly Beth pulled her arm inside the car and gripped the steering wheel with both hands. Gray sensed the threat again as he watched a gradual change come over her. Molly Beth's natural swagger was gone. Gripping the steering wheel, mascara sliding down her cheeks, she looked like a frightened little girl. Gray reached through the car window to put his arm over her shoulders. She turned to face him. Her eyes reminded him of how his mother had looked when they entered the courthouse that morning. Molly Beth's eyes were talking to him, trying to express what her mouth could not say. Gray drew back, sensing the threat again.

"What if the joke is on me and not them, Gray Boy? What if my stomach starts to pooch out in a few weeks?"

"Don't bullshit me, Molly Beth. That ain't funny."

Molly Beth looked away again, her expression reminding Gray of how she looked when she sucked on lemons. She was fighting back tears. Gray's words came out as a whisper. "Are you telling me you really are pregnant?"

Molly Beth stifled a sob, causing her to choke and cough. "Yes," came out as a throaty whisper.

Gray took a deep breath as if surfacing from an underwater struggle and blew the air out his mouth. "How long?"

Molly Beth shrugged her shoulders. "Not sure. Ten, maybe twelve weeks."

Gray made the calculations. He took several more deep breaths as he walked in circles beside the car. His father's lectures about crossing the river played in his head. Had he crossed it when he got this girl pregnant, or was the river still in front of him, challenging him to cross it now? "Okay. What do you want to do about it?"

The tissue held to her nose made the reply nasal. "Do about it?" Her tone said that the question was dumb.

Gray stopped his pacing and cupped her face with both

his hands. "We need to give the baby a name. I'll find us a place, and we can get married right away."

Gray heard the Chevy approaching again, heard the downshift that caused the twins to rack back. It was a sound he usually enjoyed and appreciated but he did not want to hear it now. He held his breath as the Chevy eased by— Cameron's Galt's head, shoulders, and one arm hanging out the window, gawking at them.

Molly Beth heard the Chevy too, but kept her eyes on Gray Boy. "You really mean that, don't you?"

"Never been more serious in my life."

"What about Halley?"

Gray winced. "She's not carrying my baby."

Molly Beth opened the door and stepped out of the car. Gray could not take his eyes off her stomach. She managed a sad smile. "You can't see anything down there yet."

Stepping into her open arms, he could not keep away the mental comparison of the embrace with Halley only a few minutes before. Molly Beth was taller, almost his own height, and she could make him feel as if every part of his body, from his toes to the top of his head, was touching a corresponding part of hers. The normal guilt he had always felt when he embraced Molly Beth melted away as he felt her hot tears on his shoulder. *I'm not crossing the river. I'm doing the right thing.*

He heard a muffled whisper against his throat. "I may regret saying these words for the rest of my life, but I have to say them while I still can. The baby is not yours."

Gray grabbed her shoulders and pushed her back to look into her eyes. "Not mine? You said ten or twelve weeks. We were going steady then."

He stepped back and put his hands on his hips. "If it's not mine, whose is it? You mean old Spooner...." He regretted the words as soon he saw the look on her face.

The red '55 Chevy passed again, heading west toward Commerce. No arms or shoulders hung out the passenger window. *Looks like the bastard may be alone for a change.*

Molly Beth sighed and nodded toward the passing Chevy. "It's his."

Gray dropped his arms, stepped farther back and stared, disbelief in his eyes. She crossed her arms under her breasts and hugged herself tightly. "It was one of those times when you were out doing things behind my back—screwing everything that walked. I was angry—wanted to get back at you. I cut off my nose to spite my face."

Gray shook his head and clenched his fists as he watched the Chevy's taillights. Turning toward Molly Beth, he saw that his once confident, brassy, fun-loving girlfriend had shriveled before his eyes into a bewildered, frightened teenager. He softened. "I'll still marry you."

Molly Beth lurched as if he had hit her in the stomach. "I can't ask to ruin your life just because I did something stupid."

He was holding out his arms, asking her to step into his embrace, when the Chevy, pipes racking, passed again. This time, it made a quick U-turn on 24, whipped onto the dirt road beside Molly Beth's car. Fats Domino declared *Ain't That a Shame* as the twin pipes stopped rumbling.

Cameron was not driving. He hadn't come alone, after all. He stood beside them before the car came to a complete stop, rolling the piece of petrified wood in his hand. "Well, Rivers. You slip out of the hangman's noose in the morning, go right back into the line of fire at night. Seems like tryin' to steal my girl has got you into trouble once before."

Gray Boy said nothing as he stepped between Molly Beth and Cameron. Molly Beth stepped from behind him to face Cameron. "Gray Boy and I were friends before I ever laid eyes on you, Cameron Galt. He's the best friend I ever had, and I hope he'll always be my friend. We're just two friends having a talk."

Cameron pointed a finger at Molly Beth. "Friends, my

ass. I saw a lot more going on here than friendship. He's had his hands all over you every time I passed by."

Molly Beth smiled at Gray Boy and he smiled back. "We're *close* friends." They said the words at the same time, causing a shared chuckle.

"You going to associate with this nigger killer; I can't stop you." He turned back toward the car and spoke to his friend, waving an arm in Gray Boy's direction. "If I was him, I'd get me a sticker to put on the back of my car window. *Nigger Killer.*"

Cameron and his friend laughed. "Then I'd put me a big Roman numeral I beside it."

Gray Boy felt his clenched fists turn loose, felt his taut muscles relax. Cameron was afraid. It was in his voice. Drifting up, he watched everything from above. He saw his father and his grandfather standing beside him, facing Cameron Galt. Drifting back down, Gray heard the sweet sounds of Griffin's violin. He looked at Molly Beth, then Cameron as the wind shifted and a rare summer breeze from the north swept over the group. The dry air soothed him, taking away his rage and the heat from his body.

Molly Beth untied the strings that held a rolled blanket behind the Mustang's seat. Turning back toward Gray, she squeezed the rolled blanket close to her chest. "For old times sake?" Gray nodded his head. She took his face in both hands, kissed him on the lips, and whispered, "Thank you," as she turned away.

She opened her car door and turned toward Cameron. "You don't own me, Cameron Galt. You never will. Now get your sorry ass in your little red car and go on home to your daddy and mama. Try to grow up some on the way like Gray Boy Rivers has done. Don't ever follow me again." Molly Beth popped the clutch, making the tires squeal a little as she pulled onto 24 and headed toward Cooper.

The Chevy rumbled to life within seconds. It stopped

beside the Mustang, Cameron's arm and shoulder out the
door, pointing at Gray Boy. "You and me—we're not done
yet." Gray Rivers smiled. The red car left ten yards of
smoking rubber and was on Molly Beth's bumper before she
reached the turn off to the old Klondike highway.

Gray hated its driver, but he could not help but admire
the sound, beauty, and power of the Chevy. "Someday, I'm
going to own a car like that one," he said to the north breeze.
He straddled the Mustang and punched the kickstart. He
raced the engine a couple of times, considering what to do.
He felt hollow, weak, and confused, but he also felt calm and
clean.

Where was the river? Did Molly Beth need help, or
should he leave her and the father of her child alone? The
motorcycle's engine idled until they were out of sight. He
pulled out of 24, raced toward them, slowed, and turned in
the driveway toward home.

17 Truman, one ankle crossed over the other, balanced the china saucer on his lap and sipped coffee from the cup. Sadie Shaw stared at him as she rearranged the lace doily on the sofa's arm. He had clumsily shifted the doily from its proper location.

"Anything else, Miz Evelyn?" Sadie asked.

"No, that will be all, Sadie." Evelyn Galt spoke haltingly, as if her mouth would not yield to the movements required for proper enunciation of her words. She took a sip from her cup, pain from the effort showing.

Truman looked around the old parlor as Sadie picked up a small tray and left the room. It had been almost a decade since he had been in the Galt home. Not much had changed. Lace was still everywhere. Lace doilies on the arms of all the furniture and at headrests; lace tablecloth over the mahogany dining table. Lace drooped from the fireplace mantle. It was clear that Buster's mother still exercised decorating power over the home that she and Tom Galt had inherited. Either that, or Buster's wife found decorating tedious.

He felt Evelyn Galt's stare boring into him before he turned to face her. "You need not worry, Mr. Bates. My condition is not contagious."

She seemed to be looking from behind a clay mask, her

eyes hooded by hardened, thickened skin. He recognized the face from pictures he had seen in the Dallas and Cooper papers when she and Buster had married, but the resemblance was slipping away. Her face appeared as a work-in-progress, a sculptor's work—with soft clay abandoned in haste, allowing the material to harden, dry, thicken, and pull away.

"Please call me Truman, Mrs. Galt. After all, the Galts and Bates go back for generations."

"Very well, you may call me Evelyn." Her lips stretched tightly across her teeth, clinging to them with every syllable.

"As to your condition, I am aware that I am in no danger from it."

"Are you familiar with scleroderma?"

"When Mother told me of your condition, I did some research." Truman hoped for a change of subject.

"And what did you find?"

Truman placed his cup and saucer on an end table by his chair, using his napkin to protect against a possible coffee ring. "I confess that I am still largely ignorant about your particular condition. I understand it is a severe form of arthritis."

Evelyn seemed to take perverse pleasure in Truman's discomfort. "Arthritis seems a harmless but ineffectual description for this monstrous disease."

"I apologize for my ignorance of the level of your suffering."

"No need to apologize. The medical profession is also ignorant. I have seen the best physicians in the world. None can tell me what causes it, or what great malady will occur in the future. Only God knows what trick He will play on me next. Having easily turned what some people considered a beautiful exterior monstrously ugly and unyielding to my movements, I feel Him working on my interior as we speak."

The bitterness and bluntness of her discourse shocked Truman. He sneaked a peek at his pocket watch. "It is approaching time for me to open my office, Mrs. Galt, uh, Evelyn. Thank you for your hospitality and the superb coffee, but...."

"I asked you here for a reason, Mr. Bates. Please indulge me for a few more minutes."

"Certainly."

"It has come to my attention that you have been making inquiries about my husband."

"Inquiries?"

Her coffee cup rattled against the saucer as she placed it on the table by her chair. "You have surely discerned that speaking, as well as movement of any kind, is painful to me. Please do not make me repeat myself."

Truman looked out the parlor window into the front yard, yearning to escape. "Yes, that is true."

"Why?"

"It is a matter I do not, cannot, divulge due to client confidentiality. I can only say that I was working in the best interests of my client."

"Why did you not come to me with your inquiries?"

Truman leaned forward, more comfortable with the conversation now. "Because of the long tradition of friendship between our families. When word reached my mother that I was making inquiries, she told me of your condition and asked me to desist."

"Your mother is a fine woman. What exactly did she say to you?"

Truman smiled. "She said to let sleeping dogs lie."

He could not be sure, but he thought a smile crossed her rigid lips. "How I wish we could. I suppose it had to come out, however, sooner or later. What do you know?"

"As I said, confidentiality...."

Her body jerked as she lurched sideways in her wheelchair. "To hell with that legal nonsense, Truman. My family is the one you are investigating. My life is on the line here. I want to protect as much of it as I can. If you help me with that, I may consent to provide you with the information you require; just tell me where I need to start."

Truman leaned back against the edge of the sofa. "I'm afraid I don't understand."

"It's simple. I'll give you the information you need about my husband's abrupt departure from a prominent position with a Dallas law firm if you allow me some control over what is done with the information."

"I can't give you any guarantee." Priding himself on interpreting body language and facial expressions as well as speech, Truman found it disconcerting to speak to this woman. Her facial expression remained rigid, her movements uncoordinated. Now, she sat perfectly still, as if any movement might cause her skin to crack and break.

"Very well, tell me what you know thus far."

"I know that Buster left Dallas and his old law firm under less than desirable circumstances. I prefer not to repeat the other information attached to that because it is not substantiated as of yet."

"Can't trust what Dad Flanagan's family told you, Truman?" Truman's surprised look told her she had hit a nerve. "I have my sources. My family is also well connected."

"What can you tell me?"

"First, I want to retain you as my attorney. I may have need of your services."

Truman smiled. "Nice try, Mrs. Galt, but that would mean anything you told me would have to remain confidential."

"As I understand it, your client has not been indicted."

"That's correct, but nothing precludes the district attorney from pursuing the issue further."

"Damn it, you're one to stick by the rules, aren't you?" She gripped the arms of her chair. "Would that my husband were more like you. All right, I'll tell you without legal restriction, only bound by the honor of the Bates family name."

"Done."

"My husband left his law firm on account of me, so to speak."

Truman listened to Evelyn's haunting tale of her illness, beginning with the first physical symptoms and concluding with the emotional devastation wrought as the disease destroyed her body and her marriage. "It is ironic that Buster's flesh became weak and soft as mine grew thick and hard."

"Why did you stay with him?"

"Let's just say that my choices were limited, Mr. Bates. I began as Buster's wife but am now little more than a kept woman—a kept woman without the usual benefits of such an arrangement." A slight chuckle escaped from deep in her throat, as if the person she had once been lurked there.

Truman's embarrassment grew deeper with each new personal revelation, and he felt guilty for feeling such immense pleasure at having his suspicions confirmed. "Was there a particular incident that ended it all and brought you back home?"

"Yes, a pregnant teenage girl—the daughter of one of Buster's partners. There were legalities involved. I have copies of the paperwork in a safety deposit box at the bank." Evelyn allowed her resourcefulness time to soak into Truman's brain. "My parents have access to the documents in question in case I cannot be reached. When and if you agree to be my attorney, I will share them with you." Evelyn was tiring from the effort of speaking.

"Why are you telling me this?"

"My father suggested it. He knows you will probably expose my husband, regardless. In the event of divorce, I will need immediate local representation. He thinks highly of you."

Truman touched the bow tie he had carefully knotted only a few hours before, wondering how news of his work had reached her father. From the corner of his eye, he saw Dr. Osler Bartlett's light-green '56 Ford Custom park in front of the house. Dr. Osler walked toward the house, derby hat at a slight tilt, a beige-gloved hand delicately swinging his cane.

"Dr. Osler. Is he coming to see you?"

She leaned forward for a glimpse of her physician through the picture window. "Yes. Strange, isn't it? My family and I searched all over the world, looking for physicians who understood how to treat this disease. Dr. Osler doesn't have the cure, but I am convinced he is more knowledgeable than any doctor in America."

Truman stood and awkwardly patted her hand. "I will leave you to visit with the doctor." He turned at the parlor door. "Why have you not divorced him?"

"As I said, I am a kept woman, used to the finer things in life. I do not want to depend on my parents or anyone else for my support. Then, there is the matter of his mother. A fine woman. Who would see to her?"

Truman nodded and opened the front door to admit Dr. Osler. Evelyn waved the doctor into the parlor and asked Truman to step back from the foyer into the parlor. "Doctor, is there not a creed somewhere that says to doctors, first, do no harm? Dr. Osler removed his gloves as he nodded.

"Truman, how about lawyers?"

"I certainly try to live by a similar code."

"I will try to see that Buster does, also." Her voice was tired. Before their eyes, Evelyn Galt shrunk further behind the clay-like mask her skin had become. As he walked to his office, Truman tried to connect the beautiful creature he had seen in photos to the woman sitting in the Galt's parlor. She was there, inside the crudely stretched clay, a skeletal framework—a sculptor's armature.

18 "You think it's dry enough to let 'em cross the Blue Bottom again or do you want to take 'em the long way around?" Rance watched for any kind of bad behavior in Jake's horse, fully expecting the horse to throw his head or fight the bit, a result of Jake's handling the reins harshly. It was almost disappointing when the gelding kept his head down, ears nodding, providing Rance with a comfortable and fast-paced walk. Even in this new territory, Scar did not spook at the new sights or the sudden flapping of disturbed bird wings. Griffin's coaching of Jake and his horse made Rance feel proud, but a little unneeded. His father had accomplished what impatience had kept him from doing.

"There's good grass up on Hurt Hill. They can graze there until up in the fall." Hack rode Peanut, a gelding that stretched to reach fourteen hands, as they moved toward deep timber, headed for Piss Elm Crossing. They had been riding for almost an hour without seeing one cow.

At the edge of the heavy timber, Rance built a loop and swung it low in front of Scar's eyes. The horse did not blink or flinch. "That boy or his granddaddy has been roping off this horse."

"You have a problem with that?" Hack said.

"Ropin's dangerous. Jake's a little light in the britches to be losing a finger or getting drug by a horse or cow."

"I don't imagine Griffin would put him in harm's way until he's ready. Ain't like you to be so overprotective."

"Losing one son and coming close to losing another makes a man jumpy." Rance pulled his horse up at the timberline.

Hack stepped off his horse. "Sorry, I shouldn't be offering my opinions until I've walked a mile in your moccasins."

Rance stepped down, loosened both cinches, and picked up the saddle and pad to give the horse's back a little air before repositioning the tack. "No apology necessary. Hack, I never thanked you for what you did on that grand jury."

Hack looked over Peanut's saddle. "Never thank me for that, Rance. You know I would do anything to help you or your family, but I voted to no-bill Gray Boy because Buster made a damn fool of himself and ruined his case."

Rance stiffened as he turned to face his best friend. "So you think he's guilty?"

"Hell, no. I didn't say that." Hack loosened his belt, unzipped his pants, and tucked his shirt back in. "But I would have voted a true-bill if it wasn't obvious that Buster was out to get him."

"What the hell does that mean?"

"Now, Rance, you know about grand juries. You know that they don't decide guilt or innocence. There was probably enough evidence to bring Gray Boy to trial. If the majority had leaned that way, I might have gone along."

Rance tightened the front cinch again and tied the loose end of the latigo strap down. "A trial, guilty or innocent, would have tainted that boy's life forever—probably destroyed this family. How could you have voted for that?"

"Okay, I made a mistake. I should have stepped away. I was determined to be fair and impartial, and that may have tipped me the other way. You're right. Voting for an indictment would not have been fair. Now, I owe you an apology rather than you owing me thanks."

Rance buckled the back cinch, leaving about two fingers space between the cinch and the horse's belly. He could tighten it later if it looked like they might have to rope something. "Ah, hell, the whole thing makes me sick to my stomach. I get about half-mad every time I pass somebody on the street, wondering if they think my son is guilty of killing somebody."

Hack had one foot in the stirrup when he saw Rance reach for his Prince Albert. That meant more talk. He stepped back down. "Time will take care of that."

"I don't think so. You know, a man spends most of his life in a community as small as this, trying to always do the right thing, never cheatin' anybody, payin' his debts, makin' his word good—then, at the drop of a hat, people believe he raised a son capable of killin' somebody and lying about it."

"I don't think anybody who really knows you thinks that, Rance."

"Do you understand what I'm feeling? It's eatin' at me so much I'm thinkin' of leaving this country."

Hack kept a hand on Peanut's hip as he walked around the little horse to face Rance. "You going to let a bitter taste in your mouth cause you to give up?"

Rance licked the paper on his cigarette and held it, unlit, in the hand that pointed at Hack. "It ain't just the thing with Gray Boy. It's bad memories with Tuck. Everything about the old house reminds us of him. Even at work, I have to pass that graveyard almost every day. I swear I can hear that baby calling me on some days."

Hack understood how hard it was for his friend to reveal himself this deeply. He pondered his reply. "Like I said, I can't say I understand, because I don't. Let me just venture something, though. It seems to me that wherever a man goes, there he is. You understand what I mean?"

"Yep. I thought about that. Papa said near the same

thing when I mentioned leaving to him. I know a man takes his troubles with him, but it seems that doing away with constant reminders might help a little. I long for a fresh start."

Hack picked up Peanut's front foot, pulled a pocketknife from his pocket, and started loosening impacted dirt and pulling out a stone. "Can't argue with that, but how about the friends you and Mattie have here? And Jake's school? You can't take that too lightly."

Rance lifted a rear foot on Scar and copied Hack's actions. "That's about the only thing holding me here. But I don't aim to spend the rest of my life working for the other man. I've always been in business for myself. I don't take orders easily."

Hack stood and rubbed his stiff back. "With the drought over, what about going back into the dairy business?"

Rance grinned as he lifted a second hoof. "I'm thinking stocker cattle and maybe a little farming. Course, this damn country seems to get feast or famine when it comes to rainfall. If I plant cotton again, it'll probably be flooded instead of dying of thirst."

"We ain't ever talked much about this, and don't take it personal, but how about the flow? I know Mr. Griffin puts a good store by this special thing lookin' after the Rivers."

Rance squinted into the sun as he looked in Hack's direction. "Those old family legends seemed sorta silly when Tuck died, I guess. For quite a while, I figured everybody was laughing at us. I beat myself up pretty good for ever believin' it. Convinced myself that those things that happened were just coincidences." Rance stopped and stared vacantly into the distance.

Hack moved close enough to put a hand on Scar's hip. "Just for the record, I never thought it was silly. You and me don't talk about religion much, but Willie Mae and I talked about it." Hack fidgeted with Peanut's reins, slapping them against his leg. "Well, we just figured it was God's way of working inside us."

Hack's Adam's apple bobbed as he forced out the last sentence. He chuckled. "That's why I always said you were a heck of a lot more religious than I ever was. I admit to being a little envious that your family seemed able to summon up divine help when it was needed."

Rance stared at Hack until his friend turned to face him. "That was hard for you to get out, wasn't it?"

"A little."

"Well, thank you for sayin' it. I never really thought about it in that light, but Jake is the one who brought the flow back into our lives. He proved more than once that a man can do it if he just tries hard enough and believes enough."

Eight hooves cleaned, they mounted and headed into the thick timber. It had not rained for several days, but low spots were still moist, causing black gumbo to build up on the horses' hooves, destroying the cleaning performed minutes before. Only a few feet onto ground that had not seen sunlight in many years, they heard the first rustling of cattle.

Rance liked working wild cattle with Hack and Peanut. The little gelding seemed to have a sixth sense about locating bottomland cattle. He knew how to keep himself and his rider out of harm's way, too. People said that Hack Gentry had bottomland cattle that he had not seen in many years. Rance knew better. The cattle were wild and dangerous to pen or work, but Hack knew them by sight. He had named most of them.

Rance held Scar in check for a moment when he spotted a mother cow and calf to his right. She had long horns that pointed straight up in a wide U-shape. She shook the horns as a warning to the men and their horses. Rance slapped his chaps and whistled at the wild cow as he pushed Scar toward her. Deciding that her threats were not going to deter the intruders, the old cow raised her tail and ran, the calf following closely behind.

"When you going to sell that mean old bitch?" Rance shouted in Hack's direction.

"Old Bell is our bell cow. She acts mean, but she knows the routine. Just about rounds up the other cattle on her own as soon as she sees it's time to move."

Rance laughed out loud. "Bullshit. That old bitch is wild as a deer. She'd put a horn in you, me, or either one of these horses if she got half a chance. Only reason you don't sell her is because you can't catch her."

Cattle were starting to move now, shaking small trees and bellowing in protest. Mother cows called their calves to them. Almost eerie silence had turned to a cacophony of sound. Peanut looked like a border collie herding sheep as he swept back and forth through big and small trees, pushing the cattle toward the creek. Scar seemed to be learning from the tiny gelding, almost competing.

Before either man could see the creek, they heard the first splashing of water and splattering of mud as Bell led the way across the Blue Bottom and up Hurt Hill to plush grass. Both men pulled up as the creek came into view. The sound of the cows crossing Blue Bottom Creek was a familiar one to Rance. He and Hack had moved cattle here for many years.

Putting both hands on the horn and stretching his legs in the stirrups, Rance allowed the sounds of bawling cattle crossing a stream to wash over him like a soft rainfall on a hot, dry day. He glanced through the trees and darkness at Hack.

Although he could see a mere outline of a man horseback in the dark woods, he knew that his friend was doing the same things, feeling the same emotions. Rance and Hack enjoyed that easy familiarity that comes with brotherhood or long-term friendship. Each knew the other's strengths and weaknesses and accepted them. Each understood that the other knew how to work cattle, allowing them to take their time as they pushed across the creek and through the open gate on the other side. Less experienced men might have rushed the cattle, causing them to turn back, run down the creek, or crowd and push over the weak fence. Not having to give instructions or worry about your partner was comforting.

"I counted sixty-seven. You?" Hack hollered the question as they eased down the creek bed. In the cattle-softened mud, their horses sunk almost to their knees, forcing them to jump with each step.

"Twenty-one pairs, three bulls, and twenty-one heifers. Might have been a steer or two mixed in with the heifers." Rance answered.

"You must have missed one. No steers, unless you been cuttin' my bulls without me asking."

"Whatever you say. You do have a few bull calves that need cuttin'."

"We'll do that later in the fall."

"Yeah. About the time they get big enough to kick hell out of us and drag us around."

Hack did not have to lean over very far in the saddle to pick up the gate. He pulled it around to close, but changed his mind and leaned it against the fence. Rance and Scar eased up the trail toward Hurt Hill and found firm footing before stopping to wait for Hack and Peanut. "How come you're leaving the gate open?"

Hack pulled Peanut beside Scar and they headed up the narrow trail. "The creek may be the only place they can get water for a couple of days. The hand pump on that trough on the hill is broken. I'll come back in the truck and fix it tomorrow."

Rance glanced back toward Blue Bottom Creek. "I'd do it now if I were you—some of your old cows or the small calves might bog down in that creek. If it rains enough to get the creek up while they're down there, they'll drown."

Hack nodded and looked at the sun. "What time is it?" Rance glanced at the sun before withdrawing his pocket watch. "I'd say about two-fifteen." He checked his watch and smiled. "Two-ten. I'm usually closer than that."

"Now who's talking bullshit." Hack looked back at the gate. "Too late to fix that pump today. By the time we ride back, it'll be time to milk. We can get by one day. Weatherman ain't callin' for rain, anyway. Besides, it would take a young flood to get the creek up high enough to drown the cattle."

The two friends followed the same routine they had followed for years, stopping on Hurt Hill to look over the bottomland valley. The valley had started its recovery from drought already, with knee-high grass waving a friendly greeting to two old friends. They had hunted, fished, ridden horses in wild chases, and worked cattle there together as boys and men.

They let the horses blow as they wordlessly soaked in the wonder of bruised nature healing itself after years of suffering. Remounted, they pointed their horses up Dogtown Road, taking the long, but drier sandy-land route to home.

Keeping his eyes on the road ahead, Hack spoke to his friend. "When you're thinking of leaving, do you ever consider what happens to the friends you leave behind?"

Rance knew that Hack was making a statement, not asking a question. The horses and their riders had worked up good sweats in the deep timber, so the cooler, drier air provided a welcome relief from the humidity and stillness they had experienced in the bottoms.

As they turned east in the ditch along highway 24 and headed for the Gentry farm, Scar began to charge the bit and prance. Peanut, usually calm in all situations, was throwing and shaking his head. The bad behavior surprised and irritated Rance. "This horse is acting like a barn-soured Shetland pony."

Hack scanned the horizon. "Storm coming. Notice how still it got all of a sudden? Clammy, too."

Rance had been too busy calming his horse to notice the

change in weather. He stood in his stirrups and looked in all directions. Hair seemed to crawl up his neck, and he felt a clammy stickiness in his armpits. "I feel it, but I don't see it. Guess the horses know it, too."

"It's still a ways off. Damn. You were probably right. I should have closed that gate.'

"Well, it's like you say; it would take a lot of rain to get that creek up much this time of year."

19 Truman was fumbling with his office door lock at day's end when he felt someone watching him. Instinctively, he turned and looked west. She was standing on the courthouse back sidewalk, dressed in a faded blue cotton dress with tiny green squares. Holding her arm across her face as if she were checking its scent, she reminded him of a shy little girl trying to hide her face. Her dress hung loose and straight, its shape interrupted only by her firm breasts. The black, shiny-but-scuffed high-heel shoes were too big. If not for the tiny straps around her ankles, they would probably slip off. He guessed they had been a gift from Evelyn Galt.

He waited for her to look away, but when she did not, he motioned for her to join him. Arm still over her face, she walked toward him. Sadie Shaw stopped a few feet short. "I seen you this mawnin' at Miz Evelyn's."

"Why yes. Miss Shaw, isn't it? How nice to see you again." Truman waited expectantly until the silence become uncomfortable. "How can I help you, Miss Shaw?"

"People say you King Ivory Hays' lawyer."

"Yes, Ivory and I have been friends for many years. He is also my client."

"Yeah, but King Ivory got money. I ain't."

"Are you in some sort of trouble?"

"Might be." Sadie dropped her arm from her face and hugged herself with both arms as she swayed back and forth.

Truman had never finished turning the key to lock the door. He pushed it open and invited her inside. Sadie's eyes widened as she took in the big office.

Truman put his hand under her elbow and guided her to a seat in front of his desk and sat in the chair beside her. "Now, tell me how I can help you with your trouble."

"I didn't mean to listen in, but I heard some of what you and Miz Evelyn said this mawning."

Truman tried to keep disapproval out of his expression. "Go on."

"'Bout Mr. Buster and all."

"What about Mr. Buster?"

"He got troubles with women."

The conversation seemed to be going nowhere for Truman. He walked to the small kitchen and returned with a Dr Pepper for Sadie. "Now Miss Shaw, in order for me to help you, you're going to have to be more specific. How are you in trouble, and what has that got to do with Mr. Galt?"

"I carryin' Mr. Galt's baby." Sadie gulped down half the Dr Pepper as if the words had scalded her throat.

Truman scooted his chair back. The familiar guilt and pleasure returned, one always accompanying the other, as he contemplated what this information meant to himself, the community, his clients, the district attorney and his wife, and to this young woman.

The calculations flooded his mind with facts and possibilities so fast that he stared open-mouthed at the young woman until she looked away. "Are you sure?" he finally said.

Sadie stared at the floor. "Course I'm sure."

Truman knew that Sadie Shaw, raised by her grandmother, was left without family when her grandmother had died last year. She lived alone in the house her grandmother had rented from Ivory. "What would you like for me to do?"

Sadie wrung her hands in her lap. "'Fraid I about to lose my job, maybe get hurt, too."

Truman leaned forward and put a hand on top of hers. "Have you been threatened?"

Tears squeezed out of her tightly closed eyelids. "Not 'zactly, but King Ivory says they likely to kill me, too."

Her closed eyes gave Truman a chance to explore her features. Her long, black eyelashes curled up, glistening with tears, as they lay wet against her caramel-colored skin. She had full, soft lips and a small mouth and nose.

Fetching. No wonder that Gray Boy had kissed her. He chased away the empathy for Buster Galt that also began to creep into his consciousness. "They? Who is they?"

Sadie opened her eyes and stared at him with surprise and disbelief. "Why Mr. Buster and that disgustin' jailer, of course."

"You think they plan to take your life? Why?"

Indignant, Sadie stood and put both hands on her hips. "Why? Why you think?"

"I confess to—and apologize for—my ignorance, Miss Shaw. Does Buster want to take your life because you are carrying his child?"

"My bein' knocked up don't seem to bother him. It's what I know." Truman's face showed his confusion. Sadie stood and looked toward the door as if she were contemplating a run for it. "You really don't know, do you?"

Truman held up his hands in a gesture of ignorance. Sadie hurried toward the door, turned abruptly before touching the knob and walked beside the wall. "King Ivory said you knew. Said all the lawyers and people in the courthouse knew."

Truman turned back and forth in his chair as Sadie paced the perimeter of the room. "Please put me out of my misery and tell me what you are talking about, Miss Shaw."

"This a fine kettle of fish. Come to a man 'spectin' to get help and he don' know shit."

"I cannot help you until you give me some information."

"You helpin' out Gray Boy Rivers, ain't you?" Sadie's voice softened as she spoke the name. "He didn't have nothin' to do with killing Spooner."

"How do you know that?"

"'Cause I was there."

Truman caught his breath and held it as if he had captured something in his head that he could not allow to escape. "Tell me what happened."

Sadie remembered it all, but she would tell Truman only what he needed to know.

Spooner and Sadie fled as they heard the sheriff's car and saw its red light reflecting on the wet pavement. Fleet afoot, Molly Beth was out of sight in a heartbeat—probably in her room, three blocks from the square, by the time Sheriff Toy Roy Robbins arrived to find Gray Boy sitting beside his motorcycle.

Spooner knew better than to try and speed out of town. Stupid white boys just called attention to themselves by racking their loud pipes and squealing their tires as they tried to escape the wrath of Delta County's law enforcement. A block off the square, he cut his lights and pulled into the parking lot of Bartlett Hospital. He and Sadie ducked down in the seat to wait.

As the rain poured on the car roof, Spooner's snuggled position against Sadie's lithe young body seemed too good to waste. Half an hour later, Spooner tired of struggling with his long legs and his pants. The rain stopped for a few minutes, allowing him to step out of the car to put them back on. Sadie pulled up her panties and pulled down the bottom of her dress.

Spooner leaned against the car window and watched. Sadie cracked the window a few inches. "You better get back in here. Somebody sees your black-ass out there, they haul us both to the jailhouse."

Spooner opened the door and sat behind the wheel. "How was it?"

"Good. Like always."

"Always? So it still good when you do it with white men?" The familiar frustration in Spooner's voice erased Sadie's smile. Spooner almost always got like this after they made love. She kept her silence.

Spooner turned to stare at her, the single hospital parking lot light affording him little more than a shadow. "Don't ever want to answer that one, does you? Do it feel better when you get paid to do it?"

Sadie moved to her side of the seat and stared out the window. "You gon' start that shit again, just take my ass on home. I ain't puttin' up with it no more."

Spooner banged the steering wheel with both hands. "Ain't startin' no shit, just askin' questions. I got a right to know."

"Shoulda never told you nuthin'."

"Told me? Hell, ever'body in the whole damn Hollow know it. You need money that bad?"

Sadie slammed the dashboard with a fist. "You promised you wadn't ever gon' bring it up again. It ain't been more'n a month, and you startin' up with your same old shit."

"I just want to know one thing. You just answer me this one question, and I'll quit talkin' about it."

Sadie turned a wary stare toward him. "And what would that be?"

Spooner grabbed his crotch with both hands. "He got one bigger'n this?"

Sadie attacked with ten fingernails, scratching at Spooner's face and eyes. Bleeding from both cheeks, he finally wrestled her into submission. Astraddle her on the front seat, he held both hands above her head. "You quit?"

Sadie was breathing in short, rapid gasps, and her eyes darted back and forth. She struggled once more with his grip before nodding her submission. Spooner released her and sat behind the wheel again, dabbing at the blood on his cheeks.

"Damn, woman, you crazy."

"You drivin' me crazy."

"I never asked you to start lettin' a sorry-assed white man get between your legs."

"I never asked for it, neither."

They sat in silence until their heavy breathing subsided. Sadie wanted to put an end to Spooner's questions, but they always returned. They were questions she did not want to—would never—answer. If he knew that she had succumbed willingly to Buster Galt, even seduced him that first time, their life together would be over.

Clinging to a thin thread of hope that would allow her to retain some degree of respect, she had told Spooner that Buster had forced himself on her that first time. He had taken her in his own house, in his own bed, professing (truthfully) his deep desire for her young, sensuous body.

Since that first time, she had always found extra cash in the envelope with her paycheck. Buster was careful not to time the payments to coincide with sexual episodes. She needed the cash and never mentioned the payments to Buster, preferring to think of them as bonuses for the way she took care of his wife and his mother in addition to her cleaning duties.

Buster soon began to talk to her as a true lover. He confided the sexual frustrations suffered by the husband of a disabled wife. Sadie saw herself as a savior of sorts, satisfying the needs of a powerful man and thereby easing the tension in the household. That was before Mrs. Tom Galt wandered into her son's bedroom at the wrong time. The senile old woman had been subject to endless, confused babbling until that day. She never spoke again—and Buster and Sadie never lay in that bed together again.

After that day, Buster sent Rube Carter to do his dirty work, fetching Sadie to him like Ivory brought a bitch-in-heat to one of his stud dogs. The cozy bedroom in a beautiful old home changed to a dusty couch or a throw rug on the hardwood floor of the district attorney's courthouse office.

The extra cash in her paycheck envelope changed to a few wadded bills pressed into her palm after each rendezvous. Buster's tender endearments and confessions changed to the grunts and lewd exclamations associated with sexual excitement. During these moments of heightened sexual pleasure, Buster began referring to her as his nigger wench. He began to demand performances from Sadie that she considered unnatural.

Spooner's flirtations had been amusing to her at first, the harmless antics of a young boy trying so sew some wild oats in her fertile pasture. She was only a couple of years older, but thought of herself as worldly. What would this randy boy think if he knew that she was having an affair with the most powerful man in three counties—a white man—in his own bedroom—in the biggest house in town?

Sadie enjoyed Spooner's increased attention, but she continued to dismiss him as naïve and immature. The first fetch-and-deliver by Rube Carter changed things. She saw Spooner with new eyes. The tall, handsome, muscular, jocular young colored boy now compared favorably to the aging, grunting, and now-peculiar Buster Galt.

As the rain started again, Spooner cranked the car and eased out of the parking lot. "Let's go sit in our spot by the courthouse. See if Gray Boy's motorcycle there. Bet the sheriff turned him loose to go on home."

Sadie shook her head, marveling at Spooner's ability to move his brain into neat compartments. He easily closed the compartment containing his jealousy of Buster Galt and opened the easier box containing the fight with his old friend. Spooner liked only to deal with problems he could solve.

"Ain't really interested in getting' close to that courthouse." Sadie squirmed in the seat.

Spooner did not know of her courthouse meetings with Buster Galt, only about the forced-and- paid-for encounters at the Galt home, and he thought those had come to an end. "We won't be there long. Just need to see if he got throwed in jail."

The Ford's bumper pushed over weeds taller than the car as he pulled into the dark lot across from Truman Bates' office. He cut the lights and looked back toward the courthouse. Gray Boy's motorcycle was parked beside the Sheriff's reserved space.

Spooner laughed and slapped one leg. "Yep, he done throwed that boy's white-ass in jail." He turned back to stare at Sadie in the dark. "Bet you a dollar he be out any minute. Sheriff don't ever lock the door on him."

Sadie kept her gaze on the weeds draping over the car's hood and standing beside the doors like dark sentinels. "You gon' just sit here in these damn weeds till he gets out?"

Spooner laughed again. "Me and him needs to settle up 'fore he goes home."

Sadie glared at him. "How you aimin' to settle with him? Had my fill of fightin' for one night."

Spooner looked toward the motorcycle again. "Me and Gray Boy, we go back aways. We settle it without fightin' anymore. Anyway, that little peckerwood knows I can whup his ass. Just caught me by surprise, is all. Bet you we be laughin' again 'fore he goes home."

Sadie looked back toward the courthouse and shuddered. "I ain't sittin' here all night waitin' for somethin' that prob'ly ain't gon' happen."

Spooner unzipped his pants. "I got something right here

to keep you busy. Come on over here, little girl, and sit on my lap. We can watch for Gray Boy and entertain ourselves at the same time."

Sadie tried to cover her smile of pleasure. "Damn, boy, you ready again? You crazy. I ain't gon'..." She was already pulling up her skirt and pulling down her panties. "You better saddle up. You ain't ridin' bareback. You hornier'n a stud rabbit..." her words drifted away as she eased one leg over the steering wheel and across his lap.

Spooner unrolled the condom, grabbed both cheeks of her butt, and eased her down. Sadie dropped her head to his shoulder and nuzzled his neck until she felt him tense.

"What's that?"

Sadie turned her head toward the window. Heavy breathing and rain had fogged it. "You hear something?" She rubbed her palm against the car window and stared into Rube Carter's leering face.

Three loud raps of Rube's billy club against the window brought a scream to Sadie's throat. Spooner turned and saw the fat jailer's face inches from his own.

"Damn! What the hell?" He struggled to free himself, but he and Sadie were wedged tightly against the wheel. Extreme pleasure had turned to excruciating pain as they struggled to uncouple.

Rube opened the door, grabbed Sadie's arm, and pulled. The inside of her knee caught the wheel as Rube dragged her across Spooner's trapped body. When she straightened her leg to keep it from breaking, the reflexive action caused her to kick Spooner in the face. Falling in the mud was almost a relief until she looked up and saw Rube's face.

"Leave her alone, you sumbitch." Spooner heaved his legs to the ground and lunged for Rube, forgetting about his pants—they dropped to his knees—he fell forward into the mud beside Sadie. Instinctively rolling away from Rube while shucking the condom and pulling up and buttoning his jeans,

225

he was on his feet quickly. Ready to fight, he stepped toward Rube and saw the gun inches from his nose.

"Come on, pretty boy. Been wantin' to stop your clock." Rube smiled behind the gun.

Spooner stopped and looked at Sadie. She was on her feet now, clothes and body covered with mud, stems, and leaves.

Keeping his eyes and his gun trained on Spooner, Rube wiggled his billy club in Sadie's direction. "Come on over here beside me, little girl. Afraid I got to take you in."

"What the hell for?" Spooner shouted.

"You best keep your mouth shut, boy. This ain't none of your business. Just be glad I ain't arrestin' you, too. Pull your pockets inside out and be quick about it. Got to check for weapons."

Spooner complied, withdrawing a pocketknife, two condoms, and some change. Rube nodded toward the Case bone-handle knife. "That's pretty. Hand that over here to the girl."

Spooner handed the knife to Sadie. "What's she done bad enough to be arrested for?" He tried to calm his anger and fear enough to bring humility back to his voice.

"I could name several things if I was amind to, but you're too damn ignert to understand the law, boy. We'll just call it whorin' for your ignert ass." Rube put his arm around Sadie, pressed the billy club against her throat, and began walking backwards away from Spooner.

"Don't let him take me, Spooner." Sadie's words were throaty, ominous.

"Shut your mouth, wench. You'll be wakin' decent people that live around here—bad enough you doing the nasty right in their back yards. You put that pocket knife in my pants pocket."

Rube turned sideways and smiled at her as she dropped the knife into his pocket. Closer to the courthouse, he walked faster, half dragging Sadie along with him. Spooner watched helplessly, his fists clenched, his muscles frozen, his mind racing.

As Rube and Sadie reached the first courthouse step, Sadie broke free, screaming at Spooner. "Get help. He takin' me to Buster."

The flying billy club caught her on the anklebone and dropped her to the ground. Rube smiled as he saw her fall. Throwing that club was the only physical thing his fat body allowed him to do well. Rube slapped her hard against the buttocks with the club as she rose and meekly followed him up the courthouse steps.

Their steps echoed through the deserted courthouse as they walked through the large foyer and toward the stairway. The familiar sound of Rube's billy club and keys banging against the stair railing combined with his heavy panting.

Sadie knew the drill, but she sensed something different tonight. *Maybe it's the smell.* The familiar odor of Pine-Sol, musty books, mildew, and stale urine seemed stronger tonight. *Maybe the rain is causing it. The man usually stinks of sweat, but he smells putrid tonight. No, it's not just the smell. It's somethin' else.* She swallowed hard to keep from gagging.

They reached the third floor landing, and Sadie reached for the door. Rube shoved her forward. "Not here, girlie."

"Why not? We always meet on the third floor." Sadie's trembling voice told that she knew the answer to her own question.

Rube paused in front of the locked stairwell door that led to the top-floor jail and swung one of his three key ring chains forward. He turned toward Sadie and moved the chain in suggestive swings across his pelvis. She looked back down the stairs.

"Don't even think about it, wench." He pulled the billy club with one swift motion. "This little baby will drop you before you're down a flight." Usually clumsy, he opened the door with precise, almost agile, movements. He bowed and indicated the dark stairway with both arms. "After you."

Sadie entered the pitch-black stairway and listened as Rube turned the key to lock it behind him. She was trapped. "Mr. Galt ain't gonna like the way you treatin' me."

Rube pushed her against the wall and pressed his body against hers. "Well, now, we ain't ever gonna find out what Mr. Galt thinks about this, girlie. 'Cause we both gonna keep it a secret." He shoved the club against her throat. "Ain't that right?"

Sadie nodded as he released the club. He pointed toward what she assumed was the stairway leading to the jail. "Now git on up there."

"Can't see a damn thing."

"Don't need to. Just reach out and touch the walls and feel with your feet. You fall, I'll catch you."

Sadie imagined the leer that must be on Rube's face. She took her time with each step, trying to buy time to think— time to find a way out of this—time to keep from falling backward into the embrace of this vile, repugnant man.

20 "Could I have another Dr Pepper?" Sadie's throat was dry from reliving her personal nightmare. Truman, impatient to learn what Spooner had been doing while she was dragged up the courthouse stairs, sprinted from the refrigerator with another Dr Pepper.

Spooner's mind raced as he watched Sadie being forced into the courthouse. He needed help, but he knew that help was not coming. There was no time to get Ivory, even if he could get home on the muddy roads. The sheriff's car was gone, and he had no idea how to contact him. Gray Boy's motorcycle was still there. Gray would help him if he could just get up to the jail. Gray's cell would probably be open. How would he get to the top of the courthouse? Gray Boy had told him the stairs going to the jail were always locked.

There was a phone booth on the Piggly Wiggly parking lot across from the courthouse, but he did not know anyone who had a phone. The rain was soaking him—making him cold. He scaled the courthouse walls with his gaze, but saw no way to climb them. The tree on the front lawn had limbs that almost reached the courthouse, but they would not hold his weight. He thought of breaking a window, but which one?

He did not even know which floor Sadie was on. Still, he had to do something. He had to get closer to Sadie, and he had to get out of the rain, now coming down hard.

He ran to the courthouse and walked down into the sheltered basement walkway. Being out of the rain lessened his sense of panic. He was at least closer to Sadie. Maybe she would cry out. Maybe he could shout for her, and she would answer. No, the fat jailer would hear his shout—and he had a gun.

A movement in the shadows startled him. As his eyes adjusted to the deeper darkness of the basement walkway, he recognized the outline of a person. The stooped, jerky movements of Bo Creekwater brought a sense of relief.

"Bo. What are you doing down here?"

"Thet you Pooner, uh huh?"

"Hell, yes, it's me. What are you doing down here in the dark and wet? "

"Waitin' on Toy Roy, uh huh."

"Why you waitin' on the sheriff?"

"Sleep in da' jail tonight, uh huh."

"Jail? When you got a nice warm bed at yo' grandma's?"

"She sick, uh huh."

"When the sheriff comin?"

"He 'posed to take me ridin' 'fore bedtime, uh huh."

"'Fore bedtime? You know what time it is?"

"Uh huh." Bo pulled his pocket watch out of his pocket by its fob and started toward the light from the street lamp.

Spooner pulled him back. "Never mind. I know what time it is. Get back out of the rain, dipstick. Still dumber'n dirt." Spooner regretted the words as soon as he spoke them. It had been almost six months since he had seen his old playmate. "We need to go huntin' again, soon's this rain stops. Maybe the coons will come back after this here rain. Right, Bo?"

Bo nodded eagerly. Hunting was the one thing he did

better than Spooner—or anyone else. "Uh huh." Folks said
he could track a piss-ant up a mountain, down the other side,
and bring it back dead or alive.

"Listen, Bo, we're wasting time. You see that fat jailer
taking Sadie into the courthouse?"

"Uh huh."

"Know where they went?"

"In the courthouse, uh huh."

"Shit, Bo, where in the courthouse?"

"Bo can find 'em, uh huh."

They took the basement stairway to the first floor,
Spooner gently hurrying Bo's clumsy steps. In the deserted
first floor foyer, Bo's hunting persona captured his body. His
stooped frame straightened as he pointed to the wet steps
leading up the stairs. They followed them to the third floor.

Spooner tried the door to the fourth floor stairwell.
"Damn."

From his large key ring, Bo felt for a key in the dark. He
opened the door on the first try. Spooner patted him on the
back and put a finger to his lips. "Shhhh."

After Bo stumbled on the first two steps, Spooner held
him by the shoulders, their combined bodies squeezed against
the walls of the narrow stairway. Spooner turned the doorknob at the top of the stairs and found it locked. He turned
toward Bo without speaking. Bo opened the door on the
first try again.

Spooner lay down on the small landing beside the door,
eased it open, and listened. Nothing. He pushed the door
a little farther. The squeak echoed down the stairs. Light
poured from the jailer's office into the hallway in front of
him. He could not see all of the office, but it appeared to be
empty.

Bo punched the middle of Spooner's back with a stubby
finger. "Listen, uh huh."

Hearing nothing, Spooner turned to see what Bo heard.

A single finger pointed upward. Irritated, Spooner whispered, "What?"

"Stopped raining, uh huh. They outside, uh huh."

Spooner knew better than to doubt Bo's instincts. He eased to his feet, walked through the door, and peered into Rube's office. It was empty.

"This my bed, uh huh." Bo's whisper startled him. He had pushed open the door to the first cell and was sitting on the cot.

Spooner looked down the hall at the row of cells. He had not even given thought to possible prisoners other than Gray Boy. He eased past three empty cells until he saw him.

"Gray Boy," he whispered. No response. *Out cold. Useless.* His plan evaporated as he rattled the cell door, trying to awaken his friend. The door was locked. Without help from Gray Boy, he had no idea how to rescue Sadie from a man carrying a gun and a club. He looked back at Bo, sitting on the cot, staring at the wall. He kneeled to be closer to Gray's head and whispered his name again, louder this time. When he shook the edge of the cot, a small round object rolled against the cell door. A baseball.

Spooner tried to pull it between the cell bars, but it was too big. Using his long fingers, he eased the ball along the bars to the larger, pass-through hole above the lock and pulled it through. It was not a weapon, but it was all he had. Rocks or baseballs, he knew how to throw. The baseball might be just enough to distract the fat jailer.

He turned back toward Bo, intending to tell him to stay put. Bo was still sitting on the cot, facing the wall. *Probably in one of his trances.* Spooner stepped past the other cells, relieved to find them empty.

As the outside door closed behind Spooner, Bo left his cell and followed. Surprised to see his old friend lying in the floor, he stopped at Gray Boy's cell, peered inside, and returned to the jailer's office for the keys to Gray's cell door.

Light rain began falling again as Spooner stepped outside. He held the baseball like a weapon as he searched the walkway for signs of Rube or Sadie. Nothing. He wished for Bo's hearing and nighttime eyesight, but he was too unpredictable—could get them both killed if he got in the way. He eased along the inside perimeter of the walkway until he heard the sounds. Muffled cries—Sadie. A huge cardboard box, a picture of a water-cooled window fan on its side, completely blocked the walkway. The cries were coming from inside the box.

Spooner reached for his pocketknife to cut the box open, forgetting that Rube had taken it from him. Even if the box held his weight, Rube would likely hear him if he tried to crawl over. He had to get to the open end so that he could rush Rube. As he turned to circle the building, Sadie cried out again. There was no time to circle the entire courthouse walkway.

He felt the rough concrete of the narrow outside wall. The top ledge formed an inverted V—hard to balance enough to walk standing up. He stuck the baseball into his back pocket and jumped enough to sling his left leg over the narrow outside wall. He rose on all fours, intending to crawl past the box and surprise Rube on the other side.

The rain had turned years of accumulated tree and bird droppings into slime. Spooner's feet slipped on the wetness as he straddled the wall, causing his crotch to slam against the wall's sharp contours. The baseball shot over the wall like it had been projected from a slingshot.

Spooner, stifling a scream, felt as if he had mounted a razor blade. Hearing another muffled cry from Sadie, he decided to right himself and walk the wall like a tightrope. In dry weather, it would have been almost easy for Spooner.

He balanced his feet sideways on the narrow surface and took two steps. Confidence growing, he reached out for the third step. Because of the rain and thunder, he did not hear the whistling sound the billy club made as it spun in the air toward his ankles. He heard the sharp crack the wood made as it struck home—felt the pain. He screamed as he went over the edge and screamed again as his neck struck the first limb. He felt nothing when he slammed into the dog wallow. He did not hear the hollow sound of the billy club falling back against the cardboard box or the clattering sound of wood against concrete as it rolled off the box, fell onto the walkway, and landed at Rube Carter's feet.

Sadie stopped her squirming when she heard Spooner cry. She shuddered and tried to scream as she heard the shuffling footsteps, the grunting as Rube Carter bent over to pick up his stick. "Came right back to Daddy, didn't you Billy Boy?" He walked over and stared at Spooner's limp body under the streetlight. "Hurt yourself, bad, didn't you, boy?"

Bo Creekwater heard Spooner's cry, too. He watched until Rube Carter had picked up his billy club, then eased the door quietly closed.

With Spooner's knife, Rube cut around the edges of the cardboard box and pulled back the side. Sadie lay on the floor of the box, her hands tied behind her back, her panties stuffed into her mouth. The now-familiar snuff-and-spoiled-fish smell of Rube Carter's breath drifted past her ear to her nose. "I'll pull these drawers out of your mouth; you promise to behave."

Sadie's eyes were wild. She could not summon the courage to nod. She finally managed a shrill, muffled sound as she struggled against the cuffs that held her hands behind her back. A small rope connected the cuffs to her feet.

Rube chuckled. "Buckin' like a calf about to lose his balls. Whassa matta, lil'girl? You ain't got no balls to lose." He pulled the panties out of her mouth and smiled, revealing his tobacco-stained teeth.

His expression changed as he placed Spooner's knife against her throat. "You got two choices, Missie. Want to join your boyfriend down there in that mud puddle?"

Sadie shook her head.

"I can throw you over the edge right now, you know. Lovers quarrel or somethin' like that." He eased the panties out of her mouth. "Or you can come visit me like you do Buster."

Sadie's eyes showed her fear and revulsion.

Rube's voice became almost a whimper. "Not as often, of course. Just once in a while. I don't need much."

Sadie nodded. "Untie me."

"You say anything, anything atall, to anybody, I swear I'll tell everybody about you and Buster." Rube grunted as he stood up. "Then I'll cut your damn throat. Ain't nobody gon' take the word of a nigger whore against a white police officer, anyways. You know that, don't ya?"

"I do. How do I get out of here?"

Truman was starting a Dr Pepper of his own as Sadie finished her second one. "How do you know how Spooner found you?"

Sadie put her bottle down on the desk. "I found Bo moanin' over Spooner's body when I left the courthouse to run home. Bo likes me—told me everything. His grandma and mine were friends. 'Sides, he ain't as stupid as people think."

Truman took off his glasses and rubbed the bridge of his nose. "One thing troubles me. How can you say for certain that Rube caused Spooner to fall? You say you were tied in the cardboard box."

"That cardboard box was wet from rain. Easy to get my feet under it, then my head. I saw him throw that billy club, all right. Saw Spooner fall over the side. Bo saw the whole thing, too."

Truman stared over Sadie's head as he contemplated the

next question. "Did Rube rape you?"

Sadie stood and leaned over the desk, voice raspy and angry. "Rape? All that fat hog done was waller and grunt on top of me, tryin' to do somethin' he couldn't get done. He heard Bo's voice before he could really pester me. That just gave him an excuse to walk around the jail and come up behind Spooner."

Truman's face colored. "Has he bothered you since that night?"

Sadie sat back in her chair and shook her head. "Ain't him that bothers me so much. It's Buster Galt."

"I think we should discuss this with the sheriff. Perhaps get you some protection."

Sadie's features contorted. "Please don' do that. I needs that paycheck. Safest place I can be is at the Galts. I sleep downstairs close to Buster's wife and mama when I stays overnight. He don't dare say nothin' to me as long as them two needs me."

"Well, then why did you come to me for help?"

"I don't wants to go up to the courthouse ever again. Don't wants Mr. Buster to ever send that pig to fetch me like a bitch dog."

"I think we can take care of Mr. Rube Carter, but I must warn you that Buster will probably be caught up in the same net. Your affair is bound to come out."

Sadie twisted the ends of her hair. "Thinks I can still keep my job with Miz Galt? I wants to keep this baby, but I gon' need some help—money, I mean."

"I can't guarantee anything, Miss Shaw, but I will do what I can to get support and protection for yourself and your unborn child."

Sadie sat up a little straighter and managed to smile at Truman.

Truman leaned forward and put one hand over the other on his desk. "Forgive me, but I have to ask this. Why did you not seek help for Spooner?"

Sadie's eyes widened with indignation. "What I gon' do, run back in the courthouse and get the law? Maybe tell the district attorney or the deputy sheriff? They the ones done killed him."

"Yes, but how did you know he was already dead when you came out of the courthouse?"

"I ran out to check on Spooner right away. Found Bo bawlin' over his body. Grabbed me and wouldn't let go. I listened as long as I could about how he had helped Spooner, but I needed to get out of there. Offered to take him to his grandma's, but he said he couldn't leave his brother. Kept saying Spooner was his brother."

Truman leaned back and put his hands behind his head. Information about the brothers was intriguing—filled with power. It was not new to him, of course. It had been more than ten years, but the trip was as clear in his mind as if it had been yesterday. He had kept the results of his investigation secret for over a decade, even from the client who had hired him to go to New Orleans in search of his wife. Now he wondered if he had made a mistake by keeping that secret.

Truman chanced a glance at the swarthy man sitting beside him in the family Buick. His mother would probably never ride on that seat again if she could see the passenger now sitting in her usual spot. Charlie Freeze looked nondescript in his overalls—skin the color and texture of tobacco leaf, high cheekbones, bluish bags under his black eyes, sunken cheeks.

Truman had politely requested that the man not smoke inside the car, but he had either forgotten or ignored the request. He was not exactly smoking so much as he was making love to his cigarette. Truman stole glimpses out of the corners of his burning eyes as Charlie pushed and pulled the wet cigarette out of his mouth. He used his tongue, not his fingers, to do the pushing and pulling. It brought to mind a child sucking on a peppermint stick. With each pull and push of the cigarette, smoke emerged from the man's nose and mouth. Truman expected it to start coming out his eyes and ears with each push.

"Are we finally on the right street, Mr. Freeze?" Truman had guided the Buick along the back streets of Bossier City, Louisiana, for almost an hour. Archie Freeze was trying to get him lost, but Truman prided himself on his sense of direction. They had been going in small squares through back streets and alleys.

The circuitous route was obvious, and Truman's patience was growing thin as the quality of the neighborhoods gradually declined from lower income to high crime. He took a deep breath and told himself to be calm. After all, he had followed the cold trail left by Ivory's wife all the way from New Orleans. A few minutes more were not going to spoil his victory. If only God had given him fearlessness and brawn to accompany his gift for detective work.

Archie answered his question by pointing a skinny arm toward a small shack at the end of the gravel path that was marked as a street. Apparently, Bossier City's funds for paving had expired a few blocks away from this neighborhood. Truman parked the Buick several yards short of the house.

It looked pretty much like most of the other houses around it. Enough paint remained to tell that the house had once been green with yellow shutters. The shutters hung askance; the front door, veneer peeling off in strips, was cracked a few inches. Windows were open to let in some air—or let the hot air out.

Truman turned toward his passenger. "Are you sure this is where she is?"

The man looked at Truman as if he had been insulted. Truman nodded, pulled off his eyeglasses and replaced them with dark shades. He pulled the brim of his hat down as low as he could without bending his ears and put his hand on the door handle. "Shall we?"

Archie Freeze shook his head. "Don' need me for this. I got no truck with that woman."

"But how can I be sure that this is the woman I am seeking?"

"You lookin' for King Ivory Hays' woman. Knew her then; knows her now. She right inside that door."

Truman slipped the keys from the ignition and put both hands on the steering wheel. "Will you still be here when I get back? I may have some more questions."

"I'll wait one hour under that tree over there. No more."

Truman kept a hand on the brim of his hat to partially shield his face as he walked across the street and up the gravel path that led to the front door. There was no porch, just a small wooden step that the ground was reclaiming, one side at a time. Truman stepped on the uneven board and knocked politely on the partially open door. No response. He knocked a little louder.

The unmistakable sound of a woman's voice answered the louder knock. No words, just a little moan. Truman waited a respectable length of time for someone to come to the door. He turned to look at Archie, who was waving both hands in a shoving motion, urging him to go inside.

When the door did not respond to a polite push, Truman put his shoulder against it and shoved. The warped door slid across the worn linoleum a few inches. Many forced openings had scraped an arc-trail across the floor covering and through the wood underneath. Truman shoved it back enough to slide in. He removed his shades and waited for his eyes to adjust to the darkness.

"Anybody home?" His voice reflected his nervousness.

"Whaddaya want?" The feminine moan had turned coarser—young vocal cords burned from smoke.

239

Truman, eyes adjusted, followed the voice. He found her in the living room, curled up on a small couch, watching snow on a small rabbit-eared television. There was just enough sound to recognize organ music from a daytime soap-opera. "Mrs. Hays?"

The woman flinched at the sound, but was slow to come out of her fetal curl. "Ain't nobody here by that name. Wrong house, Mister."

Truman removed his hat and looked for a place to sit. The only chair in the room was covered in clothes. With his finger and thumb, he moved a pair of panties and sat on the edge of the chair. "No need to be frightened, Mrs. Hays. I am here to take you home. Ivory sent me."

The woman rose to a sitting position on the couch, drew her legs to her chest, and wrapped her arms around them. Truman felt his face warm as he turned his head slightly to keep from staring at the shadow between her legs.

"Don' call me by that name. It too early for customers, but I can make an exception. After I pleasure you, you be on your way."

The girl's voice was becoming normal now, recovering from sleep. It sounded familiar. Truman removed his eye-glasses from his coat pocket and slipped them on. He studied the girl's face. Her youthful beauty was well hidden underneath red-streaked eyes lined with yesterday's mascara. Her once perky mouth had turned down, and lines had formed around little firm pouches at each end, as if she had shaped muscles trying to hold up the corners.

Yes, she was well hidden, but Truman's mind cleared away the years of misery and abuse as he recognized her. "Why, Susie Blandon. You were barely out of your teens the last time I saw you."

"You all mixed up with your names, ain't you, Mister? First, I be Hays, now I be Blandon. My name is Susie Waters."

"I'm sorry, Susie, but I never forget a face or a voice. I would know you anywhere. You left Delta County when Bo was just a baby. Apparently, Mr. Archie Freeze has made a mistake. He knew I was from Delta County, so he found me a Delta County girl. I'll bet the scoundrel has already left. " Truman stood and turned toward the door.

As he eased himself sideways through the door opening, he heard the girl's voice, but could not understand her. He stepped back into the living room. "Excuse me."

"I said ain't no mistake been made. Don't go jumping on Archie Freeze, else he be jumping on me. S'pose you paid him to find me."

"I did."

"All right. You found me. What you want?"

"I don't quite understand."

"How many ways I got to say it? I am who you think I am. I be King Ivory's wife, too."

Truman, stunned, eased farther into the room. "Ivory asked me to bring you back."

"Ain't goin' back."

Truman sat back down on the corner of the chair and studied the ragged edges of the rug under his feet and the slivers of dried mud embedded in its fibers. "Are you Spooner's mother?"

Susie's eyes drew tight and slanted as she looked away and stared at the wall. "He hurt or anything?"

"No. Spooner is a fine, handsome boy. Wouldn't you like to come home to Delta County and see him?"

She looked at him as if he had taken leave of his senses. "How 'bout you jus' bring him down here to see his mama. Don't you think he'd be proud?"

"What about Bo? Are you curious about Bo?"

Tears streamed. "He been a terrible burden to my mama?"

"Beulah is a survivor. Bo is a fine hunter, like his father."

"Still ain't goin' back."

"I suppose it would be awkward to take you back to face two husbands and two sons. Does either husband know that you married them both?"

"Awkward?" Susie smirked. "Awkward, my ass. Hell, Mr. Bates, Chock and Ivory would fight over who got to kill me."

Truman felt the familiar warm surge of power and guilt when Susie recalled his name. Her story was information best kept in his growing storehouse of knowledge. He would file it away in a neat compartment for possible future use. The greater good would be served by not telling anyone, even his client, about Susie Blandon-Creekwater-Hays. He would, of course, tell his client the truth—that his wife was a whore— possibly a diseased one, but not the whole truth.

21 It was twilight when Rance unsaddled Scar at home. He rubbed the horse's back dry with a ragged saddle blanket and shucked a few corncobs for him before walking to the house.

"How did he do?" Jake's voice startled him. Rance had not seen him sitting in the dark side yard.

"How did who do?"

"Scar."

Rance grabbed the back of Jake's neck and squeezed lightly. "About as good as any young horse I ever rode. Looks like you inherited your grandfather's touch with the reins."

The gelding had been a mess when Rance brought him home from a cow sale for Jake's birthday—dull coat, hide cut by kicking hooves, eyes wild and frightened. Scar was head-shy, too, and spooked at any movement or sound. Gray Boy wanted to name him Spook, but Jake insisted on Scar, after Doc Sixgun's horse on his favorite radio program.

Following his father's instructions, Jake had patiently groomed him, rubbing every part of his body, lifting each foot twice a day for a month. Finally, he was allowed to mount him in the deserted cow lot by the dairy barn. His father and grandfather supervised his rides in the lot until the horse and Jake seemed ready to venture out of its confines.

The simple sentence that echoed in Jake's ears, *You inherited your grandfather's touch*, was adequate reward for his efforts.

"Shy's acting funny today, Daddy. Won't come out of his house. Been in there since dinner. He never does that in the daytime. You think he's sick?"

Rance peeked in the doghouse. Only the tip of Shy's nose protruded from the door. He glanced toward the southwest horizon, looking for signs of the storm that Scar and Peanut had seemed to sense. The sky was a smoky gray, as if a fire was smoldering somewhere. The air was still and heavy with moisture. Rance, a man who did not sweat easily, felt a bead of sweat run down his spine.

"Shy knows a storm is comin'. Maybe a cyclone."

Lightning danced around the horizon at dark, circling them like torches carried by an approaching army. After supper, Mattie walked around the house, searching the sky for answers. "Could be heat lightning. I don't hear any thunder. The clouds are not moving." Always frightened by bad weather, Mattie hugged herself and stared at Rance as if she expected some type of weather forecast from him.

Rance stood on the porch and scanned the southwest sky again. "Storm usually comes from that direction this time of year. This one seems to be comin' from all directions. Better check out the storm house."

He lifted the door to the back yard storm cellar and entered. Mattie saw the flash from his Zippo lighter, then the distinctive glow from a lantern creeping up the steps of the cellar. Rance followed his shadow up the cellar steps. "I'll just leave that lamp burnin', just in case—plenty of oil in it. I'll put it out at bedtime if the storm hasn't hit by then."

The lamp was out, and everyone except Mattie had been asleep for hours when she heard the house creaking and popping. She got out of bed and checked on her sons before scurrying to the windows, staring into the blackness for some sign of the danger she felt.

Rance was reluctant to get out of bed, and she met stiff resistance from Gray Boy. Even Jake protested, arguing that the danger from spiders and snakes in the cellar scared him much more than the storm. He protested when she started to close the front door and cut off the welcome breeze that brought an end to the heavy stillness that had made sleep difficult. Jake liked storms, but he knew this one was different when the wind surged against the door and pushed his mother back.

The wind entered the house like a hungry lion, ripping the sheets from his bed and carrying them down the dog-run. Speeding droplets of rain caught up in the wind gusts stung him as he helped his mother to close the door.

Rance had closed the other windows and roused Gray Boy when they returned to the kitchen. Lightning or wind had taken the electricity, so Mattie lighted a coal-oil lamp and set it on the kitchen table. She argued for going to the storm cellar, but Rance protested that the wind was too high to open the cellar door without getting it blown from its hinges. Mattie lost the argument, three to one. The boys wanted to return to bed, but Mattie wanted them all in the kitchen, as if she could hold their hands and keep the storm from blowing them away.

For more than an hour, the wind roared over, around, and through the house, shaking the dishes on their shelves, rattling pots and pans, and slamming the lightning rods against the roof and corners of the house. They felt as if they were onboard a charging locomotive without an engineer. Something outside seemed to be sucking all the air out of the house. When the heavy rain began slamming against the house with each gust, the roar of the wind lessened slightly, and they nervously joked about getting off the train and onto a leaky ship.

The air returned as they placed pots and pans under all the leaks. When the rain slowed enough for him to walk outside at just past daylight, Rance found eight inches in the rain gauge. "Gray, you need to get crackin'. No tellin' what kind of damage we got."

Mattie turned from the skillet of bacon she was frying. "You goin' to work early on a day like this? Shouldn't you check to see what damage we have around here first?"

"Already did. Papa's house and barn are still standin', and so are ours. Looks like we missed the brunt of it, but I'll bet there is some serious damage close by. That roaring noise sounded like a cyclone."

Rance and Gray arrived at the county barn at hour early. Their short drive had proven Rance right. Trees and power lines were down; remnants of houses and barns were scattered along highway 24. The north windows had blown out of the county barn. Rance and Gray were cleaning up the mess when they heard a horn honking in front.

Dad Flanagan walked in the barn before they could investigate the honking. His nasal voice sounded hollow in the windowless barn. "Willie Mae Gentry is across the street at the store. Says Hack left at daybreak to ride Peanut down to the Blue Bottom. She's worried he ain't already back."

Rance dropped the lug wrench he had been using to clean the shards of broken glass from a window. "Damn. He went down there to close that gate—worried about his cows getting caught along the creek and drowning." Rance spoke the last sentence to himself, leaving Jake and Dad behind as he ran toward Willie Mae's '48 Chevrolet.

"What time did he leave?" Rance put his hands on the cab above Willie Mae.

The lines in Willie Mae's face seemed deeper today. "Daybreak. I tried to make him wait, but he's afraid the rain isn't over."

"Ridin' Peanut?"

Willie Mae smiled. "Of course. He thinks that little horse can climb the highest mountain, swim the deepest ocean."

Rance sighed. "That's pretty much right. Never saw
a better bottomland horse than Peanut. He'll take care of
Hack. Tell you what—I'll follow you home—if he's not back,
I'll saddle Jake's horse and see if I can go help him. Probably
decided to work on that old pump while he was down there
and needs my help, anyway."

Hack was not there when Rance followed Willie Mae into
their driveway. He knew that it was too early to worry much
yet, but he also knew that Blue Bottom Creek had to be out
of its banks and running fast. It was already too late to reach
Hack by car or truck. After asking Willie Mae to drive over
and tell him if Hack returned within the next hour, he left to
get his horse ready.

When forty-five minutes had passed, Rance and Griffin
had saddled their horses, tied on extra ropes, and were ready
to go. Rance reheated the morning's coffee, and they stood
on the porch, nervously sipping the bitter brew, watching for
Willie Mae's car.

The distant roar of running creek water, seldom heard at
the house, was nerve-wracking. When an hour had passed
without sign of Willie Mae, they loaded Scar and Buddy and
headed for Dogtown Road.

They parked where the pavement ended, unloaded the
horses, and rode southeast in silence. Within a few minutes,
they could hear the roar of floodwaters again. The raging
current was shaking trees as it sped toward the Sulphur River.
When they reached the edge of the railway bed, the horses were
knee deep in water. They pushed the nervous horses up to the
rails and stopped.

The land they had once farmed, explored, and hunted
was now a lake. A charging current, carrying small trees in
its wake, had replaced the lazy, meandering stream that had
been Blue Bottom Creek. "If the water wasn't moving so fast,
I'd say we had ridden all the way to the Gulf Coast and were
staring at the ocean." Griffin uttered his first words since

mounting Buddy.

Rance shifted in the saddle. "Never seen it like this before. You?"

"Nope. Well, talkin' about it ain't gonna find Hack. Looks like the only chance we got is to follow the rail bed." Griffin pointed Buddy down the railroad tracks.

"What about the trestle? The horses won't cross it."

"Maybe we'll see him before we get that far. That gate he aimed to close is right on the other side of Piss Elm Crossing, and we can see the bridge from this side of the trestle." Griffin shouted without turning his head or slowing his horse.

Rance eased Jake's nervous little gelding along the bank of the rail bed, trying to avoid the rails and the crossties that held them. When Scar started losing his footing as the bank gave way under his hooves, he scrambled across one rail and walked between them on the crossties and rocks. "Well, boy, you're smarter than I thought."

Piss Elm Crossing came into view just before they reached the trestle. Only the banisters of the old wooden bridge were visible, and they were struggling against the current. Guy wires extended from each corner of the bridge to the four giant elm trees that gave the crossing its name. Griffin shook his head in wonder. "Always thought those wires were a waste of time and money till today."

"We have to think like Hack. The gate he wanted to close is under a lot of water. What would he have done in these conditions?" Rance scanned the water and area for signs of Hack or Peanut.

"Probably wasn't this bad when he got here. If it rained a lot more upstream, that water might not have gotten here until up in the morning. If it was up, he would have tried to get out the way we came in—or turned around and gone home the way he came."

Rance pulled and released Scar's reins to hold him still.

"Water had to be up some, but probably just enough to allow Peanut to swim it. If he saw cattle stranded down there, Hack would have tried to move them back to the top of the hill. I've seen him swim Peanut across some pretty swollen waters before."

Griffin nodded as he removed his hat. He wiped the sweatband with the end of his wild rag. "He's probably stranded, but safe, up on Hurt Hill."

Rance breathed a sigh of relief. "That's what I think. He's up there thinking what kind of hell I'm gonna give him for doing something this stupid."

Griffin chuckled. "If he's up there, we can't reach him. He'll be there till this water goes down."

Rance smiled as he stepped off Scar. "Whatever sandwich he packed is gonna be too wet to eat. He won't starve, but he's likely to get mighty hungry before he can ride, or even swim, out. Even old Peanut won't buck this current."

Griffin reached for his Bull Durham sack. "At least he can stay dry in that old shack up there."

Rance handed Scar's reins to his father and walked toward the trestle. "Before we go back, guess I'll climb up on those banisters and see if I can see anything." He put a slippery foot into the railings and climbed to the top of the trestle banister. The top ledge was wide enough to stand on.

When he gained his balance, he cupped his hands over his mouth and shouted Hack's name several times. The roar of the current was his only answer. Shrugging in Griffin's direction, he knelt to get a handhold before climbing back down. Straddling the top ledge, he paused to sweep the creek and bridge once more.

"Papa, you see that? Looks like a set of horns."

Griffin stood in his saddle and followed Rance's instructions until he also spotted the horns. " I see her now, she's right at the water's edge. That's got to be his bell cow, don't you think?"

"It's definitely Bell. Looks like she drowned. Calf too,

probably." Rance scanned the bank in front and behind the dead cow, searching for any sign, other than stupidity, that might tell why the cow drowned. A few feet away and just above the cow's horns, he saw a movement in the dark shade. He rubbed his eyes, trying to coax more distance from them. He grabbed the banister's ledge with both hands as weakness overwhelmed him. "Damn. That's Peanut." The words escaped as a whisper.

Peanut seemed his usual calm self as he stood belly deep in the water. He was high enough on the trail to Hurt Hill to avoid being swept along by the harsh current, but still in danger from a sudden rise in the boiling turbulence or from mud giving way under his feet. Rance glanced at his father and knew at once that he had seen the horse, too. Head bowed, Griffin was easing down into his saddle.

Rance climbed down from the trestle on shaky legs. Griffin had already uncoiled a part of his rope and was tying a slipknot around his waist. Rance put his hand on the saddle's pommel. "What do you think you're doing?"

Griffin indicated Peanut's location with a head gesture. "You know as well as I do that Hack goes where that horse takes him. I hate to say it, but he may be right over there by him. If he is, we can't wait for the coyotes or the turtles to get him."

Rance slapped the saddle skirt. "I'll just camp here until the water goes down. You go back to the house and bring back a rifle. Flooding brings out the anger in a lot of critters, including snakes. No way to reach him now without getting ourselves killed."

Griffin patted the rifle scabbard on the other side of Buddy. "No need to go for a rifle, I brought one. I think I saw a rope bobbing in and out of that water by the cow. It ain't likely, I admit, but Hack could be tangled up in it and still alive. We got to try. Now."

Rance silently chided himself for not considering the

possibility that Hack could still be alive and needing help. "You're right. Maybe I can let the current carry me close enough to grab hold of something. You ain't going in that water." He loosened the rope on Scar's saddle and started tying it around his waist. "Course, if Hack is over there, I don't know how we can get him back to this side."

Griffin rode closer to him. "The main thing is to see if he's tangled up and needs help. Could be passed out and not drowned."

Rance nodded as he completed the knot around his waist. "Let's not go off half-cocked. Buddy's got a lot better chance of swimming that creek than either one of us does, so I need to hold onto him and let him swim us across. You hold onto the rope in case I lose my grip on the horn."

Griffin dismounted, removed his rifle from its saddle scabbard, and leaned it against the trestle banister. He tied his two ropes together and nodded toward the rail trestle. "Before you go, take that rope off your waist for a minute and walk across that banister. I'd feel better if you tied one end of the rope to something that ain't going to move just in case I can't hold on to you. I ain't as young as I used to be, and I'd hate to live knowin' I let you drown."

Rance nodded. "That's a good idea. We'll tie the two ropes to that end and the single rope to this end. If it looks like I can't handle the current, we'll let the short rope stop me and you can pull me ashore. If it looks like Buddy and I can handle it, you untie or cut it. The long rope should let me get all the way to Peanut."

Rance eased across the trestle. As he pulled the knot tight at the other side, he heard the sounds of Buddy's shoes clashing with the rocks on the rail bed embankment.

Griffin shouted and waved at him at the water's edge. "Hurry up and get back over to this side. Be ready to cut that rope."

"What the hell do you think you're doing, Papa?" The

question went unanswered as Griffin eased Buddy into the water, slipped out of the saddle and held onto the horn as Buddy swam and allowed the current to carry them along. Rance barely made it across the trestle in time to untie the knot. He held the rope as it slipped away, letting it burn his hands as punishment for allowing his father to go into that water. As the end of the rope slipped away from his palm, he felt his father's life leaving with the rope.

He ran to the other side and picked up the second rope. Griffin had forgotten to remove his hat, and it was the only thing Rance could see above the water. When it stayed beside Buddy as they swiftly moved toward Piss Elm Bridge, he knew it was still on Griffin's head. He watched the agile old man cross over the horse and guide him toward the opposite bank. Buddy struggled to follow his master's instructions.

When Griffin and his horse went out of sight, Rance felt the rope grow tight, then slack. He climbed the banister again for a better look. He wanted to shout and clap when he saw Buddy leave the water and sink to his knees in mud as he climbed the opposite bank toward Peanut. Griffin held on to the horse's tail and allowed Buddy to pull him up.

Griffin saw what he expected to see, but still groaned as he stared at the murky water lapping inches above Hack's gray face. The muddy current and the trash that came with it had already done serious damage to Hack's body. From the looks of things, he had been dead for a few hours. Griffin had figured that something besides loyalty and good training had kept Peanut standing in belly-deep water in a trance-like state.

He patted the small horse's head and rubbed his muzzle. "Easy boy." He ran his hand down Peanut's front leg until the horse squealed in protest. The horse was standing on three legs. Griffin dismissed the two wide, dark trails running from Peanut's side to his belly as mud until he discovered the two punctures. Bell had stuck him with both horns.

He traced the rope from the saddle horn to Hack's neck,

gently uncurling the unintended loop it had made around his throat. He followed the rope all the way to Bell's horns. Too impatient to wrestle with the wet, tight rope, Griffin cut it.

He stood and breathed deeply as he coiled the rope, glad that Rance was too far away to see what had happened to his friend. The scene reminded him of a Charlie Russell painting on an old calendar that hung in his bedroom. He liked the painting so well that he kept it long after the calendar had expired, but he had considered the wreck of cattle, horses, and cowboys portrayed by Russell as unlikely to happen in real life.

Everything that could possibly go wrong when a man works cattle with a rope had gone wrong in that painting and here in real life—and death. Looking at his dead friend, the dead cow, and the injured horse, he knew that Russell's wreck was indeed possible.

The ornery old bell cow had probably refused to leave her dead calf. Hack had roped her to drag her away from the floodwaters to high ground. With the rope on her horns, she had not run away like most cows would have. She did the unthinkable—she charged. Peanut, defenseless on the slippery banks of the creek, was an easy target. The horse and rider surely fell when the horns struck. When the cow ran back to her calf, she caused the rope to form a loop that caught Hack's neck. The cow and the horse had held the rope tight until Hack and the cow drowned.

Using Hack's slicker, Griffin wrapped the body and laid it gently over Buddy's saddle, tying it securely with the rope that had killed its owner. He checked the rope still tied around his waist and shouted at Rance. Using hand signals and shouts, they decided to try to swim Buddy across the creek, using the current rather than bucking it.

Minutes later and several yards downstream, the stout old horse pulled his cargo and himself up the other slope. Rance, waiting in the mud, grabbed Buddy's reins and led

him to safety on the railroad tracks. The horse snorted and
shook violently when he knew his swim was over. Rance
fiercely grabbed the slicker wrapped around Hack's body to
keep it from falling off the horse and down the slope. Mother
Nature would never give Hack back if he fell into her arms
again.

Griffin looked away to allow his son time with his friend.
He heard a suppressed groan, a muffled shout of anguish,
before Rance spoke to him in a raspy voice. "Thought you'd
bring Hack back on Peanut. You decide to go back and get
him later?"

Griffin's headshake was almost imperceptible, but Rance
understood what it meant. "We need to get on home. It's
gonna be dark before we get him to the funeral home. Willie
Mae don't need to see him like this."

Rance led Buddy down the tracks toward the trestle.
"Hell. I forgot we're on the wrong damn side of the trestle."

Griffin patted Buddy on the neck and whispered in his
ear. "Those boards are close enough for him to cross if he
just will." And he did.

On the other side of the railroad bridge, Griffin picked
up the rifle he had leaned against the banister and walked
back across. The first shot from the rifle seemed to silence
the roar of running water and echo down the creek through
the deep bottomland. Rance flinched from the pain as if
the bullet had entered his own body instead of Peanut's. He
imagined the air leaving Peanut's body, his legs giving way
underneath him. The second retort from the rifle pierced
Rance's ears, searing the folds and creases of his brain as it
made its way to that chamber he liked to keep locked—the
chamber where Tuck's death and other painful memories were
stored.

22 Gray stopped his hammer in mid air when he saw the sheriff's car coming down Klondike's main street. He was nailing up plywood that Joe Max had bought for the broken windows at the county barn. The sight of Toy's car still rattled him. Toy's face was pale as he ran, belly bouncing, into the barn. "Gray Boy, where's your daddy?"

Still wary, Gray felt a sense of relief. Maybe Toy had not come to arrest him again. "He went off with Willie Mae this morning. Haven't seen him since."

"Where'd they go? We need to find him in a hurry." Toy waved a piece of paper at Gray.

Gray stared at the paper, imagining an indictment or arrest warrant. "Hack went down in the bottom this morning and hasn't come back. Daddy went looking for him, I imagine."

Toy paced in a circle. "Damn. How about you? You know how to drive dozers, don't you? "

"Some."

"Think you can get us down to Ivory's junk pile?"

"Ivory's? He's in the deepest part of the bottomlands. Joe Max said the creek's way out of its banks just about everywhere."

Truman Bates weaved his way through the water and grease on the concrete floor and took the piece of paper from Toy. He pushed it toward Gray as if it were a greasy rag.

Gray read the bold letters drawn in black crayon.

I have your son. Bring your jailer and come for him.

"So, who wrote this?"

Toy pointed his thumb toward the door. "No time to tell you now. We need to know if there's a dozer close to the Hollow and if you can drive it in there."

"Yes to both questions, I guess. Daddy and I left one down there a couple of days ago. They didn't tell me why, but I think Joe Max wants us to push some dirt up around a couple of bridges that are close to washing out. Probably too late for that now. As far as driving it into The Hollow, depends on how deep the water is. I can try."

Truman took the paper out of Gray's hand, patted him on the shoulder, and pushed him toward the car. "You sit in the back seat with me. Bo's sitting up front with Toy."

Gray looked over the seat at Bo as he entered the car. "Hey, Bo. What are you doing here?"

Toy spun the tires and threw them back against their seats as the Ford squealed toward The Hollow. "Bo's my hunter. You get us there; Bo will help us with those damn dogs. He might know how to find the Galt boy, too."

Gray turned toward Truman. "Wait a minute. You mean that note was talking about Cameron Galt?"

Sadie Shaw had been shaking when she handed the sealed envelope to Evelyn Galt. Ivory had asked her to deliver it to Buster. "Tell him who gave it to you," he had said. But Sadie had not spoken to Buster since Spooner's death, and she decided to give the note to Evelyn instead. Evelyn read the note, rolled her chair to the phone and asked the operator for 126, the number for Truman Bates' law office.

"Come at once," she had said. Truman called Toy seconds after reading the note. Siren blaring, they had left Cooper for Klondike.

Gray eased back in his seat. "Let me get this straight. Ivory has Cameron Galt's prick-of-a-son, is threatening to maybe kill him, and you want me to help out somebody that I dream about killing with my own hands?"

Toy glanced back at Truman. "Better tell him the whole thing."

Truman made mental calculations of his ethical and legal obligations to Gray Boy, Sadie Shaw, and Ivory. The conflicts, real and potential, were too many to consider. The gravity and emergency of the situation required quick thinking and decisive action. He told Gray Boy everything Sadie had told him.

Gray blew out a small whistle like his father made when he was tired. "Damn, I hate to say it, but that's the best news I've had in a long time. Mother said that Buster had it in for me because of Cameron. She was just half-right."

He scanned the inside of the car, checking for sympathetic ears. "He had it in for me to cover his own ass. Screwing Sadie—using that fat bastard Rube Carter to do his dirty work."

Gray's emotions overflowed, making it hard to sit still. He was animated, angry, and happy. He banged the back of Toy's seatback. "That fat bastard musta killed him while I was passed out in the cell. I knew I heard somethin'. Told him I did."

Gray's voice trailed off until he was mostly speaking to himself. "He let me take the blame, even testified against me. Idiot Rube Carter."

Toy stared at Gray in his rear view mirror until he stopped his chatter and sat quietly in the seat.

"Toy, I always told you that Rube was lower than pond scum."

Toy's chins waggled as he nodded. "Turns out you were right. Don't hold it against me. High-class folks don't just line up for jobs like that, Cuz."

As the car left the pavement and started bouncing its way down the dirt road toward The Hollow, Gray tried to absorb what he had been told. "Still don't see how you get from there to here, though. Seems to me like Ivory is the hero in this thing. He lost his son and is just trying to right a wrong. Probably plans on whipping the shit out of Buster when he gets there. Hope he's probably already done the same to his lousy son, too. Anybody needs a good ass-whupping, it's those two."

Toy seemed to be wedged tighter than usual between the steering wheel and the seat as he struggled to keep the car in the ruts. "We'll drive her till she sticks or drowns out before we start walkin'. How far did you say that dozer was, Gray Boy?"

"Toy, you ain't listenin'. Ivory's got more than a hundred dogs down there, and I wouldn't give a hair off any one of their asses to save those two from getting punished. Why are we going to all this trouble for two people who need to get what's comin' to 'em? When the water drops, you can drive down here and pick up the pieces that Ivory leaves." The mental image of the bruised and battered Cameron and a handcuffed Buster gave Gray a warm and fuzzy feeling.

Ignoring Bo's superior hearing, Truman lowered his voice. "Because Bo says Ivory is likely to kill both father and son. Says Ivory killed Susie, Bo's mother, and Chock, his daddy, one right after the other. Claims to know where both are buried."

Gray, wide-eyed, stared over the seatback at Bo, who was

fixated on something out the side window. Gray realized that Bo's usual chattering and repetitive questions were missing today. He pointed at Bo and looked at Truman. "What makes you think he....?"

"We can't be sure, but his story is credible and makes sense. It's been rumored ever since Chock Creekwater left and never returned. Your daddy told you the stories, didn't he?"

"Yeah, but he didn't say anything about Ivory killin' anybody. He said Bo's mother ran off, and his daddy went after her and never came back."

Truman reached over the seat and put his hand on Bo's shoulder. "That's supposed to be how it happened, but Bo says his daddy did come back—and he brought Bo's mother back with him. Problem was, his mother was Spooner's mother, too." Truman's eyebrows arched as he smiled. The familiar feelings of pleasure and power mixed with guilt filled him.

Gray turned in the seat to face Truman. "Wait a minute. You mean that Bo and Spooner are half-brothers? They have the same mother, and nobody around here knew it?"

"A few people in The Hollow might have guessed, but they were probably too afraid of Ivory to say anything." Truman moved closer to Gray Boy and whispered. "It's not so far-fetched when you think about it."

"Bo's mother probably remembered Ivory before he left for the service. He was possibly her hero. She got pregnant with Chock's baby—Bo here—while Ivory was gone. When she ran off, she changed her name, put on some makeup, and looked up Ivory down in New Orleans."

Truman eased back in his seat to allow Gray time to process the information. "Ivory hadn't seen her since she was a child, so he didn't recognize her. They got married and had Spooner. When Ivory told her he was coming back to Delta County, she had to run away again."

"Why?" Gray asked.

"She couldn't come back here and introduce Ivory to another husband and son she had abandoned."

"So she ran off again. Okay, but how did Bo's daddy finally find her and get her to come back with him?"

Truman pondered the legalities of what he was about to reveal, rationalizing that the exigency of the situation warranted emergency release of information for the general good. "Ivory hired me to find her a few years back. Many people do not know that research of this sort is something I enjoy."

Truman put a hand beside his mouth to deflect the sound from Bo's ears. "I found her living in squalor in a rundown house in Bossier City."

Toy kept his eyes on the road, but leaned back enough to be heard. "So why didn't you bring her back then?"

"She refused to come. When I told Ivory she was practicing the world's oldest profession and possibly diseased or deranged or both, he elected to leave her there."

Gray made a sucking sound by pressing his tongue against the roof of his mouth. "But Chock found her and brought her home. Did he know that she was Ivory's wife, too?"

"There is no way to know for certain, but I am sure that Chock did not know that until Ivory saw them together when they returned. If my sources are correct, she was in the advanced stages of syphilis and much too addled to tell him anything. I doubt that she knew who Chock was. He likely lured her home by simply giving her food and a few kind words."

Gray shook his head. "But Ivory and Chock Creekwater both married her. I can't believe it. Didn't the folks in The Hollow know that Ivory had married Chock's wife?"

"Remember, Ivory himself did not know that he had married Chock's wife. He did not even know he had married Susie Blandon. He had not seen her since she was a child, so she was able to change her identity and get away with it when she sought him out. Besides, discussion about King Ivory's wife was a recipe for trouble in The Hollow. He never told anyone what happened to his wife, preferring that folks think she had died rather than run out on him."

"But you knew, didn't you, Truman?...and all." Toy asked.

Truman eased back against the seat. "Yes. I'm afraid I succumbed to Susie's wishes. I thought it would be imprudent to advise Ivory of my complete findings. I thought I was possibly saving lives. Seems I only delayed the inevitable."

"So how did Ivory kill both of 'em?" Gray whispered the question.

Toy stopped the car. "That the dozer you're talkin' about?"

Toy got out of the car, slopped through the mud and opened Bo's door. They headed for the dozer. Gray turned toward Truman, waiting for the answer to his question.

When Bo and Toy were out of earshot, Truman continued. "Bo says Ivory shot both of them with a twelve gauge. They returned in the dark of night. Chock apparently went directly to where his son was staying. Nobody knew they were in the junkyard, or even in the county, so Ivory did it before anybody in The Hollow saw them."

Gray stepped out in the mud and leaned through Truman's open window. "Damn—and Bo saw that?"

"Bo and Spooner were returning from hunting, heard the shots, and looked through the window of Ivory's shack. They didn't see him shoot them, but they saw him standing over their bodies with a shotgun."

"Why did they not say anything?"

"Who knows for sure, but Bo said some things to make me think they swore a blood oath as brothers to never divulge what they had seen."

"Can't believe neither one ever told."

"Think about it. Spooner was afraid of his daddy, but he seemed to love him. A young boy doesn't want his daddy taken away, no matter what he has done. To be fair, Ivory seemed to treat Spooner well. He was even a good substitute father to Bo when Chock left to search for his wife. Bo—well, Bo was just loyal to his brother. Afraid of Ivory, too."

Gray boy nodded, wondering what he would have done if it had been his father who had killed someone. "You comin?"

Truman, filled with the twin emotions again, shook his head. "Afraid I would not be much use in that mud jungle. Besides, I promised Toy I would come here with him, but now I have to tell Buster Galt that Ivory has his son."

"Can you drive mud roads?"

"I grew up in Delta County, Gray Boy. Believe it or not, I've been in and out of the woods before."

Gray slopped through the mud toward the dozer as Truman crawled over the back seat to avoid getting his shoes muddy. Behind the wheel, he leaned out the window and called Gray back. "I wonder, Gray Boy, if I could ask you a question. Do you think ...by withholding the whole truth from Ivory, that I was somewhat responsible for the deaths of Susie and Chock?"

Gray looked toward the dozer, Toy and Bo. "No way you could have known what was gonna happen. If you had told Ivory back then that his wife was married to Chock before she married him, who knows what would have happened." Gray was surprised as Truman began skillfully backing the car down the muddy ruts Toy had made on the way in.

23 Toy helped Bo to a standing position beside Gray Boy's seat on the big Caterpillar. Shivering with anticipation, Bo held on to one of the steel pipes that supported the driver's canopy. Gray Boy was almost disappointed when the dozer cranked on the second try. He patted Bo's shoulder as he revved the engine and prepared to move. Toy stood on the left track.

"Toy, you might want to move over here on the platform unless you want to try walking that muddy track backwards all the way there." Gray Boy smiled as Toy stepped gingerly to the platform. "One slip and I might run over you before I could get stopped."

Toy's need for his skills with the dozer, the sense of danger, and Bo's obvious fear filled Gray Boy with a sense of power. Still, the emotions he had sought most of his life conflicted with his hatred for Buster and Cameron Galt. One had ruined his life; the other had tried to take it. Why should he help them now?

Toy pointed a huge finger in a southeastern direction. He leaned down and shouted in Gray Boy's ear. "I figure that U in the Blue Bottom that surrounds Ivory's place to be right about there. Head straight for it."

"You mean you want me to leave the road?"

"Already been told that the bridge is out. In this weather, the unused pastures are probably better than the road, anyway."

"What about the fences?"

"Run over 'em. We're trying to save a boy's life. Fences can be repaired."

Gray Boy had secretly yearned to use the destructive power of the dozer every time he drove it. He worked the steering levers and drove it across the ditch, running over barbed wire as he crushed posts under the dozer's tracks. It was exhilarating.

"We'll be there in a few minutes, Toy. Better tell me what you plan to do."

"Ain't exactly got a plan. Just aim to drive right up to the king's shack and shoot his ass or whip hell out of him. We'll take that boy and come on back home."

"Ain't you forgettin' about Ivory's shotgun? I hear he's got a lotta guns out there."

Toy stared at his two young charges, considering how their presence might affect his actions. He was not afraid of King Ivory or his guns, but he had not considered the danger to these two young men. Bo remained trance-like as he stared in the direction of Ivory's junk fortress. His free hand was between the buttons on his shirt, massaging the pouch that hung around his neck.

Toy shouted over the diesel's clatter. "Guess I wadn't thinkin' about you two boys. Best pull this thing over and let me walk from here."

Gray Boy stopped and allowed the engine to idle. He nodded toward the junk fortress coming into view. "You got to have us, Toy. You can't even find Ivory's shack in that maze of junk. Besides, the dogs would kill you before you got close to him. Like you said, Bo will show us the way and calm the dogs. I'll get you in there with the dozer. Then Bo can find me and him a place to hide."

Toy looked in the direction of his car and Truman, out of sight now, as if the lawyer could send him instructions by telepathy. Dr. Olen Bartlett's word came back to him. *Instinct.* He gave a reluctant nod. "All right. Don't know about risking two boys to save one, but I can't just wait till Ivory kills the Galt kid. That poor mama of his has got enough on her shoulders without losing her son. You shoulda seen her this morning...and all."

Gray Boy had never thought much about Cameron having a mother, only a father who was just as vile as his son. He eased the dozer forward. "This diesel engine ain't exactly good for sneakin' up on Ivory."

"It'll still be a big surprise when Ivory finds it in his front parlor. Any shootin' starts before we get there, just point this thing in the direction of his shack and bail off. Take Bo with you and get under something. Bo knows all the hidin' places in this junkyard."

Feeling Bo's tug on his shirtsleeve, Gray Boy pointed the dozer in the direction Bo indicated. Water was ankle-to-knee deep throughout the junk fortress, most of it moving fast. Gray Boy tried not to notice the water moccasins struggling against the current in the shallow water in front of the dozer as he pushed his first pile of junk and widened the narrow trail that Bo had pointed to.

Squawking crows joined buzzards flying out of the compound amid the din of the dozer's engine and barking dogs. The grunting and squealing of pigs joined the chorus as they approached the bedspring and sheet-iron fences of Ivory's hog pens. Chickens, forced from their roosts, sought refuge from floodwaters on the junk piles. The dozer pushed aside appliances, wrecked cars, and other metal scrap as it straightened the bends in the trail.

When the load in front of the dozer obstructed his view and threatened to fall back on them, Gray Boy pushed it aside and backed up to begin again. He slowed the Caterpillar and glanced at Toy as Ivory's shack came into view. Ivory's best dogs stood in their guard positions on each side of the winding trail. Standing in their assigned spots, they seemed unaware that their chains had been removed.

As the dozer entered the lane, the dogs charged from all sides, trying to jump past the Caterpillar's tracks and reach the human invaders. Most never topped the moving tracks; those who did were carried to the ground and crushed or thrown aside. Gray Boy cringed and slowed as he heard the dogs' last yelps.

Toy, red-faced with jowls flopping, shouted, "Never mind the dogs. Keep going."

Following Bo's pointed hand, Gray directed the dozer toward the west end of the shack. The U-shaped bend of the Blue Bottom had disappeared under the floodwaters, and Ivory's house looked ready to slide into the creek behind it. The whole house moved when the dozer hit the left side. The porch crumbled. Gray Boy stopped the dozer's forward progress and shouted at Toy.

"She'll either topple over on us or fall into the creek if I keep going. Anybody inside is likely to drown."

Toy nodded as he stepped out on a track. "Bo, call them dogs off so I can get down."

Bo stepped out on the track and jumped to the ground, splashing mud and water. The dogs gathered around him, licking his hands as if he fed them every day.

Toy stepped onto the porch. "You boys find a place to hole up. Rest of this is up to me. If I ain't out in a few minutes, go back for help." Gun drawn, Toy entered the dark hallway.

Gray Boy hesitated as he stood on the dozer track. Bo waved him down. "Jump, Gray Boy. Dem dogs ain' gon' hurt nobody. Uh huh."

The diesel engine died as Gray jumped. *Out of diesel, probably.* The roar of charging water, squawking chickens, and barking dogs replaced the clattering reverberation of the diesel engine. Gray Boy searched the water swirling around his ankles for angry water moccasins.

Bo started walking between piles of metal discards as if he had never left the junk fortress. He turned to wave when Gray Boy did not follow. "Come on. Know good, dry place. Uh huh."

Gray Boy stared at the carnage left in the dozer's wake. Sharp, torn metal protruded at all angles from the disturbed sculpture of junk that his father's friend had created. He could not chase away the image of snake fangs buried in his ankles and a dog's fangs in his throat. Bo had a way with the dogs, but they might get separated in this quagmire of junk, mud, and water.

He turned back toward Ivory's shack. The east side of the porch had been lifted as the west side fell. The house teetered on the brink of the creek, but the east porch was dry. The choice was easy—fangs and dogs—or the house and King Ivory.

He jumped on the porch and waved for Bo to follow him. Bo shook his head and stayed where he was, surrounded by dogs, and oblivious to the water that swirled around him. Gray Boy gave him an angry stare and a firm wave. "Come on, Bo." Bo reluctantly came to the porch.

They pushed aside a maze of intertwined daddy-long-legs and wiped years of accumulated grime from a porch window. Gray Boy felt a spurt of adrenalin as he imagined Cameron inside the shack, peeing his pants.

He cupped his hands against a pane and pushed his face between his hands. No movement in the dark, dusty room. "Stay right here and wait for me. I'm gonna see if I can find Toy."

Bo ignored the instructions and followed Gray Boy down the dark hallway. Gray Boy's sense of smell reacted to the stifling air, sending a trickle of bitter liquid down his throat and causing his eyes to burn and water. He tried, but failed, to suppress a cough just as a gunshot covered the noise. Toy's guttural voice traveled down the hall as if it had been shot from the gun. The sounds were chased by the thumps and cracks of furniture breaking as two giants struggled. Gray Boy started toward the noise, but Bo's voice stopped him.

"In here. Uh huh." Bo walked through an open door in the hall and began pushing aside mattresses, ragged quilts, and piles of newspapers. He stopped when he uncovered a small, single bed perched on a wooden floor that had been rebuilt inches above the rotted old floor.

"My old bed. Uh huh." With tender movements, he eased the bed off the wood onto the dirt and pointed down.

Gray Boy stared in confusion. "What are you pointing at?"

Bo stepped on the wood floor, pulled his pocketknife and ran it down a rectangular crack in the floor. Gray Boy saw the outline of a door and helped him to lift it. When the door cracked open, Bo stepped back and cowered against a pile of old newspapers in the corner of the room. Gray Boy stared down into the blackness and thought of the snakes. An odor of rotting food and fetid water wafted past his nose.

"What's down there?" he whispered.

"Gun. Uh huh." Bo tossed him a box of matches he carried next to the cigars in his shirt pocket.

Gray scratched a match against the box's striker and held it down in the black hole. A crude stairway disappeared in the darkness after three wooden steps. Gray stepped down and waved the match around as he tried to adjust his eyes to the new level of darkness. The match illuminated a room similar to the storm cellar he hated at home.

"Shit." A slight puff of wind blew out the match. He dropped the box, swept the floor with his hands until he bumped it, picked it up with shaking hands, and lighted another one.

The roar of the creek echoed here, and water lapped

against the wooden walls of the underground box he seemed to be standing in. Light from the match flame flickered and jumped against the walls of the room, as if laughing at his fear. He tried to take a step, but stumbled and almost fell.

The ground was covered in something besides dirt. The last seconds of the flame revealed a coal-oil lamp on a shelf behind a row of fruit jars. *Why did they call it canning when they put up vegetables in jars?*

He lighted another match from the dying flame and picked up the lamp. With shaking hands, he removed the globe and found the handle to raise the wick. The globe fell as the wick came to life. The lamplight revealed a packed dirt floor covered in rotted potatoes and onions.

Bo's shaking voice shattered the silence. "See dat shotgun? Uh huh."

"I don't see no damn shotgun. Where's it supposed to be?"

"Little shef on da south wall. Uh huh."

Gray tried to get his bearings, struggling to remember which way was south. Kicking away potatoes, he turned until he saw it. He set the lamp on the shelf, removed a rusted, double-barreled twelve gauge, and broke it open.

Loaded. *Wet as it is down here, wonder if it will fire?* He snapped it shut and retrieved the lamp. As he started up the steps, Bo waved him back down.

"Dat tunnel go all the way to the kitchen at the back. Sound like that wher' Toy at... Uh huh."

"What tunnel?" The words had barely been whispered when he saw what appeared to be a corncrib door at the back of the room. Brushing aside onions and potatoes to make a flat surface for the lamp and the shotgun, he put the matchbox in his pocket and used both hands to pull back the crude door.

Stooping to enter the tunnel, he thrust the lamp and shotgun ahead of him like shields. Stumbling as he took an unexpected step down, he imagined himself falling into a deep well under the shack. Water seeped into his boots as he sloshed toward the sounds of two big men crashing against walls and floors. Close enough now to hear their grunting, he saw streams of light speckled with columns of dust and dirt drifting through cracks in the floor into the tunnel ahead of him.

The light gave him courage to hurry his pace. Trying to run with his head ducked, he stumbled over something in the floor and fell. The lamp fell into the water, leaving him with only the filtered light from the floor cracks. He pulled Bo's matchbox from his shirt pocket, found a new match, and pulled it along the striker. No flame. A second match...same result. His fingers told him he was down to three matches. Welcome light filled the underground coffin when the third match struck. He almost dropped it when he saw what he had stumbled over.

24 Spooner's blank stare returned to haunt him as he studied the lump he had stumbled over. A long duck-cotton sack full of something heavy and lumpy lay in the floor across the tunnel. The bottom half of the sack was underwater, its shoulder strap floated, undulating with the water.

Gray eased the match's flame along the sack's length until he saw a pair of feet, bound by rope and black tape, protruding from the open end. Punching his finger about where he figured the ribcage was, Gray sat back in the water when the body moved. "Damn." The match burned the end of his fingers.

Shaking, he managed to light another before the flame went out. He leaned the shotgun against the wall and reached into his pocket. Grateful for his father's training and discipline about keeping a sharp knife, he cut the tape and rope around the feet and started a cut along the sack's middle until he reached the bound hands. As he cut the tape and rope that bound the hands, the hands began peeling away the remains of the sack.

Gray held his breath until he found himself eye-to-eye with the gray-white face of Cameron Galt. Cameron bumped his head against a floor joist when he tried to straighten.

His blond hair was caked with mud; his frightened blue eyes accentuated his feminine facial features. Cameron's face darkened as he struggled for breath, seeming to forget that Ivory had stuffed his shorts into his mouth and taped them there. Gray pulled the briefs out of Cameron's mouth and dropped them in the standing water. The match burned his fingers again as he glimpsed a hint of gratitude in Cameron's eyes.

Gray put a finger to his lips and said, "Wait here," as he picked up the shotgun and pointed toward the light ahead. He had not noticed that the sounds of struggle from the room above them had stopped until his own sloshing interrupted the silence.

Breaking the shotgun again, he draped it over his neck in order to use both hands. Using the sidewalls for support, he elevated his feet above the water and pushed forward in longer, quieter steps. Cameron, too stiff and weak to accomplish this, stayed behind.

Gray Boy quickly found himself on the stairs that led out of the root-cellar tunnel. He closed the shotgun and pushed the double barrels against the door at the top of the stairs. Falling debris and mud from dirt dauber nests made him close his eyes as the door creaked open. He pushed it up enough to look out.

The trapdoor opened on a porch just outside the kitchen. The sound of floodwater mixed with the grunts and squeals of hogs allowed him to crawl to the kitchen screen door unnoticed. He crouched to get his breath and listened.

The boards under his feet vibrated as he sensed a very big person moving away from him. Chancing a peek through the screen, he saw Ivory, shirtless in faded overalls, wrapping black tape around Toy's head, mouth, and eyes. Toy's entire body was tied to a chair with tape and rope. Hesitation had gotten Gray hurt before, so he crashed through the screen door without thinking, the shotgun leveled at Ivory.

Gray's voice sounded weak. "Turn him loose."

Ivory stepped away from Toy and faced Gray. "Evenin' Gray Boy. Wondered who this fat lawdog had brought with him. I was downstairs when I heard you comin'."

Gray glanced in the direction of Toy's grunts and the scraping of the chair he was tied to. Toy was staring at them through tiny slits between strips of black tape. A used shop rag was stuffed into his mouth and taped over.

Gray nodded toward the sheriff as he spoke to Ivory. "Cut him loose."

King Ivory smiled, revealing his widely spaced teeth and pink lips that seemed to turn inside out with his grin. "You on the wrong side of this thang, Gray Boy. These people done killed my boy and tried to do the same to you. Why you helpin' them? You should be helpin' me."

Gray felt the tug of Ivory's words, raising the shotgun to his shoulder as if it could fend off Ivory's logic. "Nothin' against you Ivory, but you still need to turn Toy loose."

Gray stepped back when Ivory took a step toward him. "Stay back, Ivory. I ain't afraid to shoot you."

Ivory held up his hands in a gesture of defeat. "Easy now, Gray Boy. Me and yo' Daddy been friends a long time. 'Sides, you ain' gon' shoot me."

Ivory pointed a finger at the shotgun. "Why, that my old shotgun from the root cellar, ain't it? That won' fire. Been rustin' down there in the damp for lotsa years."

Gray cocked both hammers of the shotgun and leveled it at Ivory's chest. "Guess we'll find out. Now untie Toy." Toy squirmed in his chair and grunted.

Ivory dropped his hands to his sides and his eyes narrowed as he looked away from Gray toward the screen door. His arm jerked toward Cameron standing outside the door. "This boy here—you know what kinda trash he is. I just trying to set things right—for you and for me. Let's take this little worm and go after his daddy and Rube Carter."

"Let me have the shotgun before he talks you out of it, Rivers." Cameron directed a stare full of hate and fear at Ivory as he shouted through the screen door.

Gray kept his eyes on Ivory as he answered. "I'll hold the shotgun. You got a pocketknife?"

"No."

"Get Toy's out of his pocket and cut him loose."

Cameron hesitated before pushing the screen door open. Ivory narrowed his round eyes and stared at him through slits as he came into the room. Cameron flinched and jumped back when Ivory made a threatening stutter step in his direction. He backed across the room, making a wide circle around the big man. Toy squirmed with impatience as Cameron pulled back tape to dig in his pocket for a knife.

"Which pocket, Sheriff?"

Toy shook his head and nodded toward the kitchen counter. A butcher knife lay next to a pitcher and bowl. As Cameron walked toward the knife, Bo, shivering, stepped into the room from the hall.

Ivory used the distraction to step behind Cameron and deliver a kick between his legs. Cameron dropped to his knees, then fell to his side, groaning from the pain.

Gray pointed the shotgun above Ivory's head and pulled one trigger. A dead click. As Ivory advanced toward him, he pointed at Ivory's knees and pulled the other trigger. Another click. Ivory grabbed the shotgun and slapped Gray with an open hand. Gray stumbled over a nail keg and dropped to the floor.

Ivory stood over him and dropped the shotgun on his stomach. "Tol' you it wouldn't fire. Don' want to hurt you, boy, but I will. I aim to revenge Spencer's killin'. You got yo'self in the way."

Cameron struggled to his knees before Ivory's shoe cracked a rib and sucked the air out of his lungs. He dropped back to the floor.

Ivory stood between the two prone boys. "You boys stay where you is." He pointed toward Cameron and spoke to Toy. "Takin' this 'un to the cou'thouse roof. Throw him off, 'less his daddy and Rube Carter come for him."

Bo whimpered as he turned to run back down the hall. Ivory took three quick steps and pulled him back. He pulled Bo into the room and wrapped an arm around his throat. With his other hand, he snapped the leather string that held the pouch around Bo's neck.

He whispered into his ear. "You broke the blood oath, breed. Now dogs gon' bite off yo' balls and chickens gon' peck yo' eyes out. Just like I tol' you." Bo exhaled a small whimper as drool dripped from both corners of his mouth. Ivory pushed him away and tossed the pouch at his face.

He grabbed Cameron's shirt collar and pulled him up. "Stand up, Little Buster. Looks like you done pissed yo' pants. You walkin' outta here under your own steam, or I gon' have to slap you and throw you over my shoulder again?"

Gray heard the screen door squeak and the sounds of sloshing footsteps. When he looked up, he saw the wet boots. They squeaked as Rance stepped through the screen door. Rance kept his eyes on Ivory and Cameron as he walked toward Gray. He picked up the shotgun from Gray's chest. "You hurt?"

Gray's cheek was still red from the slap. He raised himself to an elbow, rubbed his cheek, and ran a finger along his gums. "No, just stung a little."

Rance broke the shotgun and checked to see if it was loaded.

Ivory took a tentative step toward him. "That ol' gun won't shoot, Rance. Ask your boy."

Rance took both shells from their chambers, tossed them on the floor, and snapped the gun shut. "Don't want it going off accidentally." Rance put both hands around the barrel and placed the gun lightly on his shoulder like a baseball bat.

Ivory kept his grip on Cameron's collar. "Don't want no problem with you and yours, Rance. Just had to tap Gray Boy when he got in the way. Coulda hit him harder, but I didn't." Rance stared at his old friend without speaking.

Ivory tried again. "Good Book says eye for an eye. I figure that means a son for a son, if I can't get at his daddy and Rube."

Rance nodded, still holding the gun on his shoulder, Gray standing beside him. "I understand how you feel, but I think you need to untie Toy and let things run their course, Ivory. I expect things are not that bad for you, yet."

Ivory looked at everyone in the room before turning back to Rance. "You gon' get in my way, Mistuh Rance?"

"Never expected things to turn out this way, Ivory." Rance nodded toward Cameron. "You hurt that boy anymore, or kill him or his daddy, things will go real bad for you. I probably can't, but I aim to try to stop you."

"All I done so far was spank his naked ass and stuff his drawers in his mouth. Aim to do a lot more."

Cameron rolled to his side and grunted. "He made me strip, then beat me with an old razor strap till I bled."

Ivory covered the distance between himself and Rance quickly, but not before Rance could set himself in a batter's stance. He swung the rifle butt toward Ivory's knees. Ivory, expecting a blow to the head, was caught by surprise.

The wooden stock broke away from the barrel as it struck. Ivory shouted in pain and stumbled, but he was gaining his feet again when Rance brought the barrel down against the back of his neck. Ivory dropped to the floor.

In his excitement, Toy turned over the chair he was taped to and floundered on the floor, grunting mangled cuss words. Gray unwrapped the tape around his mouth and pulled the shop rag from his mouth. Toy gagged and spit as the rag came out.

He jerked his head toward Ivory. "He out?"

Breathing hard, Rance stooped to look at Ivory. "I'm pretty sure I felt at least one kneecap break. He ain't totally out, but I don't think he's too dangerous right now."

Toy struggled as Gray Boy cut away tape and rope. "Yore daddy was always handy with a baseball bat." Toy finally stood and flexed his elbows back like a rooster crowing at sunrise. His nose was split down the middle, one eye was nearly closed, and both lips were swollen and bleeding. He moved nail kegs until he found his pistol that had dropped on the floor during their struggle.

Toy pointed it at Ivory. "I know this gun will fire. Sumbitch nearly killed me."

Ivory grunted. "I'd 'uv wanted you dead, you be dead."

Gray Boy felt a strange sense of camaraderie as Cameron limped around the room, bringing him tape and material to use as binding. Gray tied Ivory's wrists and feet, then wrapped his body until the tape ran out. Toy pointed the gun at Ivory until he was satisfied that the big man was under control.

Gray Boy stood and looked at Toy. "What was that shot I heard before?"

Toy's swollen face got redder. "Caught me by surprise when I busted through that door. He was waitin' on me. My gun fired when we was wrestling. Last man that whupped my ass that bad was my daddy."

"If he knew you were coming, why didn't he just shoot you?" Gray asked.

"He didn't even have a gun. It was like he just wanted to whip hell outa somebody. Buster didn't come, so he took it out on me."

Rance pointed at Toy's gun. "He knew about that gun. He could have killed any one of us at anytime. I don't think Ivory really wants to kill anybody. He just wants Buster and Rube to pay a price."

Cameron held a hand against his broken rib as he struggled to speak. "Let's get out of here." Gray turned toward his former nemesis. Cameron's eyes were still wild and frightened, his hair and face were matted with mud, and his clothes were soaked from lying in the tunnel. He reeked of urine.

Bo dropped to his knees and picked up the leather pouch that Ivory had torn from his neck. He crawled to Ivory's body and, with shaking hands, found the leather string around Ivory's neck. With a half-grunt, half-scream, he pulled so hard that he fell back with a pouch in each hand. Standing, he pulled a third pouch from the pocket of his baggy pants.

He held the three pouches above his head and began turning in circles, his face reddening more with each turn. His face screwed up as if he wanted to scream, but could not. Spittle dripping from his mouth, he walked over to Ivory's unconscious body, kicked him hard in the ribs and let the scream escape. He continued screaming as he crouched to pound Ivory's body, the pouches held tightly in his fists.

Gray whispered to Toy, "You think he might hurt him?"

"I hit that hard-headed sumbitch with everything I had, and it didn't hurt him. Let Bo get it out of his system."

Rance gently pulled Bo's arms away from Ivory and looked at Toy. "Why are there three pouches and what's in 'em?"

"Truman tell you what Ivory did to Susie and Chock?" Toy asked.

"Told me some of it on the way out here."

Toy pointed toward the pouches that Bo was still clutching. "The third one belonged to Spooner. Bo got it the night Spooner died. Me and Truman had a hard time understandin' Bo, but it seems like Ivory knew the boys had seen him kill their mama and Bo's daddy. After the killin', he made 'em gather up three stud dogs, a guinea hen, and some its eggs."

Toy waited for the questions. Rance was impatient. "Ok, Toy. You have our attention. Get on with it."

Toy looked at Cameron and Gray. "He killed the dogs

and cut off their balls right in front of Spooner and Bo."
Another long pause. "Then he wrung the head off a guinea
hen and poured the blood from the head over the hen's eggs.
He took the dog's balls, the bloody shells, and mashed it all
up together."

Cameron's face was showing disgust as Toy paused again.
"Then he rubbed it all over their faces, chests, and hair."

"His, too?" Gray asked.

"His, too. When he finished rubbin' it all over 'em, he
poured what was left of the bloody shells into those pouches—
them pouches are made outa the dog sacks, you know."

Cameron, his face contorted with pain, inched a little
closer. "Dog sacks?"

Toy nodded and stared at Cameron as if he had asked a
very dumb question. "Sure, the little sacks where males carry
their balls. Ain't you got one?"

Cameron's face grew warm. "That's called a scrotum."

Toy shot him a confused look. "'Round here, they're
sacks. Anyways, Ivory pours this nasty mess of blood and
shells and feathers and balls into these sacks and ties one
around all their necks. Then they swear some sort of blood
oath to keep it all a secret. He threatened 'em with some
kinda mumbo-jumbo curse if they ever told about the killin'."

Another pause. "Told 'em that devil-dogs would come
and bite off their balls and chickens would scratch their eyes
out if they broke the oath and told about the killin's. Scared
them boys shitless, I 'magine."

Rance leaned the shotgun barrel against the kitchen wall.
"Did Bo tell you what Ivory did with the bodies?"

"Yep. They did that abracadabra right over their graves."

Cameron had started to shiver a little. "I want to go
home. I haven't had anything to eat all day. My parents will
be worried sick."

Toy shook his head. "Expect you're right about your
mama. Don't give a red rat's ass what your daddy thinks.

Hell, boy, I guess you still don't know why you're here, do you?"

Cameron pointed toward Ivory's prone form. "While he was whipping my ass, that big buck told me some bullshit about my daddy killin' his son."

Toy gave Gray Boy a sidewise glance before turning back to Cameron. "We'll let yore mama tell you 'bout that later. Right now, we best bundle up King Ivory Hays' big ass and head outa here."

Gray was still thinking about the blood, feathers, and testicles. "The dozer is out of fuel. How are we going to carry Ivory out?"

Toy bent over Ivory to see if he was still breathing. "'Bout the only way to get him out is on that dozer." He checked the knots and tape that secured him before straightening.

He rubbed a finger along his gums to make sure his loose teeth were still there. "You say Truman brought you out, Rance?"

"Yeah, but he left as soon as he dropped me at the road. He called the Hopkins County sheriff before we left. He's waiting at Dad's to show 'em the way."

"Since we're stuck, we might as well see if we can find those bodies. Save me from comin' right back out here. Where's that root cellar?"

Rance stepped closer to Cameron. "I expect you better stay here. Can I trust you to watch Ivory?"

Cameron nodded.

"He moves or starts to get up, just shout."

Gray showed Toy and Rance the root cellar and tunnel. Bo refused to go in the cellar, but he shouted instructions about the graves' location from above. After using a pickaxe he found in a corner of the cellar to break the hard surface, Toy and Rance soon found the first piece of evidence with a shovel.

In an hour, the cellar floor was littered with bones. Gray

was surprised when a sweating Toy was able to begin ar-
ranging the bones into male and female skeletons. Toy was
placing a female skeleton, some hair still attached, at the top
of the line of bones when they heard voices from outside.

The sun, finally poking through the clouds, was in Gray's
eyes as he stepped out on the porch, so he heard the sloshing steps before he saw him. Joe Max Rainey trudged toward
them through mud and water, dodging sharp metal edges of
junk that had been disturbed and cut. The water had receded
slightly and was barely moving now, but Joe Max's fast steps had
wet his overalls to the knees.

Gray waved to him. "I'm sorry about the dozer Joe Max,
we just...."

Joe Max shouted over him. "I brought diesel. I'm surprised you got this far with that old dozer. I never leave fuel
in it... people steal...everybody all right in there?"

"Yeah. Toy got beat up, though. We got Ivory tied up—do
you know what he did? We been diggin' up...." Gray stopped
as his father stood beside him.

He looked down at Rance's best boots. When Rance
turned toward him, he noticed the red rims around his eyes.
Were those there earlier? "Why did you come out here in your
best boots, Daddy?"

Rance looked down at his soaked boots. He had torn a
hole in his best khaki pants. Mattie would not like that.

"You find Hack all right?"

Rance put a hand on Gray's shoulder. "Your Papa and I
found him too late. I was getting' dressed to go back to the
funeral home when Truman came by and said you were out
here." He reached down to give Joe Max a hand as he stepped
on the sloping porch before turning back to Gray. "We've got
to get you home. Your mama's probably frantic."

25 The rest was easy. Before leaving Ivory's shack, Bo found the courage to walk down into the root cellar and drop the three pouches on his parents' bones. His slumped posture straightened as he walked back up the steps and stood where his bed had been. Nobody noticed that he had not had a seizure during the whole episode.

Back in Cooper, in front of the sheriff and a couple of other witnesses, Truman asked Rube Carter to borrow a pocketknife. When Rube was stupid enough to pull Spooner's bone-handled Case out of his pocket, Sheriff Toy Roy Robbins pushed him against the courthouse wall and slapped on the cuffs.

When Buster Galt refused to resign his position, Truman Bates solicited the governor's assistance. The governor appointed a lawyer friend from Sulphur Springs as a special agent for the state attorney general to clean up the mess in Delta County. The agent heard the evidence against Buster and made him an offer he could not refuse—face possible charges of rape, procurement, and lying to a grand jury—or resign. Buster refused again. When the agent said the charges would be made public, Buster resigned.

He vacated his office and left town the next day.

Criminal charges were never brought against him, prompting locals to talk about "honor among lawyers." Truman Bates agreed with the governor's special lawyer, determining that evidence was insufficient to prove exactly when Buster found out the true cause of Spooner's death. Rube Carter's word would probably not be enough to convince a jury.

Rube Carter pled guilty to a reduced charge of manslaughter and was on the wrong side of a cell door in Huntsville State Prison by spring. He felt safer there—away from Buster's wrath.

For her part, Sadie just wanted to forget. She quietly moved into the Galt house, taking up residence in Buster's abandoned bedroom to await the arrival of her baby. Evelyn Galt assured her of a permanent home and a paid position assisting in the care of herself and Buster's mother.

The elder Mrs. Galt seemed to recover some of her former mental capacity when she was told that another child would live under her roof. Evelyn thought it prudent not to tell the old woman that the colored child to be born was her own grandchild. Cameron also thought it best to delay telling his mother about her yet-to-be-born grandchild.

King Ivory was held in county jail on kidnapping and murder charges. A new grand jury failed to indict him for murder. One would-be lawyer on the panel kept citing the statute of limitations, seeming not to hear when the prosecutor explained that the time limits did not apply to murder. The grand jurors, heady with power, used logic instead of law to make up their minds. The murdered woman, after all, was an addled whore who had abandoned two children and two husbands. As for Chock Creekwater, he should have known better than to go off to a Louisiana whorehouse and return with a crazy, diseased whore. King Ivory may have done the community a service. Bo was certainly better off with his grandmother than he would have been with his derelict, immoral mother.

Ivory *was* indicted and tried, however, for his kidnapping of Cameron Galt. Fathers themselves, the judge and jury at his trial took special note of the grievous and unjustified killing of Spooner, his only son. Ivory had not, after all, inflicted serious physical harm on Cameron Galt, and a man has a right to defend his own. They found Ivory guilty and sentenced him to two years in prison.

As the time arrived for Ivory's transfer from the county jail, paperwork kept getting lost or mixed up. Truman Bates, the new district attorney, and newly-elected Sheriff Toy Roy Robbins, respecting Ivory's need to remain close to the site of his son's death, found ways to keep him there.

It became sport for spitters-and-whittlers on benches around the courthouse to stare and point at the courthouse roof in the afternoons. King Ivory's head could be seen above the wall as he strolled along the rooftop walkway where his son had fallen to his death. If no strangers were present, the whittlers would repeat King Ivory's story to themselves.

King Ivory, they said, could fly off the roof whenever he pleased, but he chose to remain because Spooner's spirit walked there each morning at 2 a.m. Toy, it was said, left the door to Ivory's cell unlocked so that he could join Spooner in their predawn stroll. Truth be known, Toy left the cell door unlocked so that he and Ivory could enjoy a regular game of checkers.

Hack Gentry's funeral, they said, was the biggest Delta County had ever seen. It was certainly the biggest Jake had ever seen. Jake never made it inside the church. Adults filled all the pews. His father and mother got to see it because Rance was a pallbearer, and Mattie was asked to sit with the family. Jake probably learned more about Hack from the discussions outside the church than he would have from the preacher inside, anyway. Grown men, including his father, openly wept at Hack's gravesite.

Griffin had not mentioned it to anyone, but Dr. Olen

Bartlett noticed his peculiar gait at the funeral. The old man had hurt himself swimming that current. The support timber under Piss Elm Bridge was under water that day, so neither Buddy nor Griffin could be blamed when Buddy swam too close. Griffin had been crushed between his horse and the timber as they swam back with Hack's body.

When Dr. Olen asked about the peculiar way he walked and the grimace of pain on his face, Griffin admitted to possibly *breaking an egg* somewhere inside. The pain got worse before it got better, but then it leveled off. Dr. Olen wanted to locate and possibly repair the damage, but Griffin refused. He liked and trusted Dr. Olen, but he had no use for hospitals and refused to be cut on.

Buddy got fat and cantankerous when he was left out to pasture—prone to buck. Griffin said he probably also broke an egg. Believing that a man who could not or would not ride a horse did not need to own one, he sold Buddy to a man who lived in Oklahoma, just on the other side of the Red River. It was a sad day for the family when the man loaded Buddy into that trailer and drove away. Even Scar seemed to be crying. The little gelding called his pasture mate for days. Jake, crying without shame, swore that Buddy was staring at him, asking for help, as they pulled him away. Griffin was the only one who did not shed a tear.

Three months later, Jake was gathering kindling for the woodstove when he saw him. The sight of a lame horse with no bridle or saddle, limping up the driveway as if he knew where he was going, stopped Jake in his tracks. Scar recognized him right away and nickered a greeting, but Jake did not recognize the scarred and gaunt, ribs-showing horse until he saw the expression in Buddy's eyes.

Jake begged his grandfather to keep the horse, to reward him for traveling across the Red and walking almost eighty miles to return home. But it was no use. A deal is a deal. The horse was allowed to recover at home, and then returned to its rightful owner.

For Griffin, keeping the horse would have been crossing the river, the invisible law of integrity he had learned from his father and passed on to his children and grandchildren. Jake did not understand and was disappointed in his grandfather's decision, but Rance told him that Griffin considered Buddy's life intertwined with his own and did not want to see the old horse die.

A close brush with prison and the sight of death and real violence took the piss-and-vinegar out of Gray Boy for a while, leaving him content to stroll the lake with Halley and sit by her in church. The events in Ivory's junkyard in The Hollow had changed his hatred of Cameron Galt to indifference. Whenever the old rage returned, he imagined Cameron bent over, taking his licks from Ivory's razor strap.

Gray decided that driving heavy equipment was not going to be his life's occupation. It could never again hold the thrill it had the day he knocked down fences, leveled mountains of junk, and crashed into a house. When the piss-and-vinegar returned, he grew more aggressive with Halley in their rare private moments, and he could feel her resistance weakening. It was a battle he could not keep from waging, but one he did not really want to win.

He was sinking again—losing direction. At Halley's urging, he found himself standing in line to register for the fall semester at East Texas State College in Commerce. A crisp one hundred dollar bill, enough for tuition and books, saved by Rance and Mattie, burned a hole in his pocket. When he finally reached the front of the line, a smiling young man in a blue blazer, white shirt, and blue and gold striped tie, extended his hand.

"Freshman?" he asked.

Gray nodded and shook the hand. The young man smiled as he took a blue beanie from a stack on the table between them. He placed the beanie on Gray's head. Gray turned to look at the throng of young people standing in line at tables set up along the perimeter of the gymnasium floor. The beanie made him feel silly. More or less to get out of the way, he took a couple of steps sideways and examined the catalog of courses he had been given. After reading the description of a few courses, he pulled the beanie off his head, handed it and the catalog to a pretty young girl in the line, smiled, and walked out of the building.

As he swung a leg across the Mustang and prepared to kick the starter, a tent-shaped sign next to the motorcycle squeaked as it swung gently in the breeze. Uncle Sam beckoned with a finger pointed directly at Gray Boy. An hour later, he was signing preliminary papers to join the Marines.

Once the shock wore off, Rance was pleased that his son had finally made a decision, any decision, about his future. Mattie cried, but she was proud, too. Jake, still getting used to the new softer-gentler Gray Boy, beamed as he imagined his brother leading men into battle. He tried to push thoughts of what his brother might leave behind for him aside. Maybe the Mustang, but certainly his room.

Gray, with time on his hands, picked up his guitar again and practiced with Griff and his friends. When Jake heard he had become the designated singer for the group of old men, he laughed out loud. Trish had always encouraged his singing. She bought him a big reel-to-reel tape recorder to record his music.

It was a long goodbye. Too long, Jake thought. Joe Max Rainey surrounded Gray's hand in a crushing handshake when he learned that he was leaving to serve his country. Gray Boy was sure that Joe Max was just glad to be rid of him and his courting of his adored daughter. Pleased with the news that he might be relieved of his constant vigilance when Gray Boy left for the Marines, Joe Max even allowed Halley to visit the Rivers' house after both sets of parents had assured supervision.

On Gray's last night at home, they sat on the divan in the dining room, smooching as they watched the used portable Philco television that Mattie had bought with sewing factory wages. Jake was banned from the living room. He sat in the yard until Gray Boy left to take Halley home. Halley cried a lot. Mattie cried a lot.

As the days wore on and the new wore off, Gray grew anxious and irritable. When he sold the Mustang, Jake was almost glad when it was time for his brother to go. The actual leaving was a disappointment. Jake had imagined a parade or a cheering crowd, but it was not like that. There were not even any uniformed soldiers to take him away.

When they left for the bus station, the seats in the family Ford were filled again for the first time since Trish had left home to marry. Halley rode in Trish's former place. They kissed right in front of the family, and Halley cried some more. Jake thought she was beautiful, even when red-faced with crying.

Gray Boy kissed and hugged his weeping mother, embraced his father and grandfather. Jake was afraid his father was going to cry. Last, he grabbed Jake by the scruff of the neck and pulled him close. Jake had never been that close to his brother unless they were fighting, not even when they slept in the same bed. He smelled different today, as if the anger, with a smell of its own, had left him. He was gone in a puff of Trailways smoke. And Jake had to turn away from the rest of them.

Back at home, Jake went directly to the bedroom he and his brother had shared until he moved into the dog-run with Tuck. It was his alone now. He plopped on the bed, put his hands behind his head, and allowed it all to sink in.

Curious, he examined the tape recorder that Gray had left on a table by the bed. He studied it several nights without touching it. There would be hell to pay if he broke it, and it did look delicate. Two days passed before his discipline gave way. He switched the knob to its on position just before bedtime. He jumped a little when he heard *Don't be cruel, to a heart that's true. I don't want no other love... baby it's just you I'm thinking of.* He was fumbling with the volume knob when his mother walked into the room.

Jake relaxed a little when he saw her smile. "I just turned it on...."

"You know who that is?"

Jake was insulted. "Yeah, that's Elvis Presley."

"Listen closer. That's your brother."

There were many songs on that tape and a couple of others that Jake found later—Gray Boy singing like Elvis, Dean Martin, even Perry Como. As the absence grew longer, he invited Jake and Jerry to listen. They thought it was Elvis, too. The boys decided that Gray Boy would be famous someday.

Gray Boy was soon home again, dimples deeper and longer, smile changed from cocky to confident, burr haircut. How could one boy have changed so much in such a short period of time? They called it basic training. Always well-built, Gray Boy had put on ten pounds of muscle.

At the kitchen table, Jake stared at the black hair that seemed to have sprouted overnight on his brother's arms, marveling at the sinews that waved underneath. His split lips and scabs on his knuckles mesmerized Jake. Asked for an explanation by his mother, Gray dismissed her with something about insulting remarks another recruit had made about Texas. It all made Jake want to go to basic training himself.

Gray was smoking openly now, and he casually did tricks with his Zippo and a Winston rolling along his knuckles before popping into his mouth. Rance flinched, but there was little a smoking father could say to a young soldier-son who smoked in front of him. Mattie, of course, knew he had been sneaking for a long time. There was a syrupy reunion with Halley. Gray was treated like a hero-returned-from-the-wars at the Rainey household.

Jake was disappointed when Gray shucked the Marine uniform for his jeans and penny loafers as soon as he got home. He did not put the uniform back on until it was time to leave again. Same bus station, maybe even the same bus. The leaving was different this time. The first seemed to hurt everyone else; this one seemed to hurt Gray Boy.

26 The trip to West Texas was ostensibly to answer an oft-repeated invitation from Mattie's sisters and their families. The three of them left on a cold, gray January day, with Jake excited about traveling to the places he had heard Papa Griff speak of all his life. He watched his parents' moods and conversation change as dramatically as the countryside.

As the stately oak trees and gently rolling land gave way to the flat, vast, almost treeless prairie of West Texas, something changed inside the car, inside his shrunken family, that Jake could not identify. It seemed that Rance and Mattie were traveling back in time, a time before they suffered the loss of a child and the threatened loss of another. Jake felt his presence was the only thing that kept them from slipping back to the time before him, leaving them as newlyweds, moving toward a great adventure in this sparsely settled land.

He stayed quiet and still, sensing that something was happening—something that he was not part of and could not control. He rode the peaks and valleys of their revelations, taking comfort in the changed tones of their conversation, recalling something familiar in the words and gestures. This is how they were before Tuck died. They made no attempt at concealment, allowing him to eavesdrop on this adult conversation that simultaneously frightened and comforted him. He had never known, and could not understand, the guilt they felt when Tuck was taken from them. He had not considered his father's deep rage and bitterness at the community that was willing to accuse Gray Boy of murder.

Jake marveled as his mother alternately laughed and cried as she recounted her quest to understand Tuck's death. Jake had been an unwilling traveler on her journey, listening to screaming evangelists and his mother's plaintive rendering of songs about death. Each parent seemed surprised and relieved that the other understood, even shared the same feelings. Pain and bitterness seemed to float out the car windows to be whisked away by the cleaner, drier air. With each cleansing revelation, the mood gradually lifted like the land was lifting under the car.

Jake's ears popped (or he imagined they did) as they reached the higher elevations of the Caprock. The mood in the car was ebullient, almost silly. Jake was invited to join them as they discussed the tremendous toll taken by the drought and the cruelty of Mother Nature to follow it with a flood. They all spoke softly as Rance for the first time, recalled the loss of Hack Gentry to the flood and of Papa Griffin's heroic efforts to save him. Jake tingled with pride.

He told his own stories about the dairy and the deep cracks in the bottomland cotton patch, and he was gratified when his parents seemed to listen with interest. Jake was fighting sleep when they pulled into Mattie's sister's yard. He stepped out, felt the dry wind pepper his face with small specks of sand. He watched the windmill turn, listened to its creaking, blowing away the only life he had ever known.

27 March 21, 1957
Dear Son,
I wanted to call you from Camp Lake store, but did
not want to discuss these things in front of the nosey
old men who sit around the wood stove there. Making
a long distance call to another state would make me
nervous enough without having to deal with eaves-
droppers. I would surely forget to tell you all that I
have to tell.

My hand is trembling, so I hope you can read my
writing. I do so ache to hold you in my arms as I try
to find a way to soften this message. The thought of
what I have to tell you cuts so deeply into my heart
and soul that the pen in my hand feels like a razor
blade that will surely cut this sheet of paper as my
shaky hand writes these words. We lost Halley last
Saturday night. The Raineys are devastated, as I
know you are at this moment. If only I could reach
across the miles to comfort you. Halley drowned, or
suffocated, in their cistern.

I remember your mention of the strange smell coming
from their cistern. Joe Max thought it was because
the cistern's brick walls needed cleaning. He made a

special swing attached to a rope and lowered Halley down with a bucket and brush to clean it. (You must not blame him for your loss. It sounds terrible now, but it seemed safe enough at the time. Joe Max is too big to get through the opening—and nobody could pull him up if he did.) She fainted almost as soon as he lowered her and dropped into the water.

They're not sure yet, but they think the smell was coming from butane. A leak in the line going to their house had somehow seeped into the cistern. I guess that a lot had already accumulated down there, enough to make her pass out without warning.

The fire departments and emergency crew from Commerce and Cooper got there as soon as they could, but it was too late for sweet Halley. We called your base as soon as we found out, but they said your outfit would be gone for two days and that we could not talk to you until you returned unless an immediate family member had died or was at death's door.

I hate for you to find out this way, but it was our only choice. She will be laid to rest at Shiloh by the time you read this. When you come home soon on leave, we will visit her. We will take you into our arms and comfort you. Those words, as I write them, seem so awful and cruel; they tear my heart in two. I ache for you so. Please remember that we love you. Joe Max is blaming himself, of course, and he and the family are reaching out to your daddy and me, because they know we understand the loss of a child. He said he so wanted you for a son-in-law.

Show this to your officers and ask them to let you come home.

All our love,
Mother and Daddy

◈   ◈   ◈

Losing Halley was almost like losing Tuck again. The
euphoria from their West Texas trip had lasted until the
Rivers reached Dallas on the trip home. The trees and
changing landscape of Northeast Texas did not seem as
beautiful as they once had. When Halley died a short time
later, the shake-your-fist-at-God anger they had worked so hard
to set aside crept back into their lives. Jake was frightened
when he recognized signs of the downward spiral he had
witnessed when his little brother died. This time, he had no
brother or sister to reassure him.

Nobody said it, but Jake suspected that something was
terribly wrong with his family. The evidence was piling
up that God was angry with them. Death seemed to swirl
around the family like the plague of locusts he had heard
about in Sunday School. They managed to survive the death
of one of their own, only to have it followed by Spooner,
Hack, and now Halley. It was dangerous to enter the Rivers'
family circle. The house grew cold again.

Gray Boy came home a week later. The Rivers feared that
their son and brother would return to them angry and bitter
at his loss. He came without notice, fresh from hitchhiking
all the way from North Carolina. The scars of fistfights
healed, hair grown out a little, he looked a little bruised
and numb, but not angry or bitter. When Jake came home
from school and saw him sitting on the divan, his brother
reminded him of a Christmas package delivered by the
postman—welcome, but damaged.

As promised, the family visited Halley's grave. The
Raineys and the Church of Christ preacher came along. Jake
felt as if he was attending Halley's funeral all over again. Gray
must have felt the same way because he seemed uncomfortable
and anxious to get it all over with. When they returned
home, he borrowed the family car and returned to the

cemetery for his private time with Halley.

He left before dawn two days later, leaving a note for the family that he would hitchhike back to base. Gray's silent leave-taking was like a splash of cold water for Mattie. She was not done with mothering her damaged son. She needed that—to ease her own pain.

28

September 21, 1957
Dear Son,
I miss your letters, but appreciate the postcards and the picture of you on the parade ground. We are so proud of you. Once again, I write with trembling hand, but not because of a great sorrow. Your daddy and I have decided to try something new. We have sold the farm and house and signed a lease on a place in Oldham County in West Texas. This probably won't come as a complete shock to you, since we have talked about the prosperity out there many times. We need a new start and can't seem to find it here. Too many bad memories, I suppose.

The move will be hard on Jake, but he's young and will adjust. We're going to wait until the Christmas break to take him out of school, but we must be in our new home by the beginning of the New Year. There's maize stalks to shred and winter wheat to look after on the farm we are leasing.

I hate most of all to leave my baby in that cemetery, but Tuck has whispered in my ear that he is coming along. Hack's death seemed to take the fun out of life here for your daddy, and we were barely able to

*offer any help to the Raineys when they lost Halley.
When we visited there last year, the flat prairies of
the Panhandle seemed to offer opportunities. Those
wind-swept plains seemed clean and pure, somehow,
and I think I heard the wind beckoning us to come.
In case you think I have lost my mind, the farming
seems good, too. I know you are scheduled to come
home before we leave. I want you here once more,
so we can sit down to a meal as a family in this old
worn-out house one last time.*

*All my love,
Mother*

Jake displayed little emotion when he heard of his
parents' decision to move. He had heard it all before. They
always talked about moving away, but never did. As he
listened, his parents shrunk in his eyes, seemed pitiful with
their dreams of a new start somewhere far away. When they
said that the house and farm had been sold and that his
grandfather was moving into town, he stalked from the room
because he was too old to cry.

For the next few weeks, he managed to put it out of his
mind and soak up the special attention he received from
his parents. He began to brag about his impending move at
school and enjoy his friends' expressions of remorse. They
even threw a going-away party for him during recess one day.
When the teacher announced that the half-hour party was
over, Jake began to feel lonesome. School and his friends
would go on without him.

It was awkward when Gray Boy returned again just before
Christmas. A load of furniture had already been taken to the
Panhandle, and the Rivers were more or less camping in their
home. Gray seemed irritated that his usual hero's welcome
seemed a distraction now.

After a short Christmas celebration, attention returned to packing and loading. Rance and Mattie seemed embarrassed when they had to leave for their new home before it was time for Gray Boy to return to the Marines. Mattie drove the car packed to the windows, and Rance drove a borrowed grain truck full of their other belongings as they headed down the driveway toward 24. Jake and his brother stood on the porch of the almost-abandoned house and watched them drive away.

"Looks like somethin' out of *Grapes of Wrath*," Gray Boy said. He walked out to the pickup and pulled the .22 rifle from behind the seat.

"What are you gonna do with that?" Jake asked.

Gray put a finger to his lips and motioned for Jake to follow him. In the bedroom they had shared for many years, they sat on the floor where the bed had been and waited for the sound of a rat running across the ceiling. When one finally scampered across, Gray fired several shots with the semi-automatic.

"Always wanted to do that."

Jake smiled, but he hoped that his brother would not fire any more shots into the old house. To Jake, the house had feelings. Everything about it reminded him of Tuck. He could not escape the feeling that he was leaving his little brother to live here alone.

They took their time hitching the trailer and walking out to put a halter on Scar. Gray pushed the sliding door to the dairy parlor open and walked inside. Jake followed him in and watched as his brother ran his finger along the dusty ledges of the stanchions. He heard the hum of the electric milkers, the bawling of cows. Jake had carved his name and initials into lots of wood surfaces, and he ran his finger along every letter. He caught Gray's stare for a second, but he looked away when he thought he might cry.

In the old hay barn, Jake slipped the halter on Scar as Gray Boy lifted the blanket and saddle from the corncrib for the last time. Gray threw the tack into the pickup bed as Jake loaded his horse into the trailer. Shy was watching from the cool dirt under the front porch and came running at Jake's whistle. He was over the tailgate and lying on the saddle blanket before Jake snapped his fingers.

Jake felt good when Gray opened the passenger door, inviting him to use his new hardship driver's license. They rode to Commerce and Papa Griff's house without speaking. Jake had visited his grandfather's house in town a few times, but Gray Boy had never seen it.

"Looks just like the one on the farm." Gray Boy said as they stopped in front.

"Seems smaller to me." Jake thought the house looked sadder, too. Country houses, with the green of pastures surrounding them, didn't seem to need paint as much as houses in town.

They unloaded Scar and walked around the side of the house. Griffin was in the back yard, kneeling over an open fire. He spoke without turning. "You boys stand some Dutch oven biscuits and cobbler?" Griffin was dressed in his usual jeans, boots, and wildrag, but something was missing. Jake tied Scar to a fencepost in the back yard.

They sat on the porch and ate biscuits, beans, and fried ham from plates in their laps and washed it down with cold fresh milk from the cow that Griffin kept in his back yard. Jake pointed at the cow as he wiped the last of the peach cobbler from his plate with a finger.

"You allowed to keep cows in town?"

Griffin took Jake's plate and dropped it into the pan of hot water he had placed on the coals. "Never asked."

Dishes washed and put away, Gray Boy and Griffin took the two rocking chairs, and Jake sat on the edge of the porch. The December air was crisp and light, but not cold enough to make them want to go inside. Thoughts and memories hung heavy in the air, and the two grandsons waited patiently for their grandfather to give them voice. The old man finally spoke. "Kinda chilly out here. You boys about ready to turn in?"

"No," they answered in unison.

Griffin rocked easily and stared at his milk cow. "Notice the scabs are gone from your knuckles. Your teeth take back a hold?"

Gray Boy ran a finger along his gums. "Yep. They're about back to normal now, but I sure had to be careful what I ate for awhile."

"Accomplish anything by nearly givin' up your teeth?"

Gray turned in his chair and looked at his grandfather in the fading light of day. "What do you mean?"

"You've always been a fighter, Gray Boy, and I have to admit I took a good deal of pride in your standing up for yourself, but you've been doin' it too long."

"When do you quit fightin'? You and Daddy always said to stick up for what's right."

"We did, at that. Never thought you were payin' attention. But your daddy and me both learned a little late that just fightin' ain't the measure of a man. You should have learned that the first time Cameron Galt whipped your butt."

Gray pulled a pack of Winstons from his pocket, then thought better of it. "How do you mean?"

"Did Cameron's being able to whip you make him a better man?"

"Hope not."

Jake had sat for many hours at his grandfather's feet, listening to his lessons to live by. It had never occurred to him that his brother had received the same teachings. Getting to eavesdrop on this grown-up lesson was almost as good as the peach cobbler.

Griffin untied his wildrag, slung it out, and used it to clean his glasses. "It ain't always how a man fights, how good he can rope a steer, or how much money he's got that says the most about him." Jake could barely make out the wink that his grandfather directed toward him. "It ain't even about how many women he's bedded."

Gray stopped rocking and turned to face his grandfather. "What is it then?"

"It's how many people that love him and how many people he's helped in some way or another. How many family, how many friends."

The old man was slow to get up; his back seemed difficult to get straight. When he walked into the house, Jake was afraid he was going to bed. Jake listened for the creak of bedsprings, but he heard the squeak of fiddle strings instead. He felt better when his grandfather shook his old fiddle close to Jake's ear. Griffin knew that Jake always wanted to hear those snake rattlers inside. Griffin had told him that the rattlers soak up humidity and keep the fiddle from warping and being hard to tune.

He touched the strings with a slight tease and turned the tuning knobs as he spoke. "You boys will be going off in different directions tomorrow. Don't ever forget where you came from."

He grinned as he turned toward Gray Boy. "Think you can still play your aunt's old guitar? It's inside."

Gray returned with the guitar and began strumming and tuning. They played until Griffin announced it was time to turn in at midnight. Jake pleaded for just one more song, a slow one.

Griffin drew the bow across the strings lightly and the strains of *Red River Valley* drifted out into the thin air. Gray stopped strumming and held his guitar—his mellow voice little more than a whisper at first. *From this valley they say you are leaving...we shall miss your bright eyes and sweet smile.*

Jake shivered a little as he listened to his brother's voice grow stronger, revealing the emotions that hung heavy in the light air. He and his brother would go in different directions tomorrow; never to return to the home they had grown up in. Their grandfather would be left behind, an old cowboy living in town, without his horse... *and the cowboy that's loved you so true.*

Jake gave his brother the other bed and slept on a pallet of quilts beside his grandfather's bed. As he struggled with sleep, the moonlight reflected off a pair of spurs hanging on the wall across from the window. Now he knew what had been missing about his grandfather.

They were up at daylight, the boys pitching in to help with bacon and eggs. With frost on the ground outside, they cooked in the kitchen. Griffin, a wistful look in his eyes, reckoned that there might be snow in the Panhandle when Jake arrived. The possibility of snow had not crossed Jake's mind.

"Why don't you come with me out west, Papa?"

Griffin used a fork to turn a slice of sizzling bacon. "No, I reckon not, Bolivar. I've already been east to west and back again. That's enough for one life, I guess."

Scar, fed and watered, jumped into the topless trailer without hesitation. Jake closed the gate and turned to his grandfather. "What kinda music you hear on a day like this, Papa?"

Griffin stood on the porch and whistled softly. "Harmonica—playing traveling music—train whistles and wheels chugging." Their goodbyes were awkward, with handshakes turning into hugs. Nothing could be said this morning that would be better than what was experienced last night.

Gray Boy, older in his uniform and polished shoes, was subdued as they drove away. Jake's home run ball, perched on the wood stand Rance had carved, sat between them. Gray Boy was supposed to ride with Jake until they reached Amarillo, but the brothers knew what Mattie and Rance did not. Gray had overstayed his leave by one day, and he needed to depart from the Cooper bus station to make it back to base on time.

Jake knew that he was probably crossing the river, but this occasion seemed worth the trip. His brother trusted him to make the trip alone, and he could not say no to Gray Boy this time.

At the bus station, Jake studied the red line drawn by his father from east to west on the Texas map. Gray Boy, a mature Marine now, pulled a Winston from his pocket and lighted it with his Zippo. The sun warmed them a little as they leaned against the '56 Chevrolet pickup that Rance had bought with proceeds from sale of his farm equipment. Jake could still blow smoke with his breath.

"Shy, come back here." When Jake saw Bo Creekwater walking toward them, a baseball cap crooked on his head, he knew that calling the dog was of no use. Shy jumped into Bo's waiting arms. Jake and Gray followed.

"You gon' catch that bus and go back to war, aintcha'? Uh huh."

Gray smiled. "That's right, Bo, but there ain't no war to fight just now."

Jake reached out and touched the top of Shy's head. "Know what, Bo? Me and Shy are headin' to West Texas. I hear they got lots of coyotes and wolves out there. Shy could get himself eaten up. You think you could keep him here till I come back for him?"

Bo's eyes brightened. "Uh huh. I take him home right now...fix his bed, uh huh." Bo turned and trotted away before Jake could change his mind.

Gray turned to Jake. "Can't believe you just gave away your dog."

Jake watched Bo and Shy until they disappeared around a corner.

"Look up there." Gray Boy pointed toward the jailhouse walkway. King Ivory appeared to be staring at them from his perch.

"Think he really can fly off there like people say?" Jake asked.

Gray Boy waved at the prisoner. "I imagine if King Ivory could fly, he'd be long gone."

The Continental Trailways bus blocked their view as it slowed and clattered between them and the courthouse. As it eased past them to park, a red '55 Chevy pulled up beside the courthouse. Gray Boy stood away from the pickup, dropped his cigarette, and ground it out.

Cameron Galt looked toward them as he stepped out of the car. Molly Beth Galt, carrying a small child, stepped out of the passenger side and walked to the back of the car. To keep hesitation from changing her mind, she walked into the street, headed for Gray Boy. Jake heard his brother take a deep breath.

"Damn. She looks as good as ever."

Molly Beth stood in front of him for several seconds, holding her son, before speaking. "I wanted you to meet my son. This is Tom Galt, Jr....for his great-grandfather."

Gray held out a finger for the yellow-haired, blue-eyed boy to grab. "Good lookin' kid, Molly."

Jake stared at his boots during the embarrassing silence that followed. Gray finally nodded his head toward Cameron across the street before speaking to Molly. "You doin' okay?"

Molly Beth's eyes misted as her mouth formed a smile that was bigger than necessary. "We're doin' great. Just heard you were here for maybe the last time, so I wanted you to meet my son."

Gray looked into her eyes, winked, and smiled. "Still got our blanket?"

"I'll always have that."

Gray took another deep breath and crossed his arms as if he needed to hold them away from her. "What's Cameron doin' these days?"

"Finishin' college. Wants to go to law school. We live in Dallas now. Just home visiting the folks for Christmas."

The bus driver came out of the station with a cup of coffee in his hand. He nodded toward the duffle bag at Gray Boy's feet. "Goin' with me, Soldier?"

Gray, locked into Molly Beth's eyes, nodded. The driver opened the baggage compartment on the bus and tossed Gray's duffle inside. The airbrakes released and sent a cloud of steam rolling over them. Molly Beth touched Gray's arm and ran back across the street. Gray watched her until she reached her husband. He returned Cameron's slight wave.

Gray turned to Jake, put his hand on top of his head, and let it slide slowly down to his jaw. He gave him a soft slap on the check. Jake felt his brother's coarse hand squeeze the back of his neck. "You write me, Little Brother."

Jake, hands inside the front pockets of his Levis, thumbs hung over the edge, took a deep, rasping breath, and nodded. Gray turned and walked toward the open bus door. As he jumped on the first step, a girl yelled from an open window on the passenger side of a moving black '57 Chevy. "Hey, Soldier. Need a ride?"

Gray's dimples deepened as he turned back toward Jake with a slight jerk of his head in the girl's direction. "Guess it's up to you now, Jake." He made a short, two-fingered salute at Jake as the doors closed. Jake watched the bus until it was out of sight. The red Chevy was gone when he turned back.

Gray Boy's leaving seemed to take Jake's strength, and he leaned against the pickup until he was soaked with the cold. When he started to shake, he climbed into the pickup, checked the map, and headed west.

The sun at his back seemed to guide him as he slowed and entered the Klondike turn-off, headed for the cemetery. He stopped at Tuck's grave. Too cold to step outside, he pressed his nose against the fogged window and stared at the small marker. Wind whistled through cracks in the trailer floor. Scar stamped his hooves with impatience and cold. Jake mouthed "So long" as he pulled away.

If you enjoyed this book,
use the form on the next page and order autographed
copies for others.

Quick Order Form

Order online: Online Order forms for all of Jim Ainsworth's books available at www.jimainsworth.com

Credit cards accepted online through secure Pay Pal.

Order by mail: Season of Harvest Publications
2403 CR 4208
Campbell, Texas 75422

Please send:
Quantity   **Amount**

_____ Rivers Crossing @ $25.00 $ _____
(# 2 in the Series)

_____ In The Rivers' Flow @ $15.00 $ _____
(# 1 in the Series)

Sales tax if shipped to Texas @ 6.75% $ _____

Shipping charges @ $2.00 per book $ _____

Total (Send check or money order) $ _____

Credit card purchases (Check One) ☐Visa ☐MC
Name as shown on card _____
Exp. Date _____Your Signature _____

Ship Books To:

Name _____
Address _____
City_____ State _____ Zip _____
Telephone _____ e-mail _____
Autograph instructions _____

DATE DUE